# ACES

# ACES

## A NOVEL OF WORLD WAR II

BY

# ROBERT DENNY

DONALD I. FINE, INC.

NEW YORK

Library of Congress Cataloging-in-Publication Data

Denny, Robert.
    Aces : a novel of the world at war / Robert Denny.
    p.  cm.
    ISBN: 1-55611-225-4
    1. World War, 1939–1945—Fiction.  I. Title.
    PS3554.E575A65  1991
    813'.54—dc20                 90-55336
                                     CIP

Manufactured in the United States of America

10  9  8  7  6  5  4  3  2  1

Designed by Irving Perkins Associates

General Johannes Steinhoff quote from *The Final Hours*, Nautical & Aviation Publishing Co. of America, Baltimore, Md.

*For Bruce Lee, Dwight,*
*Ed, and the others*

# Foreword

ALL novels and films about war are lies. They lie because, to entertain, they compress into days or hours events that occur infrequently and over long periods of time. In wars, any war, the most common experience is waiting rather than fighting. So it follows that the most common emotion is not fear or anger but boredom. Except for its isolated moments of action, the experience of war is portrayed more realistically by *Waiting for Godot* than by *Platoon* or *Rambo*.

A second reason why war stories lie is because their authors use them to advance their personal political agendas. For example, if all you knew of Vietnam was what you read or saw in recent stories about it, you would think it was the bloodiest war America ever fought.

But compare it to World War II. In Vietnam, one of every 41 Americans who served there became a casualty; if not killed, he was incapacitated by wounds, injuries or illness. In World War II, it was one in 15.

In this novel, I've tried to lie as little as possible by concentrating on an event that happened late in World War II. It was the unexpected

vii

appearance of a fantastic German weapon—a superplane that flew a third faster than our fastest fighters and three times faster than the bombers with which we were battering German factories, railroads and oil refineries.

The Messerschmitt 262, the world's first operational jet fighter, appeared in the skies of Europe in late 1944. I was flying a B-17 bomber at the time and one of them went by me so fast I thought I was hallucinating.

Fourteen hundred of these elegant aircraft were produced. Had any sizeable number been used against us when they first became available, they might have defeated the Normandy invasion and changed the course of the war. They certainly would have stopped our daylight bombing offensive. But Adolf Hitler forbade his pilots to use the 262 to intercept and destroy our bombers. He ordered that it be converted into his long-sought "blitz bomber." The racehorse became a plow horse.

That order inspired the only mutiny of fighter pilots in German military history. Germany's best aces were fired; their leader, General Adolf Galland, narrowly escaped being shot. After it became clear, even to Hitler, that the war was lost, he relented and allowed his cashiered Knight's Cross wearers to form a single squadron to fly the jets against our bombers.

These facts form the dramatic background for ACES. The novel's account of the caste and class system that defined small-town life in Pennsylvania (and many other places in America) prior to World War II, is also factual, as was the destruction of that system by the war. (In this sense, Hitler did, in fact, create a New Order.)

The inferior standing of East Europeans, commonly called "Hunkies," whose men worked in the mines and whose women served as housemaids and—on occasion—as sexual tutors of young upper-class men, was part of a caste system that truly existed in America.

The historical characters mentioned in ACES—Eisenhower, Churchill, Hitler, Goering, Guderian, Speer—did, of course, exist. And, while I have created conversations for them, on the whole they acted and spoke in the manner I have depicted.

General Helmuth Karl Bernard von Moltke was a distinguished

German military figure of the past. Adolf Galland and Johannes Steinhoff, both retired generals, are alive at this writing. The dog, Wu-Shu, existed, though under another name.

Other characters are purely fictional or have been created out of assorted personalities.

I have manipulated a few dates to advance the plot but, in general, descriptions of strategy, campaigns and weapons are accurate. They have been drawn from personal experience, from interviews with Generals Galland and Steinhoff and with historians Charles von Luttichau and Earl Ziemke, and from many historical works.

Conclusions from the *U.S. Strategic Bombing Survey* and from Colonel T.N. Dupuy's analysis of comparative fighting abilities are incorporated in the remarks of the novel's General Sutter and Brigadier Brooks, though these studies were not made till after the war.

My principal deviation from historical fact in ACES is in giving the German aces one more shot at us—an additional, all-out battle of the kind Galland wanted to wage to halt the daylight bombing offensive once and for all. Looking back, it seems only fair—at least in imagination—to give them that one last chance.

He that outlives this day, and comes safe home,
Will stand a tip-toe when this day is named,
And rouse him at the name of Crispian . . .
From this day to the end of the world,
But we in it shall be remembered:
We few, we happy few, we band of brothers . . .

—Act IV, *Henry V*,
William Shakespeare


We were like dayflies who had come
to the end of their day, where the dream
dissolves into nothingness. Why did we
still fly? Whom were we doing it for? . . .

—General Johannes Steinhoff,
*The Final Hours*

# CHAPTER ONE

# MAHONING

IF it hadn't been for the depression that blighted Mahoning's economy in the summer of 1934, Mitch Robinson and Lon Amundson might never have become friends.

Though they lived a scant mile apart, the social distance in Mahoning, as in most American towns of the '30s, wasn't measured by geography or, for that matter, by wealth. For where you lived and what you did for a living depended on where you or your parents came from.

The town lay like an irregular ribbon between wooded hills ninety miles from Pittsburgh in western Pennsylvania. Jefferson Street, flanked by large and ornate Victorian houses, bisected the longitudinal axis of the town and provided its primary roadway.

Jefferson Street was where you lived if you were of English, German, Dutch or, conceivably, French extraction and could therefore qualify as one of Mahoning's elite. It was this group who furnished the political and business leadership of the community and populated the country club at the northern end of town.

Mitch, christened Mitchell Moltke Robinson, was a member of the elite. A tall, gangling youth of third-generation German and English

I

extraction, he lived in a sprawling, fourteen-room brick fortress of a house on Jefferson Street with his great-aunt Adda.

To the west, a network of streets and stores housed Mahoning's merchant class—a colony of Italian and Sicilian families who worked in the retail grocery, wholesale meat packing and beer distribution businesses. Here also lived Mahoning's three Jewish families, two of them proprietors of clothing stores, the third the owner of the town's Ford dealership.

A half mile to the east and parallel to Jefferson Street stretched the Baltimore & Ohio railroad tracks that carried coal, brakeshoes and other mining supplies between the deep-shaft mines south of town and the steel mills of Pittsburgh.

Less than 100 yards away, the ground rose dramatically into a steep hillside dotted with modest wood houses known throughout the town as Hunkie Hill. Here lived the people universally known as the Hunkies, the first- and second-generation Poles, Czechs and Slavs who had graduated from the mines to work on the railroad and in the area's machine shops. Here, too, lived a smaller group of Scandinavians who, while they did the same kinds of work as the Hunkies, occupied a distinct social classification.

Widely admired for their strength and handsome physiques— though generally thought to be of modest intelligence—the Danes and Swedes fell somewhere between the English and German elite and the Italians in Mahoning's caste system.

Lon Amundson was one of two sons of Olaf Amundson, who emigrated from Sweden with his wife to find work in the Pennsylvania coal mines. By the time Lon was born, the elder Amundson had elevated himself to foreman in a small Mahoning foundry. By now he was earning 60 cents an hour and had moved his family from the tiny, unpainted board house in Beaver Hollow they had occupied for a half dozen years.

Beaver Hollow was a slag heap atop which the coal company had perched cheaply built company houses. The miners paid rent and bought their food at the company store with company scrip. Many times in later years, Lon would drive past the settlement and wonder how the Amundsons—or anybody—could have lived like that.

The house they moved to on Hunkie Hill in Mahoning was more than twice as big. It had indoor plumbing and two coats of paint, inside and out. It even had a small back yard with grass. The rent was $30 a month but the family could breathe. And Lon's mother, who made extra money working part-time as a seamstress, could keep the house clean, something that was impossible amid the swirling coal dust of Beaver Hollow.

Lon quickly grew to be a tall, husky youth with a broad, open face and a thick shock of blond hair. He became even huskier from carrying molten iron in the foundry and loading mine-car axles and brakeshoes on trucks and mine cars.

Mitch and Lon had shared an algebra class at Wilson High School in their junior year but had never spoken at any length until one day during summer vacation at Brennan's drugstore.

At the time, Mitch topped six-three, weighed 170 pounds and was desperately trying to gain weight by drinking at least two of Brennan's thick chocolate milkshakes between meals every day. Lon was a shade shorter and a tough 205 pounds.

After the two boys exchanged greetings, Mitch broached an idea that had been on his mind. "Listen, Lon," Mitch said. "I've got an idea for doing some workouts. If you don't feel like it, okay. Thing is, I need somebody to box with. I'm getting ready to try out for a boxing scholarship up at Penn State. How about it?"

Lon shrugged. "Jeez, I don't know. I've done the usual amount of fighting, I guess—when I had to. I've never really done any boxing."

"Maybe not," Mitch said. "But you're fast and strong as hell; I've seen you play football. You'd make me work hard and that's what I need to build up my wind and stamina. We could try it and see how it goes. Whatta'ya say?"

"Well, I guess I don't mind tryin' it. The foundry's shut down this month and all I'm doin' is runnin' groceries a coupla hours a day. I could use some regular exercise."

"Oh great," Mitch said. "Look, it's about lunchtime anyway. My Aunt Adda's out visiting her friends. How about coming down to the house with me for a sandwich and some milk? We could play some

records and sit around awhile. Then we can work out in my back
yard."

"You have gloves?"

"Fourteen-ouncers. Big and soft."

They walked down Jefferson to Mitch's house. The tall oaks and
elms spread out from both sides of the street to form a leafy canopy.

"Here we are," Mitch said, leading Lon up the broad front porch of
the Robinson house. The spacious interior was cool and the hallway
bore a pleasant, aromatic smell that seemed to come from the rich
wood paneling inside. A huge staircase lay ahead. Broad and ornately
carved, it curved sensuously in a half circle and disappeared around the
landing. At the top of the landing, soft, rich colors glowed through the
leaded panes of a rosette window. Lon thought he had never seen
anything so beautiful.

"Jeez, what a place!"

"Yeah, it's nice, I guess," Mitch said matter-of-factly, walking past
polished cherrywood columns into the living room and then through
the dining room into the kitchen. Lon lagged behind, looking about at
symbols of wealth he had only imagined. A crystal chandelier. A tall
grandfather clock that ticked and tocked so authoritatively it seemed to
be saying that it, and it alone, would decide what the time would be.

Half turning, Lon saw himself in a floor-to-ceiling mirror that was
bordered with gold leaf. The bottom was fitted into a little table of
marble with legs that looked like the paws of a golden lion. He looked
at his feet, shod in Penney's cheap work shoes. Beneath them lay the
soft richness of a Persian rug. Below it, he could see at the edges, were
strips of golden oak flooring. Lon chuckled wryly. The floor of the
Amundson house was linoleum.

"Hey, come on back," Mitch called.

The kitchen was almost as big as the whole downstairs of Lon's
house. In the middle was a big oak table where a whole family could
eat breakfast. But they probably ate all their meals in the dining room,
Lon decided. Even though there were only the two of them—Mitch
and his Aunt Adda. He wasn't counting Katie Wujcik, the Robinsons'
live-in maid.

Lon had seen Katie around town but he hadn't summoned up the nerve to talk to her. Katie was a looker, with the blooming kind of skin you sometimes saw in the young Polack girls. Her dad and brothers worked in the mines.

"Listen, take what you want," Mitch said. From the oaken icebox he took a plate of cold baked ham, a slab of cheese, an uncut pound of sweet dairy butter, a crock of homemade pickle spread and a quart of raw milk. He went to the tin bread box by the window for a loaf of Katie's homemade bread.

Lon felt the saliva gather in his mouth as he smelled the yeasty freshness of the bread. Drops of moisture formed on the bottle of cold milk. The cream, thick and yellow, extended downward a good six inches. Mitch picked up the bottle, shook it vigorously, and poured two glasses. Each boy made his own sandwich and attacked it enthusiastically.

They sat in silence for a while, eating and thinking private thoughts. At length, Lon asked: "How come you decided to go out for a boxing scholarship?"

"Well," Mitch said, chewing, "it's a way to go to college. I want to go to State and State's got the best intercollegiate boxing team in the East. I'll try out for light-heavy; with my height I should have some advantage—if I can build up my strength, that is. Point is I want to go to State and get a degree and this is the only way I can do it."

Lon's eyes narrowed in disbelief. "Are you sayin' you couldn't go without a scholarship? Your aunt's got a ton of money."

Mitch shook his head and smiled faintly. "That's what a lot of people think, but it's not so. When my mother went off and married another guy, I stayed here to live with my Uncle Ralph and Aunt Adda. She's my great-aunt, actually. Uncle Ralph made lots of money from the coal and timber business when I was a kid, but he died, and then there was the stock market crash, and it all went kerplooey. We just scrape along on the little that's left."

"Be damned," Lon said. "And I thought you had nothin' to worry about."

"I hear the football scouts have been lookin' at you," Mitch said, making another sandwich. "From State and Pitt, too."

"Yeah, it looks like I got a chance."

"You've got a great chance, Lon. I've seen you play."

"Well, the main thing is to get a college education, you know. My old man says it's the only way out of Mahoning and the mines."

"Hey, you guys, what're you doin'?" The shrill voice made the boys jump. Lon hadn't noticed the small door in the corner of the kitchen. It led up to the servants' rooms at the back of the house. The door was open and Katie was leaning out, looking at the two in obvious irritation.

"You gonna mess up this kitchen just after I cleaned it up, Mitch?" she demanded.

Mitch grinned broadly at Katie, his eyes brightening. "Now, I wouldn't mess up anything for you, would I, Katie-did?" he asked suggestively. "I always try to do everything you like."

Katie stared sullenly at Mitch. Lon marveled at her coloring. Her eyes were just a little too close together, but they were a clear blue. Her hair was a dark blond, and her skin was pink and luminous, like a sun-ripe peach. She was tall for a Polack and she had long legs and nice boobs, Lon noted. She also had large hands. The mark of the working class, he thought, regarding the muscular hams at the ends of his wrists.

"Say hello to Lon Amundson," Mitch commanded. He flicked his head toward the other boy but continued to lock eyes with the girl. "This is Katie, Lon. Katie Wujcik. She's our maid."

Katie looked briefly at Lon and nodded, her color growing even higher.

"We'll clean up after we're done, Katie," Mitch said. "I always do what Katie wants."

Two months earlier, Katie had introduced him to sex; it was a common practice in the homes in Mahoning for the young men of the families to be initiated by the older servant girls. Mitch had pestered Katie unremittingly to give him what he thought of as his due.

He was nearly eighteen and she was twenty-four. He began by hanging around her in the kitchen when Aunt Adda was out walking and visiting her friends. He would teasingly stroke her arm while she was cooking or washing the dishes and she would jerk it away. Sometimes he would pop her on the shoulder with a knuckle or brush her flanks.

"You keep it up, Mitch, and I'll tell your aunt," Katie would say. "You'll catch plain hell."

"You wouldn't do that, Katie," he teased, his breath coming short. "If she believed you, she might just let you go and hire somebody ugly. You wouldn't like that, and I wouldn't either." His voice dropped. "I'd hate not to see you, Katie. I like to look at you. I really do."

The girl looked sideways at him, her eyes softening. "So you're learnin' how to sweet-talk, are you? You're gonna sweet-talk me?"

She laughed. The young tomcat would do anything to get into her drawers, she knew. And he was clearly an embarrassed virgin. She smiled and shook her head. She'd probably let him, but it was risky. Adda Robinson would fire her in a minute if she thought her beloved Mitchell was fooling around with the family maid. One night a few weeks later, Mitch summoned up his courage and tiptoed quietly into her room. He and his aunt slept upstairs in front rooms that were separated by a wide hallway. Katie's room at the rear of the house was reachable through a connecting bedroom on the side where Mitch slept.

She woke with a start when he opened the door, but she knew instantly who it was. He stripped off his shorts and wriggled under the covers with her. "Katie," he whispered hoarsely. He reached for her and took her strongly in his arms. She felt a rush of excitement, her skin prickling across her body. But she held him away with her hands against his chest and whispered fiercely in his ear.

"You're goin' to do exactly what I say, you understand?"

He nodded.

"You say one word, just one word, to anybody, anybody at all, you understand?" she said, striking his chest sharply with her fist. "You do, you'll never lay a finger on me again. Never."

"Okay," he said meekly.

"You promise? Word of honor."

"Yes. Please, Katie."

"Wait." She climbed across him, stood up and stripped off her night-gown. Then she reached around into her tiny bathroom for a large towel. Getting back into bed, she slid it under her. As they touched, she could feel his body trembling.

"Okay," she whispered. "Now I'll teach you how. Kiss me nice. Not like that. Softer, like this. That's better. A lot better. Jeez, Mitch, don't grab like that, it hurts. That's no fun for me. Slow down, will ya? Give me your hand. Like this. And here. Slowly, Mitch. Slowly. Oh yes, that's nice. Just like that. Oh, yes, yes. Take your time now. I'll touch you, too. Don't jump, relax. Oh, boy, but you're hard. You'd better come on in. I'll guide you."

"Oh, Katie."

"I know, honey. Try to go slow."

It lasted about a minute, as she expected it would. But, like most healthy teenage males, he was ready again within fifteen minutes. With her coaching he lasted longer the second time. The third time she had an orgasm.

"How do you feel now?" she whispered, stroking his thick dark hair.

"Oh Katie, it was wonderful. I had no idea it was so hot. So . . ."

"I know, honey. You go back to your room now. Real quiet. And remember what I told you."

"I will, Katie," he said. "Dear." He stooped and softly kissed her lips before he left. She had to chide him next day for looking moonstruck around her. The old lady was absent-minded and a little flighty sometimes, but she wasn't dumb. The mooniness wore off after a few weeks. Then Mitch began to grow cocky. He started taking her out in the country at night in his aunt's Buick. They would drink rye or orange gin out of a pint bottle and then climb in the back. That was okay, but she didn't like the showing-off he was doing with this new kid, Lon.

"Lon and I are gonna put on the gloves and work out some," Mitch was saying with a grin on his face. "Maybe the three of us oughta take a ride in the car tonight. We could all work out."

Lon lowered his head in embarrassment. Katie flushed angrily. "You watch your dirty mouth, Mitch Robinson! You talk like that again and you can do your ridin' around by yourself from now on."

Katie slammed her door and went upstairs. Mitch shrugged and smiled. "Women," he said manfully. "C'mon, lemme show you my records." They went upstairs and Mitch put some of the new Dorsey Brothers records on his electric vic. They still had one of the old hand-crank models at Lon's house.

An hour later, they went outdoors and put on the gloves. It became apparent immediately that Lon's advantage in weight and strength was cancelled by Mitch's superior hitting power. Lon marveled that his skinny opponent could get so much leverage in his punches. Lon had fought on the slag heaps; he knew what to do. He kept his left glove high and his right near his cheek and circled counter-clockwise away from Mitch's cocked right hand. By pumping his left indefatigably and crossing the right occasionally, he gave Mitch a busy, moving target.

But Mitch was faster with his hands and his blows stung. In one sudden charge, Mitch ducked beneath Lon's left, dug a hard right to the body, hooked a looping left to the jaw and dropped the heavier boy on the grass.

"You okay?" Mitch gasped, stepping back.

"I'm all right," Lon said, getting up slowly. "Cripes, that was a hard punch."

They continued moving and snapping punches at each other. Mitch's breath began to rasp in his throat. Finally, he had to hang onto Lon's muscular arms and rest to recover his wind.

A hoot of laughter came from above. The two boys stopped and looked up. Katie, her eyes mocking, leaned from her window. "The people from Hunkie Hill are tougher'n you thought, huh, Mitch?"

Mitch nodded, laughed and collapsed onto the grass. "I gotta admit it. Lon's strong as an ox."

"Mmm, yeah," she said. "Maybe you oughta start leadin' a cleaner life."

Mitch nodded and smiled. "I'll start tomorrow. Tonight, let's the three of us run up to Rosedale. We can have a dance or two and a coupla drinks. Okay, Katie?"

She made a face. "Lon doesn't wanta do that."

"Sure he does. You'll come, won't you, Lon?"

"Well, gee, I don't know," Lon said.

"Oh come on, Lon. Wouldn't you like to come with Katie and me? Don't you like her?"

Lon blushed. "Oh, sure. I mean, she's real pretty."

"Oh, you guys!" Katie snorted, unable to hide her pleasure. "Well, if he wants to come, I don't mind. But I havta get in early, Mitch. You guys are on vacation but I have to get up early and do laundry and everything."

"Absa-tively," Mitch said. "We'll meet at the post office at eight."

Katie shut her window. The sound startled the sparrows nesting in the thick ivy on the walls and they burst out in a cloud.

"My money!" the boys said simultaneously. If you said it first, it meant good luck. Even the oldsters in town muttered it under their breath when they saw a flight of birds.

———

After bathing, dressing and combing his hair, Mitch went downstairs to spend his ritual hour with Aunt Adda before dinner. She had just returned from a visit to Leila Crosby's house two doors away. There, the older women of the neighborhood, all in their sixties and seventies, had spent the afternoon gossiping and laughing and drinking lemonade. Some afternoons, they had a glass, sometimes two glasses, of sherry. They seldom spoke on the telephone; they simply walked out and visited each other. They were the aristocracy of Mahoning; they belonged to the Daughters of the American Revolution, played poker one night a week and had a huge communal dinner once a month.

Mitch loved the dinners. Each woman brought her specialty. Aunt Adda would usually bring a large baking dish of scalloped potatoes, golden brown on top and rich with butter, and a creamy rice pudding. He could usually count on sampling a steak and kidney pie, a fragrant crock of sauerbraten, a country ham glazed with cider and brown sugar and chicken baked in cream. During hunting season there would be roast duck and venison or groundhog and, sometimes, bear steak.

There were always three or four kinds of potatoes, homemade rolls and biscuits and, during the summer, smoking hot ears of freshly picked corn and serving dishes of fresh peas and beans and okra. For dessert, there were usually custard and cream and fresh fruit pies; Mitch especially liked the rhubarb pie. Just thinking about those dinners made his mouth water.

Aunt Adda took off her wide-brimmed hat, peeled off her white cotton gloves and sank into her favorite chair. The reflected light from the late afternoon sun touched her face. Her skin was remarkably smooth and free of wrinkles for a woman of sixty-seven.

She smiled warmly at Mitch, sitting opposite her. "Why don't we have a glass of that nice, fresh cider before dinner?" she said. "Don't get up, dear; I'll bring it in."

By the time she returned from the kitchen, the light had moved to the painting on the narrow wall between the fireplace and the doorway. The somber face in the painting seemed to brighten and come alive as the sun touched it. It was a family heirloom and Aunt Adda loved to talk about it. Today was no exception. "Baron von Moltke— or perhaps he was a Count, I've never been sure—well, at any rate, von Moltke was a great military genius and a great writer, too. One historian called him one of the 'most eminent masters of German prose.' " Aunt Adda's voice always rose to the level of declamation when she said these words. "So you have many talents in your bloodline, Mitch. Later, when you're older and established and Germany settles down a bit—I don't know what to think about this Hitler fellow, goodness knows they need a strong leader after all they've been through, and some of the British, like Mr. Chamberlain and Eden and even some of our own people have said they think he's a brilliant statesman but, my goodness, all those shootings and executions that've been going on, and now with the old President dead he's called himself Führer or whatever that word is—well, what I mean to say is, I hope sometime you'll go over there and look up our relatives. I must say I regret never having done that. But I'll feel better knowing you have."

"I will."

"There's such a strong family resemblance in this bloodline," she said. "Why, there may be a young von Moltke over there right now who looks just like you. Wouldn't it be fascinating to find out?"

———

By nine o'clock that night, Mitch, Lon and Katie were passing a fifth of orange gin back and forth as they sat in the dark in Aunt Adda's Buick Century. The car was parked on a dirt trail in the trees at the edge of the B&O railroad dam just out of town. They had come on Mitch's dare to go skinny-dipping and they were sipping the gin to help them lose their self-consciousness. The woods were deep and fragrant. Crickets chirped. An invisible bullfrog croaked nearby.

"Knee-deep," Lon intoned.

"Now I know what Lon reminds me of," Mitch said.

"No, siree," Katie said. "Lon's handsome. He reminds me of Dick Powell and Dick Powell's *very* romantic."

"Oh hell," Mitch said, reaching for her. "I'll show you what's romantic."

"No," she said, pushing him off. "I've changed my mind."

"What?" the two boys asked in alarm.

"I've decided that Lon looks more like that new guy in the movies. Nelson Eddy."

"Nelson Eddy. My God," Mitch said, relieved.

Lon laughed. "I don't sing so good. Now who does Mitch look like? Don't say Wallace Beery or he'll make us walk home. How about Clark Gable? Does he look like Gable?"

Katie looked at Mitch coolly, then smiled gently. "Well, take off Gable's mustache and Mitch does look a little like him. At least in the face."

Mitch knew it was nonsense, but he was pleased anyhow. "Hey, great! But who does Katie look like? Not Greta Garbo, she's too sad. I know! The girl in King Kong. The one that Kong peels the clothes off of, like a banana. Fay Wray. That's who Katie looks like."

"Yeah I think you're right," Lon said. "Katie does look like Fay Wray."

"Oh you guys!" Katie laughed, vulnerable to flattery in a world where sex was abundant but love was in short supply. "Listen, did we come out here to take a swim or were you'uns . . ." She caught herself too late, hating the sound of the Hunkie phrase. "Were you guys just foolin'?"

"No, no," the boys protested manfully, heaving themselves out of the car. Mitch realized he was getting drunk. He had trouble unbuttoning his shirt; when he tried to take his pants off, he stumbled and nearly fell. It was dark at the water's edge and the three bodies were silvery in the dark. Katie plunged in, surfaced and yelled: "Jiggers, it's cold."

The boys plunged in after her. They swam about, pushing each other and kicking and laughing. Treading water, Mitch pulled Katie to him and kissed her wet mouth. She responded, laughing, then pushed him away and kissed Lon. Running into the shallows, they splashed water at each other until Katie, choking, turned and ran to the car.

"I'm freezin'!" she wailed.

"Here!" Mitch said, throwing her a towel. "I put towels in the trunk." He strode to Katie and began drying her back and legs.

"You can help, too, Lon," she giggled. He did.

"I'm still cold," she said, wrapping the heavy towel around her body. "Let's get in the car and have another drink."

They climbed in the car and huddled together. Though his stomach was bubbling uneasily, Mitch took another pull at the bottle and began rubbing her legs. Minutes later, the two were in each other's arms; shortly afterward, they climbed into the back seat. Lon, excited and embarrassed, looked straight ahead. He was keenly aware of their murmuring and thrashing about. Abruptly, it stopped. Then he heard Katie tell Mitch to come on if he was coming. In answer, Mitch groaned.

"What's the matter?" Katie demanded, exasperated.

"Sick," Mitch complained. "Feelin' sick."

"Then get out, damnit! Don't you get sick in here. Get out!"

"Awright, awright." Mitch lurched from the car and staggered to a large tree nearby. Leaning against the trunk, he began retching.

"Jeez," Katie said disgustedly. "Some big lover." A moment passed. Lon peered through the darkness. Mitch was a weaving shadow, holding the tree trunk.

"Lon." The voice was low and inviting. It gave him goosebumps. "Lon. Come on back."

"Oh, Katie. I'd like to. But Mitch."

"It's not up to Mitch; I decide who I'm goin' to be with. And right now I'm tellin' you I'm back here all alone and lonely. Look, Lon."

He turned and looked. Her eyes were blue and luminous. Her slim, naked body shone like silver in the gloom. She was infinitely desirable.

Without a word, he climbed into the back seat and they fell together in a tangle of arms and legs.

Lon drove on the way home. Katie sat quietly beside him, her hand on his knee. Mitch, sick, jealous and miserable, was crumpled in the corner of the back seat. When they arrived at Mitch's home, Lon turned off the lights, coasted silently into the gravel driveway and switched off the ignition.

"I'll walk home from here," he said in a low voice. "Will you be able to get Mitch upstairs all right?"

"We'll go in the back and I'll just point him up the front stairs," she whispered. "I don't want the old lady to wake up." She smiled sensually. "It was fun, Lon. See you."

"See you, Katie."

In her bedroom at the rear of the house, Katie fell into a drugged sleep. Mitch passed out in his bedroom and lay across the bed in his shorts. But his unconscious mind bubbled with anger and frustration. An hour later, his emotions forced their way through his stupor and woke him. He sat up, groaned and held his head. Then he padded, barefoot, to the bathroom, splashed water over his face, rinsed his mouth and set out for Katie's room.

"Move over," he commanded, shoving her with his knee.

"Hell, no," she replied wearily. "Go back to bed."

"C'mon, Katie," he said in a rough voice. "You did it for Lon and now you're gonna do it for me."

"I'll do it for who I damn please, when I please, Mitch Robinson," she spat, "and that isn't now or you. You get out."

"You move over!" he demanded, his voice rising.

"Shut up, you fool!" she whispered fiercely. "You'll wake up your aunt and ruin us both."

Without answering, the boy stripped back the covers and threw himself on her. They wrestled savagely and her nightgown tore.

"Goddamn you!" she cried, tears streaming down her cheeks. "Goddamn you!"

"That's enough!" The voice turned them to stone. Aunt Adda stood in the doorway in her bathrobe. Her hair, usually carefully curled and combed, was frizzy and unkempt. Her eyes were round and staring.

"Go to your room, Mitchell," she said harshly.

"Aunt Adda . . ." he began.

"Now, Mitchell." Head down, he padded away.

"Katie."

"Yes, ma'am." The girl cowered silently in her bed, her covers pulled up to her chin.

"You be out of here before breakfast. I'll put your money on the kitchen table."

"Oh, Mrs. Robinson!" Katie wailed.

"There's nothing to say, Katie. Just get yourself and your things out of here. Early." She turned and left Katie sobbing into her pillow.

Mitch was waiting in the hall as his great-aunt arrived at the front of the house. "Aunt Adda," he said tentatively. "Please. It was my fault."

"I'm sure there's plenty of fault to go around," Aunt Adda said. "Some of it is my own for letting such a situation develop in this house. But we're not going to talk about it tonight. You just go to bed, Mitchell. Now."

He did, though he slept only fitfully. In the morning, his head ached horribly and he felt as if he had a cold lump in his stomach.

"Aunt Adda, please believe me," he said at the breakfast table. "I caused the whole thing myself. It wasn't Katie's fault at all. She was trying to make me leave when you came in. She didn't invite me or want me there."

"Drink your tea, Mitch. You need something in your stomach. I wish you'd try a soft-boiled egg."

He shook his head.

"Mitch, you were drinking last night; you smelled to high heaven when I saw you. You'd been out somewhere with Katie, hadn't you? I heard what you were saying, you know." Aunt Adda looked at him sadly, her brown eyes soft. "Mitch, my dear, you've been with Katie before. You know it and so do I, so please don't insult me by telling me a lie." He sat silently, looking at his tea. "Perhaps you did make the first move," she said. "You're a young male and I know what that means. But Katie is a grown woman. She knew better. She deserves exactly what she got, Mitch. And even if that weren't the case, she could hardly stay on in this house, could she?"

"Oh Aunt Adda," Mitch wailed. "I feel just awful."

"I'm sure you do, Mitch," she said. "And you deserve to; I'll say that. You have to learn you can't expect to act promiscuously and not do harm to others and yourself. And it's that much worse when you do it with someone of a different class."

"Class. That sounds like we're still living back in Europe in some old feudal system," Mitch said. "That's why our people came over here, to get away from that class business."

"I don't know about that," she replied. "I just know we're better off staying with our own."

Later that morning, Mitch walked uptown to Brennan's drug store. The quiet house had become unendurable. Aunt Adda had gone to a D.A.R. luncheon. Katie was gone. There was no place else to go. Lon was standing outside the drug store when he arrived. Without a word, the two began walking toward the town square. They came to a halt at one of the World War I cannons at the entrance to the square.

"Gee, Mitch," Lon said. "I'm awful sorry about what happened. I hear your aunt kicked Katie out this morning."

"Oh crap. Is that around already?"

"I guess it is. I heard it up on the Hill."

"Oh crap. That's terrible."

"It sure is. And listen, I'm sorry also about—well, taking your place last night. Seems like I couldn't help myself."

Mitch waved the apology away. "Forget it. It was my fault entirely. I acted like a horse's ass."

"Don't be too hard on yourself, Mitch. I'm sorry as hell for Katie, but, you know, neither of us was a match for that girl. Hell, we're still kids and she's a woman. But I *am* sorry."

"God, so am I. I wish I could do something to help."

They walked disconsolately through the park. "You want to box today?" Lon asked.

Mitch smiled wanly. "You kidding? One poke in the gut and I'll heave again. I'd like to start up again tomorrow, though. I really want to concentrate on that from now on. I need to get in shape to qualify for that tryout at State. At least it'll keep me out of trouble."

Lon laughed, relieved. They were still friends. Mitch never saw Katie again. He heard she left town shortly afterwards. Somebody said she went to Cleveland with a friend to find work.

Weeks later, he began seeing Betsy Bowers. It started when they sat and talked with mutual friends in one of the booths at Brennan's. When the others left, she invited him to walk home with her and play records. He began going to her house regularly. After Katie, the relationship seemed a tame one, but there were compensations. He and Betsy came from the same social group; they could talk about things. They listened to the latest records on her new Majestic automatic record changer and she taught him how to dance.

Betsy was a tall, slim, dark-haired girl with freckles and slightly uneven teeth. She had enrolled at Hunter College in New York and she dressed in what Mitch vaguely recognized as good taste. She also drove him around in a beautiful blue Packard convertible with leather seats. *That* was neat.

They danced to the songs from the new show, Roberta—"The Touch of Your Hand" and "Smoke Gets in Your Eyes"—and to a great new song called "Dancing in the Dark" that had a nice steady beat. Betsy taught him some of the steps that were coming out of New York; she said they were influenced by a new dancer named Fred Astaire. She taught him fast walking steps that were executed as a smooth glide, and the grapevine step in which one foot circled around another as they moved sideways. She taught him a back-dip where he pulled her into him, dipping down and leaning forward a little from the waist to hold his balance. Best of all was the side dip where he wheeled around and, steering his partner with his grip on her left hand and her waist, pulled Betsy into a low dip facing him but beside him.

Dancing was a new kind of fun for Mitch. After an early period of awkwardness, he suddenly acquired the springy, confident balance and sensitive use of hands needed for good ballroom dancing. Betsy was extraordinarily light-footed. She had a rangy, athletic build with very small breasts, slim hips and long, shapely legs. Mitch liked to run his hands over her legs, a liberty she permitted after they started necking.

They started necking one afternoon after they had danced awhile and were sitting on the couch listening to a record made by a new skinny kid singer named Sinatra. He threw one arm along the top of the couch behind her and she snuggled into him. Unconsciously, he dropped his hand to her shoulder and squeezed her affectionately. At his touch, she turned toward him, her face close to his, and shut her eyes. Her lips were half open and he could see the slight irregularity of her front teeth. Her breath smelled of toothpaste and Camels; she smoked a pack a day. For an indecisive instant he sat immobile. Then, as her eyes began to open in surprise, he moved to kiss her. Her arms slid around him. It was pleasant, Mitch decided, but not nearly as exciting as Katie's hot, deep kisses.

He had to work at it to feel excited with Betsy. But he liked her. She was sweet and considerate, and he was impressed by her lack of class-consciousness. She invited Lon to her house as soon as she found out the two boys were friends.

Lon fit easily into Betsy's crowd. Whether it was a natural ease of manner or confidence born out of his athletic accomplishments, Mitch couldn't decide. But he was pleased to have the company of Betsy and Lon in the same circle of friends. Mitch also was amused by the fact that several of the girls were openly attracted to Lon, though they were going steady with other boys at the time.

Mitch discussed it with Betsy. "It gives me a kick to see the way some of your girl friends get bug-eyed around Lon and his muscles."

Betsy grinned. "Yes, I'm afraid Jonesy breathes a little hard when Lon's around. Lon isn't making a play or anything. She's the one doing it." She looked at Mitch appraisingly. "And maybe she's not the only one in that situation."

"What do you mean?" He knew what she meant.

Betsy smiled gently. "Sometimes I think I'm the only aggressor in this—what shall I call it?—relationship of ours."

Mitch talked about it with Lon one afternoon after they had finished boxing six two-minute rounds and were sitting on the grass. "I swear to God, Ace, sometimes I wonder if I'm a damn hypocrite or just weak-minded. I was a whole different personality with Katie. All

hands and hot breath and horny as hell. With Betsy, I'm cool and
casual and she makes all the moves. I hardly recognize myself."

"Well, it seems to be working pretty well for you," Lon said. "And
I got to thank you for getting me invited into her crowd. I sure never
thought I'd be sitting around in any of Mahoning's Main Street houses,
talking and dancing and drinking cokes and beer."

"Well, you've made a real hit with Betsy, I can tell you that. She
even asked me if I thought you'd like to play some tennis on the
family court."

Lon sat up straight. "*Tennis!* Jesus H. Christ! My old man would
croak, the idea of his dumb Swede football player son playing tennis!"

"Well, she used to play and she wants to start up again. She said
she'd teach us. She's got racquets. All you need is sneakers. And you
can help me roll the court. It's made out of red clay and you have to
roll it with a big heavy roller. It'll help build up the pectorals." Mitch
laughed briefly. "Maybe I oughta get Betsy to push the roller. She
could stand to build up her pecs."

"She's a little small up top, I guess."

"You guess? There's damn near nothin' there."

"Well, you're the man who should know."

"Well, you're the only man I'd tell, Ace. They're just little points,
you know. She gets all hot and bothered when I touch them, but I
don't see why."

"It bothers you going with a girl with small boobs."

"Yes it does, damn it. When Flo bends over in one of those dresses
—she does it deliberately, as we all know—I feel like one of these days
I'm going to grab one out of her dress and start chewing on it."

Lon laughed. "I'd like to see that. You'd really stink out the party."

"Wouldn't I though? I know it's silly, but it bothers me. Suppose
Betsy and I got married. I'd be looking at other girls' boobs and
thinking about boobs and dreaming of fields full of boobs. Walking
through them barefoot."

Lon hooted, jumped to his feet and, lifting his legs up and down,
pretended to step daintily through the mammarian field conjured up by
Mitch. Mitch aped his friend's movements and the two tip-toed gro-

tesquely around the yard, laughing. When the joke wore out, they sat down and chuckled.

"Seriously, though, Ace," Lon said, "you could do a whole lot worse than marrying Betsy. I think she's a real good-lookin' number and a nice girl, too. If you don't want her, move aside and give *me* a shot."

Mitch shrugged. "Problem is, I don't know what I want."

"My money!" Lon shouted. Mitch looked up. The sparrows had burst out of the ivy on the side wall of the house and settled into formation as they flew overhead.

The issue remained unresolved. By now, Mitch was seeing Betsy three or four nights a week and having sex at the end of every date. If they were alone, they'd drive out to the country club, have a few drinks at the bar and dance to the juke box. Afterwards, they would jump in her car, put the top up and drive with the lights off to a grove of trees at the foot of country club hill. The darkness was inky black and it smelled of pine. They would neck awhile and he would unbutton her dress and suck her breasts. Then she would pull off her panties, help pull his slacks down, straddle him and ride him as he held her buttocks. He always got an erection and he always had an orgasm, but the pleasure never quite reached his heart.

For Mitch, the stimulation of sex with Betsy paled beside the excitement he felt at the arrival of the German pilot in his Waco-10 biplane.

The German's name was Othmar Kraus; he was a barnstormer who came for a few days to offer rides for fifty cents apiece. Like others before him, he used Potter's pasture southwest of town because it was a flat expanse of grassland and had an old, unused barn on it that could be used as a hanger.

Kraus had been an ace—he said he was and the boys wanted to believe him—in Richthofen's Circus in World War One. He looked like a fighter pilot was supposed to look—broad-shouldered, compact, tough. His eyes were blue and surprisingly bright for such an old man. The boys judged he must be forty.

Kraus wore an old leather jacket, a faded army shirt, wool officer's jodhpurs, and a pair of ancient but highly polished military boots. On his head was a leather pilot's helmet and padded goggles. And, of course, he spoke with a thick German accent.

Mitch and Lon caught a ride to the pasture and watched as a procession of passengers went up to buzz over the town. Eventually, there was no one left on the field with Kraus but Mitch and Lon. The two boys had pooled their money, finding only fifty-five cents in change. Mitch turned and held it out to the pilot, gesturing sideways at Lon and himself.

Kraus looked at the money, smirked, and said: "This is for *both*?" The boys nodded. The pilot shook his head. "Please, sir," Mitch said. "It's all the money we have today and we really want to fly. Together. We could squeeze into your cockpit together."

The German began shaking his head again and Lon blurted: "And we'll help you—run errands, wash the plane, get gas, whatever you want." Kraus stared at them for a moment and a small smile crossed his face. "You want to fly, *ja*?" The boys nodded and mumbled assent. "And you will do work (it sounded like "verk") for me?" They nodded vigorously.

Five minutes later, the boys were gasping with excitement as the Waco cleared the trees and roared over the nearby dam, gaining altitude. The sky above seemed to expand and the world below turned into a child's playroom. There was a toy train below, chugging along; there was the business section of the town, now a collection of tinker-toy buildings with the afternoon sun glinting from its windows. They zoomed over one of the tall towers of the town's abandoned iron works and Mitch, looking down the shaft, felt a sudden surge of vertigo.

After they landed, the boys helped Kraus pull the biplane into the hanger and swabbed oil from the engine cowling and fuselage. The next day, they borrowed Aunt Adda's car to bring the pilot sandwiches and cans of gasoline. Every day or two, when he had finished with his paying passengers, Kraus took the boys for a ride. One day he went up higher than usual, depressed the nose till the engine and wires began screaming and then pulled up and kicked the Waco over into a snap-roll, spinning it once on its longitudinal axis as the world turned in a tight circle.

Before they could get their breath, he shot into a breathtaking dive and pulled upwards into a half-loop, rolling out on top. Kraus laughed heartily when they landed and the boys tumbled, white-faced, from the cockpit. "Okay," he said, waving them toward the barn. "Come sit. I give you something." After sitting them on crates in the barn, he produced small silver cups and filled them with brandy.

Kraus traced the last flight maneuver with his right hand. "The Immelmann, ja? That was our best combat trick; we get a lot of Tommies that way." Sitting on a barrel, the German became reflective. "This Waco okay but not like the Fokker. Like a shark, that one. Two Spandau machine guns arranged so to fire past—through—the propeller. We had many kills. Many."

Kraus took a pull from his flask and shook his head. "We had the best!" he said firmly. Abruptly, he stood. "We *were* the best!" he said in a loud voice. "The best in the air, the best on the ground, too!"

Mitch spoke before he thought. "But you lost." The German looked at him balefully and the boy cringed. After a bit, the German nodded. "*Ja*," Kraus said. "But we didn't lose the fighting, *kinder*, we lost by our government."

Kraus' voice rose again. "We were betrayed! Stabbed in the back! By the bankers, the Jews! Always the Jews!" He pointed at the boys accusingly. "Then the *verdammt* Versailles treaty, they take our territories, our factories, our lives . . ." He took a deep breath, sat down, and began speaking softly. "Now a new day comes. A new leader. Not so nice in some ways, maybe, but necessary. To clean out the traitors, the Jews. To restore to us our, our . . ." he struggled for the word . . . "*stolz*, our . . ."

"Pride?" Lon volunteered.

"Ja, pride," Kraus said. "*Stolz. Hochmut.* So," he said, leaning forward conspiratorily, "we fight this World War over again, *over again*, and this time we win. You will see."

Kraus rose and, shedding the conversation like an uncomfortable coat, smiled like a genial host saying goodbye to guests. "So it has been good fun today, *ja*? I thank you for your help. You are good boys. So, for now, goodbye. *Auf wiedersehn.*"

On the way home, Lon said: "You know, Ace, that got real—I

don't know—creepy, almost. It was like Captain Kraus has got this stuff, this mad-on, all bottled up inside, that nutty business about the Jews and like he's ready to go to war right now today."

Mitch nodded. "Boy, I'd hate to be in his gunsight." He grimaced. "I can't believe all the Germans feel like that. If they did, imagine what could happen."

"Things would sure hit the fan, wouldn't they?"

When they went back to the field the next day, the German and the Waco were gone. The barn was spick and span; it was as if he had never been there at all.

The episode dimmed in importance when the Penn State boxing coach phoned and agreed to give Mitch a tryout. It was successful and Mitch was given a full scholarship.

With his height and punching leverage, Mitch became the top light-heavyweight on the team during his freshman year. When his sophomore year began, Mitch elected a major in English literature.

Meantime, Lon had become Pitt's No. 1 halfback. The boys stayed in close touch throughout their college years, getting together on holidays and during vacations when they weren't working at summer jobs.

By the summer of 1939 Mitch was still seeing Betsy sporadically and Lon was dating a looker from the Hill, a half-Italian, half-Irish girl named Josie. What amused both boys was the fact that each was attracted to the other's girlfriend.

"It's really nutty," Mitch said. "Neither one of us ever seems to be satisfied with what we've got."

"Yeah," Lon sighed. "Course all this is likely to be—excuse the expression—academic pretty soon. The way ol' Hitler's torn across Europe—in what, *two weeks?*—it looks like England's next. Then whatta *we* do?"

"Jeez, those Germans sure can fight, can't they?" Mitch asked, feeling slightly guilty and proud at the same time of his ancestral bloodline. "But why should *we* get sucked into it?"

"You should hear my old man," Lon said. "See, Olaf remembers the first World War. He keeps shakin' his head and sayin', it's the same thing all over again. The Germans; we'll be next, he says."

"No disrespect," Mitch said, "but I don't really think so."

Mitch was wrong. He was a graduate student at State on December 7, 1941, and Lon was assistant football coach at Wilson High School when Japan attacked Pearl Harbor. Four days later, Germany declared war on America. The two talked excitedly by phone.

"You're not goin' for a student deferment, are you?" Lon asked.

"Hell no," Mitch said. "I'll tell you what sounds neat. There was this Air Corps recruiter on campus yesterday and he showed us some films. It looks real exciting. You and I could enlist over at Dubois for the aviation cadet program. We'd pass the physical easy and, hell, we ought to be able to pass the written test. Become a pilot, a *real* honest-to-God *ace*. How about it?"

"Gee I don't know," Lon said. "It's all so quick."

"Listen, Ace, you know we're gonna be in this thing, sooner or later. Let's do it the way *we* want. Go to Germany and bomb Hitler's brains out. I may be part German but he's got it coming."

"It sounds good, Mitch, but—jeez, it's an awful big decision to make all of a sudden."

"I think it's the only one we *can* make," Mitch said. "I'm going to do it. C'mon now; are you with me?"

Lon hesitated and then smiled into the phone. "Sure, Ace. Let's do it."

———

Two thousands miles to the west, in San Francisco, Alvin Google made the same decision. Alvin, at 19, thought of himself as a warrior. If he had had the power, he would have transformed himself into a medieval *wu-shih* or *samurai*. All his life he had reveled in stories of man-to-man combat. In school he had been a marginal student except when the unit of study was history and it involved a war. And then, for the moment, he became outstanding. The public schools didn't teach Eastern history. So it was a revelation to him, at the age of fourteen, to learn about Shaolin Temple boxing.

He had already been taught Western-style boxing by his father, a taciturn, hard-bitten man with whom he lived after his mother died. His father was a lean, sinewy dockworker who supplemented the meager family income and satisfied his appetite for violence by fighting periodically in winner-take-all fights at the local saloon.

By the time Barney was fourteen—his schoolmates gave him the nickname from the comic strip—he could whip any boy in school. Except, he found out one day in the schoolyard, a Chinese boy his own age. They were playing. Barney was laughing and pushing the boy. And suddenly he found himself flat on his back. In some fashion, the boy had swept Barney's feet from under him. Now the boy was standing over him, smiling.

Barney rose, intensely interested. He gestured to the boy to raise his hands, raised his own, circled and threw a left followed by a right cross. The boy easily blocked the left from the outside and, swaying to the left, crossed his right arm with Barney's oncoming right, grasped his wrist and pulled sharply down, sinking into a crouch. Barney found himself falling forward. As he tried to straighten, the boy uncoiled. His arms shot upward; the palms of his hands struck Barney's chest. The blow, given added force by Barney's upward momentum, lifted the American boy off his feet. He landed heavily on his back, the air exploding from his lungs.

The Chinese boy stood over him again, smiling slightly. Barney rose, taking deep breaths. "I've never seen nothin' like that before. My old man hasn't either. Would you teach me?"

The boy's name was Wing. After considering the request for a moment, he consented to show Barney the two maneuvers he had used. Barney realized that one was some unusual form of wrestling, the other something that mixed wrestling with boxing.

"Teach me more of this," he pleaded.

The Chinese boy smiled slightly and shook his head. "This takes many years of faithful training," he said. "Westerners don't have the patience. Besides, it would be impertinent. I have no right to teach this art, even if I could. I'm only a novice."

"Then take me to someone who can teach me," Barney asked. He asked Wing every day for a month, but the Chinese boy always smiled and shook his head.

Then, one day, Wing looked at him seriously when Barney asked the ritual question. They were sitting on a fallen tree trunk at the edge of the playground. "Barney," he said quietly. "I've spoken about you many times. To my master."

"Your father?" Barney asked.

"No, my master, my teacher," Wing said. "At first he said it was impossible, a white boy taking such instruction. But I begged his pardon every day and told him respectfully that you had asked again. Yesterday he grew very angry and shouted at me when I asked. But then he said, 'Very well, bring this strange white boy to me. We will dispose of this matter very quickly.' 'You won't hurt him, will you, master?' I asked. He gave me a sharp hit on the head; it made my head ring. He said, 'I will hurt you, you worm, if you speak disrespectfully to me again! Now bring me this annoying boy!' "

Wing opened his almond eyes wide and shrugged. "So you can come today if you like, Barney. If you don't want to, I will understand."

"Oh gosh," Barney breathed, jumping to his feet. "You bet I'll come."

"All right," Wing said. "But you must behave properly. You will take off your shoes before you enter the practice room. Be sure your feet are clean. When I introduce you to the master, you will bow. Not like that; from the waist, like this. If he puts out his hand, you can shake it. Otherwise, just bow. Don't forget."

Barney met the master in a large empty room over a cluster of tiny stores in the heart of Chinatown. The place smelled funny, a little sour and spicy, like some kind of cooking Barney couldn't identify. He and Wing reached the practice room by walking up a long, narrow flight of stairs. A dozen Chinese boys in loose cotton uniforms were doing some kind of slow dance or drill in their bare feet.

The master's name was Mr. Chang. He was a lean and bandy-legged man of middle height. But it was his face that caught Barney's attention. The eyes were dark and piercing and the face was finely chiseled with high cheekbones and a thin gash for a mouth. A flat thatch of black hair capped his head. Barney was surprised to find that Mr. Chang spoke no English.

When Barney straightened up from his bow, he saw that the thin gash of Chang's mouth had lifted at one corner. The master, hands on hips, surveyed him silently for a moment, a sardonic expression touching ·the chiseled face. Then, abruptly, he gestured for Barney to strike at him. When Barney hesitated, the Oriental scowled and gestured savagely. Obediently, Barney set himself and threw the right hand as his father had taught him. Chang seemed to sway like a shadow, deftly caught the boy's wrist with one hand and, pivoting from the waist, thrust his free hand, spear-fashion, into Barney's armpit. A blinding pain shot through Barney's chest and he gasped for breath.

The master looked at Barney for a another moment. Then, turning, he looked at the Chinese boys who were kneeling nearby, watching, and pointed to one. The boy sprang to his feet, approached and bowed, first to Chang and then to Barney. Barney, who was careful not to rub his aching armpit, looked inquiringly at the master. With a brief nod and gesture, Chang made it clear that the two boys were to spar.

The Chinese boy lashed out with a high kick. Barney caught it instinctively on his forearm and began to circle. Out of the corner of his eye he saw the thin gash lift into a smile. The Chinese boy's eyes widened suddenly and Barney braced himself for a second kick. When it came, he blocked it, slid beneath the outstretched leg, yanking it upward, and kicked the boy's other foot out from under him. The boy fell heavily on his back.

The master clapped his hands. When the boy failed to rise quickly enough, Chang grabbed him by the collar and flung him toward the others. Another boy was summoned to spar. This one tried a snap kick to the groin, which Barney blocked, and followed with a swift one-two punch, left and right. Barney blocked the first, slipped the second, and counter-punched sharply to the stomach. The boy fell to the floor, gasping.

The master shoved the second boy toward the kneeling students, moved in front of Barney and gestured for him to spar. Barney realized quickly that Chang was imitating the actions of the two students. The high kick flashed at his head like a whip. It touched him lightly, like a kiss, and was gone before Barney could react. Then the snap kick to the groin. Barney partially blocked it but the man's hard fists followed so swiftly that both landed lightly before he could get his hands up. Barney instinctively tried to counter. The master caught his wrist and pulled, simultaneously blocking one of Barney's ankles with the flat of his bare foot. Barney somersaulted and landed on his back. Pulling upward on his wrist as Barney was about to land, Chang broke his fall so that there was little impact.

As Barney scrambled to his feet, Chang dropped his hands and grunted. *This is how your opponents should have fought,* he seemed to be saying. Chang seemed to come to a decision. Abruptly, he waved Barney toward the Chinese boys. He was to join them. A broad smile broke across Barney's face. Barney started to move toward the other boys, turned back and bowed. Again the thin gash lifted. Settling into place beside the other boys, Barney stole a glance at Wing. His friend's face was composed but his eyes were merry as they flickered toward him. Barney had become a student.

By the time he graduated from high school, three years later, Barney had learned 170 distinct bodily postures divided into the five styles of Shaolin Temple boxing. The Tiger style, Barney found, concentrated on the sudden mobilization of bones and muscles, like an angry tiger springing from the woods. The Leopard style required great leg strength. The Snake demanded the cultivation of an inexhaustible supply of breath and an unending succession of supple movements. The Crane required the developed ability to stand on one leg in a variety of postures.

In the floating movements of the Dragon style, Barney found the mysterious source of energy called *ch'i.* It was useless, he found, to try to understand it intellectually.

His friend, Wing, who served as interpreter for Chang's few verbal explanations in Chinese, couldn't explain it beyond saying that *ch'i* is a force.

"It is centered in the navel," he said. "When you master it, it will provide great force at the moment you need it."

"You mean strength?" Barney asked.

"No, not strength," Wing said, shaking his head at such Western stupidity. "Force, power, which comes suddenly when summoned. Strength is never used in the Dragon."

Once, Barney foolishly tried to ask the master, by means of gestures and the few Chinese words he had learned, what one of the movements meant. He wanted to know whether it had a practical application to fighting. Chang cuffed him across the head and stalked away. Wing explained afterwards that it was a fundamental breach of etiquette for a student to ask such a question. If one of the Chinese boys had done it, he would have been dismissed instantly. It was only because of Barney's racial ignorance that he was allowed to stay in the class.

Learning such things came only with long, hard-earned experience, Wing said. They would reveal themselves in time.

It was a week before Chang would acknowledge Barney's presence in the class. When he did, he ordered Barney to stand in the horse-riding posture, back straight, knees well bent, for a half hour. The pain became intense, almost unbearable. Afterwards, Chang motioned for Barney to stand erect with arms extended horizontally to either side. For another hour, Barney stood, arms extended at shoulder level, his left palm up, his right one down, till his shoulders felt as though they were on fire.

Barney had to use all his willpower to keep his heavy arms from sinking. To allow them to drop, he knew, would disgrace him. As he stood immobile, the other boys moved around him in their drills and movements. They seemed not to notice him, but Barney knew they were watching to see how the strange Western boy bore up under the ordeal.

Barney was drenched with sweat. His lips and knees trembled. Then, toward the end of the hour, something remarkable happened. In desperation he imagined that, instead of trying to hang down, his arms were being held *up* by strings hanging from above. When he succeeded in believing it, his arms became light. A thrill shot through him. He had found a way to deflect pain and acquire a small measure of mastery over the physical world. He felt almost as if he were floating in the air.

Chang's voice returned him to earth. Focusing his eyes, Barney saw the master standing before him, the thin mouth turned up at one corner. He nodded and Barney let his arms fall. The master looked at him for a moment, nodded again and walked away.

As time went on, Barney learned that the Western fist was an inferior instrument for fighting. The fingers were more effective as prongs or knives. The flat of the hand made a slashing sword. The heel of the hand became a hammer. The feet were deadly weapons, too. With them, the Oriental fighter had an enormous advantage over a Western opponent; he had four hands to fight with instead of two. Still, Barney told Wing, he had no confidence that he would know what to do in a fight. "All we do are these forms, these drills, and I don't even know what they mean," he complained.

"Each of these forms is a story in itself," Wing explained patiently. "I know only a little of them myself. But as you move from one posture to another it is as if you, perhaps a traveler, have been attacked, first from one side, then the other. As you wheel around, swinging, crouching, kicking, slashing, you are defeating the attacks and responding."

"But what good is it if I don't know what I'm doing?" Barney asked.

Wing smiled. "A very great master once said: 'I cannot tell you how I defeat the enemy; I only do my exercises.' "

Barney found out what this meant the afternoon his father was killed. He had seen his father only a few times over a period of several weeks. They seldom spoke to each other; his father had seldom shown him any warmth—he had little to offer—and had offered him advice and instruction only in the Western boxing in which the man excelled. He provided Barney with a cot in his room to sleep on, and he doled out enough money each week, just barely enough, for Barney to buy food for himself. For the rest of his needs—a minimum wardrobe and a few pennies in his pocket—Barney worked at a variety of odd jobs.

His father, Barney realized by now, was an embittered man, frustrated by the knowledge of greater talents than he had been able to use. A warrior by nature, he should have become a professional fighter rather than a mere barroom brawler. Barney thought that if his father had been lucky enough to have been born Chinese and grow up as a *wu-shih,* a man of arms, he might have become a respected personage like Master Chang.

Barney went down to the docks to find his father. It was payday and his father would give him his week's allowance if Barney found him before the day's drinking began. Barney arrived to find his father in a fight with a larger, heavier man. Both had been drinking. A crowd of dockworkers ringed the pair, shouting encouragement to one or the other.

Both men were unsteady, a condition that gave the larger man the advantage. Twice, using his weight, he bulled into Barney's father, mauled him and pushed or knocked him down. The second time he rose, Barney's father was bleeding from his nose and one eye. The larger man, now confident, rushed him again. This time, Barney's father sidestepped the rush, ducked the swinging arm and hooked twice sharply to the stomach.

The large man doubled over, wheezing. Barney's father followed closely, hammering the man's face with punches. The man fell against the stacks of boxes and bales they had unloaded earlier. It was then the big man saw the longshoreman's hook lying on a bale. He clutched it, stepped forward and swung it at Barney's father. It pierced the skull with a terrible crunching sound. A moan rose from the crowd. Barney's father fell like a tree, blood streaming from his head. Insane with rage, the burly man raised the hook for a second blow.

Without conscious thought or effort, Barney darted forward, his body moving smoothly in the sequences he had learned. One upraised arm blocked the descending hook. Barney's other hand uncoiled. The heel of the hand struck the man a hard blow under his heart, knocking him off his feet. Rolling over, the man clambered to his feet and charged, swinging. Barney blocked his wild punch from the outside and, pivoting from the waist, swung his left arm loosely, bringing all the weight of his body with it. The edge of his hand struck the man's kidney with tremendous power. As the man staggered and turned, Barney's right arm followed like a spear. The tips of the fingers shattered the big man's larynx.

The man collapsed, strangling. His face turned a deep red, then purple. His eyes bulged from his face. Barney turned to his father. His father's face was a dull gray color; his eyes were half closed. Barney fell to his knees and felt for his heart; then, as he had seen the Oriental master do when someone had been knocked senseless in a match, he felt for the pulse in the neck. There was none.

A hand grasped Barney's shoulder and he looked up. A man Barney recognized as one of his father's co-workers was staring into his face.

"Get outa here, kid!" the man said. "There's nothin' you can do. Your old man's dead and so's the other guy. They killed each other. You weren't even here, understan'? You don't wanna go to no reform school, so get the hell outa here now. Don't even go back to your room."

Barney got up and left, a feeling of confusion and wonder spreading through him. Death had come so easily. As he made his way through the streets, he tried to understand his feelings. He felt regret at his father's death, but not sorrow. He felt neither regret nor remorse at killing the other man. Barney also was aware of a certain irresistible feeling of—what? Elation? No, that would be unworthy. Power? No. Fulfillment. Yes, that was it. He had done what he had trained himself to do when it had to be done.

Half an hour later, Barney realized that he had returned to Chinatown and the practice room. He opened the door, which was never locked, and entered. There was no one there. He took off his shoes and sank into a kneeling position against the wall. He was still sitting there, asleep, when the master shook him by the shoulder and woke him.

Barney never knew whether Chang had found out what had happened, though it seemed likely, given the effective network of communication within the Chinese community. Barney was moved into Wing's family's tiny apartment to live. He left Chinatown during the next year only to visit the public libraries. There, he read extensively about Eastern beliefs and cultures, recognizing in himself the developing attitudes of a Buddhist and the character of a *wu-shih*.

From the Japanese, he absorbed the warrior's code of Bushido. Bushido taught that death was unimportant. The mind is trained to the death of the self. Accepting this, one could lay fear aside forever. All that one should fear, if that was the word, was dishonor. Honor lay in the warrior's life, in doing one's duty, whatever that turned out to be, and defeating the honorable opponent.

From Zen Buddhism, Taoism and Confucianism, Barney plumbed the mysteries of life and death. The Book of Change taught him that life continues to change and evolve and, in a true sense, nothing and no one ever dies. In the Upanisads, he was told that, following a temporal life, the soul, depending upon the behavior displayed in that life, goes either to Brahma or into the womb of a woman to be reborn. Birth is identical with death; if you are going to fear one of them, you should fear birth.

The Hindus taught him that there is no direct opposite to life. More importantly, *there is no death.* Only birth, growth, decay and renewal. *The cause of death is birth.*

Barney was surprised to find that Westerners had thought along parallel lines. Heidegger, he found, proclaimed that, to live a productive life, one must confront death and lay it aside. The stoic emperor, Marcus Aurelius, taught that one should not worry about living a long life because that is impossible to do. All that we mean by life is what we perceive of it, and we can live only in the present. The past is gone and cannot be relived. The future is not here. Consequently, whether we live one day or one hundred years, it makes no difference. All we can truly live is the sliver of *now.*

As he moved silently through his exercises, day by day, Barney wondered: if life is largely an illusion and death doesn't exist, if we are to live in perpetual cycles until we achieve a higher level of being, then how should we live our lives? The Dhammapada said that "even Buddhas do but point the Way." But which Way? Buddha's final words were: *Strive mightily.* To do what?

When World War II came, Barney felt that he had found the answer. There was an honorable duty to perform and he had undergone the most important part of the training to do it. The issues of the war seemed clear enough. One nation, led by a barbarian warlord named Adolf Hitler, had invaded its neighbors and proclaimed itself superior to all others. Now it had declared war on the United States. The question was not whether to serve but how. The concept of aerial combat fascinated Barney. Given the disappearance of swordplay and sustained hand-to-hand fighting, flying seemed the closest thing modern war could provide to honorable single combat.

So he decided to enlist in the Army Air Corps and become a pilot. Investigating, he found that his lack of college would not be an obstacle if he could pass a rigorous physical and written examination emphasizing English, questions of logic, mechanical aptitude and mathematics. Since math was his weakest point, he called upon Wing, a superior student, to drill him every day for six weeks in algebra, geometry and trigonometry. One week later, he went to the recruiting office, easily passed the physical, scored highly in the written exam and was accepted as an aviation cadet.

Barney's acceptance filled him with delight. Now he would become a warrior in fact as well as spirit. And he would play a part in the defeat of this new barbarian Warlord of the West.

# CHAPTER TWO

# The Warlord

HAGGARD and dull-eyed, the Warlord sat listlessly at his desk in a barren room in the *Wolfsschanze,* his sprawling Wolf's Lair headquarters in the pine forests of East Prussia.

The news was terrible, unbelievable, and it had driven him into a deep depression. The campaign to create a New World Order, which had begun so brilliantly in 1940, had ground to a disastrous halt by late 1944.

His face was gray and bloated. His left arm and hand twitched uncontrollably. From time to time his entire left side shuddered with spasms. The room echoed his disharmony. It was bare of furniture but for a nondescript divan, a plain wood desk, a small armchair. The ugliness of the gray concrete walls was relieved only by furring strips to which dark wood paneling had been attached. For visitors, the darkness inside the windowless bunker created a painful contrast to the sunlight that filtered through the trees outside.

The darkness within was of his own making as well. The peculiar magnetism that had once radiated power and inspired fear now filled the room with gloom and an almost palpable atmosphere of hatred and frustration.

The Warlord tried to rise from his heavy chair, trembled violently and then sank back in the seat with a curse. A year ago, even six months ago, he would have made his morning decisions as he paced about the room with his secretary following him, reading from dispatches and taking notes. Now he had become so weak that walking even a short distance exhausted him.

He looked balefully at the reports he had called for. In the West, American forces had reached the Rhine. In the East, the Russians had reached the Danube and were driving into East Prussia. To the south, the Germany armies had been driven from Greece. In the Norwegian fjords, the mighty battleship *Tirpitz,* pounded by British bombs, had capsized and drowned a thousand German seamen.

But they were nothing compared to the casualties the *Wehrmacht* had suffered since D-Day. Nearly a hundred divisions destroyed; more than a million German soldiers killed.

He looked glumly about the room. Within a few days, he would have to pack up and leave the *Wolfsschanze,* its twenty-foot-thick concrete walls, its guest bunkers, tea house and flak tower. He would order it blown up. His private train, the *Führersonderzug Brandenburg,* was waiting now on the siding with two locomotives, a *flakwagen* car equipped with cannons and separate cars for his baggage, his bath, his conferences and himself.

His staff was frantic for him to leave. The Russians were within bombing range; if they knew where he was, they would undoubtedly try to drop paratroops and capture him. The thought made him snarl. He would go to his *Adlerhorst* headquarters near Frankfurt and, if that, too, were threatened, he would be forced to return to his ruined Chancellery in Berlin and spend the rest of the war living like a prisoner in the reinforced concrete bunker beneath it.

There were two more status reports, companions to each other. He lifted them with trembling hands. One described the devastating effects of a raid by 1,000 American bombers on the synthetic oil refineries at Bohlen and Zeitz. The other assessed Germany's fast-developing oil crisis. The oil fields of the East were back in enemy hands. Production from the synthetic oil plants in Germany was dwindling daily under the bombing in spite of heroic twenty-four-hour-a-day efforts to keep them on line. The Politz, Magdeburg and Lutzkendorf refineries were operating at 20 percent of capacity. Because of the fuel shortages, counterattacks had to be canceled, tanks were being abandoned in the field; some were even being drawn by horses. New Luftwaffe pilots could be given only fifty hours' training before being sent into combat.

He struck the desk. One thousand bombers! Who could have imagined what would rise from the Pandora's box when he declared war on America! It was his destiny to conquer, he had always been sure of that. But now? He shook his head angrily. There had to be a way out; he had always found one in the past.

Pulling himself erect, the Warlord pawed through the papers on his desk. Somewhere here he would find the solution. The manpower report; he scanned it and threw it aside with a curse. Fifteen-year-old boys were manning the Reich's anti-aircraft batteries now. The new Hitler Youth Division, the 12th SS Panzer, was manned—manned!— by boys of twelve and thirteen. Wherever salvation lay, it clearly would not be in manpower.

Strategy? He grunted; there was no room left for maneuver. Germany was being squeezed like an orange from both sides. What remained? He pondered and finally nodded. Technology. New weapons, secret weapons. *Miracle weapons!* He said the words aloud. This is where the solution had to be found! He searched impatiently for the reports on research and development, snatching them up and examining them one by one.

The Mouse, the 100-ton tank. It had been his pet project, but Speer lacked the men and materials to produce it now. He threw the piece of paper aside. The Power Egg, the 600-mile-an-hour rocket plane. The Allies had bombed out the assembly works. He tossed it aside. The Arado, the new jet-powered bomber with the BMW engines that could reach England and knock out the accursed American and British air bases. He pondered it for a moment. No; if he told Speer to switch production to the Arado now he would have to give up his V-2 revenge rocket. And pilots would have to be trained to use the new bomber. Too late for that. His hand flicked it away.

The Gotha flying wing; the scientists claimed it would produce a radar image so tiny it would be invisible to anti-aircraft gunners. Nonsense! Who cared what the enemy gunners saw? They wouldn't see anything at all if the Luftwaffe did its job and wiped them out. The hand flicked sideways again. Another report: the ram-jet. He peered at it irritably, trying to understand it. The scientists described a "space plane" that would take off normally, escape the earth's gravity—he snorted with derision—and bounce along atop the earth in a sort of orbit, coming down anywhere in the world within two hours. They were testing a scale-model design in a wind tunnel.

He crumpled the report and threw it on the floor. The last thing he needed was something that would fly to China at some time in the future! He needed something that would help him here and now.

The two-stage A-10 rocket to bomb America; the scientists called it a true intercontinental ballistic missile. He pronounced the words silently. That was more to his liking, but it would do nothing to solve the problems at hand. Perhaps later. He laid it carefully aside. There were two reports left.

He picked up the first and cried out in anger. Another heavy water experiment to make a *verdammt* atomic bomb! He had told them and *told* them he wasn't interested in nuclear physics, *Jewish* physics, he called it! That's why he had driven the Jewish scientists into exile in the first place. The fools would never learn! He balled the paper up in trembling hands and threw it across the room.

The last report. He looked at it and sighed. The pestiferous Messerschmitt 262 project again. A twin-engined jet aircraft, the first of its kind, the so-called wonderplane. It had been available for a year and a half. When a test-flight demonstration was staged for him in March '43, he had watched the thing rip across the field at an unbelievable speed—twice the speed, they said, of the ME 109 fighter, half again faster than the fastest Allied fighter or any propeller-driven aircraft.

But he didn't want a fighter! He wanted a bomber, the *Blitz* bomber the Luftwaffe had been promising him and failing to deliver, for years. When he ordered the new wonderplane converted to his long-awaited *Blitz* bomber, the unthinkable happened. His fighter aces, led by Galland, that pampered, thirty-three-year-old movie idol of a Luftwaffe general, *mutined.* If Galland and the others hadn't been national heroes, he would have had them shot out of hand. Instead, he told Göring to fire them.

Now the report said the bomber pilots had been unable to make any real use of the 262; that 1,000 of the propellerless airplanes—about a quarter of them assembled—were simply sitting around in hangers and forests and quarries. The report also stated—gratuitously, he noted—that Galland and his fellow mutineers were still unemployed. Drinking and chasing women, he thought disapprovingly. Useless, all useless. And yet . . .

His eyes came alive and began to flicker incandescently in the strange way that had impressed and frightened so many. Perhaps Providence, which had guided his hand so many times, had directed him to this report. It was all that was left. If that were the case, he would assume that Galland had been right after all. He would assume that the best of Germany's remaining aces, given this so-called ME 262 wonderplane, could do what they claimed and stop the obscene Allied air offensive. If they could, it would give him time. Time to restore Germany's fuel production; time to rebuild the nation's shattered transportation system. And then he could do again what he had done so brilliantly before—go on the attack. The course of the war would change.

He struck the desk decisively with a palsied hand. Very well! He would order the pilots to give him a demonstration. He would order Speer to supply enough ME 262s for the task. Then he would tell Göring—Göring! he sighed with disgust at the thought of the drug-ridden ruin his paladin had become—he would tell Göring to put Galland and his band of mutineers back to work. Give them the new jet airplane they said would allow them to work wonders. Let them prove it or die. Adolf Hitler smiled faintly. Let them prove it *and* die.

———

At his desk in his headquarters office in Berlin, Minister of Armaments Albert Speer picked up the phone.

"Put me through to General Galland, please. Yes, I'm holding. General, Speer here. Yes, fine, fine. General, I have something to tell you.

That shipment you've been wanting so much? Well, you'll be getting part of it very soon. Half a loaf, you know, better than . . . What? Yes, from the very highest quarter. You'll be getting the news officially from a bit lower down. These days, he's much lower down. Remember to be surprised. Glad to do it, don't mention it. Just thought you'd like to know."

Speer hung up and peered reflectively at the slim, aristocratic face in the mirror across the room. This was the first chink in the dike, the first sign that the Führer was finally willing to show as much concern about the defense of the Reich as about attack and revenge.

It was horribly late for such a conversion; unless something miraculous was done to stop the Allied bombing, Germany's oil supply would simply vanish by spring. He knew the figures by heart. Between March and September, synthetic production had fallen from 132,800 barrels a day to 18,500. Aviation gasoline had dropped from 50,000 barrels to 2,500. Soon it would be even less. And the thousands of new tanks and locomotives and airplanes that the talented Reichsminister of Armaments had succeeded in manufacturing in caves and underground factories with slave labor would sit impotently where they were stockpiled.

The only hope now lay in stopping the bombing. With even a few days' relief from this horrible battering from the air, his engineers and chemists could work wonders. Even now, the giant Merseburg-Leuna refinery was coming back on line. But for how long?

If Galland's aces could just pull it off now—prove that even a handful of new-generation fighters could destroy a large force of heavily escorted bombers—he would quickly provide larger numbers of the jet fighters. Then, maybe then, he could persuade the Führer to divert enough resources to allow production of a second weapon that would surely stop the cruel bombing of Germany—the *Wasserfall,* his new electronically guided, breathtakingly accurate ground-to-air rocket. Except for the death of Adolf Hitler, that was what he wanted most.

———

Reichsmarshall Hermann Göring, his huge body bulging like an overstuffed sausage in a white uniform bespangled with medals, waddled slowly through the great room of Karinhall, his fabled castle and hunting lodge, now his rustic refuge from the scorn of the Führer.

He lifted his fleshy jowls and peered lovingly at the stolen Rembrandts and Goyas that hung on the walls near the stuffed heads of elks and stags that had once wandered into his gunsight. Possessions like these were what he loved most now. He raised a pudgy hand and admired the sapphire ring he had chosen from his jewel box. His paintings, his jewels, his model railroad, his private zoo—all things of beauty, all welcome escapes from bomb-shattered Berlin, his frightening Führer and the *Götterdämmerung* of the Third Reich.

He stopped and surveyed himself in a gilt-bordered full-length mirror. He was unaccountably nervous today. Partly, he knew, because his doctor had cut his daily intake of paracodeine pills to thirty. And partly, he admitted, because of the impending arrival of *Generalleutnant* Adolf Galland.

The order that Galland was to be returned to duty had surprised him; there had been no forewarning. It had also humiliated him; the Führer hadn't deigned to telephone him and give him the order directly, as he would have done in the old days. Instead, the call had come from that odious office toady, Bormann. Still, it was the Führer's order and must therefore be obeyed.

For Galland he felt both sorrow and anger. The man was so much like what he himself had been in World War I—a handsome, rakish, devil-may-care combat ace. Once he had considered Galland his protege; it was he, after all, who had persuaded the Führer to promote Galland to General of the Fighter Command at the age of thirty. In turn, he had basked in Galland's admiration for what an energetic Hermann Göring had done to create the powerful Luftwaffe.

All that good feeling had been destroyed by the mutiny and by Galland's unpardonable behavior when Göring gave the fighter pilots a tongue-lashing for failing to turn back the American bombers. (It was nothing compared to the abuse that the Führer had heaped on *him*.) Galland had actually torn the Knight's Cross from his neck and thrown it on the Reichsmarshall's desk.

There would be no such theatrics today. He smiled grimly to himself and moved slowly to a corner of the room where he lowered his huge backside into a heavy, throne-like chair behind an oaken table. Today he would be neither tolerant commander nor friendly mentor. Today he would be the stern judge, the dispenser of justice.

He straightened in his seat, tugged at his uniform jacket and took a deep breath to calm himself. Galland strode through the door exactly two minutes later. The trim figure stopped, came to an exaggerated posture of attention and threw Göring a casual Luftwaffe salute. Göring returned it with a flick of the hand and pointed to a seat opposite the desk.

The Reichsmarshall watched coolly as the younger man seated himself. Galland hadn't changed; still the ridiculously crushed officer's cap, the black hair, the nose that had been flattened in a stunt-flying accident, the rakish black moustache that seemed to captivate women and the Brazil cigar that Galland now impudently took from a silver case and began to roll in his fingers.

"General," Göring said without preamble. "I have decided to allow you to return to active duty. Furthermore, I have decided to allow you to fly the 262 as a fighter-interceptor." He watched Galland's face carefully for reaction. The eyes were opaque but, for an instant, the lips tugged upward at the corners. Damn the man! Had somebody tipped him off? He grew even sterner.

"Let me make clear the conditions under which this will happen. I authorize you to form a squadron—a single squadron, do you understand? You'll give us a demonstration of your ability to bring down the American bombers with this so-called wonderplane you've made so much trouble over. You'll show us what you can do. As the Americans say, put your money where your mouth has been."

"May I choose my own pilots, Reichsmarshall?" Galland asked blandly.

"Go and recruit those unemployed fellow mutineers of yours. Get them out of the rest camps and the bars and put them back to work. Report to General Koller of the Luftwaffe General Staff in Berlin— you've dealt with him before; he'll cut orders for the men you want. He'll also arrange the transfer of a suitable number of jet fighters to your command, as well as the mechanics and other support facilities you'll need to set up your base."

"Where will we be based?" Galland asked.

"Wherever you like. The further away from here the better. That brings up the second point. Once you're set up, you'll have no further communication with Fighter Command or anyone else in the Luftwaffe. You'll be in a state of quarantine. I'll expect periodic reports from you, of course." He waved a bejeweled hand. "That's all. You're dismissed."

As Galland rose, Hermann Göring smiled faintly. "You'll end this war the way you began, Galland. You started as a lieutenant and squadron leader. You'll end it as a lieutenant-general and squadron leader."

Galland threw him a salute, turned and strode to the door. As he touched the doorknob, he turned, his dark eyes dancing, and said, "Reichsmarshall, have you ever read the American Uncle Remus stories for children?"

Startled, Göring answered: "No, I haven't."

"When you have time, Reichsmarshall, I commend to you the one about the rabbit and the briar-patch. *Wiedersehen.*"

———

The wonderplane, the Messerschmitt 262, was a machine of breathtaking beauty. It seemed more the work of an inspired avant-garde artist than the product of engineers. The fuselage, painted a mottled gray-green camouflage, was abnormally slim. The nose was shaped like the end of an artillery shell; the tail was a rakish triangle.

The engines—should they really be called engines?—were extremely long, slim pods suspended beneath the wings. There were no propellers at all. Simply a turbine that sucked air into the front of the pod and expelled it with great velocity at the rear. At the front of the turbine on each engine was an ingenious little electric motor that was started by hand. It fired up the turbine. The assembly was, by definition, a jet engine. There was nothing else like it on any airfield in the world.

Looking at it, Luftwaffe Colonel Karl Walther von Moltke felt curiously humble. Ordinarily, Moltke was untroubled by such feelings. He came from a proud and revered Prussian military family. At twenty-seven, he was an ace with thirty confirmed kills; twenty-two of his victims had been four-engined bombers. As commander of a Focke Wulf 190 *Sturmgruppe* unit, he had engaged in the most difficult type of air-to-air combat and survived.

He also knew that he cut a dashing figure in his dove-gray uniform. He was tall for a fighter pilot and broad-shouldered, if thin, and had a striking face with dark, wide-set eyes, heavy eyebrows, a generous mouth and strong jaw. But for his devotion to his beautiful wife, Elise, he could have had his pick of the frantic, thrill-seeking women he encountered at ground control, on trains or in the bomb-wrecked cities.

All of this normally combined to create a sense of considerable self-esteem. But, today, he felt it oozing away like air from a punctured balloon. His first look at the wonderplane was reason enough, but there were other reasons as well. One was the officer who was standing beside him, briefing him on the operation of the new aircraft. He was the famous *Oberst* Johannes Steinhoff, one of Germany's most famous fighter pilots.

Steinhoff, Moltke noted, was the perfect Aryan. He was athletic and blond, with fine Nordic features. He was also a prodigous combat pilot; he had shot down 176 enemy aircraft and had been decorated personally by Hitler.

A third reason for Moltke's attack of humility was the group of men who sat, talking and laughing, in a semicircle 100 meters behind him across the grass field. There, lounging in old deckchairs in a weed-grown patch of open field, drinking tea and eating coarse army bread with gooseberry jam—my God, like laborers on their lunch hour—was the most imposing group of airmen he had ever seen together. Every one of them held the Knight's Cross. Every one was an ace.

Sitting in the center of a group of twenty or so behind a rickety table with a field telephone on it was the most famous fighter pilot in Germany—Lieutenant General Adolf Galland, until recently the Luftwaffe's General of the Fighters. Here he sat in exactly the same manner that the newspapers and cinema and postcards had captured so often—the crushed cap, the gray leather flying suit, the yellow silk scarf, the famous cigar. Galland had waved the cigar impatiently at him when Moltke arrived at the field and approached the group to report for duty.

"For God's sake, man, we don't stand at attention here," Galland said. Some of the men laughed. "Sit down." He pointed with his cigar. "There's an empty chair; it's got a broken back; mind you don't fall out of it."

Galland turned to his pilots. "Gentlemen, this is Colonel Karl von Moltke, late of the *Wilde Saus* and, until recently, commander of a Focke-Wulf *Sturmgruppe* with an impressive record. For those of you who've been spending all your time lately in bars and fighters' rest homes, the *Wilde Saus* were night-fighters, chasing RAF bombers on bright nights. They made a lot of kills till they were weathered out.

"A few of you, I know, served in the *Sturmgruppes*. Those who didn't should know that they were, and perhaps a few still are, elite units—ME 109s and FW190s equipped with cannons and extra armor-plate for the pilot. Their mission has been to blow the American bomber formations apart by boring in and firing till they're at the point of ramming—a tactic based on the Japanese kamikazes, actually. Not that we believe in actually ramming; at least not yet. We may be crazy; we're not quite *that* crazy." The men laughed.

"Colonel Moltke, or should I say Baron?"—Galland grinned and Moltke felt his face flush—"this handsome devil beside me is *Oberst* Johannes Steinhoff; he is the official training officer of our little squadron of experts—*Kommando Jagdverband* 44, by name."

The general used his cigar to point at each man in turn. "We also have with us *Oberst* Barkhorn, who has somehow fiddled the records in order to claim 300 kills on the Eastern and Western fronts; Count Krupinski, who helped invent those *Sturmgruppe* tactics you've been using; *Oberst* Lutzow, who told Göring to his face that he should step down; *Major* Hohagen, just back from hospital with a bit of steel in his skull . . ." He turned to a blond officer with a black student's cap pulled low over his eyes. "Is it steel or plexiglas?"

"Plexiglas," the man said.

"Well, there you have it," Galland said cheerily. "You'll meet the others in time. For now, you should meet one of our wonderbirds over there." Galland pointed to the other side of the grass field. Beneath a row of trees sat a line of sleek twin-engined airplanes.

The general stared at them for a moment and his face darkened. "If we could have just had those kites a year ago, along with the rest of it —the fast-firing cannon, the new rockets we'll be using—*what* we could have done!" His voice became a growl. "It hardly bears thinking about."

Galland picked up the chipped Wehrmacht mug from the rickety table in front of him, stared into it and sipped his tea. "Well," he said at length. "Steinhoff, why don't you show our new friend around? Maybe you should offer him a ride."

It was then that Steinhoff and Moltke had walked across the field to the new airplanes. Earth embankments had been built around some of them on three sides. A dozen 262s had arrived in sections on railway cars; soon there would be as many as fifty. But some lacked parts, and mechanics were still assembling most of the rest.

"As you can see, it's only a grass field and we're only a squadron," Steinhoff said. "But it's a squadron of experts and it's headed by a general, a very special one. Not long ago, he was head of the Fighter Command."

"I feel greatly honored to be here, Colonel."

"We want people like you, Karl—you don't mind if I use your first name? That's why we invited you to join us. You've had a fine record and we knew your *Sturmgruppe* was out of action."

Moltke laughed mirthlessly. "They had plenty of new aircraft to give us but they couldn't manufacture new pilots and finally the deliveries of octane stopped. So the unit shut down."

"We're the last and best of the Luftwaffe, Karl." Steinhoff's voice was curiously gentle. "Our aim is simple: to protect what's left of our cities, of our culture, to the best of our abilities. We'll do it with this." He walked up to one of the airplanes and patted the fuselage as if it were the neck of a prized horse. "This kite will fly 200 kilometers an hour faster than either the Mustang or Thunderbolt," Steinhoff said. "Twice as fast as our old 109s. Nearly three and a half times faster than the Boeings."

Moltke raised his eyebrows in surprise. "I had heard less, and I didn't even believe *that*."

"You'll see for yourself, Karl. Another thing: this propulsion system becomes more efficient at altitude rather than less, contrary to our old reciprocating engines. With the 262, we're able to fly higher and faster than anyone on earth. Enemy fighters can't attack us; they can only try to get out of our way. And with good reason: our armament is fantastic. In the aircraft you'll fly today, you'll have four 30-millimeter cannons. Not the old 20s. These shells will punch a hole in any armor known. And, by the time you go up again, the armorers will have fitted wooden rails to the wings—for the new 55-millimeter rockets they've developed for us. Each airplane will carry twenty-four of them. Assume you approach the bombers from the rear at high speed. You fill the luminous gunsight with the bomber. If you've got it in the gunsight, wingtip to wingtip, your distance is 1,000 meters. Release the rockets and it's a 100-percent kill, Karl. Because the explosion covers a space of ten meters high by fifty meters wide, the size of a house. There's no possible way for the bomber to escape, and you may get two or even three with one salvo if they're in tight formation."

"Incredible," Moltke breathed. "But what about fuel? The Luftwaffe's starving for it."

"We're lucky there," Steinhoff said. "First, the general has all sorts of connections. Second, our kites don't use octane gasoline. They burn a crude fuel made from brown coal. It stinks like the devil . . ."

"Made from coal?" Moltke asked incredulously.

"Yes, the stuff's called J-2 fuel. It's something like heating oil with an admixture of octane gasoline, I understand. Every kind of fuel's in short supply, of course, but nothing's as scarce right now as octane gasoline. That's one of the reasons—I'm sure the biggest reason—we've been called up to fight. To defend our synthetic oil plants."

"And this is the perfect aircraft for the job."

Steinhoff smiled. "Nothing's completely perfect. There are some weaknesses you should know about. First, the kite is very slow to gain momentum, particularly on takeoff. Run it up slowly, hold it with the brakes, and then let it roll. Use the whole field. If you try to pull it up too soon, you'll kill your speed," he smiled grimly, "and yourself. The angle of attack of the wing when the aircraft's rolling on the ground is less than the angle of attack when you're flying at stall speed. So the kite won't come off the ground by itself; you have to pull it off. When you do, do it very carefully—one or two degrees' incidence will lift it. When you get off, push the stick down slightly to pick up flying speed. You'll accelerate slowly at first, but soon you'll be flying faster than any prop-fighter pilot has ever flown. Be very careful banking; you can pass out. You've never felt a G-force like this. At high altitudes, try to avoid touching the throttle at all. You might blow an engine. Don't exceed 870 km. Also, be careful not to dive too steeply. The kite has no dive brakes and you'll not only miss your target— your controls can freeze on you."

"Good God," Moltke said. "That's quite a sackful of cautions."

"Yes it is," Steinhoff said. "You have to handle the 262 gently. Would you like to take this one up and make a circuit or two?"

Moltke felt his heart accelerate. He felt like a student pilot again. "Now?"

"Why not?" Steinhoff raised a hand to a mechanic who came running from a nearby earth berm. "Don't do anything fancy. Just familiarize yourself with the way it handles; takeoff, landing, turns, banks. Keep your eyes open, of course. Don't let a stray Ami fighter hit you from above."

"Should I shoot a few touch and goes?"

Steinhoff considered. "No," he said. "You really need the whole field for takeoff, so you'd have to land very precisely at the edge. Leave that for later."

Moltke smiled to hide his excitement. "Well then, wish me break-a-leg—wish me luck."

"*Hals und Beinbruch.*" Steinhoff waved a hand and walked away.

Moltke moved to the left side of the airplane's slim fuselage, placed his foot in the step and heaved himself into the cockpit. Inside, he wriggled around on the parachute to find the most comfortable position. He adjusted the height of the seat to bring his eyes to the exact level of the luminous gunsight. Whether he used it or not, it was best to be ready.

Moltke pulled on his shoulder harness and seat belt and fastened it.

Buckling his helmet under his chin, he picked up his oxygen mask and snapped it into place. Now the instruments. He set the altimeter for the correct barometric pressure, turned on the radio and moved the stick and rudders to make sure the controls were free. At last. He gave a hand signal to the waiting mechanic on the ground below. The mechanic started the electric motors and the turbines fired and began making a heavy humming sound. Not at all like a gasoline engine turning a propeller. The smell of coal oil drifted past the cockpit.

Engine temperature normal. Pressure normal. He closed the cockpit hatch and the mechanic stepped away. Moltke advanced the two throttles slightly. The airplane moved forward. Carefully, he staggered the throttles so that the 262 turned into the wind and toward the line of flags that marked the takeoff strip. He looked across the field toward the men lounging in the broken-down chairs. Steinhoff, standing apart from the others, threw him a jaunty salute.

Moltke took a deep breath to relieve his tension and concentrated fully on what was at hand. *Now.* Slowly he ran up the throttles until the turbines screamed. Dust billowed up around the airplane. When the rev counter reached 8000, he released the brakes and began to roll along the grass field. *My God, but it's slow getting started.* Steinhoff was right. The 262 bounced and jolted, the undercarriage thumping from intermittant contact with the ground. The airplane tried to wander; he corrected with the rudder. He kept rolling and bouncing. A thread of fear began moving through him. *When would it take off?* The end of the field was coming up. *It would have to be now.* He pulled back very slightly on the stick and the 262 lifted into the air. Wheels up. He kept the nose flat, as Steinhoff had advised.

The kite began to move, sluggishly at first. Then, as if it had just awakened, the air speed indicator began winding up at an unbelievable rate. He pulled the stick back slightly and began climbing at a high rate of speed. The shattered city of Munich lay below, a thin ground mist covering it with gauze, like a lightly bandaged wound. To the south, a blurred vision, the snow-shrouded Alps.

Moltke swung in a wide circle as he climbed. The sound—no, the absence of sound—fascinated him. All he could hear was the air rushing past. It was like flying a glider; but no glider had ever moved this fast. What had General Galland said about it? It was as if angels were pushing you.

He swiveled his head; above there was mixed and broken cumulus and stratus cloud cover. He sailed through a hole and looked quickly around again. Nothing. He banked the 262 gingerly and soared, climbing, through a huge cumulus cloud. So fast! A wave of exhilaration swept through him. Nothing could match this! He dropped the nose and dived through another cloud, pulling up gently when he realized the controls were stiffening in his hands. *Remember what Steinhoff said! Don't dive too steeply.* He flung himself at a magnificent, towering cloud castle, sailed around the battlements and cut a hole neatly through the tower, prepared to rescue any wraithlike maiden who emerged.

Aerobatics? Well, just a little. He dived shallowly, pulled the nose up and tapped the right rudder, at the same time pulling the stick back and to the left. The 262 rotated easily through a snap-roll. Lovely. For fifteen minutes, with only the wind as companion, he wheeled and banked and soared, savoring a freedom he had never before felt in powered flight.

"Ground control to unidentified aircraft. Do you receive?" The disembodied voice startled him.

"Control, this is Rhineland One."

"Rhineland One, what is your mission?"

"Rhineland One to Control. Practice mission."

"Victor, Rhineland One. Report any change of position."

"Returning to base, Control. Rhineland One, out."

Time to go home. He banked the jet gently, eased back on the throttle and checked his compass. It would look silly indeed if he allowed the speed of the kite to get him lost. He broke through the clouds. There was Munich, there was the field. He made a circuit and, giving himself plenty of room, made a low, careful approach, kissing the grass with his wheels. He breathed a sigh of relief, having avoided the embarrassment of a rough landing his first time out in front of the entire squadron.

Steinhoff was waiting as he taxied back to the berm. "How did you like it?"

Moltke grinned, feeling curiously like an adolescent. "It was everything you said. Wonderful."

"No problems?"

"Oh, the takeoff scared me a bit, I'll admit. It's so bloody slow developing airspeed. In the Focke Wulf, you just push the throttle and you're off the ground. Punch a button and up come the wheels. Same thing on landing; very simple." He shook his head. "You'd be a sitting duck in this kite if you had to take off while the field was under attack. But in the air . . ." He opened his hands in wonderment. ". . . unbelievable. You could attack and break off at will."

Steinhoff smiled. "We'll test that theory very soon now; shouldn't be more than a few days till we get these kites fully armed and checked out. We may send you up solo, meantime, if ground control wants high-speed recon on the bomber stream. It may bore you, nosing about up there simply looking at things, but don't worry. We'll be flying together against the pantechnicons soon enough."

Moltke laughed. *Pantechnicons.* Trucks. Ground control used that term for the Amis' bombers for some reason that Moltke had never understood. But yes. He would enjoy seeing a pantechnicon in the gunsight of his ME 262.

# Prepare for Max

MITCHELL Robinson felt the vibration of the incoming V-1 pulsing against his eardrum before the sound became audible. His ears had grown exquisitely sensitive to engine noise over the past year and the tiny undulation seemed to be coming from his pillow. Sandra, half-asleep beside him, was unaware that the bomb was coming. Soon, he thought irritably, the thing would become loud enough to wake her, as it always did.

It came. *Uh-ruh! Uh-ruh! Uh-ruh!* The pulse-jet engine made it sound like two badly synchronized reciprocating engines in the hands of an incompetent pilot. That was one reason he found it so irritating. Another was the fact that it shouldn't be in this area at all—so close to the base at Whitwick Green.

"Oh, God!" she cried suddenly, stiffening and clutching him. "What in the name of God is a buzz bomb doing *here*?"

"It's off course, that's all," he said. "It's meant for London, not Bedford. I'm surprised they still have a V-1 base operating; I can't imagine where they . . ."

"Oh, damn and hell, Mitchell, I don't care *where* the beastly thing is from," she gasped. "It's *coming*!"

The flying bomb was approaching at low altitude, its engine growing louder and more menacing. *UH-RUH! UH-RUH! UH-RUH!*

Sandra trembled violently and Robinson pulled her against him. "It'll be all right," he said.

She hit his chest with a small fist. "How in the world can you say it'll be 'all right'? You'd have to be insane not to be frightened!"

"I never promised you sanity, love," he said. "Only affection, passion—whatever I have available at the moment. I . . . ."

"Oh, God," she whispered. The engine had grown loud enough to shake the old Swan Hotel. Now it had stopped. It had run out of fuel and was diving toward town. Robinson held Sandra tightly and began counting. Thousands of people throughout England's Midlands were doing the same thing.

*One thousand and one, one thousand and two, one thousand and three, one thousand and four* . . . There was a resounding thump. Somewhere, perhaps a half mile away, there were cries in the dark followed by cheers from the town's survivors. A house, maybe two, had been pulverized. Three, five, six people were dead, others cut badly by flying glass and debris. A siren wailed; a fire truck rumbled by, bells ringing.

When Sandra stopped shaking, he got out of bed and peered out the window. It was nearly dawn, and the river and the boathouse on its opposite bank were dimly visible in pale black and white. There was no smoke or fire. The bomb must have landed behind them, somewhere in town. He looked up and down the river as far as he could see from the window.

There were no swans on the river. Where do the swans go in the winter? The hotel clerk had been astonished when Mitchell asked. "Why I have no idea," she said. "No one's ever asked such a question before. I expect I'll have to ask 'round." If he knew where the swans went, disappearing so cleverly and completely, Robinson thought, he'd go join them.

"Come back to bed, darling," Sandra said. "You'll catch your death standing there." He climbed beneath the covers and lay beside her. "The V-2s don't seem as bad," she said, snuggling against him. "The explosion is terrible and I know they do more damage, but at least they're—what do you say? . . ."

"Supersonic."

"Supersonic. You don't hear them coming so you don't have a chance to be afraid. But *you*." She pushed slightly away from him and pulled her head back to look at him. Her eyes, he thought, were so clear and green that he could make out their color even in this half-light.

"Can you tell me why on *earth* you're not afraid of the buzz bombs?" she demanded.

"Oh," he searched for the reason. "I guess it's because they're junk . . ."

"Junk?"

He propped himself up on one elbow. "The things are just too damn random to be taken seriously. They're technological junk. They're not aimed at anything in particular, they can't be aimed. So what good are they? When we go out on our raids, we have precise targets and we do our damndest to hit them. The Luftwaffe has precise targets, too: namely us. Sometimes you see the man's face in the fighter that's attacking you. That makes it very personal. But those things . . ."

Sandra laughed or snorted; it was hard to tell which. "Are we talking about professionalism or predestination, Mitchell, or just that the commander of the 205th Bomb Group is too bloody important to be carried off by a lowly buzz bomb?"

He smiled, "Maybe all of the above. Anyway, how can you really hate them so much when it was one of them that brought us together?"

A V-1 had performed his introduction to Sandra Brooks one late afternoon near Harrod's. It appeared, flying just over the rooftops, trailing a red plume. It was an unexpected, other-worldly apparition, the more so because London's traffic noise had muffled its approach. Now it was overhead and people were scattering. *UH-RUH! UH-RUH! UH-RUH!*

Robinson saw her as he turned toward the subway entrance. She stood like a doe caught in a flashlight. She was tall, with sea-green eyes and chestnut hair. Her lips were parted in surprise. She was wearing a green wool suit. Time slid into slow-motion. He sprinted to her, caught her in his arms, yanked her into the subway entrance and pressed her against the wall, shielding her body with his.

The blast was deafening. It shook the shelter. Bricks and shards of glass fell outside. A cloud of dust rose in the street. Cries rang out. Sirens sounded. Wardens and first-aid people ran by.

The woman clung to him, trembling. A long moment passed. He listened intently, feeling a faint pulsing sound begin in his ears. The woman looked up, puzzled, and then with annoyance.

The man was a complete stranger, she thought, and one of those boorish Americans to boot. They trafficked with the Piccadilly Commandos, the whores, and with the occasional shop-girl, and they spoke in the most odd and ignorant manner. Now this great giant of a flying officer was holding her tightly against the wall of the shelter, the length of his body against hers. She owed the man her thanks for pulling her to safety, but he seemed to be expecting some sort of payment in return.

"Let go of me," she demanded, trying to get her hands up to push him away.

"Listen," he said, his eyes half closed. "There's another one coming."

"It is *not*," she said. "Now will you let me go or—oh my God!" He was right. There was that horrible undulating sound again and then the eerie silence. She pressed herself against him. He was counting in a calm voice "One thousand and one, one thousand and two, one thousand and three . . ." as if he were timing a race. CRUMP! The bomb fell farther away this time. Then it was he who pulled away.

"That seems to be all for the moment," he said. "I didn't mean to alarm you."

"Alarm me?" She found herself laughing, half hysterically. "I didn't realize that Americans had the gift of understatement."

She looked more closely at the man. He was smiling gently. He was quite tall and broad in the shoulders, though thin through the body. He had a rather nice face, she decided. Interesting, too. Lean, with brows that were heavy and black. The eyes were dark and wide set. The jaw was strong, stubborn looking; the mouth was generous. For such a young man—he couldn't be thirty—he had surprisingly heavy lines at the corners of the eyes and mouth. His uniform jacket was a chocolate color; on the left chest he wore silver wings. On his shoulders were round silver badges of rank; a light colonel, she judged.

"People from another planet sometimes look a little different," he said, smiling again.

"I'm sorry," she said, embarrassed. "But we did meet rather violently and I haven't met many—well, really, *anyone* from your 'planet' till now. You must think me rude."

"I promise not to think that if you'll have a drink with me." The smile became broader. Oh dear, she thought. It's true. They do have better teeth than our men. Probably the result of better diet and more money for dental care.

"I really don't feel secure enough right now to sit down calmly somewhere and drink gin," she said. "I'd rather get to my flat. If you'd like to walk along, I won't mind."

"Be glad to." They made small talk as they walked. She did most of the talking. It was ironic, she thought. The American was the very picture of the strong, silent Western hero of the Hollywood films. When they reached her entrance, he stood patiently, smiling at her. God save the Queen, she thought. What *would* my friends say if they knew I met an American flying officer in the street and invited him up? To her surprise she heard herself do just that.

"You've been very kind, and you don't seem like Jack the Ripper. Would you like to come up for a cup of tea or cocoa? Unless I can find something stronger."

"I'd like that very much."

Upstairs, Sandra turned the kettle on and took two cups from the cupboard of her tiny kitchen. She dropped one when the next buzz bomb signaled its approach. They wound up sitting under a table in the tiny room that served for sitting and sleeping. She always crawled under it when the flying bombs arrived—unless she was in bed, in which case she simply pulled the covers over her head and prayed.

Now she was clinging to him again, trembling, as the ugly device sputtered into silence somewhere overhead. After the blast, he said: "I think I'm beginning to like these things."

"Please don't even think such a thing," she said, shuddering. It was a particularly bad night. The V-1s came every five minutes or so. It was unthinkable for Robinson to leave under the circumstances. So he stayed.

After a few hours, and following his suggestion that they stretch their legs—no ulterior motive, he declared—they moved onto the single bed and propped themselves with pillows against the wall in a half-sitting position. When a V-1 came, she burrowed against his chest.

Between bombs, they talked about themselves. Sandra did clerical work for the War Ministry. Her father, Brigadier Harold Brooks, a widower and retired World War I officer, was employed by the Ministry as a military historian. He lived in a small house in Harpenden, an hour away by train. Robinson told her about growing up in a small town named Mahoning in western Pennsylvania with his Aunt Adda, in reality his great aunt. He had majored in English literature at Pennsylvania State College. She was surprised that Shakespeare and Housman were taught at American colleges.

By dawn, the bombs had stopped coming and they fell asleep. Robinson woke first. A slit of sun peered at him from the edge of the blackout curtain over the window. They had slid down until they were lying against each other, full length, on the bed. His arm was around her and Sandra's head was on his shoulder; her mouth was open slightly. He had never seen a more beautiful face, he decided, certainly not from the range of six inches.

Her eyes opened. They looked at each other for a moment and, without thought, he covered her mouth with his.

That was six months ago and they were in bed in the room he rented by the month in the 150-year-old hotel in Bedford. The telephone was ringing. She rolled over, picked it up, spoke briefly and handed it to him.

"It's Major Carlino," she said. Carlino was the base adjutant.

Robinson spoke guardedly. "Morning, Ed. What's up?"

"Looks like we'll be having a meeting," Carlino said. "Why don't I send a car for you? No rush; is an hour time enough?"

He smiled slightly. "An hour'll be fine."

When he had hung up, Sandra moved against him. "One hour. Twenty minutes to shave and shower. Twenty minutes for breakfast. That leaves twenty minutes for us."

"Wizard," he said.

"Not wiz-erd, darling. I can't share my bed with someone who says wiz-erd. It's wiz-ahrd. Now come here."

Their mouths locked, their hands moved and stroked, as they had done many times before.

"Oh, yes. Now, please." Her breath came short. "But I warn you— if a bomb comes while we're doing it, you're going to get the most terrible squeeze."

She was right. A bomb came, and he got a terrible squeeze.

———

The mission alert came over the teletype from Pinetree in midmorning. *Await a field order,* it said. *Prepare for maximum.*

The duty clerk climbed in the watch officer's jeep and carried the message to the group commander, the group operations officer, the intelligence officer, the group navigator, the group bombardier, the weather officer, ordnance, armament, engineering, the photo unit, the cooks, the motor pool and the charge of quarters for each squadron's cluster of barracks. Soon, all of the 4,500 men on the base, seeing the herky-jerky movements of the key people, would know a mission was being planned.

Robinson waited in one of the two rickety armchairs near the pot-bellied stove in the Nissen hut that served as his office. In America, it would have qualified as substandard housing. But the stove glowed a cherry red, offering a modest cheer. A dented metal desk made a triangle in the corner. An army cot with blanket stood along the opposite wall. His regular sleeping quarters were in an adjacent hut.

*Maximum effort.* Everybody and everything available would fly. It was also his turn to lead the group. Now *that,* not the buzz bombs, was what scared him. And the prospect of his sixty-fifth mission scared him far more than the experience of the first.

"Colonel." Executive Officer Ed Carlino entered and sat down in the second armchair. Carlino was Robinson's physical and tempera-mental opposite. He was second-generation Sicilian, five-seven, 180, built like a granite block. And, like a granite block, something Robin-son knew he could lean on.

"What's on the menu, Ed?" Robinson asked.

"The man hasn't told us yet," Carlino said. "Maybe a nice interdiction mission, some railroad marshalling yards somewhere. Maybe an aircraft factory."

"The group navigator may want a little more detail," Robinson said sardonically. "Name a town in Germany that doesn't make airplanes."

"Well, all we've had on the menu lately are oil, chemicals and railroads. Maybe it'll be someplace like Leipzig; that qualifies all around."

Robinson grimaced. "No thanks," he said, sticking an unlit cigar in his mouth. "First time there we lose an engine. Second time we lose hydraulics, Campbell loses a finger. Last time we lose McGuire. I've seen enough of Leipzig."

"Your people originally came from around there, you said."

Carlino cursed himself for inviting the conversation. But it was better to encourage Robinson to talk about his lineage again than to let him brood over bad luck.

"On my mother's side," Robinson said reflexively. "My Aunt Adda must have told me about him a hundred times. General Hellmuth Karl Bernhard von Moltke." He spoke the name slowly, giving each syllable equal emphasis. "He was my great, great—ah, great grandfather. I'm never sure whether it's two or three greats. We had a portrait of the old bird in the living room, painted in 1848. She and I would sit there at the end of the day and it would sort of half light up. She'd see it and, oftener than not, start talking about him. He was a military genius, German General Staff. Invented *auftragstaktik*"—he said the word slowly and carefully—"mobile mission tactics that the Germans are so good at. But the big thing was that, according to her, I looked just like the face in the portrait. Strong bloodlines, she said. I didn't see it. Anyway, that's why they christened me Mitchell Moltke Robinson, a pretty fancy . . ."

Robinson looked up sharply. "You're playing games with me again, Ed. You *know* all this crap. I always rise to the bait!"

"I really don't remember: did the von Moltkes live in Leipzig?" Carlino asked.

"Yep. She wanted me to visit my relatives some day." He grunted. "Now I have."

"Okay, so it isn't Leipzig. Maybe another basic industry. Or maybe you'll go look for that new buzz-bomb launcher."

"Not bloody likely. This is a max."

"You still gonna lead?" Carlino asked.

"Well, I have to, don't I?" Robinson demanded, chewing on the cold cigar. "The lead teams know the rotation. Besides, I'm not ready to be a paddlefoot yet." He smiled. "No reflection on paddlefeet, of course."

"Thanks."

"So how many aircraft do we put up? Who leads the high and low squadrons? And, as long as we're talking trivia, who's my co-pilot? Ravitz has pneumonia. McGee's at Diddington with the heebie-jeebies."

"Battle fatigue."

"That's what I said."

"Taking them in order," Carlino said, consulting the clipboard he held in his hand, "we oughta get up a full thirty-six with three spares to fill in if needed. For the low squadron lead, subject to approval, Ops has picked Captain Coleman. The high squadron will be led by Major Amundson."

Robinson glowered. "Lon Amundson led the group two missions ago; he's got a bad sinus. Why should he have to fly?"

"Because everybody flies." Carlino looked up sharply. "Look, Mitch. Everybody on the base knows Amundson's from your home town. Don't act like his daddy. You embarrass him."

"Okay, okay. What about my co-pilot?"

"Already picked him," Carlino said. His dark eyes brightened but he stopped short of smiling. "Lt. Alvin Google."

"Barney Google?" Robinson barked, sitting erect. "Why, for God's sake?"

"Because he's the best pure pilot in the group, no question," Carlino said evenly. "He's good enough to be lead team and lead the group if . . ."

"If he wasn't as nutty as a fruitcake. The guys are all afraid of him, you know that. He does those crazy-looking Chinese-type slow-motion exercises, and he has that big damned dog some farmer gave him. I even hear Google's been taking the dog on missions. That isn't true, is it?"

Carlino shrugged. "Well, yeah. A couple of medium altitude raids, the crew chief told me. I understand Google got a quartermaster to modify a B-6 jacket for the dog and found a helmet for him. Even a cut-down parachute."

"Godalmighty, Ed, I know this is the Air Corps and not the goddamn infantry, but it *is* supposed to be a military unit."

"Yes, well, I understand the dog sits quietly by Google during the missions. Flak doesn't seem to bother him. And he won't wear the mask. He doesn't need oxygen, at least not at 15,000 feet." Carlino smiled. "There'll be no dog aboard your airplane tomorrow, Colonel."

"Not as long as I have my .45." Robinson chewed the cigar glumly. "Well, okay, it's Google. But he sure as hell is odd."

"There are a lotta odd people around here, Colonel. F'rinstance, on your last trip, when the fighter escort showed up? You must have had the mike button depressed. The crew heard you say 'my money,' or something. Wanta explain?"

"I didn't realize," Robinson said. "It's something that Lon and I used to say back in Mahoning. My money. When you saw a flight of birds. It was supposed to be good luck for whoever said it first."

"Makes sense," Carlino said dryly. "Last subject. Up at Wing last week I heard some scuttlebutt about a new German fighter, a new power plant of some kind that drives it a lot faster than our escorts. You heard anything?"

"Latrine rumor, probably," Robinson said. "Somebody's always talking about Hitler's secret weapons and when he's going to spring them. It's a little late for that, don't you think?"

"There's no question at this point, we've got the war won. But we're still taking casualties. I'd hate to see something pop up at the last moment that'll make things worse."

"Well," Robinson sighed, "the devils I know about are bad enough. I'm not going to worry about the devils I don't. All I want to know right now is where we're going tomorrow."

———

Reichsminister Albert Speer took a last look at the vast and intricate network of piping that processed crude oil into lighter forms of petroleum and gasoline at the great Merseburg-Leuna refinery. Then he stepped into the van that served as his portable cipher office. The clerk jumped to his feet and snapped to attention.

"Sit down, please," Speer said, "and send a short message to the Führerbunker at the *Reichskanzlei* in Berlin. I'll dictate it."

The clerk removed the cover from his Enigma machine, checked his list to determine the day's cipher settings and rotated the three small wheels in the back of the machine until their contact points were in the prescribed position.

On the keyboard at the bottom he typed in the call sign and time of origin, and then the introduction he had used the last three times Speer had radioed the Führer from the plants he had been inspecting:

P7J to SF9. 10:30 TO THE ATTENTION OF THE SUPREME COM-
MANDER, HEIL HITLER.

The clerk turned to Speer. "The body of the message, sir?"

Speer read the message from a piece of paper on which he had scrawled it. As he spoke, the clerk typed it onto the keyboard:

IT IS MY HONOR TO REPORT MERSEBURG-LEUNA BACK IN
FULL OPERATION. OIL PRODUCTION RESTORED TO 500 TONS
DAILY AS OF NOW. SPEER.

A separate alphabet was displayed in tiny lightbulbs at the top of the keyboard. Speer watched with interest as each keyboard letter at the bottom illuminated a different letter in the alphabet above. Today, he noted, the first T became J. M became P. But, since the Enigma's three wheels turned eccentrically with each tap on the keyboard, the routing of the electrical circuits inside the wheels changed accordingly. The second time T was typed it came out O. M became Q. There was no logical way to predict the pattern of letters being transmitted by

Enigma, no known way to break a code that defied the basic rules of cryptanalysis. Enigma was a scientific marvel, absolutely unique, the deepest secret of the war.

When the coded message was complete, the cipher clerk handed it to a waiting wireless operator who sent it to the Chancellery in Morse code. At the Chancellery, the wireless operator printed out the incoming letters and handed the message to the cipher clerk. The clerk checked the wheel settings for the day and typed out the coded letters on the keyboard of his Enigma machine. A companion wrote down the message that appeared in the illuminated alphabet above it.

Adolf Hitler read the message and a trickle of hope fed his ailing spirit. With Merseburg-Leuna back on line and 500 antiaircraft guns ringing the plant, things were changing for the better.

———

While the message was being transmitted from Merseburg to Berlin, a British signal sergeant who was sitting in a van five hundred miles to the west plucked the electrical signals out of the air. He and two corporals had been monitoring the frequency around the clock for three days and had become familiar with the operator's call-sign.

When they had transcribed the dots and dashes into their incomprehensible five-letter groups, one of the corporals reciphered them in the latest British code and sent the message by teleprinter to a country estate called Bletchley Park that lay forty-seven miles north of London.

There, one of the 10,000 oddly assorted men and women who worked twenty-four hours a day in nondescript wooden huts received the Merseburg message in the registration room. He copied it and sent it by courier to the intercept control room, where the supervisor looked at it and decided the call sign merited priority attention. Copies went to the crib room in an adjoining hut, where cryptographers searched for repetitive elements in messages that they called cribs.

A university professor on leave from Cambridge recorded the frequency and call sign of the Merseburg message and compared it against a stack of others that had come in over the past three days. Seeing the same call sign and a vague but unmistakable similarity in the letter patterns of the introductions, he noted his findings and sent them with the message text to cryptographers in the next hut. Sitting around the rim of a long horseshoe table, twelve mathematicians, talented chess players and professional cryptanalysts studied the new message and compared it with others that had the same characteristics.

Within two hours, the group had produced twelve pairs of letters that they thought might bridge the intricate electrical circuits between the Enigma keyboard and the illuminated lampboard.

A courier took the pairings to a hut containing four five-by-ten-foot electromechanical calculating machines called *bombes.* There, a clerk programmed the twelve pairs of letters into one of the machines by inserting metal plugs with prongs into selected receptacle slots. Then she pulled a switch and walked away.

The *bombe,* which contained twelve replicas of the Enigma's three-wheel sets, hummed through 17,576 possible wheel settings. One hour later the machine stopped abruptly. The clerk peered at a three-digit number displayed on the *bombe*'s readout, copied it on a piece of paper and sent the paper by courier back to the cryptanalysts' hut.

A professor of probability theory read the piece of paper, sat down in front of a duplicate of an Enigma machine built by exiled Polish mathematicians, set the wheels in the three-digit position predicted by the *bombe* and typed the letter groups of the Merseburg message on the machine's keyboard. The watch officer got up from his chair inside the center of the horseshoe table and watched as the clear text appeared in the array of lightbulbs.

The process that had broken the unbreakable code was called Ultra. It was the Allies' deepest secret; aspects of it would still be classified fifty years later.

———

At his advance post on the second floor of the College Moderne et Technique in Reims, General Dwight D. Eisenhower, Supreme Commander of the Allied Expeditionary Forces, sat at a raised teacher's desk and scanned a sheaf of battle reports.

He had been working since six o'clock in the morning and it was shortly after noon. The room was small and plainly appointed. Blackout curtains hung at the two windows. On the Supreme Commander's desk sat his blue leather desk-set, framed photos of his wife and son, and two black phones, one for ordinary use, the other for scrambled calls to London and Washington.

Beside Eisenhower's right hand sat a full and smouldering ash tray. By noon he had smoked thirty cigarettes. He growled as he scanned one message. Another complaint from Montgomery! That goddamned prima donna! He had a good mind to . . .

There was a quick rap on the door and his personal aide, Colonel Tex Lee, stuck his head inside.

"The PM's on the scrambler phone, sir."

Eisenhower's expressive face wrinkled in surprise. He picked up the phone. "Prime Minister," he said in the voice that had charmed thousands, "how are you?"

The voice of Winston Churchill was faint but unmistakable.

"Fine, my dear general. Are we scrambled?"

"Yes we are, sir."

"Splendid. Have you heard from Uncle Boniface today?"

Eisenhower grinned. Even over the most secure line, Churchill couldn't bring himself to use the word Ultra. He always referred to it, even in private conversations, as Boniface. The general picked up a sheet of paper that had come by courier ten minutes earlier. "I have him with me now," he said.

"As you'll see, the busy fellows have put one of the big ones back on line. A pity to leave it there, wouldn't you say?"

"I agree. I'll see what we can do."

"I've already asked my lads to do the same. Always pleasant talking with you, my dear Ike. I hope we can lunch soon, there or here. I'll ring off now."

"Goodbye, sir." Eisenhower hung up the phone and reread his copy of the Ultra message. Then, disdaining use of his buzzer, he roared: "Lee! Get in here!"

The aide sprang into the room as if propelled. Eisenhower pointed at him as if in accusation. "Get hold of Spaatz now and have him talk to Pinetree quickest. Cancel whatever they have on for tomorrow. I want the Eighth to hit Merseburg-Leuna. The RAF'll be doing the same at night. You got that? Merseburg-Leuna. Go!" He clapped his hands and the aide disappeared.

———

Thirty feet underground, in a bombproof room on a thousand-acre estate south of London called Bushey Park, also known as High Wycombe (code name Pinetree), the general heading the Eighth Air Force bomb planning team stared disbelievingly at the message he had just been handed. Then he sighed and looked up at the officers sitting expectantly amid the maps and charts that littered the table of the war planning room.

"Scrub Kassel. We're going to Merseburg."

———

The field order arrived at the base at 1830 hours during the evening meal. The teletype machine, flanked by long tables, stood against one long wall of the windowless, perpetually air-conditioned and gas-proof concrete-block operations room at headquarters. A huge blackboard hung on the opposite wall. It was divided into four quadrants; each listed the names of the pilots and the numbers of the airplanes assigned to each of the four squadrons. Three out of four would fly on a mission unless it was designated as a max-max, also called an all-out, all-out.

Robinson stood over the teletype machine as it churned out foot after foot of yellow paper. It presented coded information on target, mean point of impact, types and weights of bombs, bombing altitude, predicted weather en route, predicted opposition, the route to be followed, checkpoints, the order in which the three-group wings would fly to form the bomber stream, takeoff time and the assembly point for the division.

Robinson watched while the duty officer opened the cipher book, matched the target number on the sheet with the list in the book, and wrote the name on a pad. *Merseburg-Leuna.* The oil plant again; for the third time. Robinson grunted. He fished in his shirt pocket for his dead cigar. It was better than chewing on your hand.

His stomach was tightening and he wished he hadn't eaten. The duty officer pulled the Merseburg mission folder from the hundreds kept in the file cabinets and carried it over to the work table. He pulled out an overhead reconnaissance photo of the Merseburg area along with a transparent plastic sheet on which was printed a grid with numbers in the boxes.

Laying the transparent sheet neatly over the photo, he checked the point-of-impact number in the teletype message and located it on the grid. The huge plant sat at the western end of the city. That would be the mean point of impact—assuming they hit the target.

After a few minutes, the story was complete. "In twenty-five words or less," Robinson asked the group operations officer, "what've we got?"

"Merseburg No. 3. Bombing altitude, 27,000. Each load, sixteen 500-pound RDX demolition bombs. Wing claims decent weather, though you may encounter some icing with contrails en route."

"Shit," Robinson said.

"Takeoff time: Oh-five-hundred."

"Working backwards," Robinson said slowly, as the ops officer took notes, "crews to the hardstands at four, general briefing at three, breakfast at two, wakeup calls for air crews at one-thirty, wakeup for lead teams, one a.m. And a shit-load of work before that."

"The paddlefeet'll shovel it. You gonna get some sleep?" It was Carlino at his elbow.

"I'll sack down till one," Robinson said. "Wake me?"

"Least I can do, Colonel."

"Exactly."

As Robinson walked back to the office, more than 1,000 men began working at tasks that would keep them busy till takeoff time. MPs took up guard posts at the doors of group operations and intelligence. Security was tightened around the perimeter of the field.

Intelligence staff began to assemble maps and photos. The photo lab started copying flak position charts and mission flimsies for the thirty-nine crews. The group navigator plotted courses and distances and identified checkpoints along the way. The group bombardier calculated the bombsight settings for the bombing altitude.

Ordnance and armament crews loaded the 500-pound bombs on

trolleys at the bomb dumps and attached them to Dodge trucks that pulled the trolleys to the B-17s. The bombs were wrestled into the bomb bays of the thirty-nine airplanes. There, ordnance men screwed in the nose fuses. Other ordnance men lugged heavy boxes loaded with belts of .50-caliber machine gun ammunition and placed them by the guns. The gas truck made the rounds of the hardstands, topping off the fuel tanks and leaving a wake of high-octane fumes around the perimeter track.

Sleepy mechanics showed up to "pre-flight" the airplanes and laboriously pull the props through by hand to clear the cylinders. When they were through, the crew chiefs—mostly tech sergeants whom Robinson always considered the most dignified professionals on the base—started the auxiliary power "putt-putts" and climbed into the cockpits to check the engines. An assistant with a fire extinguisher stood outside beside the nose.

The chiefs started each of the four 1,200 horsepower Curtiss Wright Cyclone engines on each of the thirty-nine bombers and ran them up to check manifold pressure, pitch, prop feathering, oil pressure, turbo-superchargers and magneto performance. Sleep would be fitful for the airmen trying to rest in the barracks a half-mile away.

The same thing was happening at the same time on twenty other Eighth Air Force bases. A man would have to be deaf not to know that a major mission was being readied. The Germans weren't deaf. Their listening devices and agents made it clear that a major raid could be expected. Luftwaffe staff began checking probable targets and gasoline supplies, put fighter groups on alert, warned factory managers and wakened the thousands of men who manned, loaded and supplied the flak batteries stationed throughout the Reich. At this point in the war, fully one million Germans were occupied with the defense of Germany against the Allied air offensive.

In England, group weather officers checked temperatures, wind data and drift. The critical points for weather, in sequence, were takeoff conditions, target visibility and overcast conditions at the base upon return.

Carlino closed the non-coms' and officers' bars after leaving operations and told the cooks to prepare for a two a.m. breakfast for 400 men. The menu varied little: canned grapefruit juice that the men contemptuously called battery acid, oatmeal, chalky powdered milk in big tin pitchers, ersatz coffee, canned condensed milk, toast made from English bread that tasted like sawdust and watery, tasteless scrambled eggs made from an Army powder. Sometimes there were doughy flapjacks. Not that such a breakfast wouldn't have been a feast to the British, Carlino reflected; their civilians got two ounces of tea and two ounces of cooking oil a week, and the RAF didn't fare much better. Here, aircrewmen who had bought fresh eggs from nearby farmers at a whopping two shillings apiece would take one to a cook and hand it over to be fried. Over light please. Burn my egg and you die.

————

Lying on his office cot, engine sounds rising and falling in the near distance, Robinson found sleep hard to entice. He had been on the two earlier raids on Merseburg. Each time, they had knocked out 40–50 percent of the plant's production. Each time they had been hit by fighters and encountered an unbelievable curtain of antiaircraft flak over the target. Last fall, the group had lost nine bombers, 25 percent of the force. Four raids like that and your base became a ghost town. Something like that had happened at one base on one raid—the second Schweinfurt mission. Two airplanes returned. *That was all.* The deputy group commander and his staff waited disbelievingly on the deck atop the control tower for an hour, and then, moving slowly like men in deep shock, walked down the steps and wandered away. Pray God that wouldn't happen today.

Robinson did pray. He folded his hands in the dark and prayed to God for the strength of will and nerves he needed to lead the raid. Both were badly frayed. He didn't pray to be spared. That would be— he strained for the right word—wrong, unlucky, *inappropriate.* With millions of people dying everywhere in the world—maybe hundreds of thousands that day—praying for personal survival would be offensive.

————

In the cold flat she occupied in London when she wasn't overnighting in Bedford, Sandra Brooks put a shilling in the slot to turn on the gas fireplace and tried to draw cheer from its pink glow. He hadn't called and she knew what that meant. He would try to get through to her by phone next afternoon. If he was able to. She stared into the artificial fire, her handsome face a somber mask.

She had been such a happy child; she had loved her studies as much as she enjoyed outdoor games and sports. Field hockey had been her favorite. She read a great deal about ancient civilizations. She fancied that someday she would become an anthropologist or archaeologist and go on digs. The bloom of happiness faded quickly when her mother died of cancer. Then the war came and she fell in love with Alex Walker, a young British Army artillery officer home on leave. He was a quiet, generous Englishman, the sort of man she had imagined marrying someday. But that prospect disappeared in Holland. All that was left of him was a soiled badge of rank taken from his body and a dirt-smeared letter he had been writing her when the Germans counterattacked and wiped out his gun battery.

Now the American who had replaced him was in mortal danger. Mitchell Robinson was as unlike Alex Walker as a man could be, except for the essential decency of character they shared. Mitchell was a man who had done a dangerous job for too long. He seemed sometimes to be positively haunted by the memories of dead friends, though, for her, he would often come out of the shadows and become witty and downright funny in a way that seemed to come naturally to the breezy Americans.

Dear God, would she lose him, too? The thought sent a chill through her, and she drew a sweater over her shoulders. She had grown to love Mitchell Robinson, though she had no idea what would happen to them after the war—again, assuming he survived. If he wanted her to go to America with him—she was far from sure of that—could she leave her frail father, now in his midseventies? He wouldn't live much longer under the best of conditions.

She felt as if she were surrounded by death, as if she would soon be the only human alive. The enormous impact of a V-2 rocket resounded somewhere in the city and the window of her flat rattled. She hardly noticed it.

———

Robinson participated in, rather than presided over, the lead team briefings. The discussions were limited to technical details: course, altitude, checkpoints, turning points where the route zig-zagged to avoid flak emplacements and weather. It would be clear on takeoff and all the way to the target. But there was a good chance that the base would be socked in when they returned. The thought made him queasy. Trying to land in zero-zero fog was almost as frightening as being shot at. Though there was nothing quite so instantly stimulating as having a Focke-Wulf bore in at you, head-on, turn over on his back, firing his cannons at your windscreen and then split-S in front of you in the downward arc of a half-loop.

"We believe there'll be at least two hundred fifty enemy fighters, about half FWs and the other half ME 109s," the intelligence officer said. "They've got to defend this target. And there'll be some ME-110s standing off out of your gun range lobbing air-to-air rockets at you." The airmen looked gloomily at each other. Robinson kept his expression impassive and chewed his cold cigar.

"Heavy flak, of course," the officer continued. "They've moved in some extra flak batteries and you may see some ground-to-air rockets. They look like a 55-gallon oil drum coming up. The explosion is pink instead of black, like the flak."

A nice aesthetic touch, Robinson thought wryly. "What's the update on our fighter escort?" he asked.

"You'll be escorted all the way in and out. The first Mustang groups will meet you over the channel. They won't try to fly formation on you; their orders are to engage the enemy whenever they see him. When they withdraw, you'll be picked up by Mustangs and Thunderbolts."

———

Nearly four hundred men in flying gear were crowded into the main briefing hut when Robinson and the lead teams arrived. *Get it up, get it up, get it up,* he said to himself as he stepped to the middle of the stage. When you're group commander and Blue Leader on the same day, you're a one-man band. You have to strut, show confidence, make a joke, *lead.* Even if your fingertips and feet do feel numb.

The air above their heads was thick with cigarette smoke, courtesy of Camels' and Chesterfields' weekly gift of a carton to every man on the base. The men were hunched forward, watching the curtain covering the wall map. Robinson gestured and the group operations officer, Captain Porter, soberly pulled the cord and opened the curtain. Community theater, Robinson thought. The red yarn stretched from England deep into Germany, zig-zagging from leg to leg, leading finally to the initial point of the bomb run—a location picked for its sharp radar image—and to the blob that denoted the target.

*Merseburg.* A mass groan, pulled from the collective gut, filled the room. "Okay," Robinson declared. "So it's Merseburg, the oil refinery. Piece of cake." He unzipped his A-2 jacket and took a wide stance to show resolve.

Jeers, catcalls and whistles. He raised his hands for quiet. "Come on. What would a Marine say if he heard that? You want to live forever?"

"Hell, yes!" a crewman shouted, amid boos and more catcalls. *So long as they can yell and bitch and let it out,* Doc Benson said, *don't worry too much about morale. It's when they get quiet and sullen that you have to look out.* Out of the din and mass movement—hands pointing and waving, heads shaking—co-pilot Barney Google, though a slim man of medium height, suddenly became visible. He was sitting erect, his body absolutely still, a small smile on his face. His big yellow-gray eyes blinked contentedly. *Like a goddamn cat. He's enjoying this. That's why Carlino picked him for me,* he realized. *Google's absolutely fearless. And Ed knows I'm not.*

Another figure caught his attention. Lon Amundson, Red leader for the day—big, blond and broad shouldered, as a Pitt halfback was supposed to be—was smiling at him. Robinson's smile flickered back and a ripple of affection displaced his tension. *We're a long way from Mahoning, Ace. Take care today.* Robinson looked up. The noise had ebbed. They were ready for more.

"Okay," Robinson said. "Our brain trust will give you the detailed

rundown in a minute—altitudes, checkpoints, weather, probable opposition, target photo blowups and so on. Afterwards—you know the
drill—navigators will pick up maps and flimsies, bombardiers will go
over target info, co-pilots to equipment to pick up evasion kits. Radio
men are checking out the day's wireless codes, frequencies and call
signs. Gunners are being briefed separately. So I'll say my piece real
quick: I'm leading today. I've been to Merseburg twice; a few of
you've been there, too. It was rough last November; fighters clobbered
us all the way in and out. Half of our fighter escort couldn't get off
their fields in the weather that day."

Angry sounds, grumbles and curses filled the hut.

"Today will be different, I can promise you that. Two big reasons:
One, the improvements we've made in our defensive armament, particularly fields of fire at nose and tail. We didn't have the twin-50 chin
turrets last time. Or the fire extinguishers on the engines.

"Two, we'll have long-range fighter escort, guaranteed, start to finish. '47s and new model Mustangs with supplementary fuel tanks. I
won't kid you. We're going to see plenty of opposition. But *this* time
we're going to have the firepower, *and* the mobility, to defeat it. So
good luck and good hunting; above all, *hit* the damned target! And, as
they always tell me up at Wing, if I've left anything out, you may rest
assured."

There were smiles and nods, a laugh or two, a few catcalls. They
were still scared; but now there was hope.

———

Major Ed Carlino climbed the stairs to the control tower and peered
through the heavy glass that encased it. He could see, though indis-
tinctly, the X made by the intersection of the 6,000-foot and 4,200-
foot runways. The airplanes and the crew chiefs' huts at the hardstands
were shrouded in the darkness and scud that hung over the field.

"Not much to see just yet," the duty officer said. "Visibility'll im-
prove pretty soon, though."

"Hope so," Carlino said. "I don't like instrument takeoffs." A silly
comment, he thought. Who did? Three months ago, a fully loaded
bomber had blundered off the runway in the fog just before picking up

flying speed. It had crashed into the woods beyond and exploded, killing all ten men aboard. It had also caved in the end of the long runway. It had taken six weeks to repair it. A British team of army engineers diddled and dawdled with the job for a month, making tea, spreading straw and doing God knows what. Finally, Carlino blew up, kicked them off the base, and managed to get a crew of U.S. Navy Seabees to come in. They rebuilt the runway in two weeks.

During that six-week span, the bombers had to take off on the 4,200-foot runway. A fully loaded B-17 could barely make it; it was a miracle they had had no takeoff crashes during that period.

Carlino stared sightlessly at the field, his heavy shoulders hunched, his stubby hands thrust deep in the pockets of his trenchcoat. He had acted competently in that matter, he knew; he was a good executive. He also knew it wasn't enough for him. The air crews put their lives on the line every day; he didn't. There was a word for that. *Paddlefoot.* A ground officer; a nonflyer. He hated the term. One day, he vowed, he would fly a mission as a waist gunner. It would scare the living hell out of him, he knew; it could even kill him. He knew what combat flying did to the bomber crews. He saw their shocked and hollow-eyed faces as they stumbled out of the airplanes. Those who survived became old men in their twenties. Look at Robinson. He was twenty-eight, looked forty-five and acted like a man whose nervous system was shattered.

Nevertheless, Carlino told himself, he was going to find a way to experience this hell the airmen flew into every day, even if he managed to do it only once. He had prepared for it secretly by trading Scotch for lessons on operating the Brownings and by becoming a superior marksman on the skeet range.

Carlino had examined his secret desire many times. He wanted to prove himself to himself; that came first. And when he went home to Steubenville, Ohio—little Eddie Carlino, son of Mike Carlino, the barber; you know, the kid who used to run errands for Margiotti's Market, he got to be a major in the Air Corps—he wanted to be able to say—no, to *admit,* when asked—that, yes, he had flown combat. He knew what it was like to be shot at.

Less than a day's drive away in Mahoning, Pa., Mitch Robinson, another kid who had never done anything much before going into the Air Corps, would always be known as an authentic war hero. Carlino admired Robinson for what he had done; he envied him, too. And mixed with that envy was a grain of resentment. That was unworthy, he knew, but he felt it nonetheless. Flying a mission would exorcise that feeling. And, never again would he be embarrassed to be called a *paddlefoot*.

————

In the equipment room, Robinson moved slowly through the ritual of dressing for the mission. He took his wallet containing cards and papers that could identify him and placed it on his locker shelf. He pulled on his long underwear, his wool OD shirt and wool OD trousers, two pairs of socks—one silk, one wool—his coveralls, fleece-lined boots, lined helmet—oxygen mask hanging from one side—and medium-weight alpaca-and-wool B-10 flight jacket. He stuffed an escape kit, containing silk handkerchief maps of France, Belgium and Germany; phrase book; emergency rations and European currency in a big pocket. Over his head he pulled his rubber Mae West inflatable jacket and secured it around the waist and between the legs. From the locker he took two pairs of gloves. One was thin rayon, the second, wool-lined leather gauntlets. The leather would be worn over the rayon. It would be cold up there, even if the cabin heat worked. His hands felt icy already. He picked up his heavy shoulder holster with the GI-issue .45 automatic pistol hanging in it, hefted the holster and then hung it up again. A peashooter wouldn't help much today. And it weighed too much. He walked outside to the jeep that could carry him to the hardstand.

————

The green flare hissed from the tower into the dark sky just before 0500. "Start engines," Robinson said.

"Start engines," Google replied, picking up the checklist. The two men talked their way through the checklist, one saying the words as he took the required action—the other repeating them. One of the Catholic boys had told Robinson it was like being part of a mass.

"Fire guard posted."

"Fire guard posted."

"Batteries on."

"Batteries on."

"Hydraulic pump auto."

"Hydraulic pump auto."

They went through the list painstakingly. Hydraulic pressure up. Flaps up. Cowl flaps open. Master switch on. Gyros caged. Bomb bay doors closed.

"Starting Number One." A new progression. Booster pump on. Throttle cracked. Fuel mixture to idle cut-off. Props high rpm. Magnetos off. Circuit breakers on. Generators on.

"Starter on for twenty seconds. Ignition. Prime the pump." Robinson pressed the starter button and Google began pushing the hand pump. No. 1 engine whined like a fretful child, clattered, coughed several times to clear its throat and sputtered into a roar.

"Mixture to auto-rich."

"Auto-rich."

"Check oil pressure."

"Oil pressure okay."

"Stabilize at 1,000 rpm."

"1,000 rpm."

"Check fuel pressure."

"Fuel pressure okay."

They went through the same sequence for the other three engines. All four started without problems. *A bloody miracle. On a cold morning, four out of four.* The two men watched the engine instruments as the engines warmed up. Oil and cylinder head temperatures ascended into the green arc.

"Wheel chocks out."

"Chocks are out."

"Flight control locks off, exercise controls." After all of the training and all of the missions, one of the pilots managed to take off the other day with his controls locked. He got about two hundred yards off the field before he crashed into the woods and blew up.

"Control locks off, I say *off*, controls exercised."

"Radios on and set."

"Radios on and set."

They waited. Robinson took his D-ration chocolate bar out of his jacket pocket and placed it carefully on his side of the dash, its length parallel to the thick windscreen. Google, he noted, had placed a sandwich—the mess hall's horrible corned beef, no doubt—on his side of the dash. Aloft, it would freeze and curl into a U. When Google ate it —Robinson couldn't imagine wanting to—ice crystals would dance through the cockpit.

Robinson leaned forward and spread his metal-and-fabric flak jacket under his seat. It was too heavy to hang around your neck while you were wrestling the controls of a thirty-ton airplane without servo-assist. He checked the harness of the parachute. You wore the harness and, if and when the worst happened, you grabbed the chute from beneath your seat and clipped it onto your chest before you bailed out.

The crucial thing, Robinson reminded himself, was to make sure that, if your harness had rings, the chute had clips to mate to them. Or, if the harness had clips, your chute was fitted with rings. Unfortunately, some quartermaster genius somewhere had produced them both ways—probably because a congressman had a ring or clip manufacturer in his district. It was the nightmare of every pilot that, forced to bail out, he would lift the chute with trembling hands and find he had rings and rings or clips and clips. According to Division, it had happened.

"You got rings and clips, Chief?" Google asked through the interphone. Robinson nodded, looking at him.

"Rings on our fingers and clips on our toes," Google said happily. Google had a round face that looked small because his eyes were unnaturally large and bright and, given their yellow cast, attracted instant attention. He seemed to be looking out at the world through the eyes of a giant pussy cat. He wore a perpetual half-smile as if he knew a secret you didn't. Odd. Odder still, his habit of pointing a finger and thumb at you like a small boy pretending to shoot you. He did it now, while Robinson was looking at him.

"Bang," he said softly, extending his index finger toward Robinson's head. The eyes were shining. Robinson shrugged. He could have said, "Cut the shit, Google," but why bother?

Another flare from the tower. Time to taxi. With his right hand clamped over the four throttles, Robinson expertly wiggled thumb and little finger to shuffle the two outboard throttles forward. The 65,000-pound bomber lumbered forward on the hardstand. As it began to move, he pulled the port throttle back with his thumb and advanced the starboard throttle, at the same time pushing on the left rudder with his left foot and toeing down to engage the left-wheel brake. The No. 4 engine roared, the tires squealed and the B-17 wheeled sharply to the left and rolled onto the perimeter track.

Robinson peered down at the left-hand edge of the runway in the darkness. It would be a minor disaster and a major embarrassment for him to roll off the runway and bog down in the mud. It took a great deal more skill to taxi a B-17 than a B-24; the B-17 squatted back on a tail wheel so that the pilot couldn't see straight ahead on the ground. The B-24 had a nose wheel so that the fuselage was parallel to the ground while taxiing, giving the pilot an unobstructed forward view.

As Robinson moved out slowly, the deputy leader swung in behind him. The No. 3 man in the lead flight pulled in behind No. 2. The sequence was repeated over and over—each pilot watching for the call letters on the tail of the airplane passing by—until the lead squadron was taxiing in trail toward the head of the runway. When the twelve airplanes had gone by, the leader of the high squadron would taxi out. When the high squadron was in motion, the low squadron would form up on the taxiway. The three spares would taxi out last. They would fly behind the group, ready to fill in if a bomber aborted before the group reached the point of no return. If no one aborted, the spares would return to base.

The bombers would take off exactly thirty seconds apart, making sure they held to predetermined headings, rate of climb and airspeed to avoid overrunning each other in the clouds.

Robinson and Google waited at the head of the runway. *At least you can see to take off.* "Tail wheel locked."

"Tail wheel locked." When it was time for business, Robinson noted thankfully, Google was all business. They went through another checklist sequence. Parking brake off. Cowl flaps trail. Flaps up.

Robinson peered at the checkered van, now dimly visible, that was parked by the tower. A green light blinked from the Van Aldis lamp in the doorway. *Takeoff.*

Robinson stood on the brakes, holding them down, and walked the throttles slowly to the firestop. Google reached across with his left hand and blocked them open. Robinson's legs trembled with the strain as the airplane, shaking and shuddering like a huge, reined-in horse, tried to break free.

When the bellow of the engines became a scream, he released the brakes. The bomber leapt forward. Google called out the speed. "Fifty . . . sixty . . . seventy." Robinson had elevator control at sixty and eased the wheel forward to raise the tail and save the tail wheel.

"Eighty . . . ninety . . . a hundred . . . one ten. Red lights coming up."

Warning lights denoted the end of the runway. Robinson pulled back softly and the B-17 reluctantly left the ground. "Wheels up," Robinson grunted.

"Wheels up." Google hit the landing gear switch and the wheels rumbled up into their wells. They slid into the low-hanging clouds immediately and water droplets spattered the windshield. Robinson eased back on the throttles and Google set the prop controls for the long climb at 500 feet a minute. The water-laden clouds painted the windows gray and it grew dark inside the cabin.

Robinson kept his eyes on the artificial horizon. The instrument's tiny pair of wings, hovering over a bar, told him the attitude of the airplane. Periodically, his eyes swept the flight instruments. He held the airspeed at 125.

On his own initiative, Google called the crew on the interphone and had them check in, starting from the tail. The tail gunner, waist gunners, ball turret gunner, radioman, the engineer in the top gun turret, the navigator and bombardier in the nose. Make sure they were awake and listening. Twenty minutes later he called them again.

"We're at 10,000," Google said. "Go on oxygen. Acknowledge." One by one, they acknowledged. Robinson became aware that Google,

oxygen mask in place, was leaning sideways, pointing his thumb and
forefinger at him silently. He was probably saying "bang" in his oxygen mask. Robinson nodded, lifting his hands from the controls.
Google took them and Robinson snapped his mask in place; the first
few whiffs always tasted of rubber.

"Keep it," Robinson said through the mike. "We'll be on top in a
few minutes."

"Jawohl, Colonel," Google said.

They climbed steadily, rocking and shaking as if they were driving
up a steep, bumpy road in the dark. At 17,000 feet, the opaque gray
began to swirl and boil. Streaks of purple and gold appeared. A tiny
thrill shot through Robinson; it always happened this way. The murk
turned suddenly to white. The clouds exploded soundlessly away and
the airplane, dripping water, rose from the darkness into a dazzling
upper world of blue and gold and white. The sun was blinding and
both pilots groped for their sunglasses.

The upper world was a place for angels. Above them arched a sky of
brilliant blue, etched in a few places with thin ice-crystal tracings of
frozen cirrus clouds. As far as the eye could see at their altitude tow-
ered massive fairy-tale castles and mountain peaks of virgin-white cumulus clouds. Robinson looked at them with yearning. He wanted to
get out and sit on one and never go down again. When he was in
advanced flying school in Florida, flying a stripped-down bomber that
handled like a fighter, he loved to fly around and through the peaks,
sometimes sinking into the dense carpet of cloud-cover below so that
only his head was above it.

Sunlight glinted and sparkled from the water droplets flecking the
wings and engines. The propellers had become perfect circles of silver
mesh. It was a moment of total beauty, producing a feeling of pure joy
that the people in the gray world below could never know. Pilots
never talked about it, but, when this moment came, they turned instinctively and smiled at each other. Robinson had never known a
pilot, however insensitive a clod he might be on the ground, who
failed to respond.

He looked at Google. There came the forefinger and thumb. The
man's emotional range is limited, Robinson decided. But he can fly.

Google leveled off 2,000 feet above the cloud banks, reducing power to 30 inches of manifold pressure and 2,000 rpms. Robinson nodded approvingly, set the fuel mixture to auto-lean, closed the cowl flaps and turned the booster pumps off.

They headed toward the Alconbury radio beacon signal and began making a slow, shallow circle five miles wide. Thirty seconds later, the deputy leader popped out of the clouds and began cutting across the diameter of the circle to take a position on Robinson's right wing. Brabank, the pilot, shuffled the throttles expertly, catching up, slowing down and then sliding into place less than ten feet away. He would continually adjust the throttles, eyes intent on the leader, anticipating turns with hand and foot pressure on rudders and ailerons, to stay in tight formation all day long. At altitude, sweat would run down his face and soak through his long johns, sometimes freezing and making him feel alternately hot and cold.

No. 3 appeared, taking up his position on Robinson's other wing. No. 4 slid into the space just below and slightly behind Robinson's tail. That pilot would look almost straight up all day. On the way to the target, he would be looking at the sun. Nos. 5 and 6 appeared and settled on either side of him.

It took fifty-nine minutes on the giant merry-go-round before every member of the group got aboard. At the stroke of sixty, all thirty-six airplanes were locked tightly into three squadrons, each with twelve airplanes in four flights of three.

Robinson held up his hands and placed one on his wheel and the other above the throttles. Google relinquished control and Robinson banked slowly toward the Wing assembly point twenty miles to the east, the group turning with him. At the designated buncher beacon, the circling began again. Robinson fell into trail behind the lead group of the wing. The third group slid slowly into place behind his group.

The massive combat wing turned toward the designated Division assembly point at the coast. Exactly two hours after takeoff, the Eighth Air Force headed eastward across the English Channel and into an orange sun. The fantastic procession stretched for a hundred miles and shook the earth below with its passing.

"Set up autopilot," Robinson said. Google turned to the oblong

Minneapolis Honeywell box at the end of the control pedestal and began centering the dials to control pitch, yaw, roll, bank, climb and descent and make the B-17 fly straight and level. The autopilot had to be tuned delicately, allowing for just enough slack to prevent the airplane from wandering and, in rough air, from overcompensating and jerking the wingmen around. Google pulled the master switch. With a jerk and a tremor, the automatic pilot seized the controls and began flying the airplane.

Robinson took his hands from the wheel and began adjusting the engine throttles. His ear had told him they were out of sync. He leaned to his left so that he could see the spin of one propeller superimposed against the other. A gray shadow moved steadily through the silver mesh. Watching the shadow, he tinkered with the No. 1 and 2 throttles until the shadow slowed, stopped and disappeared. Google nodded, turned to his right and did the same with 3 and 4. The throbbing stopped. The engines were humming together now, a bass quartet singing in unison.

The radioman attached an oxygen bottle to his mask, climbed carefully to the bomb bay and pulled the safety pins out of the bombs. The belly gunner, the size of a jockey, crawled into his tiny ball turret and cranked it down so that he was hanging beneath the fuselage of the bomber.

The gunners waited expectantly for permission to clear the guns. Robinson gave it. Thirteen .50-caliber machine guns chattered briefly, shaking the ship and dropping spent casings throughout its length.

The sun made their eyes water and ache as they moved across France and toward Germany. Their route had been plotted to avoid the worst known flak concentrations on the way in. But you never knew when fighters would strike. It was particularly dangerous on the way in. They could drop out of the sun. No matter how many guns you had aboard or how good your crossfire pattern, it would be too late by the time you saw them rip through the formation.

The thought made Robinson uneasy. Where was the damned fighter escort? They had it so damned easy. Sleep until the bombers pass overhead—*we've* already put in half a day—then get up, have a quick breakfast and overtake the bombers before they get to the enemy coast.

You couldn't help but resent the bastards. But when you met one in a bar, you wanted to hug him.

"Friendly fighters, nine o'clock high." The call came from left waist.

"My money," Robinson said automatically. Unsure of whether his mike had been open, he looked at Google. The big yellow eyes blinked happily at him.

# CHAPTER FOUR

# The Cauldron

THE rising sun woke Karl von Moltke as it crept across the bedroom window of the lodge. Instantly alert, he turned and watched the rays creep across the bed and touch Elise's hair. For a moment he debated whether to take her in his arms and enjoy the special warmth of early-morning love. Reluctantly, he decided against it; it was time to leave.

Maintaining separate quarters even a mile from the airfield was a privilege he did not want to abuse. He had a perfectly good Wermacht-style one-bedroom with bath in a billet at the edge of the field and only one other pilot that he knew of was keeping his wife nearby.

Moving quietly, he padded into the bathroom, washed and shaved, and came out. As he pulled on his uniform trousers, he watched the sun touch his wife's blond hair and seem to set it ablaze. Five years after their marriage, he still marveled at her beauty.

He had pulled one boot on when she spoke. "You left our bed without waking me," she said accusingly.

"It's a clear morning and I need to be at the field," he said.

Elise Joanna von Moltke sat up, stretched and yawned. Moltke watched appreciatively as her full breasts strained against the thin silk of her green nightgown. In a moment, she rose, moved to a makeshift vanity table and began brushing her long hair. The strokes of the hairbrush slowed and she looked at him through the mirror. "I wish you didn't have to go."

He smiled, hiding his impatience at resuming a familiar conversation. "It isn't a matter of wishing, Elise."

She swung around and faced him. "Karl, you know I'm happy that you were able to take this lodge so we can be close to each other, and I don't intend to be a whining *hausfrau*. But I have to question, honestly, why you volunteered for this duty. Your *Sturmgruppe* was disbanded; you served with distinction, great distinction. This terrible war is lost. But we have money, we have connections in Switzerland; we can still get across the border." Her voice rose. "Karl, for the love of God, we're young and we love each other. Why shouldn't we go and live our lives? What are you staying for? Surely not for the Führer!" She spat the last word like a curse.

He winced as if she had fired a dart at him and then sat down and looked at her. "The Führer . . ." he began. "It's not for the Führer. Not any longer."

"Once it was," she said flatly.

"Once . . . it was different, Elise. So very different. You know that." His voice took on a pleading tone. "But now . . ." Unaccountably, his voice choked in this throat and his eyes filled with tears. "Sometimes—sometimes I feel as if we were living in a dream, as if we were all hypnotized in some way, and now we're awake and it's turned into a nightmare." He walked to the window and gazed at the snow-capped mountains in the distance.

"It was so exciting," he said in a low voice. "When we were young. The years in the Hitler Youth, the war games, the training in gliders."

"And there was the Führer," she said gently.

He nodded. "The Führer. Like . . ." he searched for words ". . . a *God;* even more than a God. Kind, all-powerful. He was reclaiming our lost territories for us, righting the wrongs that had been done to us by the French and English, protecting us from the barbarians in the

East." He realized he was reciting the old dogma, but he felt compelled to finish. "And he was doing it for *us*, for the youth of Germany."

"I know," she admitted. "We heard it all the time. From the classrooms and the books and the instructors at the *gymnasium*. How couldn't we believe? And don't forget the people's receiver."

"The people's receiver," Moltke said slowly. "It had just been invented—what an advantage it gave him—and he put one in every kitchen in Germany so he could talk to us every day. Could he have seduced us so quickly without the radio?"

"He had the rallies."

"God, yes, the rallies," Moltke said, staring sightlessly into the past. "At Nuremberg that day, when we knew the Führer was coming, we craned our necks . . ."

"Adoringly."

"Yes, adoringly, we got a glimpse of our wonderful, mystical leader. And how we marched and played for him!"

She laughed. "You were still such a child and you had the job of beating that big bass drum for your cadre."

He smiled ruefully. "It was a great honor. I was very proud."

"I can still see your face, all wrinkled up like a monkey's and shining with sweat, your hair in your eyes. You were so intense, so very serious. You were adorable."

"I remember *you, liebchen*. You and the other girls in your pigtails and white dresses, doing those exercises to music in the stadium with those silly balls you bounced back and forth. You were beautiful."

His face became somber. "I can't remember exactly when it changed. He was such a brilliant politician, smarter and nervier than all the rest. He moved into the Rhineland with a handful of troops and the French were afraid, even with their big army, to stop him. Then Austria and Czechoslovakia. Why not? The German people were united once again. Besides, he put seven million unemployed to work; things were better for everybody."

"Except for the Jews."

"Yes, except for them. But that's an old story, Elise; it goes all the way back to the Inquisition and the Crusades. Look at how the Dutch and Poles have always treated the Jews. Adolf Hitler didn't *invent* the idea of making them scapegoats; he just *used* it. But nobody imagined what could finally happen to them. *Nobody.*"

Moltke's face turned dark. "I don't think I realized what had happened to them, to *us,* until some of us toured the factories we were supposed to be protecting. I'll never forget going to the Farben plant at Auschwitz and seeing the workers there. Wretched, sick, emaciated men; women, too, they were little more than skeletons, and they stank like goats! But they were *human beings,* Elise. Even in medieval times we didn't treat people that way."

"It's the people he has around him," she said.

"He *chose* them, Elise. Göring . . ."

*"Der dicke."*

"Yes, fatty. And Himmler; the man gives me the creeps. So does Bormann. When I saw them together at the Knight's Cross ceremony, I couldn't believe that *they* were our leaders." He shook his head slowly, marveling. "And the change in Hitler . . . As a boy I remember that sad face, those gentle, wise eyes, his smile, that beautiful voice. And then to see him last year as close as *this.* The eyes flickered in a way that made him seem insane. He snarled and shouted at the people around him in the foulest way! I couldn't *believe* what he had become!" He shook his head in disgust. "And the way he had the generals executed after the bomb plot—with *piano wire*! Horrible. They even arrested my cousin, James. He's criticized the government, but he's never *done* anything. They're still holding him, you know."

Moltke began pacing the room, his hands together under his chin as if in prayer. "Sometimes I have the strongest feeling. Remember that summer we drove through the *Schwarzwald*? On the way to the Black Forest, we stayed at that little hotel in Bad Krozingen . . ."

"I remember. The room overlooking the courtyard. Very romantic."

"We drove over to Staufen and climbed that little mountain to explore the ruins of Doctor Faustus' castle."

"Fascinating," she said. "But why . . ."

"Faustus sold his soul to Mephisto. Somewhere in those ruins there's supposed to be the imprint of Mephisto's cloven hoof."

She shuddered. "Good thing we couldn't find it."

Moltke nodded slowly, his face bleak. "I think we've found it now. We've found the demon, too. He was here all the time."

Elise looked around uneasily. "Karl, this kind of talk frightens me. For what you're saying and for—for the person you're saying it of. We'd better be careful."

Moltke laughed mirthlessly. "We're safe here, at least. No one knew we were taking this lodge, Elise. Even I didn't know it till I saw it from the field sitting up on the hill across the way. He stood up and straightened his uniform. "Anyway, you asked a question, *liebchen,* really two questions. Who am I still loyal to, and why do I keep fighting? When any of us who wear the Luftwaffe uniform make a trip or go on leave, people—ordinary people—look at us oddly, sometimes scornfully. Some actually say: 'Have you fellows stopped flying? Where's the Luftwaffe?' Can you imagine what that does to us? 'Where's the Luftwaffe?'

"Our loyalty is to the people. We have a duty, to the extent we can carry it out, to protect them, to save our cities and countryside from complete destruction. I also have a loyalty—you know that—to my family, my profession. The Moltkes have served Prussia and Germany for centuries. I have a duty to my ancestors and my profession at arms. I am . . ." he groped for the words.

"A warrior," she said resignedly.

He raised his eyebrows and smiled. "Yes, a warrior. And a warrior must fight for his people."

A klaxon sounded from the field. Elise started and then stood up. Moltke picked up his gloves and sheepskin coat and went to her. They embraced. A few seconds later, there was a rap at the door.

"*Herr Oberst,* your car is ready."

"Coming, Willie." He turned to Elise. "That damned car they gave me burns wood and converts it to gas for fuel. Can you imagine?"

———

The bass chorus of the B-17's engines vibrated reassuringly in Robinson's chest. Five miles below, the ground unrolled like a vast tapestry of green and brown. The windows of the tiny houses caught the sunlight and winked a false welcome.

Robinson pressed the mike button. "Pilot to navigator."

"Navigator."

"Doroshkin, what's ground speed and ETA?"

"The jet stream is giving us a tailwind of 100 mph today, so ground speed is 275. We should arrive at the target, at approximately 10:01, assuming no diversion."

"Roger, navigator." Another hour to go. Flak had been light so far and, miraculously, there had been no fighter attacks.

"Right waist to pilot.

"Pilot to waist."

"There's a B-17 flying alone, way out of gun range, on a course parallel with ours. It's painted black and I can't see any markings. I don't think it's one of ours." O'Kane had the best eyes in the crew.

"Can't be," Robinson said. "It's gotta be a captured 17, flying recon for the Jerries. If it moves in, shoot. Shoot at anything that comes in and points its nose at us. Pilot to crew; acknowledge." They called in, one by one. A bogus B-17 had slipped into a First Division formation a week ago and shot down the airplane beside him before being spotted. The bandit escaped, unfortunately, by diving into a cloud. And there wasn't time to decide whether an ME 109 was really a P-51 Mustang or a Focke-Wulf was really a P-47 Thunderbolt when they were flying at you. They looked too much alike to take chances. Better to shoot a friend than die from failing to recognize an enemy; that was the unwritten rule.

Robinson's stomach cramped momentarily when they reached the German border. Here was where the yellow-nosed German fighters had met them the first time. Now there was peace, or at least the illusion of it. Robinson noted that vapor trails were beginning to appear. When the conditions were right—or wrong—the super-cooled water droplets suspended in the atmosphere would condense as the hot engines plowed through the frigid upper air. Plumes of vapor would form behind every engine. They were pretty to look at in photographs, but they drew a precise trail for flak gunners and fighters. Even worse, if icing conditions were severe and the plumes grew into heavy clouds, bomber groups would find themselves flying through dense fog they

couldn't climb above. Wingmen would become gray shadows struggling to hold formation, and the target would be obscured.

Today, Robinson noted thankfully, the vapor trails dissolved a few
hundred yards behind each airplane. There would be no cloud buildup.
And now they were within a hundred miles of the target. Could a raid
on Merseburg actually have become a milk run?

The answer came, literally, like a bolt of lightning. Flashes of light,
like exploding flash bulbs greeting a celebrity, appeared dead ahead.
Four voices, Robinson's included, spoke simultaneously: "Bogies at 12
o'clock level."

Six Focke-Wulfs, cannons firing, raced toward them, wingtip to
wingtip, at a closure rate of 600 miles an hour and plunged through the
formation. The B-17's nose and top turret guns thundered, shaking the
airplane. Robinson involuntarily hunched forward, gripped by animal
panic, as the enemy leader pulled up at the last possible second, missing
the B-17's nose by inches. The bomber's tail guns pounded as the tail
gunner shot at the fading fighters.

Robinson's left wingman rocked with an explosion and the bomber
wobbled outward and then crabbed back into place. Robinson's heart
banged alarmingly against his chest; he struggled to slow his breathing
and regain control of himself.

"One of the low element ships got hit," one of the crewmen yelled.
"He's got an engine windmilling and he's rolling over."

"No. 3 took some damage," another voice said. "It looks like somebody in the cockpit was hit. I can't make out . . ."

"Pilot to crew." Robinson recovered his stability in anger. "Stop
chattering and keep your eyes open."

"Another wave at 12 o'clock!" someone called.

Again, the flashes, then dots that grew into hungry sharks. The
Focke-Wulfs swept through the formation once more. Explosions
sounded. The bomber rocked and slewed.

"Pilot to crew. Report damage."

"Tail gunner. I think he took a piece of the tail above me."

"Belly to pilot. I can see something flapping back there."

"Left waist to pilot. ME-110s pulling up at 9 o'clock, just out of
range. They've got rockets."

Robinson swiveled to the left, noting irrelevantly that, when he did, the warm air exhaled from his oxygen mask froze in a strip across the side window. A twin-engined ME-110 turned toward them and fired an air-to-air rocket. A huge blob of black with an angry red center appeared off the left side of the lead squadron. Another ME-110 turned in; another rocket was launched. A B-17 disappeared in an orange and black explosion. Bits of the airplane and its crew fell out of the cloud, and the cloud drifted backwards as the bombers plowed ahead.

Abruptly, Mustangs fell on the ME-110s from above. One German blew up, another lost a wing and rolled over. A third caught fire and the pilot bailed out. Robinson saw the man hit the stabilizer of the aircraft and spin away, his parachute unopened. The image imprinted itself on Robinson's memory. The German was wearing light-colored coveralls and they were covered with blood.

"Bogies coming from six to three level," a voice called. A string of ME-109s turned at 90 degrees and banked toward the bombers to make beam-on attacks. The B-17's heavy Browning machine guns chattered. The bomber shook. Something that sounded like hail peppered the airplane.

"I got the sumbitch!" O'Kane called from the right waist. "He's smoking!"

"Heads up!" Claiborne yelled from the top turret. "They're coming in train." Firing broke out throughout the ship again, gunners calling to one another.

"Shorten your bursts," Robinson ordered. "And stop yelling."

*Where's the goddamned escort?* Robinson said to himself. As if in response, a horde of Thunderbolts slid into the scene and the sky suddenly filled with clawing, diving, turning airplanes. Smoke blobs began to stain the air. The army of American fighters quickly took control of the battle. Soon the combatants swirled away and disappeared. But another bomber was trailing smoke from an engine.

"Pilot, I think we've lost four so far.

"Roger." Robinson didn't ask where the information came from.

"Navigator to pilot."

"Pilot."

"Pilot, thirty seconds to IP. Turn right to 89 degrees on my mark:

seven . . . six . . . five . . . four . . . three . . . two . . . one . . . mark."

"Turning on IP," Robinson said. The initial point marked the beginning of the bomb run. He turned the turn-and-bank dial on the autopilot a fraction to the right, watching the compass heading swing as he did it. *Slow and easy,* he reminded himself. *Don't crack the whip.* If you turned too sharply, the ships flying formation on the outside of the turn would fall behind and bend their throttles forward frantically, trying to keep up.

For the ships inside the turn, it was even worse. A sharp turn would force the inside wingman and the element flying on the lead bomber to bank very sharply and reduce power to avoid running into the leader. In a heavy airplane, that maneuver could quickly lead to a stall. The bomber would fall off on a wing and have to dive to pick up flying speed and regain control. By then, assuming he hadn't collided with another ship on the way down, he would be alone. A lone bomber would last as long as a side of beef thrown to a school of sharks.

"Pilot to bombardier," Robinson said, leveling out. "You got it."

"Roger, pilot." The bombardier engaged the clutch that coupled his Norden bombsight to the autopilot and began flying the airplane. He made small corrections in course and altitude by turning two knobs on the bombsight. Shutting out the fury that was going on outside, he bent over the bombsight and peered through the telescope. Merseburg lay ahead. A smoke bomb dropped by the lead wing zig-zagged from altitude to the ground, marking the target. Carefully, Fisk centered the target in the crosshairs of the sight. Now everything was automatic. Computing the instant of release, it would trigger the bomb drop at the right instant. An intervalometer would space the fall of the sixteen 500-pound bombs, each drop registering as a red light on the bombardier's display panel.

Robinson pressed the mike button. "Open bomb bay doors." They swung open. The ship rocked with the extra drag and ice-cold air began to spread through the airplane.

"Do we have chaff aboard?" Fisk replied affirmatively. Chaff was the name given to cannisters of aluminum foil that were hung on several of the bomb racks. Opening, the cannisters strewed hundreds of thousands of strips of foil that slowly floated to earth, turning enemy radar screens to snow as they fell.

"Bombardier to radio. Turn on strike camera."

"Radio, Roger. Camera on." The radioman switched on the bomb-strike camera mounted in a well beneath his compartment. An electronic pulse from the bombsight would trigger the camera at the instant of release and the camera would take six pictures of the target at six-second intervals.

"High rpm," Robinson said, his throat gravelly with tension.

"High rpm," Google replied. He shoved the four prop levers forward to the stop. At their emergency war power setting the engines made a terrible grinding sound that pilots hated; it always sounded as if they'd blow up. It was a wonder, Robinson thought, that they didn't do it more often.

Robinson looked ahead. The fighters, friendly and enemy, were gone. No matter how violent the action, they always disappeared on the bomb run. The reason lay ahead. The sky was an oily black and it seemed to boil around the lead bomber groups ahead. Five hundred flak guns on the ground fired incessantly at the bombers as they moved into range. When their radar screens became jammed by the chaff, they switched to a preset box pattern of flak coverage. It was like watching an approaching thunderstorm and knowing there was a tornado hiding in it.

*Choong! Choong! Choong! Choong!* The bomber rocked. Four ugly black L-shaped clouds appeared a little high and to the left. They were too close when you could hear them.

Four more explosions burst, this time off to the right, and shrapnel hit the airplane like a giant fistful of stones. The cloud ahead grew larger, blacker, more frightening.

"B-17 hit in high squadron," a gunner called. Robinson craned to the right in time to see a stricken bomber nose up sickeningly. Flames swept across the cabin and fuselage and it fell out of formation and began spiraling toward earth. A man in a chute tumbled out; it was afire.

*Don't let it be Lon's ship,* Robinson said to himself. *Please, God, not Lon Amundson.* He peered upward again. Red Leader's ship was still in place. He was grateful and ashamed at the prayer. One of his crews had gone down. He had no right to feel relieved. But he did.

Robinson looked at the target ahead. Black smoke was spewing from the ground at the edge of the city. The lead groups must have hit the refinery. A quarter-mile away, he could see the red tile roofs of the town. The windows winked in the sunlight. What were the people doing down there? Hiding in shelters or cowering in their cellars?

A long trail of pink smoke shot up from below. *They're shooting at us, that's what they're doing down there.* The object exploded in a huge pink burst the size of a house just between the lead and low squadrons. *A ground-to-air rocket.* By some miracle, it appeared not to have hurt anybody. If it had landed in the formation it would have been a different story.

Explosions burst around the lead squadron. Again the sound of stones being thrown against metal. A whimper escaped from Robinson's throat. He looked quickly to make sure his mike was closed.

"Left waist to pilot. Right waist is hit; it's his shoulder and arm, I think."

"My arm," a voice grunted.

"Pilot to left waist. Weaver, give O'Kane a morphine shot and a tourniquet if he needs it. Keep him warm. You'll have to cover both waist positions."

Robinson knew the instructions were unnecessary but he was supposed to give them. Flak rocked the ship again. *Would this goddamn bomb run ever be over?* They were flying through a huge black storm in which the raindrops were flying shards of metal.

The B-17 lifted sharply. "Bombs away!" The bombardier cried. "You got it!"

Robinson seized the wheel and Google flipped off the autopilot. Robinson forced himself to stay on a straight and level course for five more seconds to allow the group to toggle their bombs on his drop. Then, slowly, far more slowly than he wanted, he pressed the left rudder and turned the wheel to the left, pushing it forward at the same time to put the big airplane in a shallow, turning descent to get the group out of the flak zone as quickly as possible. Now the flak was bursting above them. They were safe until the fighters came back.

Something flashed past his nose at an unimaginable speed. It was gone before he could open his mouth to speak. But he knew it had been gray-green and sleek. It was nothing he had ever seen before. *And it wasn't anything of ours.*

Voices cried out. "What was that? What the hell was that?"

"Did you see that? It went past us like a bat out a hell! What the hell *was* it?"

"Pilot to crew. Knock it off. We'll find out later." Robinson switched to the bomber channel. Cries and yells filled the air. Whatever it was had been seen by a dozen or more crews. And now it was gone.

"Blue Leader to group," Robinson said, forcing his voice to be calm and authoritative. "Get off the air. Maintain radio silence. And close up. Close up." In their excitement, the wingmen had wandered out of their tight formation.

The thing was gone. But what the hell *was* it?

———

Moltke sighed in disgust and pulled on his leather trousers, zipping them snugly around his ankles. He rested against the berm and pulled on his fur boots. Then the bulky, plush-lined leather jacket. He started to sling his 9mm pistol belt around his waist and then changed his mind and handed it to his batman.

"Sometimes it happens, *Oberst,*" Willie said.

"No one's fault," Moltke grated. He was frustrated and furious. The electric motor at the head of one of the turbines had malfunctioned and it had taken the mechanic half an hour to repair it. A half-hour after ground control had expected him to take off. Now his observations would be of little use to control. But he would go anyway. He chafed at the inaction. He hadn't flown against the bombers in two weeks. All fighter pilots—be they German, American, British, even Russian—were hunters by temperament. And he wanted to hunt.

The mechanic peered around the engine, smiled and raised his hand in mock salute. Ready at last. Moltke was off the ground within minutes.

"Control, Rhineland One. My horse was lame. I'm riding now."

The voice that came back was flat and metallic, even bored. "Rhineland One, further recon unnecessary at this time. Pantechnicons attacking Merseburg, sector two–one–B. Suggest you observe and advise any unusual developments. Over."

"Control, this is Rhineland One. Victor." Control was giving him busywork. Very well, he would fly this remarkable airplane there and try to make something useful out of it.

He climbed up into air so thin that his now–obsolete Focke-Wulf would have mushed and staggered in it. Only the pesky, elusive British Mosquitos could fly so high. He raced northward, hearing only the sound of the wind. Near Merseburg the spectacle spread out below him like a wide-angle photograph taken from space. The four-engined Boeings moved toward the city like beetles, trailing silvery threads of vapor. Knots of swirling fighters, like fleas. The Amis were clearly getting the best of it, and why not? They outnumbered the FWs and old 109s at least five to one. A huge black cloud of flak speckled the air above the town. Below, oily black smoke gushed from the ground; fires flared from the buildings below. A scene from Hieronymus Bosch.

Abruptly, Moltke became angry—at the Americans and their malevolent bombing; at his countrymen for blundering into a world war; at himself for sitting alone and impotent at high altitude, like a neutered cat. *To hell with it.* He was more than a pilot. He was an *ace.* He was flying a virtually invulnerable aircraft. And he was carrying four fully loaded 30mm cannons. *Orders be damned.*

Moltke stood the 262 on one wing and looked down, selecting a group to attack. *That* one. He would smash the leader. *Now.* He depressed the nose and dived. The beetles rapidly grew larger on the heavy glass of the windscreen. He put his eye to the gunsight to center the lead bomber. Suddenly it was much too big and he had to skid sideways in a near-panic. He missed the bomber by inches and dived past it.

*God in Heaven!* The rate of closure was so great. And he had forgotten Steinhoff's admonition. Be careful of steep dives. The kite has no dive brakes. The controls can freeze. They were freezing now. He had dived far below the bomber formation. He dived through a cloud. He was alone, fighting for control of the 262. The airframe shuddered and the leading-edge flaps popped out. He had exceeded maximum speed. He pulled back hard on the heavy stick; it was like lead. It began to respond. He tried to bring the nose up in a slight turn and groaned. The force of gravity pushed relentlessly, crushingly, on his head and shoulders. He felt as if his spine was being pushed through the seat. His eyes stood out of his head. Everything turned gray and red and finally black.

His vision returned an instant later. The 262 was wandering about but it was more or less in level flight. Moltke breathed deeply. His face and body were bathed in sweat. *An expensive mistake; one that I won't make again.* He looked around quickly. It would be an ignominious ending for himself and his wonderplane if he were shot down by some anonymous American fighter that dived on him from above.

There was nothing around him. He advanced the throttles gingerly, banked and swept upward again through a cloud. Before him lay a whole group of Mustangs. Effortlessly, he sailed through them. Astounded and panicked, they broke apart and banked wildly in a dozen directions. The bomb group he had tried to attack lay above him now. Very well, he would attack from below.

Moltke tried to adjust in time to get the leader in his sights. He cursed. Again he was too fast. He had to learn to fly this beautiful, *verdammt* machine. He swung his nose slightly to the right. The high squadron leader filled his luminous gunsight. Now. He pressed the trigger on the control stick and his cannons thumped. The bomber lurched; pieces flew from the big aircraft, smoke began pouring from an engine.

Moltke swept past the bomber without seeing whether it was mortally wounded. He circled, slowed and peered down to take a look. Red tracers suddenly appeared off his right wing. *What in hell?* He banked away and advanced the throttles. He had been caught rubbernecking; he had neglected the oldest lesson of all. *Look up. Look around. Keep looking.* There was the bastard, an American Mustang. The fighter tried to climb with him. Impossible. Keeping an eye on him, Moltke soared high above the Mustang. The pilot lost sight of him. Now the Mustang was joined by his wingman. Very well. Moltke put the 262 in a shallow dive, *keep it shallow this time,* and fixed the fighter in his gunsight. Just so. He pressed the trigger. The Mustang exploded in midair and became an orange cloud that turned black and drifted away.

Control spoke as if it had been watching him. "Rhineland One, this is Control. Any observations?" Did he detect a note of sarcasm in the voice?

"Rhineland One. I was attacked by a Mustang and shot him down." The literal truth.

There was a pause. Then Control said: "How's your juice, Rhineland One?"

*My God, fuel.* He checked quickly. "I'm low, Control. Going home."

"Victor, Rhineland One."

———

Robinson felt sick; his stomach shrank into a cold knot. That Buck Rogers thing, some kind of manned rocket, had flashed through the formation again, this time from below. He saw the shadow dart upwards between the lead and high squadrons. He saw Red Leader lurch and yaw. A large hole appeared just forward of the cabin and No. 2 engine began windmilling and spewing oil. Then Red Leader slipped backwards.

"Copilot," he said hoarsely, depressing his mike button. "Can you see Red Leader?"

"Yeah, Boss," Google replied, swiveling to his right. "He's got some holes around the nose and cabin and he's lost No. 2. His deputy is taking the lead. He's still flying, though."

"Waist to pilot. Red Leader seems stable for now. Oh, wait. Some little friends have moved in to escort him."

Robinson sagged with relief. Friendly fighters would shepherd Amundson home. "Set up autopilot," he said, looking at Google. "Let down at 500 feet a minute." He didn't trust the steadiness of his hands right now.

"Mind if I fly, Chief?" Google asked.

Robinson shrugged. "No." Google took the controls, adjusted the throttles and RPMs, and held the airspeed at 170. Robinson saw his eyes crinkle at the corners. He was smiling again. *At what?* Robinson pounded his numb hands together. Everyone in the plane—hell, in the group—knew of his preoccupation with Amundson's safety. He knew it was wrong to let it become palpable; but he couldn't help it. He had talked Lon into joining the Air Corps. He had promised the Amundsons he would look after him; people were always asking that and such promises were always made. But, looking into Olaf and Frances Amundson's eyes, and shaking hands with Lon's younger brother, Steve, Robinson had meant it. When he rose to the command of the 205th, he had pulled some strings at Wing and arranged Lon's transfer from a group that had been decimated.

Now this. *Pray God he isn't dead or hurt bad.* The group commander couldn't call the ship and ask unless he was going to contact every plane in the group and ask who had been wounded. And that would be insane. He would have to wait.

Time unwound. He glanced at Google. He was obviously enjoying himself. Gliding gently, going home, empty of bombs and more than half empty of fuel, the bomber was light in his hands. He had the feeling he could slow-roll it if he wanted to. But what would his wingmen do? The thought made Google chuckle.

The coastline and channel were approaching. Robinson looked at the altimeter. 10,000 feet.

"Pilot to crew. Come off oxygen." He unsnapped his mask and wiped away the crust that had formed on his lips. He could smell cigarette smoke drifting through the ship as the crewmen lit up. This was the moment that everyone savored. He picked up his frozen D-ration chocolate bar, unwrapped it and bit the corner. It was delicious; his stomach relaxed a bit. Maybe Lon was perfectly okay. He took another bite. The bar was incredibly rich, the one item of GI food he really liked. After he had finished eating it, he turned to Google.

"Want me to take it?"

"Just as soon keep it, Chief." Robinson nodded his assent. He reached across the pedestal, unwrapped Google's frozen, U-shaped sandwich and handed it to him. Google nodded, took it with one hand and bit into it. Ice crystals exploded throughout the cabin and Robinson could hear him munching like a horse eating an apple. Or a cat eating a mouse. The thought dampened his appetite slightly, as he reacted to the image and to the certainty that the sandwich was stringy GI corn willy.

Robinson made another intercom check with the crew. O'Kane's wound was superficial. Nobody else had been hit. So much for the good news. The bad news lay ahead. He could see it as they crossed the channel and radio confirmed it after checking with Control.

The afternoon sun still shown above and lovely cumulus clouds showed traces of pink and purple. Below them, however, lay a suffo-catingly thick gray blanket of cloud cover. Not a hole or rent in it. And it stretched all the way to the ground.

Google had leveled off at 16,000 feet to keep the group, now flying a loose formation, above it. When they reached the letdown point, Google looked inquiringly at Robinson.

"Want me to take it now?" Robinson asked. Google shook his head, a small smile parting his lips. His front teeth showed. They were small and shaped like a horse's teeth. Robinson had half-expected to see long incisors.

"Carry on," Robinson said. He didn't know whether to be relieved or not. He didn't want to have to make still another blind letdown; yet he hated to sit helplessly, like a passenger, his life in another pilot's hands.

The group made one circuit around the beacon and then the three bombers that made up the low element of the low squadron peeled off one by one, banked and disappeared nose down in the undercast. A minute later, another three. Then another. The lead squadron would be next, and then the high squadron. Once in the clouds and blind, each airplane would be on its own.

Robinson took one last, longing look at the sparkling sun and the colors it painted on the high clouds and airplanes and then they banked over and plunged into the darkness below. Doroshkin calculated the course to the base and checked it against the muddy radar image of the ground below. Every pilot hated and feared blind descents. England was such a little island and the airfields were so close together that their traffic patterns nearly overlapped. So many airplanes were coming down in such a small space.

The murk became dark gray. The blind bumping and jolting continued for fifteen minutes. The crewmen kept a sharp watch from their positions to guard against collisions.

"There's a barrage balloon in this sector," Doroshkin warned. *Was that a large gray shape on the right? Or a piece of dark scud against a lighter cloud? No matter, it's gone now.*

Google was talking to the tower now. They were getting close. It would be a blind approach. "You're on the nose, Blue Leader," the tower man said. "Keep that rate of descent. You'll see the ground from about thirty feet up. Crab a little to your left. That's good." "Flaps down," Google requested.

Robinson hit the flaps switch. "Flaps down."

"Gear down," Google said. Robinson checked the warning light; it went out. "Gear down and locked."

"High rpm," Google said.

Robinson shoved the prop levers forward. "High rpm." They were nearly down, almost safe.

*Christ!* A huge apparition loomed up out of the fog. A B-17, coming directly at them. Robinson grabbed at the controls, but Google was faster. He shoved the wheel yoke forward, standing the big aircraft on its nose. They could hear the roar of the other bomber's engines as it swept over them, its wheels just missing their cabin.

Robinson's heart beat like a hammer. He fought to control his breathing. He looked at Google. Intense concentration, nothing more.

"Tower to Blue Leader, you're coming into the clear. Get your nose up." The clouds broke. The runway appeared; to the side, the tower and operations buildings. All drab and gray; all suddenly beautiful. Google wrestled the bomber over the runway and chopped the power. Air speed was 115, then 110.

Robinson would have pulled the wheel back in his lap and dumped the airplane on the runway. Google, in an elegant maneuver, shoved the wheel forward quickly and then eased it back, kissing the runway lightly with the main wheels. The tires squealed briefly, rolled, and the big tail settled back on its wheel.

"Unlock tail wheel," Google called.

"Tail wheel unlocked," Robinson responded, reaching down and pulling the lever. Google tramped on the brakes, blasted an outboard engine and slewed quickly onto the taxi strip to make room for the B-17 that was settling onto the runway behind him. Robinson killed the inboard engines. They taxied, slowly now, to the hardstand. It had been nine hours since takeoff.

Robinson experienced a familiar, irrational sense of guilt. Sergeant Callahan, the crew chief, a man for whom perfect was barely good enough, would be waiting like a long-suffering parent expecting the worst from his errant child. The pilot had taken Callahan's beautifully prepared airplane out again, and again he had brought it back smeared with oil and punctured with holes. And there he stood beside the hardstand, his big head turning slowly from side to side, his weather-beaten, countryman's face pursed in displeasure, a sight before which even a group commander felt abashed.

Robinson's legs gave way when he dropped from the hatch onto the concrete. Many aircrewmen would have rubbery legs for a few minutes after landing. Robinson's feeling of numbness would last longer.

The jeep pulled up, Major Ed Carlino behind the wheel. Robinson called O'Kane, who was clutching his arm and looking pale, and told him to get in. He told the crew chief quickly about the damage; the large hole in the vertical assembly was clearly visible. Robinson scanned the field. A red flare. An airplane with serious injuries aboard. The ambulance crept forward to intercept it. It taxied off the runway on a taxi strip and cut all four engines.

"Bad day?" Carlino asked.

"Bad enough," Robinson said. "And we saw something I've got to report."

"I know," Carlino said. "We've already heard about it. But they'll want your report."

The muted roaring of engines suddenly grew louder. Robinson peered up into the murk. There was a thunderous crash. A midair collision. "Oh, God," he whispered. Then he stepped back. "Out of the jeep!" he yelled. "Back here! Here!"

He pulled O'Kane back into the shelter of the B-17's big wing. Carlino was close behind. Time seemed suspended; Robinson felt as though he had been turned to stone.

Then it began. Pieces of metal began falling over the field. A heavy engine thumped to earth on one of the taxi strips. The whole tail section of a B-17 crashed to earth in the middle of the field. Robinson recognized the insignia of the nearby Podington base. Another engine landed, this time on the short runway. A turret with machine guns in it was next.

Then there were *things*. A helmet with something in it. A shower of blood droplets over one part of the field. Parachutes. A boot with a leg in it flopped onto the edge of the hardstand. Bits and pieces of people fell over a large area. Robinson shifted his weight and was horrified to feel something crunch underfoot. He lifted the boot and, though he didn't want to, looked down. *Teeth.* His stomach convulsed. One of the gunners bent over and began vomiting. The terrible rain stopped. A B-17 about to land went back to full power, milked up its flaps and went around. The tower had closed the field, leaving the exhausted pilots circling dangerously overhead until the runway could be cleared. Trucks, ambulances, jeeps, even bicycles, were racing toward it to do the job.

"Let's go," Robinson said hoarsely. "Get O'Kane to the medics. Google, come with us. I want you to give intelligence a report on that thing that attacked us. I'm going to the tower to check the incomings. We've got to clear this mess off the field fast."

They handed O'Kane over to one of the ambulance teams on the way. The jeep lurched to a stop in front of the headquarters building and Google got out.

"Good job today, Google," Robinson said. "Hell of a job. You can fly with me next time."

Google blinked happily at Robinson. He extended his thumb and forefinger. "Bang," he said. His all-purpose greeting, farewell and salute. Robinson watched him walk away and shook his head.

"Colonel." Carlino's black eyes were somber.

"What?" Robinson asked warily.

"Amundson came in; that is, his copilot did. Major Amundson was hit in the upper back and chest by cannon-shell fragments. Doc Benson said he should live, assuming no complications; they gave him a lot of blood to replace what he lost. But he's got a collapsed lung and considerable damage to the right shoulder and upper back muscles."

Robinson wilted. "Where is he?"

"They've taken him to Diddington. They have the right people there for the surgery. When he's ready, assuming everything works out all right, they'll transfer him back to our hospital here."

*Oh God,* Robinson thought despondently. *What will I tell them back in Mahoning?* He thought about it and decided to wait a day or two until he had the full story. It was one thing to say Lon was hurt, another to say he was hurt but he'll be all right.

———

Moltke landed with his fuel gauge indicating empty. He climbed out of the cockpit and looked appreciatively at the beautiful gray-green airplane before walking away. It felt good to stretch his legs. He walked into the barracks that sat on one edge of the airfield. Upstairs were rooms for the JV 44 pilots. The downstairs was a combination meeting room and bar where they spent their time off duty.

The bar was noisy and full of cigarette smoke. Moltke detected cigar smoke, too, and quickly spotted the source. General Galland, cigar in mouth, waved him toward the table he was sharing with Steinhoff. Moltke could read nothing in the face beneath the rakish Luftwaffe cap.

"Sit down, Baron," Galland said with that familiar edge in his voice. Moltke sat erect in the empty chair. Galland smiled and said: "Oh, for God's sake, man, relax. I told you there's no place for formality here. Have a cognac." He produced a glass and filled it.

"But," he said, peering closely at Moltke, "I would be grateful for your personal report on that incident today. You told Control you shot down a Mustang. In self-defense, was it?"

"In a manner of speaking," Moltke said.

*"In a manner of speaking,"* Galland repeated, pronouncing the words slowly as if they contained a profound meaning. "I see. And did you shoot down anything else in self-defense today?"

Moltke took a deep breath and looked Galland in the eye. "Sir, I made an attack on the leader of a Boeing group and missed. Almost lost control of the kite. When I recovered, I came up from below and made a hit on the high squadron leader. I don't know what the extent of damage was, but he was smoking. When I passed him and circled around, the fighter shot at me. He almost got me."

Galland took the cigar out of his mouth and looked at it thoughtfully. The corner of Steinhoff's mouth twitched as he raised his drink to it. "Were you informed before takeoff that you were not to attack today, that you would use your cannons only in genuine self-defense?"

"Yes, Herr General."

"You disobeyed that order, then. Why, Moltke?"

Moltke paused to compose his reply. "I got off late and was unable to perform the re-con. Sitting up there doing nothing, I became angry. I'm a fighter pilot. I was fully armed. The bastards were smashing the oil refinery and the town around it. I felt the need to—to *help,* and this was the only way. So, yes, I disobeyed my orders. Sir."

Galland's eyes brightened. He turned to Steinhoff. "Macky, we have a mutineer with us. *Another* mutineer." He turned back to Moltke. "So, Baron, for disobeying a lawful order, I must punish you. Your sentence will be to shoot down at least one Boeing, preferably two, your next time up. Do you think you can endure that?" He handed Moltke the glass of cognac.

Moltke smiled and heaved a sigh of relief. "*Jawohl,* Herr General."

Galland raised his glass and the two followed suit. "Up the mutineers," the general said.

# CHAPTER FIVE

# Command Decisions

A cold wind blew a fresh snow shower across Mahoning and turned the air to milk as Adda Robinson returned to the house after her morning walk. The old brick house was imposing at any time. But when the oak trees that lined Main Street were bare, it loomed among its neighbors like a fortress. Today, it seemed an especially welcome haven.

The morning walk was always a pleasure. There was always someone to greet, and it was fun to see Jane Dinsmore driving a horse and buggy. It was a lovely idea, actually; gas rationing gave you just three gallons a week for your car. But it was really quite cold and raw today, as western Pennsylvania tends to be in late winter and early spring. And, though she huddled as deeply as possible into her old fur coat and hat and fleece-lined boots, the cold gets to your bones when you're seventy-eight. She was looking forward to stoking up the coal fire that smouldered perpetually this time of year in the marble-inlaid fireplace in the living room.

Now it appeared that there might be something worth sitting by the fire and drinking another cup of coffee over. Ben Woodfield, the

106

mailman, was standing on the steps of the broad front porch with a smile on his face. In a small town like Mahoning, everyone knew everyone else's business and expected to share in it.

"Something good for me, Ben?" she called as she approached the steps.

"I'd say so, Mrs. Robinson," the mailman said. He held up a wrinkled envelope. "It's got one of those APO box numbers on it. The handwriting looks a mite familiar to me, but . . ."

"Oh, stop that spoofing, Ben," she said, taking the envelope from him. She studied the writing. "Oh my, yes. It's from Mitch all right—I mean, *Colonel* Robinson."

The mailman peered expectantly at the letter. "Wonder if it says anything 'bout Lon Amundson. That was a terrible thing."

"Well, I don't know yet, do I, Ben?" Adda Robinson said. "Do you have another letter for the Amundsons?"

"Well, yes I do," he said.

"Well, I'm sure they'd like to have it," she said, smiling. "If they don't tell you what it says about Lon today, I'll tell you what I know when you come back tomorrow, all right? Right now I'm going inside to get warm and read it."

Before opening the letter, she made a small ceremony of stoking up the fire, arranging the old claw-arm chair just so and getting a hot cup of coffee with plenty of thick cream. When she was settled, she slit the envelope carefully with her letter opener—she saved every one that came—andspread out the two-page letter. Tears sprang to her eyes when she saw the handwriting:

*Dear Aunt Adda,*
*I'm sorry it's taken me so long to write this time. It's been awfully busy here. As I said before, my job is something like being the mayor of a fair-sized town. There's so many people to see and so much paperwork to do here in the office.*

She recognized the ploy and loved Mitch for presenting it. It was his way of telling her that he wasn't in any serious danger any more. But, knowing that it was a ploy, she also knew that it could be only half true.

*Lon is getting much better, and I'm getting a letter off to the Amundsons today. It should arrive at the same time yours does. It was a freak accident, as I think I told you, and he was pretty badly hurt there for a while, but he's come back to our base hospital now to recuperate. After we fatten him up a bit, he'll be given a leave to go home for a month. Wish I could come with him. Bet you wish I could, too. Anyway, Lon will be all right. He won't play football again very soon, but then he wouldn't be doing that anyway.*

*As for myself, I'm quite well. The food isn't like Mahoning, but there's plenty of it. And I get a lot of help in my work from Ed Carlino. I've written you about him before, you'll recall. He's from Steubenville. A wonderful guy. Now, I know, you'll be asking what kind of family does he come from? Well, that's been a natural thing to ask up till now for people like ourselves in Mahoning, but I really believe that kind of question—the old business about bloodline and breeding—will never be asked again after the war, even in Mahoning. And I think you'll come to agree later on that this is all to the good.*

*What about the war, you're probably asking? Well, I don't think the censor will mind my saying that it's almost over, at least in Europe. The Germans are incredibly tough people, the Moltkes on both sides included, but they're about out of gas. Literally. After all, it's 1945 and they've been fighting for six years, if you count Poland. I wish something could be done to wind up the war without going through all this attrition—that is, this costly chipping away at troops and factories and resources.*

*However, as the waiter up at the Elks used to say, that's not my table. I'd better go back to work now. Give my best to everyone. And love to Mrs. Crosby—I mean Aunt Leila. I guess I'm still supposed to call all of your old buddies "Aunt."*

> *Stay well.*
> *Love,*
> *Mitch*

Adda Robinson smiled and wiped her eyes again. She was glad to hear about Lon. Mitch couldn't have been sugarcoating that too much, because Lon would be coming home for everyone to see. And Mitch sounded as if he were all right. Even if he was laying it on a bit thick when he talked about all the paperwork—unless, of course, it meant letters to the mothers of dead aircrewmen, and that was a thought she didn't want to think.

Still, her keen antenna detected signs of distress beneath his cheery monologue. And his handwriting was sprawling, almost spidery. It had deteriorated a great deal over the past year. She smoothed out the letter and shook her head. She did hope this terrible war would be over soon. She didn't know what a bemedaled, twenty-nine-year-old colonel in the Air Corps would do in Mahoning after taking off his uniform, but she would gratefully worry about that later.

For now, she would do whatever she could to help buoy his spirits. She thought for a moment and then nodded vigorously. She would go to the kitchen right now and bake him a big devil's food cake. It was his favorite kind and it was moist enough so that it wouldn't dry out too terribly in the APO mail. The cake would be a real treat for Mitch. She smiled happily as she walked to the kitchen. She was pleased with her decision.

———

Reichsmarshall Hermann Göring, a specially tailored double-breasted version of the dove-gray Luftwaffe uniform buttoned across his huge stomach, strode jauntily into the Führerbunker at *Adlerhorst*, the Führer's Eagle's Nest headquarters near Wiesental. Behind him walked Reichsminister of Armaments Albert Speer, who by contrast always seemed lean and ascetic when he was with Göring. Outside, the men noted, SS men were loading furniture, radio equipment, files and furniture into SS trucks for delivery to the Führerbunker beneath the Chancellery in Berlin.

The meeting room was bare but for a single chair. The two men stood in front of it and waited. Göring quickly became restive; it was ridiculous, he knew, but he felt like a small boy who had been called before a stern headmaster and knew his bottom soon would be stinging. Speer, he noticed with irritation, seemed calm and composed. Five minutes later, the Führer arrived with Bormann trailing behind him, notebook in hand. The Supreme Commander's face was ashen, the body seemed stooped, the right arm hung almost uselessly at his side. He shuffled to the chair and fell into it, his head back, as if exhausted.

His eyes closed, he spoke in a dry, emotionless voice: "What is your report on the Merseburg-Leuna air raids?"

"My Führer," Göring said heartily, "the toll of Boeings and Lancasters continues to grow. As of this moment, we appear to have shot down as many as seventy-five bombers. When they first gave me the report they said the ground was literally covered with the wreckage of the enemy planes. At first I didn't believe it, but now . . ."

The Führer waved him to silence. "What did the raids do to production? That's all I care about. Speer?"

Speer took a deep breath, cleared his throat and paused for a moment to summon his courage. "My Führer, I regret to say that the American and RAF raids have destroyed approximately 75 percent of the production we had restored."

Hitler's eyes snapped open. "Why?" The voice suddenly became a scream. "Why? Where was the Luftwaffe?"

Göring's face turned white; he stuttered momentarily as he tried to speak. "The Luftwaffe fought bravely, my Führer; we took heavy losses."

*"Why?"* screamed Hitler, sitting erect in his chair, his eyes blazing.

Speer spoke quietly. "Three reasons. First, the American bombers are much better protected now; they seem to have an inexhaustible supply of first-line fighters and pilots to fly them. Not as good as our old pilots, perhaps, but few of those are left. That's the second reason; the Luftwaffe is much weaker. We can't provide enough gasoline to resist every air raid or even to train new pilots properly."

Seeing Hitler shaking his head angrily and preparing to interrupt, Speer spoke more rapidly. "Third, the manager of the plant failed to turn on the fog machine. The Americans had a clear picture of the target through their bombsights."

"Sabotage!" Hitler bellowed. "Question the man rigorously and then shoot him!"

Speer smiled faintly. "It wasn't sabotage, my Führer, simply an exaggerated case of professional myopia. The man's a chemist. He says he needed to test the humidity content of the air to set the fog machine for maximum effect. He was still testing from the factory bunker when the bombs began to fall."

Hitler's mouth opened and closed, like that of a stranded fish. Göring sighed and massaged his temple with a bejeweled hand. "Don't shoot him," he said as if to himself. "That would be a mistake. The man's too valuable; I have a place for him. I've been thinking for some time of forming a committee of idiots—military and industrial—so that I can consult them on our plans. Then I'll know that, whatever they recommend, we'll know to do the opposite." He shook his leonine head.

Adolf Hitler sprang to his feet and began to scream. Foam flecked the corners of his mouth. His body shook. Göring quailed and Speer instinctively stepped back a foot.

"Idiots! Incompetents! Fools!" Hitler bellowed. "That's what I'm surrounded with. Incompetent ministers and cowardly pilots and treacherous generals!"

"We did what we could . . ." Göring began timidly.

Hitler rounded on him savagely. "You? You can do nothing—nothing!" He lifted a shaking finger and pointed it at Speer. "I order you now to convert all fighter aircraft factories to the production of antiaircraft batteries."

He turned contemptuously to his quaking Reichsmarshall. "I am disbanding the Luftwaffe fighter arm, forthwith. Your pilots are useless. I will keep only the new jets, assuming they are making some sort of contribution. I want a report on what they are doing in two days' time. Do you understand?"

Göring nodded, seemingly too frightened to speak. Hitler swung back to Speer. "You will use the Luftwaffe's men and materials to produce more antiaircraft guns for the defense of our hydrogenation plants. Do it now!"

"Führer," Speer said. "I have a highly advanced antiaircraft gun—actually a new ground-to-air rocket, the *Wasserfall*—that will ride an electronic beam up to nearly 17,000 meters, through clouds and fog, with amazing accuracy. Much better than our conventional . . ."

Hitler swung his head from side to side. "I don't want to hear about that now. Do what I've told you. Expand antiaircraft production and get Merseburg-Leuna back in operation immediately. Now get out! I have no more time for this!" He flung an arm out in a gesture of dismissal and closed his eyes.

Outside on the terrace it was cold and Speer gathered his greatcoat collar around his throat. Göring stood, stock-still, head down, like a beaten dray horse.

"Don't worry about your fighters," Speer said. "I'm staying over-night. I'll go back to him tomorrow with good news of some kind—a temporary production increase, a small victory, there'll be something in the battle reports—and get him in a better mood. He'll rescind the order about disbanding the fighters when I point out that I can't build heavy AA guns with light-frame metal fabrication for making fighters. And we have to have fighters, whatever their efficiency these days, to help protect our explosive plants. There's no point building AA guns if we won't have ammunition for them. The fighters at least can intercept some of the bombers before they get to the plants and drop their bombs. I'll also tell him that I'll convert half of our heavy locomotive production to AA work. That'll appease him." Speer stared into the distance. "When I have his agreement, I'll bring up the *Wasserfall* again. We absolutely must get this weapon into production."

"He won't approve it without a demonstration," Göring said sullenly.

Speer nodded. "He's going back to Berlin. I'll put one on for him there."

————

The long-legged Fieseler Storch plopped down on the grass field and taxied to the table around which the group of aces sat. Out of the passenger seat of the light aircraft struggled Göring. Pulling down his wrinkled Luftwaffe jacket and adjusting his peaked cap, he strode to the table. The pilots got to their feet and stood in varying positions of attention.

The Reichsmarshall's fleshy face stretched in a sardonic smile as his eyes swept across the group. One year ago, they would have popped-to and stood like ramrods. Now . . .

General Galland stepped forward and threw Göring a casual salute. Göring touched his cap with the baton he had taken to carrying. Steinhoff and Lutzow stared at the Third Reich's Number Two man with naked disdain.

"Will you sit down, Reichsmarshall? Or we can take a car to the inn and have refreshment, if you like," Galland said.

"I have little time," Göring said. "Let's walk away a bit from the others." Galland pointed toward the earth berms protecting the airplanes and they moved slowly toward them. The Reichsmarshall had considered the conversation carefully. If there was any hope of salvaging his reputation with the Führer, it apparently lay with the jets, and that meant Galland.

"General," he said; "I want to confess error." The fat man swallowed. "And to apologize." Galland looked at him warily. "I was wrong not to support you more firmly on the *Blitz* bomber business," Göring said. "I misjudged you. And I'm here to try to make it up."

"That's good of you, Reichsmarshall," Galland said guardedly.

"Not at all. First, I want to tell you that I gave you the best possible report in a meeting with the Führer yesterday. I told him I would return with a positive report on your activities. Can you give me one today?"

Galland nodded. "I can. We have twenty aircraft operational and fully armed, cannons and the new rockets. I have twelve seasoned professionals to fly them and we're ready for a major sortie. Until now we've flown one at a time in reconnaissance—making an occasional solo attack—and we've flown several *kettens,* formations of three under combat conditions to test the behavior of the jet engines in formation flying. There's a built-in throttle lag that you have to get used to."

"What are your results so far?" the Reichsmarshall asked. He twisted his thick neck toward Galland and the younger man noted irrelevantly that pink face powder flecked the fat man's collar.

"We can fly through the Ami fighter escorts as if they were standing still in the sky, like balloons. Our speed is so great that, in attacks from above, the bomber crews won't even see us. In three attacks starting from the *ketten* formation, we've shot down nine bombers."

"Excellent! Excellent!" Göring said, smiling broadly.

Galland lifted a cautionary finger. "But it isn't good enough, Reichsmarshall. Look at the arithmetic. If each of us shot down—oh, pick a generous figure—fifteen bombers, what real good would it do? Assume twelve of us flying, that would be one eighty. A fine total, of course, enough to alarm the enemy, but out of one thousand bombers? Under 20 percent. More than 80 percent would still drop their bombs. The question is whether the Americans would back off the way they did after Schweinfurt. We can't count on that now."

Göring's smile faded. "I can't carry a report like that to the Führer. He'll . . ." his mind quailed at the thought.

"I have a recommendation," Galland said.

"Please," said the Reichsmarshall imploringly.

"Lift the quarantine you imposed on JV 44. Let us coordinate our attacks with Fighter Command's prop fighters. Given the thousands of fighters the Amis are putting up, we know the Luftwaffe boys can't do the job the way it's going. They're dying for nothing. They take off under fire, they come up out of the clouds blind, their cockpits are iced up, they have no de-icers or even blind-flying instruments. Worst of all, they *know* it's for nothing. And, as I say, we can't do enough by ourselves with the jets to make an important difference."

The young general stepped in front of the older man, stopped and held up both hands. "Picture this. We hit them hard, with everything, in a coordinated effort. The jets go in first, first with rockets and then with cannons, to break up the Boeing formations. That destroys their cross fire and creates confusion—more than that, chaos. Once the B-17s are wallowing around out there alone, the Ami fighters can't protect them. Our prop fighters can pick them off."

"They'll take heavy losses from the Ami fighters."

Galland smiled thinly. "They're taking them anyway."

"True."

"We have one major problem, though. If the Amis should find us here they could wipe us out. We're eagles in the sky but we're chickens taking off and landing."

Göring raised his baton. "I'll give the order today to move in two flak batteries to protect you. And I'll speak to General Koller; he'll give you an umbrella. A constant patrol of Focke-Wulfs."

Göring thrust out his right hand. Galland took it and smiled openly for the first time. "Thank you for the visit, Reichsmarshall." He peered inquiringly at Göring. "And the attack plan?"

"I'll take it up with the Führer right away. I'm sure he'll agree.

You'll have your chance to strike *der gross schlag.*" Göring's face became cherubic. "The Führer will be very pleased."

Galland's smile masked his thought: *I could care less. Just give us the chance to accomplish something.* He added: "One more thing, Reichsmarshall. Till now, we've had plenty of airplanes but not enough pilots. Now, within the last few days, a dozen or so younger pilots have arrived unannounced; some are hardly more than boys. They've heard about us and they want to fly for us. Do I have your permission to expand the squadron? Perhaps set up a second one?"

"Who would command it? Steinhoff?"

Galland grinned and shook his head. "No, I'll keep Macky and the older boys with me. I'm thinking of a younger man, someone the lads can identify with. I have a good one with a name everybody will know. Karl Von Moltke."

"Moltke," Göring breathed. "A name from Germany's pantheon of heroes. And it would help offset the embarrassment over that dissident cousin of his, James. Excellent, indeed." Abruptly, the fleshy face rippled into a scowl. "I have a favor to ask in return, Galland. It's the damnable British Mosquitos. They fly into our airspace every day without a care in the world, checking the weather and taking pictures and giving the bombers advance information. As you know, they fly too high and too fast for the prop fighters. Now the bastards have taken to coming over Berlin nearly every night, four or five of them. They drive the city's entire population down into the air raid shelters night after night. Sometimes they drop chaff to make it seem as if a major bomber force is coming. Sometimes they drop air mines to scare the civilians. Nobody in Berlin gets any sleep anymore. The Führer is outraged. If it's really true that you can fly at their altitude . . ."

"We can," Galland said.

"Then go up and get them."

———

Robinson was grateful for the trace of anemic sunlight that touched the headquarters hut as he walked toward it. His shoulders were hunched inside his leather A-2 jacket; his GI shoes crunched on the gravel. Even the palest natural illumination was welcome in the dregs of an English winter. Even when it illuminated nothing more than a flat landscape dotted with olive-drab buildings.

The U.S. Army had colored the war and everything in it olive-drab and that was probably a good decision, Robinson thought. Those rakish caps and uniforms the Germans wore probably made it too much fun to be a soldier. But no army could control the colors aloft. They were beyond the reach of military regulations.

Robinson opened the door and walked in. The stove was glowing red and Carlino was sitting in one of the armchairs, coffee mug in hand. He started to rise but settled back when Robinson waved him down.

Robinson poured himself a cup of thick, black coffee, turned it yellow with canned evaporated milk, shook in a tablespoon of brown sugar crystals and stirred it with the single teaspoon sitting on the desk. He grimaced at the harsh taste, but it granted a moment of false vitality.

"Morning, Ed. Your coffee tastes like horse piss."

"Thank you, sir. You saw the group off."

"Heard them off; the ground fog was like milk. We got the full thirty-six up, one abort. An engine accelerated on takeoff and ran away. The pilot—I don't know the guy, named Attilis, I think—feathered and swung around in the fog—very hairy—and dumped it down. Managed to straddle the field lights on one end of the runway. The tail wheel knocked out twelve of them; that's seventy-five dollars apiece."

"Was it an honest abort?"

"I think so. Engineering's checking out the engine, of course."

Carlino shuffled the papers in his hands. "Do you wanna go over the morning list, Colonel? We've got some decisions to make."

"Yeah, sure. Whatta you got?"

"First, the six new B-17Gs came in on schedule."

"Yeah, I saw them, they're beautiful."

"The primary unit is missing from the cabin heaters. At 60 below zero it'll be bloody cold."

Robinson's face contorted in disgust. "Balls."

"We've got an angry farmer. One of the pilots was supposed to be slow-timing a rebuilt engine. He buzzed the guy's farm. A cow panicked and crashed into a fence. Broke a leg, had to be shot."

"Balls."

"We've got a pregnancy claim. A mother in one of those farms near the base complained to Wing that an airman from the 205th is the poppa of her daughter's forthcoming."

"Balls."

"Wing promises us a complete stand-down for our party. Other groups will soak up our part of the effort. We're guaranteed not to fly that day. That way everybody on the base, including yours truly, can have a proper blast."

"Super. I mean su-pah."

"But there aren't enough girls to go round. The noncoms want a couple truckloads of girls brought in from the surrounding towns."

"That's just asking for trouble." Robinson sank lower in his chair and grazed over his coffee. "You can't get them out of the barracks next morning. What else you got to raise my spirits this morning?"

"I've got a G-2 report for you on that new German 262 fighter. The blow job."

"I already know about it," Robinson said glumly.

"Apparently High Wycombe thinks we're going to see more of them soon. Small flights of them have made what seem to be experimental attacks on a couple of our bomb groups. Pretty successfully, too. There's also an analysis of the 262's strengths and weaknesses."

"What's weak about the damned thing?" Robinson asked.

"The report says they're vulnerable to attack on takeoff and landing."

Robinson laughed shortly. "Who isn't? The trick is to know where they're taking off and landing from. If we know that, I haven't heard about it. Have you?"

"No."

Robinson sighed. "All right. The most important thing is the missing cabin heaters. Can we get the missing component from Wing or Division?"

Carlino shook his head. "Engineering says it'll be faster to make it here. They say they can do it. I told them to go ahead."

Robinson laughed mirthlessly. "Glad I was able to help. The farmer. Pay him for the cow and gig the pilot. Who was it?"

A pause. Robinson looked up at Carlino. Carlino looked down. "Google," he said.

Robinson hit the arm of the chair with his fist. "Google again? Gig the bastard. He's too valuable to court martial. Restrict him to base." Robinson shook his head. "He stays on the base most of the time anyway. Oh hell, Ed, you decide. As for the pregnancy, we know there's a dead cow. We don't know for sure there's a live baby, or who the father is. Who's he supposed to be?"

Carlino looked up, a wry smile on his face. "The mother's named Lieutenant Google."

Robinson stared at the adjutant. "Are you serious?"

Carlino shrugged. "It's one of the farms that backs up to the base. Apparently Google strolls around the perimeter from time to time. He stopped a few times at the farm. That's where he got his dog; Wu-shu he calls it. And apparently, if the mother's telling the truth, he got to walking around with her daughter. Apparently they stopped in the barn a few times. I'm looking into it."

"You're giving me a headache, Major. About the party, we can't deny the noncoms their fun. Let the girls come in. We'll wind up with a couple of VD cases, of course. Get Doc Benson to distribute rubbers . . ."

"He'll set up a complete prophylactic station—saddle, green soap, self-injectable ointment, the works. I've got another question, though: should we confiscate the officers' handguns before the party?"

Robinson grimaced. "No. Their .45s are GI equipment. Besides, we don't want to offend their—excuse the expression—*dignity* as adults. Some of them are actually as old as twenty-one or twenty-two. Just remind them that shooting off the pistols will bring fines and restrictions to quarters, no exceptions. I'd like to look forward to this party instead of worrying about it. How bad did it get last time? It must have been three months ago."

"Four. There was some shooting, one flesh wound, followed by a court martial. Two fistfights. A broken jaw and a detached retina."

"Oh, my."

"Oh, my" was Aunt Adda's capstone comment of dismay. It bore more weight than any casual obscenity.

"We had a rape charge, of course," Carlino continued. "And Captain Blackman, the intelligence officer we had for a few weeks? Fell in a ditch, drunk, broke his leg. He was in the hospital for a month."

Robinson stared into his empty coffee cup. "Speaking of the hospital, Ed. I wonder how Lon's doing. I haven't seen him for a couple of days."

"Doc Benson says he's doing fine. He's eligible for R&R—more than that, a trip home on a month's leave—he's going home after the party. He lost a lot of shoulder and back muscle on the right side, you know. He's still about twenty pounds underweight. But his lung's reinflated and he's a strong guy."

"How's he going to be later on?" Robinson asked. "That's the real question."

Carlino shugged. "Well, he'll never have the back and shoulder strength he had before, that's for sure. He'll have some ugly-looking scars. But he'll be okay."

"Boy, I wish I could go home with him on that leave."

"I know you do, Mitch."

"Ah well. I'm going to drop in on Lon when we wind up here." Robinson spread his muscular hands and studied them. The ends of his fingers trembled almost imperceptibly. He turned his hands palms up. There were twin rows of calluses at the tops of the palms of each hand and near the tips of the fingers. *It's really incredible. You wear two pairs of gloves and you still get blisters on the calluses.*

He flexed his hands and looked at Carlino. "If we're through, I'm going to go see Lon for a few minutes, stand by for the radio transmissions from the target, then catch a nap before they get back. I was up a little late last night."

"I wish she had a sister," Carlino said, heaving his compact bulk from the chair. "Since she doesn't, I'm going to go tend to my military duties—cabin heaters, cows, pregnant girls, parties. I don't have time for small talk."

———

The two-story frame and asbestos-shingle hospital lay at the end of Whitwick Green, as far from the engine noise of the 205th Bomb Group as it was possible to get without leaving the compound. A screen of trees helped to dampen the sound. When Robinson entered the small ward, he found Lon Amundson sitting in a chair beside the hospital bed, reading. He was wearing pajamas and a red bathrobe. The only other occupant was a navigator with a mild case of pneumonia. His bed was at the other end of the room and had a curtain pulled across it. Lon's face opened in a smile when he saw Robinson.

"How you doin', Ace?" Robinson asked, perching on the bed. "You're looking good, sitting up and everything."

"Feeling fine, Ace," Amundson said. "I can raise the right arm up to here." He raised the elbow till it was parallel with his shoulder.

"Don't rush it. You're doing great."

"I really am. I'm doing physical therapy, working out with some light weights."

"Weight is what you need. Are you eating?"

"Like a horse. It's beginning to taste good."

"That's a bad sign. I understand you're going home on R&R."

"I have mixed feelings about it, Mitch."

"I would, too. But it's SOP to take the leave. You owe it to your folks. And I want you to stop by and see Aunt Adda."

"And Betsy."

Robinson frowned. "Yeah, Betsy. I don't know what to tell you to say to her. I haven't written her for quite a while."

"Because of Sandra."

"Well, Sandra's part of it. She's a great lady, and I'm crazy about her. I think. But, oh hell, Lon, sometimes I still get to thinking about the other one—you know."

"You aren't still carrying the torch for the hometown Hunkie." It was more exasperated accusation than question.

Robinson heaved a sigh. "For Katie. The beautiful Polack. Who wound up in the back seat with my best friend while I was leaning against a tree, sick."

Amundson lowered his head and clapped a hand over his eyes. "Oh, cripes, Mitch. That was twelve to thirteen years ago. We were kids. And how many times have I apologized? A hundred, two hundred?"

"No reason to apologize. I made it happen. But I wish I could make that girl disappear from my mind. I've never felt like that again. Betsy never came close to it. Sandra does sometimes, but . . ."

"Excuse me, Mitch, but you've got to get over that horseshit. She was your family *maid*, for God's sake. It was the first time for you, or me, for that matter. You can't let that screw up, excuse the expression, every relationship you'll ever have."

Robinson nodded. "I know. I don't know why I got into it today except that talking about Mahoning and talking to you out of uniform for a change . . . Ah, well, back to business—your leave."

Amundson nodded. "Right. I want to go home, you know that. But I need to know. Will I come back here after my leave's up? I don't want to sit on my ass in some reclassification center."

Robinson spread his hands. "You know you're not going to be rassling another B-17, Lon. Not in this war." He got up and looked out at the window at the washed-out sunlight. "Tell you what, Ace. There's a lot of shit to do around here. More than you think. Maybe I could swing it where you'd give Ed Carlino and me a hand on the ground. Be my deputy, help run the base. You'd be making a real contribution."

Robinson turned to see Amundson smiling tolerantly. "You wouldn't bullshit an old buddy, would you, Ace? No, listen a minute, Colonel. I don't particularly want to fly a B-17 again, thanks anyway. But I sure as hell would like to fly one of those stripped-down P-51s or Mosquitos on long-range recon. I've *always* wanted to fly one of those wooden wonders—high, fast, light in your hands. Nobody can catch a Mossie."

Robinson raised his eyebrows. "The international weather force? Jeez, I don't know. I suppose I could lobby General Sutter up at Wing for the transfer. You'd get to live in that big old mansion at Stonehurst with the Brits and French and Poles—just like the movies said *we* were going to do."

"They lied."

"They sure did. Our whole damned generation enlisted because of

Hollywood. I found that out on my first raid. It looked like it was supposed to, but something was missing. I realized finally it was the music. Nobody was playing 'Onward Christian Soldiers.' "

"Betty Grable wasn't waiting for you when you got back to the base, either."

"Not even Greer Garson. But seriously, folks . . . I really could use you to help out here, Lon."

Amundson's smile faded. "Don't wet-nurse me, Mitch. Talk to General Sutter for me when you can, okay?"

Robinson sighed and smiled. "Okay. Listen, I'm going over to Ops and wait for the message from group. No reason not to hit the target today. Are you coming to the party?"

"I'll be there," Amundson said. He watched Robinson leave and his face grew somber. The invisible bond that had tied the two of them together for so long was chafing. It was time to cut it. He felt deep affection for Mitch, but Mitch's protectiveness had become obsessive. It was as if Mitch, prematurely aged and exalted by rank and responsibility, had become Lon's father rather than his friend.

"I don't need another father," he said. He didn't realize he had said it aloud until he noticed the orderly standing by his bed with his pills, a puzzled look on his face.

# CHAPTER SIX

# Party Time

THE 205th Bomb Group's party was roaring at full throttle by 2100. Before going to the officers' club, Robinson made a personal check of the base, taking Sandra with him in his jeep. He checked on the posting of sentries and then drove around the perimeter track and spot-checked the hardstands to make sure that no drunken crewmen had climbed into the airplanes. At an earlier party, a co-pilot got into a B-17, started its engines and taxied onto the main runway before others could block his path with trucks. When he was hauled out of the plane by MPs, he wailed drunkenly that he wanted to fly to Berlin solo to kill Adolf Hitler. A check of his record showed that he had twice turned back from the target, claiming mechanical problems. He was sent to Wing the next day and assigned to a clerical job.

Robinson also drove to the NCO club and watched while Army trucks unloaded hordes of English girls from the surrounding villages. One truck disgorged a group of husky, short-legged Land Army girls from a nearby farm. Direct descendants of the European serfs of the Middle Ages, he told Sandra. She gave him a cold look in response. He drove on to headquarters to talk to the watch officer and confirm that nothing had happened to disturb the 205th's stand-down arrangement.

"But they've already told you your group needn't fly tomorrow," Sandra said. "Surely they wouldn't go back on their word."

Robinson smiled. "A distinguished philosopher named Fats Waller once said, 'One never knows, do one?' "

The officers' club had once been a cattle barn. At one end was a lounge with couches, chairs and two gaming tables. A large stone fireplace had been built into the end wall. An addition had been built at the other end to house the officers' mess. In between was an oval-shaped bar manned by enlisted men who served as bartenders. The bar was open every evening, serving beer, gin and mixers. Off-duty officers regularly lounged around the club, many of them gambling casually at dice and cards with wads of tissue-like five-pound notes that represented more money than they had ever seen in their young lives.

When Robinson and Sandra approached the entrance, the din inside had grown so loud she instinctively moved close to him. He smiled and told her not to worry; it wouldn't be as bad as she thought.

The statement was disproven immediately. As Robinson walked through the entrance, two grinning, red-eyed junior officers seized him by the arms. A third grabbed his tan tie and, wielding a large pair of shears, cut his necktie off just below the knot.

"Party rules!" one officer yelled. Robinson nodded, the men released him, and he and Sandra walked through the throng to the bar.

"What on earth was that for?" she asked. "They ruined your lovely tie."

"An old tradition," Robinson said, examining the stub. "I didn't start it. But I should have remembered." He waved his hand toward the hundreds of officers who were drinking, laughing and gesticulating nearby. All were in dress uniforms and not one was wearing a whole necktie.

Someone, no one was sure who, had started the practice at group parties at some time in the past, Robinson explained. Perhaps his name was carved into the ceiling of the club or had been painted there with candle smoke. Hundreds of names of departed men who had finished their tours or had been killed or invalided home were inscribed there.

Robinson wedged Sandra and himself into a corner where the bar
met the wall—a spot reserved by common understanding for the CO.
From there they could watch the proceedings without being jostled.
Many of the carousing officers in the club were accompanied by English girls, some of them startlingly good-looking. The Americans had
few contacts with British men and weren't particularly friendly with
those they knew. But they were almost universally impressed by the
girls, their blooming good looks, their peaches-and-cream complexions
—the result of regular walking in the outdoors and few sweets and fats
in their diets—and their European habit of deferring to males. The
girls were, in the main, poor, and it was reflected in their dresses, some
of them obviously homemade.

Many were steadies. Most of the men had been in England long
enough to form liaisons with women they had met at community open
houses and dances. A few officers were married but had decided, after
experiencing combat and seeing the girls, to suspend their vows for the
duration.

As the evening wore on, Robinson sipped steadily at gin-and-limes.
Every time his glass was half empty, a solicitous bartender placed a full
one before him. Sandra, nestled under his arm, watched with amusement as he increasingly played lord of the manor to the officers who
stepped up, one by one, to pay their respects. Few junior aircrewmen
did; for the most part they stayed as far away from the brass as they
could. But the senior officers and lead team members walked over to
greet the group commander and say a few words that were frequently
lost in the noise.

Robinson's demeanor changed only when Major Lon Amundson
appeared. "Evenin', Ace!" Amundson shouted. "I mean, Colonel Ace!"

"Howya doin', Ace?" Robinson shouted, disengaging himself from
Sandra and throwing his arms around his friend.

"Feelin' great," Amundson yelled. "I wanted to come by. I'm goin'
home tomorrow. R&R. All the way to Mahoning. Priority air cargo."

"Oh boy," Robinson said, suddenly sobering. "You won't forget
now, you know . . ."

"Course not. As soon as I see my folks, I'll call on your aunt and everybody. I wanted to come by and say hello. It's bed instead of booze tonight. Gotta get an early start."

"Great!" Robinson said, throwing his arms around him again as Sandra grinned. "Take care, Ace."

————

No one could remember later whose idea it was to trace the outline of a young Englishwoman's body on the ceiling in candle smoke. All that anyone could recall was that a group of officers was pleading with the young woman, whose name was Jill, to leave her lovely outline where they could appreciate it each night after returning from their missions.

"You'll be an inspiration to all of us," one officer declared.

"You'll be famous, Jill," another shouted. "The men who come along after us will all want to know about you."

A third officer applied the clincher. "What it'll do, Jill, is prove once and for all that British women, without a doubt, are the best-built in the world."

Within minutes, the unsteady young woman consented to have her clothes removed. "Mind you now," she said to the goggle-eyed group surrounding her, "I don't want a single thing lost. Put all my things neatly in the corner there."

Robinson was deep in what he imagined to be a conversation with another officer about the social dynamics of small-town America as the officers shed their jackets and formed two human pyramids.

"What on earth are they doing?" Sandra said, watching them swaying back and forth. One had handed Jill up to two men at the top who were trying to hold her spread-eagled against the ceiling. As she squeaked and giggled, the two top men in the second pyramid leaned close with large candles that billowed flame and smoke.

"Mitch. Mitch, dear, do you see what's happening there?" she asked, punching Robinson's side. He nodded and kept talking.

The plan was doomed from the beginning. To get close enough to trace the outlines of the girl's body, the smoke painters had to hold the candles uncomfortably close to her. It was inevitable that an unsteady hand would scorch her flesh. The first time it happened she yelped in pain and wriggled. A dozen voices reassured her and shouted curses at the lout with the candle. The second time it happened she screamed and wriggled so violently that she slipped out of the hands of the men holding her up. She fell into the middle of the pyramid, which tumbled to the floor, knocking the second pyramid sideways and toppling the men into the crowd.

Within minutes, a phalanx of MPs cleared a path to the fallen for Captain Harvey Benson, the base flight surgeon, and his nurse, Lieutenant Kathleen McGinnis.

"What happened?" Robinson demanded.

"That's what I've been trying to tell you," Sandra said. "Things got out of hand and I'm afraid that poor girl is hurt."

"Why does she have her clothes off?" he asked. Sandra rolled her eyes. After Benson had examined them, the moaning girl and an unconscious officer were carried away on stretchers.

Benson and McGinnis approached Robinson. Benson was a sandy-haired, pear-shaped Air Corps physician of forty who frankly loved his life on the base and the distinction that being the oldest man in the group gave him.

"She was lucky," Benson said. "So were we. She has a few second-degree burns of her side and arm and a minor contusion or two. But her reflexes are okay; she'll be all right. The officer may have a concussion, though. He'll be off duty for a while. We'll keep them both overnight."

"But this whole thing is ridiculous," Sandra said indignantly.

Kathy McGinnis nodded and smiled faintly. "This is a kindergarten, my dear. That's what you have to remember."

Robinson took a deep breath and struggled to focus his eyes. "Anything else?"

"A broken jaw in the NCO club. We'll be minus a gunner for a while. And somebody was firing his Colt outside a barracks. The MPs got him before he could hurt anybody."

"Not so bad then."

"Not yet, anyway."

"I've got something bad, Colonel. Real bad." It was Major Ed Carlino. "They've called us out."

Robinson, suddenly alert, wheeled and scowled at his adjutant.

"Whattaya mean, 'Called us *out*?'"

Carlino looked at him steadily. "I mean the Wing has sent through a message saying it's an all-out-all-out and we have to fly, stand-down or no stand-down. I called them on the scrambler and verified it. No exception. Every available aircraft, they said. Whatever we can put up."

Robinson slammed his glass on the bar. Sandra winced. "Shit!" he shouted. "The double-crossing bastards!" He rubbed his hands over his face. "God*damn* them." He straightened up and looked at Carlino. "What's the drill, then?"

"First, we close the bar. Here and at the NCO club. Then make a general announcement and schedule the briefing. Send the MPs to get the lead teams. Roust everybody out of the clubs and bunks."

"Ah hell," Robinson said. He took a deep breath. "Okay." He spoke slowly as if reciting an old lesson. "Then get the ground crews to the hardstands. Armorers to the bomb dump. Women off the base. Controllers in the tower. Intelligence and photo crew to the ticker and the lab."

"Anything I can do, Colonel?" Benson asked.

"Can you get any of these people sober?" Robinson asked. "Including me?"

"Not really. It takes time to oxidize all that alcohol. Getting something to eat would help absorb a little of it. Get everybody on oxygen as soon as they get into the airplanes. Kathy and I can screen as many people at the skill positions as there's time for—check eyes and reflexes: can they focus their eyes, touch their nose, walk a line, that kind of thing. That's about all we can do."

"All right," Carlino said. "I'll find the mess officer and get some breakfast cooking. Check them over on their way out of the club."

Robinson unfastened his mutilated necktie. "Whose turn is it to lead?"

"Warrington," Carlino said. "But you can forget him; he's out like a light; I checked. Frisbee's next in rotation, but he's on leave. We'll have to move down a notch. Let a squadron leader—maybe Morse—take the lead. If he can fly."

"Ah hell," Robinson said wearily. "I'll go.

"Not a good idea, Colonel. You've taken on a load tonight. It'll be some hours before your head clears."

"Eddie's right, Mitch," Sandra said. "Please don't fly."

Robinson turned and threw her a look that made her quiver. "I'm sorry," she said. "I didn't mean to trespass."

Carlino blew out his cheeks. "All right, Colonel, you're the man with the fuzzy balls. I'll round up some kind of crew for you. Starting with a sober copilot."

"Where's Google?" Robinson asked.

"Don't know," Carlino replied. "Haven't seen him. He may be off the base."

"I'll fly copilot for you." Robinson turned to see Amundson standing beside him.

Robinson looked at him hard and shook his head. "You're through flying F-17s, Lon. Forget it."

"Come on, Mitch," Amundson protested. "You need me. I'm cold sober and a lot fitter than you are right now for flying. You got no right to turn me down."

Robinson shook his head impatiently and strode toward the door. "Gonna wash up and get into my gear." He turned to Carlino. "I'll see you at the mess hall."

Amundson caught up with him at the door and blocked his way. "Wait a minute, damn it!" he said. "You got no right to pull rank on me at a time like this. No right to wet-nurse me either. I'm not a damn baby!"

"Oh, Lon," Sandra said softly. A knot of men had clustered around the two angry officers.

"Major," Robinson grated. "Get your ass outa my way. You're not fit to fly a B-17. You shouldn't be flying *anything*. Matter of fact, I wish I hadn't arranged that dumb-ass transfer of yours to the recon group."

Amundson's face hardened. "So now it comes out, doesn't it? You've just gotta run my life for me, don't you?"

"This isn't the time, Lon," Carlino said, taking him by the arm. "Let's go."

"No, damn it!" Lon said, shaking him off. "We're gonna settle this now."

"Get out of my way, Major," Robinson said. The exchange happened in a matter of seconds. Robinson pushed Amundson sideways. Amundson, losing his temper, threw a clumsy left hook at Robinson's jaw. Slowed by alcohol, Robinson only partially blocked the blow. But, moving automatically, he counter-punched sharply to his friend's stomach. Lon went down gasping and retching.

"Oh, God," Robinson said, crouching beside him. "Lon, I'm sorry. I'm really sorry. I don't know what happened."

Carlino pulled Robinson to his feet as Benson squatted beside Amundson. "He just had the wind knocked out of him," the medical officer said. "He'll be all right."

"Come on, Colonel," Carlino said. "He knows you're sorry. We've gotta go."

After they left, Benson walked Amundson around to help him catch his breath. Sandra turned to Kathy McGinnis. "There seems to be no one else to ask. Do you think I might stay overnight? Might I wait for Mitchell in his office?"

Kathy McGinnis nodded and smiled. "I'm sure it'll be all right, dear. It's going to be a long night around here. There's a cot in there. There should be a blanket on one of the shelves. You might as well try to get some sleep."

———

By the time Robinson arrived at the airplane in his flight gear his head was aching like an infected tooth. It was dawn and a milky light filtered through the trees at the edge of the hardstand. A rag-tag group was waiting. The regular members of his crew who showed up were red eyed and seedy looking. Three others were visibly ill at ease and awkward in heavy flying clothes. One was Ed Carlino.

"What's this, Ed?" Robinson demanded. "Why are you in flight gear?"

"This is your crew, Colonel, and I'm your left waist gunner."

Robinson shook his head disgustedly. "You're no such damn thing. This is ridiculous."

"Ridiculous it may be, Colonel," Carlino said stoutly. "But if you want a left waist gunner today, you're lookin' at him. I'm all there is."

"Sometimes I think everybody in this damned outfit is crazy!" Robinson yelled in frustration. "Do you have any more surprises for me?"

"As a matter of fact, that gentleman there you may recognize as Captain Cohen, the engineering officer. He's our tail gunner. And of course you know Captain Maniglia. Right waist."

"The Catholic chaplain?" Robinson asked in horror, peering at the ascetic face beneath the flight helmet.

"Good morning, my son," Maniglia said, smiling faintly. "I thought it might be time to render unto Caesar. Besides, you need live bodies."

"This can't be happening," Robinson said.

"Shall I preflight the lady?" The question came from Google, who had been standing in the shadows beneath the wing. Robinson nodded, looking at him with the mingled relief and concern he had come to feel whenever the placid little pilot with the large yellow eyes appeared.

"Google turned up a few minutes ago," Carlino said. "He was sleeping in a farmhouse across the field when he heard one of the crew chiefs run up an engine. *That* farmhouse. So he got up and came over to see what was going on."

"Good, I guess," Robinson said. The men were looking at him expectantly. "All right," he said, raising his voice. "We're going to fly together today because you're all there is. I'm not completely sober and some of you are worse off. Three of you don't belong aboard this airplane, any airplane, drunk or sober. So we have to stay in tight communication." To his irritation, the last word came thickly from his tongue and he repeated it carefully. "Com-mun-a-kay-shun."

"Go on oxygen as soon as you get aboard and put on your headsets. Stay on the intercom frequency all day. When Google or I ask for a check-in, respond by position, starting from the tail. Answer by position. If I say, 'pilot to right waist,' that's you today, Father, you say 'right waist to pilot.' Got that?"

The chaplain nodded. "Yes, my son."

Robinson sighed. "Look, Father—I mean, Captain—on the ground you can call me 'son' or 'sir' or 'skipper' or even 'hey you' if you want. But, in the air, call me 'pilot.' As airplane commander, never mind group leader, I can't be the waist gunner's son. Okay?"

"Yes, my—yes, sir."

"All right; let's get aboard."

The 205th managed to get fourteen bombers in the air. Another couldn't be started; it wasn't clear whether there was an engine malfunction or the pilot couldn't remember the starting procedure. Still another bomber taxied off the perimeter track and bogged down helplessly in mud.

Robinson, his head aching horribly in the thin air aloft, called for a check-in as soon as the skeleton group had formed up and left the Alconbury Beacon. Cohen and Carlino tried to answer at the same time. Maniglia started to call the pilot "son," but caught himself and garbled his response.

"No, goddamn it!" Robinson said angrily. "Do it again. Pilot to crew. Check in. From the tail, one position at a time."

The second time it went off properly until it was time for the navigator to respond. After Robinson had called him twice, the bombardier broke in to say that Doroshkin had fallen asleep and couldn't be roused.

When they reached the German border, heavy clouds began to develop and, with them, icing. Huge contrails blossomed from the hot engines and formed opaque streams of ice crystals. Soon the group was flying in dense fog. The pilots peered at dim shadows to hold formation.

Robinson depressed the mike button. "Pilot to bombardier. Fisk, what was the last update on weather over the target? Doroshkin should have brought a flimsy aboard."

"Got it here. Wing said this low-pressure front was moving eastward ahead of us but they thought we'd get to the target before it went zero-zero. They predicted some icing, but not this bad."

Robinson grunted. If it stayed like this, there would be little flak and no fighters, friendly or enemy. But what good would it do if they couldn't hit the target? Then he realized to his horror that he couldn't remember what the target was.

"Bombardier," Robinson said cautiously. "Review target data."

"Well," the bombardier said, puzzled at the request, "it's Magdeburg, the oil refinery there. ETA, an hour and a half from now. They want a tight bomb pattern, but, in this stuff, I don't know . . ."

"Is Doroshkin awake yet?" Robinson asked.

"No, sir," the bombardier answered.

"I'll signal the deputy to take us the rest of the way."

It wasn't necessary. A recall order came a few minutes later from Pinetree. The radio operator relayed the message to Robinson. The attack on the primary target was cancelled, repeat, cancelled. Fifteen minutes later, the attack on the secondary target was cancelled, too. They wandered around in the fog for another thirty minutes trying to find a suitable target of opportunity until the Wing leader decided to call that off, too. The day was a total loss.

Robinson swore to himself. Any casualty today would be a waste. When a son was killed, the folks at home seldom cared where and how it happened. The fact of the tragedy was enough to occupy them. To the airmen, the circumstances mattered a great deal. Getting killed in combat was undesirable but understandable. You could live—or die— with that. But getting killed on a mission with no purpose, or lumbering off the runway during a blind takeoff, or colliding in midair— those kinds of deaths were especially detested.

An hour after they had headed back toward the channel, Robinson's No. 4 engine began running rough and losing power. Google tinkered with it and diagnosed the cause as icing. Then Cohen developed an ear blockage and, with it, intense pain. A gunner with an ear block would be useless in a fight.

"That's it," Robinson told Google. "Tell Brabant to take over the lead. We're taking the ship down to 10,000. See if we can shake these problems. Shouldn't be any fighters around in weather like this."

Google called the deputy, who was flying on their right wing. Robinson called the crew and said they'd be going home alone. Travelling westward in a shallow glide, the B-17 emerged from the fog into broken clouds. At least you can see the ground, Robinson said to himself. But the ground could see him, too. There was a series of sharp cracking noises and four oily black puffs with orange centers appeared off the left wing. A four-gun 88mm antiaircraft battery had picked him up.

Robinson's heart hammered and he tried to concentrate. He knew what to do. It was like boxing. Instead of leaning away from a punch and allowing your opponent to step in and deck you, you stepped into it, blocking or slipping, to counter. It was the same here. Instead of turning away from the flak burst, you turned sharply into it to spoil the gunner's opportunity to correct his aim.

But his hands and feet wouldn't obey his brain. He sat and sweated. The next barrage burst just off the right wing and splinters banged against the fuselage. He tried to turn again and, again, seemed to be paralyzed. Abruptly, Google leaned across the pedestal, flicked Robinson's right hand from the wheel and seized the controls.

The action broke the paralysis. Robinson slumped in his seat. Google rotated the wheel to the right, stood on the right rudder, pressed the yoke forward and put the big airplane into a turning dive to the right. Four explosions banged overhead. Google went to full RPM and full throttle and pulled the bomber's nose up sharply. Four black bursts appeared directly ahead. A climbing turn to the left. Four bursts to the right. Another diving turn, this time to the left. The bursts fell behind and overhead.

By now, they could see new explosions in their path ahead. The gunners had telephoned ahead to the next battery. They would be tracked all the way to the channel. Fighting to control his breathing, Robinson punched the mike button: "Hang on!" he yelled to the crew.

He didn't ask for acknowledgement, but it came simultaneously. "We're with ya, skipper!" Who was that? "Y'got it, Mitch!" Was that a Steubenville accent? Somewhere in the garble, he heard a sonorous voice intone, ". . . my son." Robinson looked at Google. He was grinning and sweating heavily. Flak bursts exploded around them; the heavily loaded B-17, heavy in his hands, twisted, dived and climbed to avoid destruction.

The black quartets followed and tracked them. Periodically, something like gravel spattered against the ship. Robinson looked at Google. His grin had become a rictus, his breath came in gasps. Once, he depressed the mike button by mistake and a deep rasping sounded through the intercom. The airplane, still carrying its bombs, was too heavy for these aerobatics. It needed to drop them.

Robinson squeezed down hard on his fear, inhaled slowly and deeply and took back the controls. "Pilot to navigator or bombardier, whichever. Where the hell are we?"

"Bombardier to pilot, I've been tracking us. That's Dortmund over there."

Dortmund. He remembered this industrial region all too well. Struggling to suppress his feelings of panic, he vowed to make something of this ruined day even if . . . his mind refused to finish the thought. He banked the bomber sharply to the right, put it into a shallow dive and barked: "Open bomb bay doors."

The additional drag would slow the airplane even further, but it wouldn't be for long. "Bombardier. Gelsenkirchen is just north of Dortmund. Synthetic oil plant; we hit it before. Can you get a fix on it?"

Fisk's voice was high, excited. "Pilot, I can. I see it. Give me a minute." It was a long minute. One flak burst exploded uncomfortably close, rocking the airplane.

"Level out now! Two degrees to the right! Hold steady! I'm going to salvo!" Fisk shouted.

"Do it!" Robinson grated.

The bombs fell free in a clump. The bomber rose, suddenly light in the hands. Robinson stood the bomber on one wing, looking down.

"Bingo!" Google shouted, seeing the bombs burst below. "Great shot!" Cheers rang through the interphone.

A quartet of flak bursts rocked the B-17. Someone cried out in pain. Robinson dumped the nose, banked to the left and headed for the deck to spoil the gunners' aim. In the shallow dive, they reached 275 miles an hour. They leveled out and skimmed over what seemed a vast, confused battleground covered with smoke and murk. And then they were roaring over towns and trees. Occasionally, a rapid-fire aircraft gun would send up a stream of 40-millimeter cannon shells. Jinking and turning, making frequent changes in course, they escaped further damage.

And then they were over the water, leaving a string of disappointed antiaircraft gunners behind. Google was calling the crew for an injury or damage report. They acknowledged, one by one. Carlino had been gashed along the cheek by a hot flak fragment. Robinson laughed aloud. Good God, he thought, I'll have to put him in for a Purple Heart and he'll always have a scar so people will know he was wounded in combat. Better it had been in his butt.

It was dark by the time they reached the English coast and they were low on fuel. Robinson had no idea where they were. Doroshkin tried to sit up and plot a course but only a deranged pilot would have used his calculations.

"I'll call Darky," Google said. Darky was the name the British had given to their ingenious radio navigation system to help wayward pilots. It was made up of a network of tiny, low-powered transmitters. Each had a range of only three miles, so that, when you called one, it knew approximately where you were. To contact Darky, you simply turned to the Darky frequency, began circling, and asked for help. The station would answer you only if you identified yourself three times.

"Hello, Darky; Hello, Darky; Hello, Darky," Google called. "This is A for Able, A for Able, A for Able. We are lost, lost, lost. Bearing to Whitwick Green, please, Darky."

They circled in the deepening darkness. The horizon had disappeared. No lights could be seen. Flying in England's wartime blackout was like looking into a cave.

A woman's voice broke the silence. Speaking in clipped British English, she said: "Darky calling A for Able. Turn to 225 degrees and fly for six minutes. Follow the light and make the standard DREM letdown. Do you read, A for Able?"

"Roger, Darky. A for Able out." He turned to Robinson. "Shall I take it, chief?" Robinson nodded; his hands and feet had grown numb.

At the end of six minutes a point of light appeared just to the left of the nose. Google turned toward it. As he reached it, a second light appeared, again to the left. When he reached the third light, there was another. Now a string of lights began to form an arc. They were in the entryway of Britain's unique DREM airfield lighting system. Each light was hooded and could be seen only from a predetermined angle.

Google began letting down at 300 feet a minute. A marauding

German night fighter above them might know from the radio transmissions that a lone B-17 was coming into his sector. But, unless he
accidentally turned on the same headings at the same speed and rate of
descent, which was almost impossible for a fighter to do, he would be
unable to see either the lights or the bomber.

The arc became a funnel of lights leading toward a runway. As they
flew down the funnel, the runway lights snapped on. The B-17 touched
down and rolled and the lights snapped off. A jeep with a hooded light
illuminating a Follow Me sign appeared and led them to the taxi strip
and the hardstand. One by one, they plopped out of the airplane.
Robinson, dropping from the nose hatch, landed heavily. Google
dropped light-footedly, like a cat. Fisk had to lead Doroshkin through
the bomb bay and out the back door. The three ground officers, talking
animatedly to each other and shaking their heads, stepped out of the
back. Cohen, the engineering officer, knelt down and kissed the
ground. Maniglia, the chaplain, began to do the same thing but halted
midway, in a small genuflect. Robinson, watching, understood. He
would have liked to kiss the ground too.

Robinson's jeep pulled up with the flight surgeon behind the wheel.
"Good news, Colonel," he said. "Everybody's back. You're last in. No
casualties."

"Thank God for that," Robinson said wearily. "That's good enough
for a day like this." Laughter suddenly bubbled up in him. "But you'll
have to amend that report, Harvey. Major Carlino is wounded. He was
cut by some flak and he'll bear the scar to his dying day. At least he'd
like to. Wouldn't you, Ed?"

Carlino, holding a bloody first-aid pad to his cheek, smiled ruefully
in the dark. A truck pulled up for the crew. Robinson, Carlino,
Maniglia and Google squeezed into the jeep with Benson. The chaplain
turned to Carlino. "Well, Ed, we had our mission today, didn't we?"

"Indeed we did, Father," Carlino said. "It was pretty scary there for
a while, being followed by those guns." He turned to Robinson.
"Whatta you say, Colonel? Would you consider this a tough one?"

Robinson shrugged elaborately. "Oh, well . . ." Then, seeing Carlino's face fall, he said: "Yeah, it was a tough one, Ed. Really. No
question." A smile spread over Carlino's face.

When he was finished with the debriefing, Robinson went directly to his office. As he entered the door, Sandra threw herself into his arms. "Oh, I'm so glad you're safe," she sobbed, digging her fingernails into his shoulders. "Waiting has *never* been as horrible as this. I thought I'd die!"

*So did I,* Robinson thought. Her face was drawn, her hair uncombed, her eyes red. He held her against him for a while, saying nothing, as she cried. Then he held her away from him and dried her face with his hands. "You sure are ugly," he said. "But you'll get over it."

Sandra laughed through her tears. "Lon had to leave but he told me to give you a message. He's sorry for that—'blowup' he called it—and he said he was sure you were, too."

Robinson felt a flood of relief. "Thank God for that."

"And he said, and I'll quote him in that American dialect of yours, after all this time he's still a 'sucker for your left hook.'"

Robinson, suddenly light hearted, began laughing. He laughed so hard he had to sit down. When he recovered, he got up and locked the office door and began peeling off his flight clothes. By the time he looked up, Sandra was undressing.

Later, as he prepared to take her back to Bedford, he found Google by his jeep.

"Great party, Chief," the lieutenant said. "We oughta have them more often."

Robinson looked at him wonderingly. As he did, Google slowly raised his index finger and pointed it at him. He cocked his thumb and let it fall. "Bang," he said softly. His eyes, catching the light from the supply room, glowed.

———

Stowing his flight gear in his locker, Barney Google reflected on the peculiar reputation he had acquired during his tour with the 205th. Initially, he had been disappointed to be picked for bomber duty rather than as a fighter pilot. But the need was for bomber pilots; the attrition rate demanded large numbers of replacements. He arrived at Whitwick Green during a period of heavy losses. Assigned as a replacement copilot, he quickly found himself in demand. He learned quickly, proved himself to be a superb pilot and was fearless. The qualities that set him apart from his fellow airmen on the ground made him invaluable in the air. He was offered an airplane and crew of his own but he declined, saying he wanted to remain a copilot. As a constantly available copilot, he could fly more frequently than first pilots following normal rotation.

Barney flew right-seat for squadron, group and Wing leaders; occasionally, when a high-ranking officer was flying right-seat as command pilot, Barney would serve as gunner and spare pilot. He found that the psychological demands imposed on bomber pilots—being forced to endure punishment stoically—suited him perfectly. It provided a constant review of his teachings.

Barney's only regret was that he lacked the space and privacy needed to practice his physical exercises. It was impossible, on the base, to do them without being seen. Doing the elegant, slow-motion movements of the Tai-chi behind the barracks drew undesirable attention; undesirable because the young men, being young and Western, tended to dislike, ridicule and even fear something they did not understand. One lout made open fun of Barney. Barney accepted that, but when the young man, a burly copilot named Turk, yanked him to his feet in the officers' club to test the merits of "that nutty Chink stuff" in fisticuffs, he was obliged to defend himself. A simple wrist pull and ankle-block took care of the problem, but, being witnessed by twenty others, attracted even more undesirable attention.

Consequently, Barney stopped doing his exercises physically. Instead, he did them mentally. Sitting on his bunk in the barracks, he would imagine the movements and the forms. His large eyes would stare placidly ahead; his body would move and rock almost imperceptibly; his hands sometimes made tiny motions as he walked through the patterns inwardly. But it didn't solve Barney's problem of alienation; his barracks mates knew he was sitting there doing *something,* and it disturbed them. And they absolutely did not understand a man who was not afraid of combat.

Barney finally came to accept with amusement his reputation as an eccentric. And sometimes he did something unexpected or outlandish

—like buzzing the farmer's cow, taking the dog on a mission or firing a flare in the pub—to add to it. He acquired the dog he had named Wu-shu as well as the problem with the girl when he went to the farmer to offer a sincere apology for harming the cow and to offer to pay for it. That led to ownership of the unkempt Alsatian, which the farmer didn't particularly want, and to an unexpected liaison with the girl, a blooming eighteen-year-old named Rita. As a hard-exercising warrior and—he accepted it—a man who looked more odd than handsome—he had had little contact with women. But he seemed to fascinate Rita.

"I love your eyes, duckie," she said. "They're so big; they seem to see so much. And you're not like the others on your base. All they want is what they can take from you. You're so different. You don't ask for anything."

And, since he didn't ask for it, she gave it to him repeatedly in a stack of fragrant hay in the barn. Barney tried to sift the experience through his training to decide if it was honorable. But the attitudes of Eastern teachers differed radically. Some declared that liaisons with women weakened the warrior and should be avoided. But others proclaimed that the pleasures of the body were an appropriate part of a warrior's life. So the activity continued and when Rita became pregnant, he had the administration office allot half his monthly pay to her. His presence was too impermanent to consider anything further.

Barney often wished he could use his special knowledge to help his fellow airmen overcome the fear that afflicted them, but he didn't know how to teach them in a few weeks or months what it had taken him years to learn.

He particularly wished he could help Colonel Robinson. He had come to know and understand the lanky group commander, he thought, very well. Robinson was a good man, even a brave one in Western terms, because he forced himself to do what he dreaded. He had learned how to fight but he lacked the attitude of the warrior. Robinson thought of death as a terminal condition, the end of everything that men thought of when they thought of life. So, instead of accepting death, he feared and hated it. And his emotional attachments to others made him grieve and feel responsible for their deaths in combat. Now he was trying to force the big Swede, Lon Amundson, to stay alive, and that disturbed Barney. Trying to interfere with the natural order of things was wrong and almost certainly dangerous, both to the one interfering and to the object of his actions. No good could come of it.

Sitting on a box, he stared at Wu-shu. The dog approached and laid his head on Barney's thigh. Barney ruffled Wu-shu's fur with both hands and pondered his dilemma. He couldn't imagine how to begin a conversation about life and death with Colonel Robinson or what he would say if he could. A very special circumstance would have to present itself for him to even think of trying. Meantime, he decided he would address an occasional, anonymous note to the colonel, possibly a passage from one of the Eastern scriptures. Perhaps it would help the colonel understand.

He looked deeply into the dog's brown eyes and Wu-shu looked soulfully back. There was another problem. Something new needed to be done to maintain his reputation for eccentricity. Barney thought for a few minutes and then smiled. He knew a headquarters clerk who could be persuaded by a five-pound note and a couple of cartons of cigarettes. Corporal—no, Sergeant—Wushu would soon appear as a replacement mechanic on the 205th's payroll records and begin receiving a monthly check. The check would be allotted automatically to the noncommissioned officers' club's entertainment fund. Operations would try a dozen or so times to assign Sergeant Wushu to duty and he wouldn't show up. They would ask if anyone knew him and no one would. Finally they'd check his 201 file and find that Sergeant Wushu was two feet tall, four years old, weighed seventy pounds and was a native of Alsatia. Imagine the screaming and yelling. The large yellow eyes blinked happily.

———

Lon Amundson was first incredulous and then amused at the stir he made when he arrived in Mahoning. There were very few able-bodied men left in town and, until his arrival, no combat airmen had been home on leave.

He found out what that meant the first time he walked uptown to the drug store. The trip, normally ten minutes, took an hour. Every few feet, it seemed, he was stopped by someone who was eager to shake his hand and talk to him. Everyone in Mahoning seemed to know about his injury and his thirty-day leave.

Mr. Tyson, who owned the hardware store, offered him a job as soon as Lon got his discharge. Mr. Tyson would teach him everything from the ground up and, within a few years, Lon would become his partner. Lon thanked him and said he would consider it. The older man had tears in his eyes when they said goodbye. He had lost his son in a tank battle in the Ardennes.

Mr. Winslow, the bank manager, banged him enthusiastically on the back—too enthusiastically—and said, as soon as Lon was discharged, he'd like to start him as a teller and then move him up to loan officer. The bank needs new blood, Mr. Winslow said, and Lon, being a war hero—Lon chuckled in disbelief—would draw business from all over.

Lon's younger brother, Steve, grinned broadly when Lon told him about it. "Well, why not?" he said. "Mahoning needs a hero right now —even a big, dumb Amundson. You're just lucky you didn't get your uniform torn off by one of the sex-starved women this town is full of these days."

"I'm sure you're doing your part to keep them happy," Lon said dryly.

"Wouldn't I like to?" Steve said in exasperation. "But the girl friend keeps me on a real short leash. That's okay, though." His face darkened. "What I don't like is being stopped every day by somebody on the street who wants to know if I'm really 4-F and why that is. It's a pain in the ass; after a while you get to feeling like a criminal."

The draft board doctors had detected a heart murmur during the routine physical and, over Steve's protests, had declared him physically unfit for service. Steve said that, in Mahoning, a finding like that should be published in the newspaper and plastered on the lampposts. Maybe it would stop people from questioning your manhood.

Lon's mother, Frances, a tall, big-boned woman with strong Scandinavian features and graying blond hair pulled into a bun, asked why Lon couldn't stay home for good. "You've given them so much," she said. "Why should you have to do more?"

"I have to, Mom," he answered. "I'm a skilled pilot, or so they say. And I'm still on duty."

"But you were injured so badly. Are you really all right now?" she asked.

"Nothing's wrong that some of your cooking won't fix," he said, smiling.

But his father, Olaf, waited until his wife was out shopping for groceries and made Lon strip off his shirt so he could see the damage to the back. The old man nodded and muttered to himself and said, "Well, it looks fine, Lon. But maybe you don't show your mother just yet." Lon said he knew better, with a hole in the back you could put your fist into.

The Amundson family had prospered during the war years. Olaf and Steve had got hold of a good stand of timber near Gaffney and had struck natural gas on the property. A royalty check came in every month. They bought a bigger and pleasantly modern house near the country club; it had been part of the estate of a widow who had died leaving no kin in the region. The Amundsons also reopened an old brick kiln near a clay pit in Reynoldsville and picked up the first of many building jobs.

"We're just waitin' for you to come home," Olaf said. "Amundson & Sons is going to be the first honest-to-God homebuilder in the Mahoning area."

His father proudly pointed out the mechanical features of their new home. "An automatic coal stoker in the furnace, Lon," he said solemnly, his pale blue eyes glowing.

"Yes, Pop, it's great."

"A shower bath," his father said, waving his hand toward the stairs. "We have two bathrooms now." He shook his shaggy head. Lon noticed that his hair was turning white. Olaf laughed. "Not so long ago, we did good to have one. *Inside* the house."

"It's really great what you and Steve have done, Pop. Really."

When Lon had been home a few days, he began to wonder whether he had been wise to come. It was good to see the family, but he felt as if everyone and everything he saw belonged to another time and place. He felt flickers of emotion and a peculiar sense of loss when he saw someone or something that reminded him of the old days. It was as if he were a ghost, drifting in and out of reality. And being treated as a conquering hero made him feel like a phony. He began to wear a plain olive drab shirt and field jacket when he went out; the Class-A jacket, wings and fruit salad—the airmen's nickname for battle decorations— seemed to provoke emotional responses that were out of all proportion to their importance.

When Lon walked up the steps of the Robinson home, he felt his original sense of awe return. The smell of the rich woods in the foyer recalled all the memories of boyhood. But he never expected the regal Adda Robinson to hug him as she did. He was surprised at how frail she felt in his arms and how old she had become; he resolved to tell Mitch when he next saw him.

She cross-examined him at great length about Mitch's duties and state of health. She hadn't had a letter for two weeks and she was clearly distressed about it. Lon said Mitch was fine; he just had too much paperwork to do, but the war would be over soon. She wept in her handkerchief; it seemed to Lon that his return had loosed a river of tears in Mahoning. He had become the surrogate son, husband, brother and lover of everyone in town.

He hadn't called Betsy to tell her he was home, but he knew she knew, and was waiting for his visit. He wore his Class-A uniform when he went to see her; he wasn't sure why. When he walked up the steps onto the broad front porch of the Bowers home, he paused and looked at the swing that hung from the ceiling. He remembered vividly, one day long ago, when Betsy's friends sat on the porch talking and laughing, as they did every day during the summer. Flo and her boyfriend had had a falling out and she invited Lon to sit with her on the swing. Soon they were necking feverishly. They kissed and bit each other's lips till their mouths were sore. His was swollen and sore the next day; Mitch had pointed at it and laughed.

A breeze made the empty swing move slightly and it seemed for an instant that he heard a faint echo of laughter. When was it—ten, twelve years ago? Before the war, even before college. A lifetime ago, yesterday.

Lon walked to the door and pressed the bell. When Betsy opened

the door, her mouth fell open. A spark glowed in her dark eyes for a
moment, burned hot, died and then quickly warmed again. She had
thought for an instant that it was Mitch, Lon realized. But she smiled
broadly now and threw her arms around him.

"Lon! Lon, sweetie! Oh God, I'm so *glad* to *see* you!"

She pulled him inside, hugged him hard and then helped him off
with his coat.

"Come into the living room, you beautiful man! Oh, how gorgeous
you are in your uniform. All those ribbons. But sweetie," her voice
dropped with concern, "you're *thin*. You must have lost . . ."

"About twenty pounds."

"I heard you were hurt. I talked to your mother."

"To my mother?" It had never occurred to him that a Betsy Bowers
might pick up a phone and talk to a Frances Amundson. Things certainly had changed in Mahoning.

"Yes, there was a big story about you in the Banner. You're a hero,
Major Amundson."

"Am I really? That's a laugh."

They sat on the couch and he looked at her appraisingly as she
groped for a cigarette. Still a knockout, he thought. The wide-set, dark
eyes. The freckles and quick, bright smile. The graceful, gazelle-like
physique. As she strode to a table to find a match, a ball of muscle
showed in the calf of each long, slim leg.

Plopping down beside him, she said: "How long you going to be
home, sweetie?"

"I'm on thirty days' R&R—rest and recuperation," he said. "Nothing to do but eat, drink, sleep, be with my family, see old friends."

"Well, I want you to see *this* old friend quite a lot while you're
home, okay?"

"I'll be delighted to, believe me, Bets. So tell me how you've been.
And what you're doing these days. It must be quiet around here these
days with the men gone."

She frowned and shook her head. "I don't do much of anything; a
little rich-bitch volunteer work, mainly. But don't underestimate the
old town's ability to create excitement, sweetie. For instance, old Harry

Packwood—he's at least 50—getting caught by the State police in his car, up at the dam, with Shirley Raffetto."

"Oh my ass—excuse me, my Lord. Her husband, Johnny, he's in the Pacific. In the Marines. And she's in her twenties."

"And would you believe that Billy Baldwin is sleeping around with two older married women in town?"

Lon laughed. "Billy Baldwin is just a puppy. About sixteen now. He must be in dog heaven."

"Well, that'll give you an idea of the level of social activity we have to offer these days." She smiled briefly. "As for myself, you know the old song, they're either too young or too old."

He smiled. "That's no reflection on you, Bets. As far as I'm concerned, you look, well, just wonderful." He was immediately embarrassed, feeling he had been too effusive. His concern vanished when she leaned forward and kissed him, lightly but softly. His mouth tingled. It was the first time she had kissed him on the mouth.

"That was very sweet of you, Lon," she said softly.

He looked around the room in momentary confusion; the smell of her perfume clung to him. "Hey, there's the old vic," he said. "That brings back memories."

She rose, went over to the old Majestic and began shuffling through the phonograph records. "It's about worn out, but you can't get new vics just yet. In a few months, they say. As soon as the war's over." She pulled out a record. "Do you know this one? I don't know what you hear over in England."

"Sure," he said as the music began. "That's 'Speak Low.' The Ray Noble record. I heard it in the hospital over the Armed Forces' Network."

"Of course. I didn't think of that." She swayed with the music.

"Are you up to dancing these days?"

"Sure," he said. "My wind still isn't too good, but my legs are fine."

"Well, then," she said, as she moved into his arms, "we just won't do any shagging, that's all."

They danced for a few moments without speaking. He had forgotten how smoothly and lightly she moved, "You're still a great dancer," he said at length.

"So are you," she murmured, her head resting on his shoulder. "You always were more light footed than . . ."

The sentence hung in the air and he finished it silently. *Mitch.* Neither of us can seem to get free of him. The music ended and Betsy pulled her right hand free and turned toward the record player, continuing to hold him with the other arm. "Let's play that again, okay?"

The song began again:

Speak low
When you speak love,
Love is a spark
That dies in the dark,
Too soon, too soon . . .

"Oh, *hold* me Lon!" she said suddenly, clinging to him. "I've been feeling so damned lonesome and sorry for myself. And bitter about Mitch, too. And now I'm so *glad* to see *you.*"

She leaned back and looked at him. Tears filled her eyes. Impulsively, he put both arms around her and kissed her. She whimpered once and then held him fiercely. They rocked back and forth, their mouths moving against each other. A feeling of great warmth, almost relief, flooded through him. He had wanted this for so long. Until now she had belonged to Mitch. Against his will, invocation of the name made him feel guilty.

They stood close together. Betsy's breath came in short gasps. "Oh golly, Lon," she said.

"I'm sorry, Betsy," he said.

She leaned back and looked at him searchingly. "Sorry? Why?"

"I didn't mean to take advantage. I apologize."

Her eyes narrowed. "What exactly are you apologizing for? And who to?"

His body twisted in embarrassment. "I just thought for a minute there that it was unfair of me to make that kind of a move, considering —everything."

Her eyes softened. "Sweetie, I have to say that, for an agressive man —I've seen you play football, you know—you can be pretty cautious about making romantic moves. You always were. Even when Flo was practically falling out of her dress trying to get your attention."

He smiled sheepishly. "That was kind of interesting. But, even then, to tell you the truth . . ."

"What?"

The words were hard for him to say. "I wanted *you*. All the time."

"You did?" Her grip tightened. "A woman is supposed to know those things. But you were so loyal to Mitch . . ."

"Yeah, Mitch was—is—my best friend. And you are . . ."

"Was."

"*Were* his girl."

"That's all over, Lon."

"Is it really?"

"Why don't you kiss me again and help me make sure?" They kissed, slowly and thoroughly, standing thigh to thigh. When it ended, she sighed. "I thought I was still lonely for Mitch. But now I can't seem to remember what he looks like. I guess I was just lonely. And you've changed, Lon. You were always so strong and stable . . ."

"But?"

"But you were so dependent on Mitch. You got to talking like him, acting like him."

"Now?"

"Now you're not as strong physically. But you seem much stronger as a person. You have more—don't be offended—depth, I think. I *like* the new you."

"I'm glad. I like the old, young, same you. Look, I told my folks I'd stay home with them tonight. Just sit and talk. How about our going out to dinner tomorrow night?"

"That would be wonderful," she said. "It's supposed to turn warm tomorrow. False spring, no doubt, as usual. I'll pick you up in my car. I've got five gallons of gas in the tank. You remember, the convertible."

"I sure do. I'll never forget the first time I got in it. I felt like a slave getting in a Roman nobleman's chariot."

She laughed. "I'll pick you up at six, if that's all right. We can drive out to Walston for dinner, if you'd like that. And then go to the country club."

"People'll be talking about us being together, won't they?"

She smiled. "Oh yes. They'll talk, all right."

"You don't mind?"

"God, no. I'm tired of talking about other people. Let them talk about *me* for a change. And go green with envy."

Lon spent a quiet and pleasant evening with his family. He reassured his mother for the hundredth time that the war would be over very soon and his new job, meantime, would simply be checking the weather. His days of combat were over. His father talked of his plans to expand the Amundson enterprises. After his parents had gone to bed, Steve came to Lon's room for a brotherly talk.

"What's the real story on this weather recon thing?" he asked, perching cross-legged on Lon's bed. "Isn't there really more to it than you let on?"

Lon, unbuttoning his shirt, hesitated. "Well, not really."

"But what?"

"Only that there's always *some* risk, right? The weather, a mechanical problem, and, of course . . ."

"Of course *what*, Lon?"

Lon sighed and eyed his brother. "Well, I don't want you to say this to the family, understand, but the Germans have this new jet fighter. It's an engine that sucks in air and compresses it and blows it back with tremendous force. It's a whole new thing. They say the engine gets more efficient the higher you go."

"Is it fast?"

"Yeah, it's fast. About five hundred miles an hour, maybe more."

"Oh, Lon," Steve said, dismayed. "Then why in the name of God did you volunteer for this?"

"Because, except for the new jet, the Mosquito can outfly anything they can put up. The Germans don't have many of these new planes and, when they use them, it's mainly to make attacks on the bomber stream. Besides, it's a very big sky up there, Steve. It would be like swimming in the ocean and being caught by a shark. Not bloody likely." He decided not to tell Steve it was the cannons of a German jet that had wounded and nearly killed him.

Lon looked at Steve seriously. "As long as we're talking along this line, there is one thing I want to say, Steve. I know you've been upset about being classified 4-F, feeling out of it and all, but I'm here to tell you I'm glad." Steve looked at him sourly. "No, listen," Lon continued. "The odds of survival are all in my favor right now, but there's always a risk, however small. And I want to be *sure* that Frances Amundson has a son after this war is over to give her a grandson or granddaughter. And I want to be sure that Olaf Amundson has a son to help him become the big success he wants to become in business."

"*I* want Frances and Olaf to have *two* sons after the war is over," Steve said, looking at him levelly.

Lon smiled. "Well, so do I, brother. But I feel a lot better knowing you're my insurance policy."

Betsy's arrival in the convertible created a stir in the Amundson household the next evening. Frances Amundson hurried about the living room, picking up loose belongings and plumping pillows. Peering out the window, she turned to Lon and asked if he shouldn't invite her in. Olaf kept saying "yes, yes" and following her around the room. Steve sat, smiling, like a well-fed cat.

"Listen, folks," Lon said gently, buckling the belt of his dress jacket, "Betsy's just picking me up, is all. She doesn't expect to come in. She can do that another time." His family was making too much of the occasion and it embarrassed him.

Betsy grinned as he walked to the car, climbed in and sank into the leather seat beside her. "Does it look familiar?" she asked.

"Familiar and great," he responded.

"So let's go," she said. They sped out of town to Walston, a tiny coalmining community with a dance hall where Mitch and Lon used to buy shots of Silver King whiskey for a dime and a beer chaser for a nickel. On Saturday nights the miners would come in their clodhoppers to dance the polka. The collective stomping would make the rickety old building shudder.

Atop the hill, a local widow ran a tiny restaurant in her home. You called ahead to reserve one of the four tables. You ate what she had cooked that evening. Lon and Betsy were given a salad dressed with peppers, black olives, olive oil and vinegar; homemade linguine in a mushroom sauce; a tender osso bucco; the widow's own bread; and, to top it off, a delicate zabaglione and coffee.

Lon groaned with pleasure as they finished the meal. "I haven't eaten like this in years. I'll gain that weight back in no time, and I know where it'll come back, too."

"Wherever it lands, it'll look great," she laughed.

The evening at the country club was a mixture of fun and embarrassment. They sat at the horseshoe bar with a dozen or more townspeople and drank highballs. Betsy still drank Presbyterians—rye mixed with ginger ale. Weaned off sweet drinks by Britain's gin-and-lime, Lon drank rye with clear, hard water from the Mahoning spring. The club members buzzed around the couple like bees around flowers. Clearly, two things held their attention. The first was the faintly scandalous relationship between Betsy Bowers of Jefferson Street and Lon Amundson, recently of Hunkie Hill, a liaison made even more titillating by the absence of Mitch Robinson, former lover to one and best friend of the other.

"It just goes to show you how this war is turning everything upside down," one member proclaimed loudly to a friend at the bar. "Considering all the social changes they've made in Mahoning, the Germans might as well have bombed the town."

"Damn right," his friend said. "Hitler said he was going to create a New Order, and, by God, he's done it, right here in Mahoning."

The second thing that intrigued them was the difference in Lon Amundson. They remembered him as a big, husky, smiling—well, kind of dumb—football star. Yet here was a rather frail-looking, somehow far more intelligent-seeming young man in an Air Corps uniform. The silver wings over his left breast winked in the light, making the men faint with envy. The row of colorful ribbons above the wings spoke of valor and skill and awesome aerial battles in foreign lands. The major's oak leaves clearly hypnotized one boy, home on leave, who had just struggled up to the rank of corporal. The shoulder patch sewn on Lon's dark tunic bore the exotic designation of the Eighth Air Force.

One older member, Gene Gillespie, owner of the local lumber yard, approached and put a large hand on Lon's shoulder. "Great job you boys are doing," he whispered. "Great job." Overcome by patriotism and three rye highballs, he wiped a tear from his eyes. Then, his voice strengthening, he said in a voice meant to be heard by everyone: "As soon as you boys get this war over with, we want you back here. We've got an unbelievable big building job to do here, everyplace in America—new roads, houses, businesses; you wouldn't believe how back-ordered every merchant in town is. And Lon, lemme say it now: you've got a standing offer, a *standing offer* to come in with me. A junior partnership, call it." He lowered his voice. "You know, I was going to take in my sister's boy—you remember little Clint. Well, he went down with his destroyer out there somewhere in the Pacific. Too bad."

"I'm sure sorry to hear that, Mr. Gillespie," Lon said. "Clint was a nice boy. And thanks for your offer. I've got to go back to England pretty soon, but I'll sure keep that in mind."

"You do. You do," Gillespie said heartily. He turned to Betsy and smiled broadly, displaying the false teeth that Doc Lenhart had installed years ago. "Betsy! Good to see you out, girl. *Time* you got out. Especially with somebody like Lon here."

Betsy smiled warmly, her uneven teeth giving her freckled face an elfin cast. "It's worth going out when you've got Lon Amundson to do it with." She took Lon's hand in hers. One member noticeably cocked his head, wondering: did she put some special emphasis on those last words?

Gillespie laughed a braying laugh. "You said it, Betsy. It's worth going out when you've got a boy like Lon to do it with." He squeezed Lon's arm and, laughing, walked through the door into the men's locker room. A poker game would be in progress there.

"Would you like to dance?" Betsy asked Lon, smiling.

"Sure."

They picked up their drinks and walked into the high-ceilinged main room of the clubhouse. The oak floor was bare and polished. A log fire burned in the huge gray stone fireplace. A chrome juke box stood in the corner. Lon peered at the name tabs. "Look. 'Chattanooga

Choo–Choo.' 'String of Pearls.' Boy, do those take me back. Johnny Mercer on 'Accentuate the Positive.' And look here. Eberle and O'Connell on 'Tangerine.' "

"Oh I love that. Let's play it."

He fed money into the slot and they walked away a few steps, turned toward each other, and began dancing. Another couple began dancing across the room. Others watched from the doorway of the bar.

"They're watching," he said. "I think they're trying to figure out . . ."

"How far things have gone, right?"

He laughed hesitantly. "I guess so."

"Well, let's not disappoint them." She moved closer and slowly pressed her pelvis into his.

"Good God, Betsy. They'll . . ."

"Never mind, and don't you dare pull away. You stay right there and I'll stay—right there."

"Bets honey," he said after a bit, "there's something you'd better know."

"I know. I can feel you. Why don't we go out on the porch? It's very warm outside."

They sat on the long porch that encircled the low clubhouse and smoked her Camels. Soon, there seemed to be a dozen people nearby.

"We seem to be drawing flies again," Betsy said. "Would you like to take a walk up Country Club Hill? It's wonderfully warm."

"Fine with me. But can you walk in those heels?"

"I'll take them off and throw them in the car on the way up," she said. "There. Now I'm three inches shorter. A real squirt, beside you."

"A great looking squirt." He put his arm around her waist. "Let's go."

Country Club Hill was the fairway of the seventh hole of the club's nine-hole course. The hill was so steep that a good golfer teeing off from the top could drive all the way to the green at the bottom without touching the slope. If he hooked or sliced, he stood a good chance of losing his ball in the thick stands of pine that flanked the fairway.

Lon and Betsy walked up, hand in hand. The pines were fragrant around them and there was just enough starlight for them to see their feet. She put her arm around him once when he stopped to catch his breath.

They reached the tee-off platform, both out of breath, and sat down, draping their legs over the edge. The lights of the clubhouse shone far below; the headlights of a car moved occasionally between the club driveway and the main road. The lights of Mahoning strung out like Christmas decorations along the valley and hillside to their left.

"It's time you saw this," Betsy said. "It's the best view in town."

Lon laughed. "Don't be mad if I say it's second-best. The best view, as I remember, was from those rickety porches on top of Hunkie Hill. The people up there used to say if the Jefferson Street folks knew about it, they'd come up and take it."

"Oh God, that's terrible. Did they really say that?"

"Well, yeah, that was the general view."

Betsy turned to him. "How do you feel about taking what you want, Lon?"

His heart began to thud in his chest. "Betsy, I might want more than you're ready to . . ." His voice trailed off.

She seized him firmly by the lapels of his jacket and pulled him down atop her on the grassy platform. "Why don't you find out for yourself?" she demanded.

Their mouths found each other. Pressed against each other, their bodies seemed to generate far more heat than the two of them produced. His khaki shirt was choking him and he freed a hand to fumble with the collar button.

"I'll do it," she murmured. Her slim fingers deftly unbuttoned his collar and untied his necktie. The gesture seemed incredibly erotic to him. "It's very warm," she whispered. "You should take your jacket off."

He did. Lying back, she watched him, her light wool dress clinging to her slim body. Her skirt was hiked up and one of her long thighs gleamed dully in the starlight. Instinctively, he placed his hand on her thigh. She flinched slightly and then, seizing his hand by the wrist, swept it possessively upwards.

"What you start, you'd better finish," she whispered.

"Are you really sure . . ." he began.

"Lon Amundson," she said between her teeth, "make up your mind. Do you want me or not?"

"Of course I do," he said hoarsely.

"Then come *on,*" she said fiercely. She unbuttoned the front of her dress, pulled down her bra and pulled his head to her small breasts. His mouth found a nipple. His hand grasped the mound between her thighs and she bucked convulsively. In a moment, he sat up, stripped the pants from her and pulled his trousers and shorts down below his knees. He was large and hard and she quickly made room for him as he settled into her.

Most of his sexual experiences had been embarrassingly brief, but this was different. Moving slowly atop her, loving her but feeling strangely detached, he marveled at what was happening. It was as if he had acquired a mysterious, God-like control of the night. As he moved, his head higher than hers, he saw the lights of Mahoning winking up at him. A slight breeze swept across the knoll and he smelled the pines. Betsy was groaning and digging her fingernails into his shoulders. He felt as if had nailed the two of them into the center of the earth. Or the mouth of a volcano.

He remembered suddenly that Mitch once said the way to make it last is to make yourself think of something else while you're doing it. Think about a problem or something totally different, Mitch said. Lon pressed his eyelids together. *One thing I do not want to think about right now is Mitch or being with Mitch's girl. Which, Goddamn it to hell, she is not. Not any more. She is mine. Mine. Mine.* It was happening. Betsy was calling his name, her body was heaving, her strong legs were gripping him like a vise. He came too, blindly, his breath rasping in his throat.

Afterwards, they lay quietly. "Oh, golly," she said at last. "That was incredible. I didn't know it could be like that."

"It was wonderful," he said sincerely.

She hugged him, then pushed him away. "You'd better get up now, sweetie. You're beginning to mash me. I don't know what I'll do when you gain all that weight back." Mopping himself with his handkerchief and pulling up his trousers, he was giddy with happiness. She had spoken in the future tense. This was just the beginning.

At her door, he took her by the shoulders and said simply: "I love you, Betsy."

"Oh, Lon darling," she answered. "I think I love you too. It's hard to believe, it's been so fast, but I do. And listen." She leaned back and looked at him resolutely. "I know you want to spend time with your family. You have to; don't short-change them. Just call me, anytime. Day or night. I'll be available. You know the number. One-two-nine. But don't say very much over the phone."

He smiled. "Who was it that used to listen in on the gang's calls? Helen?"

"Well, believe it or not, now it's Flo. She has the late afternoon shift on the town switchboard. So just say, how's everything, or whatever. I'll say fine. Then come over."

"But what about your family?"

"My father's away in Washington; one of those dollar-a-year war production jobs. Mother spends part of her time here, part there. She'll be there for the next couple of weeks." She paused and spoke slowly. "Tomorrow, if you want to, you can visit my bedroom."

"You know I want to."

"And you should know that your visit will be the first that any man has made to my bedroom. *Any* man."

He was exultant. Mitch had never been there. It was a part of Betsy that Lon would always have to himself. They made love every day. Some of the time it happened in her bedroom. Sometimes they pulled off their clothes and did it on the living room floor. Once, laughing and groaning, they did it standing up, pressed against the kitchen sink.

The days slid by in a happy blur. And then it was time for him to return to Pittsburgh to pick up a military air transport plane to Bangor and ride as a passenger on a new B-24 headed to England. Betsy joined the Amundsons at the train station. His mother clung to him and sobbed. Olaf hugged him roughly, like a bear. Lon and Steve shook hands and then, abruptly, embraced. Betsy had no inhibitions about showing her feelings. She threw herself into his arms and sobbed openly. "Come back soon. Please come back." The collective emotion was overwhelming. He was almost relieved to get aboard the train so he could calm himself.

———

When he landed in England, Lon hitched a ride to the 205th before reporting to the weather recon base. Mitch jumped to his feet and threw his arms around him.

"Lon! Jeez, but I'm glad to see you. Sit down and tell me about your R&R, Ace. What's it like at home? How is everybody?"

Lon told him about the changes in Mahoning's social system, and Mitch shook his head and clucked in wonder. He laughed at Lon's tale of being lionized as a war hero.

"It was goddamn amazing, really," Lon said. "But imagine what it would be like if *you* suddenly turned up there. *I* was the hero; *you'd* be a goddamn god. The whole damned town would fall on its face for you."

Lon admonished Mitch to write more often to his Aunt Adda. "She's gotten pretty old, Mitch, pretty frail and thin. She worries a lot about you."

Mitch nodded, abashed. "I'll write her every other day at least." He looked up, faintly puzzled. "What about Betsy? Did you see her?" Lon nodded. "Well, how is she?"

Lon hesitated. "Oh, Betsy. She's—ah—fine. Sends her love."

Mitch nodded.

When they parted with a four-handed shake, Lon felt a flood of warmth for his boyhood friend. All the old resentment was gone. At the door, Lon turned and threw Mitch a salute. It might be a long time before they'd see each other again.

# The Threat

THE Supreme Commander of the Allied Expeditionary Forces watched disbelievingly as the little Prime Minister put away a heavy breakfast of bacon, eggs and toast liberally smeared with the PM's favorite black cherry jam. Churchill's secretary had brought the jam, his master's personal tin of tea, an Imperial quart of brandy and a box of cigars in an army kit.

At length, the cherubic figure sat back in his chair and sighed with satisfaction. "Excellent rations, my dear Ike," he said. "Do you think we might go and see what our lads are doing?"

Eisenhower smiled. "Of course, Prime Minister. We'll take a jeep down to the river bank." Eisenhower had grown sincerely fond of Churchill and felt enormous respect for him as a statesman, but he didn't welcome ceremonial visits to forward areas when there was so much work to be done. And there was always the chance of a stray shell or marauding airplane getting through.

Still, there was no graceful way to say no. Churchill had arrived at the west bank of the Rhine the previous night with an entourage that included his secretary and valet. He said he wanted to see the Rhine crossing with his own eyes. So Eisenhower had to commandeer a nearby chateau, detail a special guard, find a competent cook and make himself available as escort.

Outside, Churchill donned his British army visored cap and a great-coat with colonel's pips on the shoulders. Then he thrust a fat cigar in his mouth and lighted it from a box of matches. Eisenhower, lean and trim in his waist-length American battle jacket, stood, hands on hips, and waited for his guest to climb into the jeep.

Five minutes later, the jeep pulled up on a knoll and they sat and overlooked the broad Rhine river. The Ludendorff Bridge at Rema-gen, over which the Americans had made their first crossing several days earlier, stood, blasted and bent, a desolate monument to German defeat. Since it had been pronounced seriously weakened by shelling, it was no longer being used. Now, companies of infantry and armored units were swarming across the river on portable treadway bridges installed by U.S. Army engineers. In the distance, billowing smoke and rumbles of man-made thunder marked the Allied advance.

Churchill smiled happily. "It's rather like sending someone a rude letter and being there when it arrives."

Eisenhower chuckled. "I hadn't thought of it just that way but it's a pretty good analogy, PM."

Churchill waved his cigar enthusiastically. "My dear general, it's plain to see that we've beaten the Germans. We've got him on the run. All that remains is to follow through."

Eisenhower nodded. "We've destroyed all organized resistance this side of the Rhine and the Sixth Armored Division's heading for Frank-furt on the autobahn. But we still have a long way to go. Many of our boys are going to fall before it's over."

He turned to Churchill, his mobile facing wrinkling into a scowl. "Two intelligence reports concern me right now. One you're familiar with from the Ultra intercepts. Something's brewing with those damned ME 262s. Speer keeps telling Göring and Hitler that he's delivering more of them and we've got a list of the pilots that've joined that JV 44 jet fighter unit. It reads like a Who's Who of the old German aces."

"Can you deal with the jets in the air, given your enormous superiority in numbers?" Churchill asked. He was careful not to say *can't*.

"No," Eisenhower said shortly. "We have to wipe them out on the ground. There's some suspicious-looking activity around Munich; as soon as we can find out with any certainty where they're holed up, I'll turn the Eighth loose on them."

"Excellent," Churchill said. "I'll ask the Mosquito lads to increase their recon sorties; we'll pay particular attention to the Munich area. We can't allow anything to happen at a time like this to interfere with your daylight bombing."

Eisenhower grunted. "Lord, *no*. Another heavy blow against the Eighth and there'd be another howl from Congress to stop daylight raids."

"The last time was after the second Schweinfurt mission, I believe."

"It's the penalty a democracy pays when it fights a war." Eisenhower smiled ruefully. "I wouldn't have it any other way, of course."

Churchill smiled wryly and examined his cigar. "I'm familiar with the problem. But you spoke of a second report."

"From our G2 officer in the Seventh," Eisenhower said, jabbing his thumb toward the right. "In the south. They have eyewitness reports of an increasing stream of supplies moving toward what they think is a redoubt area in the Bavarian mountains. They claim the Germans are planning something they call a National Redoubt with an elite force of several hundred thousand men, SS and mountain troops. An average of five long trains are arriving in the area every week, they say. A new type of gun is supposed to have been seen on one of the trains. Several POWs have even heard talk about an underground aircraft factory there."

"Clearly something to look into," Churchill said. "But surely it needn't divert us from our main task of driving on to Berlin with all possible speed." He looked at the American warily. *He's a splendid soldier and a man of great charm, but, like so many of the Americans, he's a political innocent. He doesn't realize how important the capture of Berlin will be once the war is over.*

"I'm asking for further information," Eisenhower said carefully. *Who takes Berlin isn't nearly as important as protecting our flanks and minimizing casualties,* he thought. *But now's not the time to pick up that hot potato.* "Meantime," Eisenhower said, "we'll make every possible effort to wipe out that nest of jet fighters."

"Of course," Churchill said. "And we'll do everything we can to help."

———

The Supreme Commander of the Third Reich sat, glowering, at his desk in his office in the *Führerbunker* fifty feet beneath the Chancellery in Berlin. He hated paperwork but, today, it had to be done.

An hour earlier, he had had his daily breakfast of mashed apple and milk and then walked up to the rubble-strewn garden above to inspect and decorate the twelve- and thirteen-year-old members of Axmann's Hitler Youth for bravery in battle. An air raid alert had halted the ceremony and driven him back down into the bunker. He snarled; he hated and—he refused to admit it, even to himself—feared the air raids.

Things would never have got to this state, he told himself, if he hadn't been surrounded by traitors and incompetents. Also, he admitted, he had been too soft and tolerant a leader; as an American had said in one of the cowboy novels he loved, he had been "too nice a guy." But that was all in the past.

He scratched out notes for a series of new Führer Directives. First, the officers who failed to blow up the Remagen Bridge before the Americans could cross it would be shot as common criminals. Or had this already been done? He frowned; no matter, he would issue the order anyway. Second, he would invoke *Sippenhaft;* any German soldier who surrendered or was found away from his unit would be shot and his family would be punished for his cowardice. Third, all Germans forces, large or small, would stand and fight in place unless and until they received express orders from the Führer to retreat. Any deviation from this order would be punishable by death. Fourth—he nodded vigorously as he wrote the words—since the German people had been too weak to attain victory, Germany must be destroyed. Nothing must be left to its enemies. Everything, he decided, must be blown up or burned: electrical power plants, gas and waterworks, factories and warehouses, bridges and buildings of any size, dams and waterway locks, railroads and rolling stock, all vehicles, all farm animals and supplies of any kind. Even the autobahns would be destroyed.

Meantime, he would inflict all possible damage on the enemy. He would tell Bormann to get him an up-to-date report on the new weapons. *Materialschlacht,* the battle of materiel. It could still make a difference. Speer was pestering him to witness a demonstration of his pet *Wasserfall* ground-to-air rocket. And when would that band of pampered Luftwaffe aces strike a real blow with their 262 jets? He would tell Bormann to find out.

Adolf Hitler sat back, satisfied with a good morning's work. It was time for his morning tea, a plate of sweet cakes—he loved sweet cakes —and a playtime with Blondi, his Alsatian bitch. She would have puppies soon. He awaited that event with keen interest. He would give one of them the nickname he had chosen for himself: Wolf.

———

Flight Officer Peter Hawkins watched with amusement and disdain as a Focke-Wulf, nose up and mushing in the thin air, tried vainly to climb high enough to intercept him. Hawkins snickered in his oxygen mask, advanced the Mosquito's twin throttles slightly, and left the fighter far behind. He had learned long ago that, so long as you stayed alert and maintained your altitude, no German fighter could catch you. He would have to be able to dive on you to do it and, unless you were diddling round at an altitude where you shouldn't be flying, you had little to fear. The light wooden fuselage of the Mosquito gave German radar a poor image and the twin, in-line Rolls Royce Merlin engines offered a full 3,300 horsepower when you needed it.

It was a lovely day over Germany. The billowy cumulus clouds were almost summerlike. There had been remarkably little rain for a week and the Danube, now behind him, was almost blue again. Munich, 38,000 feet below, sparkled like a field of diamonds in the sunlight. On the horizon lay the snow-capped peaks of the Bavarian Alps. Hawkins had skied at Garmisch-Partenkirchen with a group of schoolmates one summer; now, with the war being tidied up, he thought how wizard it would be to shed his RAF uniform, dig out his civvies, and go there again. The old skis were probably still sitting in the bedroom closet at Mum's. They would need a good waxing, of course. Perhaps this summer, he thought; from what he'd heard about the Allied advances, that wasn't too balmy a thought.

"Pilot, turn 15 degrees to the right, will you?" It was talkative Tony Blake, his navigator. "I want to get a snapshot of the area over there. Jerry's flying a regular patrol down there—you see?—and Control wants us to take a look-see. Well done."

"Glad to oblige," Hawkins said.

"Lovely day for snapshots, isn't it?" Tony continued. "The sun's so bloody strong today—so little vapor in the air you know—you wouldn't believe my F-stops. Super."

Hawkins held the new heading as Blake took his pictures with the big recon camera mounted in the nose. Quite lovely. He had been holding the heading for at least three minutes before he noticed that the cockpit was in shade. A cloud, his mind said unconsciously. But the shadow moved—first out, then back in—and Hawkin's trained instincts rang a silent alarm.

"What the bloody hell?" he said, swiveling his head and shoulders to the left. Just above and behind him, not twenty feet away, was an *airplane*. His jaw dropped in astonishment and he blinked his eyes to dispel the illusion. But it remained. The airframe of the strange craft was sleek; the long engines produced no propeller sheen. Cannons were mounted on the wings. An ugly Maltese cross was painted on the fuselage. And the pilot was grinning at him. A Messerschmitt 262.

The hair on the back of Hawkins' neck stood up. He hit his throttles, jammed stick and rudder to the right and thrust the Mosquito's nose down.

"What in hell?" he heard Tony yell in anger and surprise. The Mosquito heeled over, the air speed indicator winding up, and streaked toward a bank of cumulus clouds. Once inside, he flung the Mosquito in the opposite direction, holding the throttles against the stop.

He plunged through 6,000 feet and emerged in the open air. He swiveled his head again to the left and looked back. Nothing. He maintained a shallow turn, still traveling at high speed. *It's gone,* he said thankfully to himself.

"Oh Lordy." It was Tony again. "On the right." Hawkins swiveled to the right and his heart sank. The thing was flying formation on his right side. In fear and rage, without conscious thought, Hawkins flung the Mosquito toward the strange aircraft. Moltke skidded his 262 sideways and cursed at himself. *You deserved that, you damned fool.* He had fallen off to the right and he leveled out and pulled up behind the Mosquito. *Remember who you are, Moltke. You had no right to taunt an enemy. Certainly not one who's unarmed.*

In the Mosquito, Hawkins felt as if time had braked into slow motion. He felt unaccountably calm. There was really nothing more to do. He had no guns to fight with and it seemed clear that he lacked the speed to escape. Unconsciously, he leveled off. Tony was crying out but he couldn't hear what he was saying. Hawkins looked straight ahead at the beautiful Alps. *Wouldn't it be lovely to have a holiday there again? Perhaps next year.*

Four seconds later, four 30-millimeter cannon shells blew him, Tony and the beautiful wooden airplane to bits.

————

Brigadier General Harrison Warfield Sutter had the face of a falcon and, some said, the temperament to match. His eyes were light blue and penetrating and were set beneath thick brows. His nose, sharply hooked, stood out from a lean and angular face. The configuration gave him a fierce and predatory look.

Sutter was what the Eighth Air Force thought of as an elderly officer. He was fifty-two. He had been an ace in World War I with seven German airplanes, two Zeppelins and a Distinguished Service Cross to his credit. But he still had 20/15 vision, far better than the eyesight of all but a fraction of the population. Over the years, he had kept himself in trim. He was midsized and wiry and had the short-muscle reflexes of a much younger man.

Sutter was deputy commander of the 1st Combat Wing of the First Division of the Eighth Air Force, the culmination of a military career that had started in World War I. Now, in 1945, it was his job to oversee the operations of the four combat groups that made up the

Wing. The 205th was one of them, and he was on his way to visit it and its commander.

Sutter sat in the back seat of the staff car as it sped through the pleasant, rolling English countryside near Bedford. He didn't bother to look at it. His thoughts were turned inward. There was such an enormous difference between the two World Wars and, for him, all the comparisons favored the first. Aerial combat in World War I had been a direct and personal matter; you went out and fought, face to face, with an honorable enemy. Despite the losses, sometimes grievous and personal, it was—there were no other words for it—great fun. World War II wasn't. It was huge and bloody and tedious.

Part of the feeling came from his advanced age and reduced personal role, he recognized. But part of it was due to what he thought of as the debased and bland technology of the twentieth century. Take the Chevrolet sedan he was riding in. It had about as much excitement built into it as a farmer's plough.

Just compare it, he thought, with the old Model T Ford. He was a teenager when the T came out. Harry and two friends had pooled their funds to raise $800 and buy one of the sensational new cars. How many drivers today could operate its planetary transmission system? Three pedals sprouted out of the floor below the steering column. You depressed the one on the left to get into low. When you let it up, you were in high. The central pedal put you in reverse. The one on the right was the brake. To make a panic stop you hit both the reverse and brake pedals and the T would stand on its nose. You *drove* the T; it didn't drive you like a modern plain-vanilla Ford or Chevy made in 1945.

You had to start the Model T by hand. You bent down in front of the radiator and took hold of the crank handle, making sure you didn't hook your thumb around it. If the car backfired and the handle spun, and you weren't alert, it could break your thumb or your wrist. Before cranking the car, you yanked at the tickler, the wire loop that acted as the choke and protruded from the radiator. The whole process of starting and driving the T was a highly personal, tactile experience that took skill and alertness.

The same kind of comparison could be made about the combat

planes of the two wars. Sutter hated flying in the four-engine bombers. They were big and slow and you were totally deprived of the ability to maneuver. The idea of just sitting there and letting people shoot at you was more than a man should be expected to bear. It was a wonder that anybody ever finished a tour of duty. In the beginning, of course, not many did.

The World War I airplanes were very much like the Model T. When he arrived in France as a member of the Lafayette Americaine— they changed the name to the Lafayette Escadrille when Germany claimed a violation of America's neutrality—his first airplane was the Nieuport. He remembered it clearly. It had a 110-horsepower Le Rhone engine. It was a tricky little beast, but it was fast, over 100 miles an hour. He loved the sound and smell of it. The engine made little burping sounds when you opened and closed the throttle to taxi or glide. Aloft, the wires sang like violins. And there was a lovely smell of fresh glue and burning castor oil.

Even the clothes they wore were better than today's. Today, the aircrewmen dressed like laborers working at the Arctic Circle. In the old days, Sutter wore a heavy flying jacket with a big fur collar, a long white silk scarf and padded helmet and goggles. But his pride and joy was the pair of wonderful, thigh-high fleece-lined boots that had been made for him in London.

And the patrols were so much fun to fly, unlike the grim eight-to-ten-hour endurance contests in the heavy bombers.

Even starting a World War I airplane was fun. He would settle himself in the cockpit, adjust his straps and grin over the side at Bert, his misanthropic mechanic. "Switch off," he would call. "Switch off," Bert would mumble.

"Gas on," Sutter would shout, turning the switch. "Gas on," Bert would say. Bert would walk the propeller backward a turn or two to pump fuel into the cylinders. Then he would peer around at Sutter, a perpetually glum expression on his doughy face. Sutter would grin and yell: "Contact!"

"Contact," Bert would grunt. He would place his hands high on the wooden propeller, swing his right leg forward, and then yank sharply down and away.

The little engine would cough, wheeze, burp a cloud of blue flame and smoke and settle into a sweet hum as Sutter advanced the throttle. He would bump and bounce over the bare field and slide up into the fragrant air of the French countryside. He had eaten a roll and drunk a cup of coffee. After the patrol, assuming all went well, he would ravenously attack a plate of ham and eggs in the mess tent. There was nothing, and there would never be anything again, like the experience of flying an open-cockpit biplane in combat.

Sutter grunted. There wasn't any "combat," in the aggressive sense of the word, in flying a big bomber. You delivered your bombs like a dump truck unloading debris. You didn't even get to see or hear the bombs landing. And then, when you'd made your delivery, you defended yourself, as best you could, from a swarm of angry hornets.

Flying a fighter plane was altogether different. Only a paddle-foot could have designated a fighter plane as a defensive weapon. What it was, really, was a platform for a gun, or a battery of guns. You were part of the gun or—this was closer to the truth—the gun was part of you. You pointed yourself at the enemy and fired.

It didn't have to be an aerial enemy, either. It could be a locomotive, a convoy of trucks, a platoon of soldiers—hell, truth be told, it could be an old man on a bicycle or a herd of cows. Whatever it was you shot at, the act produced an instant of ferocious joy.

Sutter frowned. Why was it so joyful to kill, more sensual than sex, more satisfying than a plate of spaghetti? Was it because the pink-cheeked boys who flew those airplanes were, deep inside, malevolent killers? He shook his head. No, that was false reasoning. Nearly all young men placed in that same environment, wherever they came from, would feel the same enormous jolt. The insight came to him abruptly and he smiled thinly in satisfaction. It was the *power.* You couldn't sit in the cockpit of that lethal weapon, even on the ground, without feeling that surge of power, that hunger to *use* it, to release it . . . Sutter growled in disgust at a sudden image of one of those nosy, new Army psychiatrists with their Fruedian theories and their big eyes shining out of their thick eyeglasses trying to make something, well, *phallic* about the whole thing.

Best to drop the thought and concentrate on the business at hand. He was on his way to have a talk with Col. Mitchell Robinson and, lifting his bushy eyebrows in surprise, he realized suddenly why he had felt drawn to Robinson.

Odd he hadn't thought about it before. It was Robinson's love for his boyhood friend, Major Lon Amundson, whom Sutter had recently assigned to the international weather force. Robinson had carried his concern to an extreme, but who was he, Sutter, to criticize? Sutter had had a close friend, too—Freddie Weaver. And Freddie had been killed by a piece of advanced German technology—the Albatros.

Sutter grunted with disdain and his driver, an overweight sergeant, glanced up into the rear-view mirror to see what the old man in the back seat was doing. Never could tell about him. Probably having a gas pain or something.

Sutter shook his head. These pilots of today thought that modern war started when they arrived in the ETO. They talked about the "bloody summer" of 1943 as if they were the first military unit ever to be ground into dogmeat.

These jackrabbits had never heard of the "bloody April" of 1917. Well, April 1917 nearly wrecked the American, French and British air commands combined. It was that damned Albatros with its high-compression engine, the synchronized, forward-firing Spandau machine guns and—never forget it—the Circus tactics that Richthofen had taught the German pilots. Much like what that fellow Galland and his predecessor, Moelders, had drilled into the Abbeville boys in the '40s. Things evened out in the Great War only after the Allies came up with the Sopwith Camel and the rugged French Spad. He and Freddie were flying Sopwith Pups when the Albatroses bounced them out of the sun in a mass attack. That was one of the things Richthofen had taught them—the mass attack. Bullets stitched a path along Harry's instrument panel and fuselage before he had a chance to react. He jerked the Pup around in the tightest turn possible. You didn't want to lose altitude against an Albatros. As he rolled around, he saw Freddie clutch at his chest and fall sideways in his cockpit. His Pup heeled over into a spin and disappeared.

Harry cried out in a loud, sobbing denial of what he had seen. Heedless of what might be behind him, he plunged onto the German who had shot Freddie down. The German pilot kicked his rudder bar and jinked from side to side to spoil Harry's aim. Then he made the mistake of trying to turn inside the highly maneuverable Pup. Harry swung his nose to the left, cutting across his path, and burned him with the Vickers. The burst caught the Jerry in the head and blood coursed down his face. Then his gas tank blew up and the Albatros fell apart in flaming shreds. Harry was still crying but now there was a savage joy mixed with his grief.

These people today seemed to think this new ME 262 was the first technological leapfrog in military history. Even some of the older heads at Division were panicking. But it happened in the first World War in much the same way and, again, it was the damned Germans who made the jump. First with the Albatros and then with a dream airplane, something entirely new, called the "tin donkey." It was the Junkers J-2, an all-metal, low-wing monoplane. It was years ahead of its time and it was hardly used. Like the ME 262. The German General Staff proved its brilliance in strategy from one war to another. But it never really understood aviation.

Sutter chuckled to himself. The Germans hadn't had the sense to design a long-range bomber for World War II. If they had, the Eighth couldn't have maintained their air bases in England and there would have been no Allied invasion. The Third Reich would have lived on and expanded. Yet the Germans had a six-engine bomber, the Gotha, in World War I. It measured *138 feet* from wingtip to wingtip. Harry shot one down. It went up like a torch. That was nice but it couldn't compare with the lovely fire that consumed his first Zeppelin. The damned things were scaring London half to death with their night raids and indiscriminate bombing. They were fast and silent and could climb very quickly. They were also heavily armed and dangerous to attack.

Sutter intercepted one in late afternoon on its way to England. The Zep was flying at about 11,000 feet. When its crew saw him, they pointed its big nose up and began climbing. Harry tried to keep up and his engine began sputtering. He swore and began working the fuel pressure pump to gain altitude. Pumping and swearing, he finally climbed above the big airship. He had reached 15,000 feet and it was cold; the thin air made him wheeze. It was no place to stay for long.

He nosed over, put the gunsight on the Zeppelin's spine and pressed the firing button. The Vickers raked the length of the airship. As he shot past, tracer bullets arced after him. Banking tightly, he made a close-in, head-on attack and fired again. He swept past and turned again and saw the Zeppelin beginning to turn red and glow. It glowed brighter and brighter and then burst into an enormous ball of flame.

"Like a goddamn Chinese lantern!" he told them back at the field. He repeated the words, liking the sound of them.

"Sir? General?" It was the goddamn driver, holding the door open and peering in at him as if he were mad.

"What?" he barked, and then he realized they had arrived at Whitwick Green.

———

After lunch in the officers' mess, Sutter and Robinson went to the latter's office for a private talk and sat facing each other, coffee cups in hand.

"I'll get right to it, Robbie," Sutter said. He was the only one who used that nickname and Robinson recognized it vaguely as a term of affection. "You've seen the ME 262s."

"Sure have."

"Well, you're liable to see some more real soon. Two of them made what apparently was a practice attack on the 100th two days ago. They stood off at about a thousand yards and fired a new kind of rocket. One screwed up and missed entirely. The other hit the lead element of the group on the nose. It was a salvo, maybe twenty rockets, launched from under the wings."

"Twenty! My God!"

"Yep. That one salvo knocked out the lead plane and his deputy. One shot, two '17s. And the formation fell apart."

Robinson whispered: "Good God."

"There's more, Colonel. As you well know, the Germans have been building airplanes in underground factories, camouflaged warehouses, even in forests—dragging them out of the woods and taking them off on the autobahn. We've been damned fortunate that they've still been mass-producing the old 109s. But now we're getting some worrisome reports about 262 production. Intelligence estimates they have some hundreds of these blow-jobs in production, maybe up to a hundred ready to go."

Robinson looked at Sutter somberly. "General, if they hit us with a hundred jets, they'll blow us apart. I don't care how many fighters we put up."

"Agreed," Sutter said. "That brings me to the point of this visit. If we let anything like that number get aloft—particularly if they're armed with those new rockets as well as their cannons, it's goodbye Charley for the Allied air offensive, for daylight bombing, probably for our campaign to make the Air Corps a separate branch of the service. And it'll make this war a whole lot longer and bloodier. So we've got to find Dracula's coffin and drive a stake through his heart before night comes."

"Do we know where they're based?"

"We think we do now. We have Mosquito photos of a suspicious-looking pair of grass fields, very close to each other, near Munich. There are barracks, plus what looks like a schoolhouse and is probably a ground control center, plus a few other buildings. There are shadows that indicate camouflage nets strung over part of the area. And a Focke-Wulf squadron seems to be conducting a perpetual patrol over that sector. We hear that the last of Germany's top aces—the old boys— have congregated in that area. It all adds up. And it stands to reason they're going to hit us hard with those jets sometime soon."

Robinson felt his stomach contract. "What's the strategy, General?"

"We want to stamp them out just as soon as possible, but we need to wait for the best possible day. We need perfect visibility to hit the targets with precision. We're going to carpet-bomb those fields and the complex of buildings nearby. Anything of a built-up nature in that area we're going to knock out. We'll be heavily escorted but only part of the escort will fly high cover. Five Thunderbolt squadrons will go in lower. Their orders will be to ignore the sky and watch the ground. They'll try to catch any 262s taxiing and taking off. Five more squadrons will relieve them to try to catch any 262s coming in to land. I don't care how we get them. We've got to squash them on the ground before very many can get in the air."

Robinson stared at his coffee. "Who's going to lead the mission, General?"

Sutter smiled a grim little smile. "We are, Colonel. You and I. We're going to lead the Division. I'll fly right seat with you."

"That'll be fine, sir." Robinson's thoughts raced. *The General will be flying copilot for me. 'Would you mind terribly putting the flaps down, General?' 'Would you condescend to bring the wheels up, sir?' 'May I offer you my chocolate bar?'*

"We'll take an extra copilot," Sutter said. "I've heard some stories about the one you've been flying with. Gaggle or Giggle or something. Sounds like a strange bird."

"Lieutenant Google. He's a little odd, General, but he's a superb pilot. Excellent skills and reflexes; no nerves at all."

Sutter nodded, getting the opening he wanted. "Speaking of nerves, Robbie, have you considered standing down? You've flown more missions than a bomber pilot is supposed to fly. A fighter pilot can flap around forever. But not a man who has to sit there and let people shoot at him, day after day." Sutter leaned forward and his voice dropped. "The group commander doesn't have to fly forever. It isn't desirable. Why haven't you stopped?"

Robinson toyed with a cold cigar. "I guess I haven't really felt entitled to. We really haven't gotten the job done. A lot of good men in the 205th died trying to get it done at Schweinfurt and Regensburg and Frankfurt and—you know the places. We couldn't *do* it. We went there, we took heavy losses and then the Eighth switched us to easier targets. If we had left it at that, those losses would have been wasted."

Sutter nodded. "So now that we're stronger, you've felt an obligation to keep going back. Who's the obligation to, Robbie? The ones who didn't make it?"

"Something like that, I guess."

Sutter raised the shaggy eyebrows. "Well. I think any one of them would say by now that you've paid your dues. Unless you think you have to *die* to wash out the obligation. You don't think *that*, do you?"

Robinson shrugged. "I hadn't thought of it that way. No, I guess not. I mean, of course not."

"I don't think you're completely sure. Well, I am, Colonel. You and

I will lead the 262 extermination mission when Pinetree gives the sign and then I want you to stand down. That's an order, Robbie."

Conflicting emotions of relief, shame and guilt washed over Robinson. "Yes, sir," he said at length.

"I want you to stay healthy, Robbie," Sutter said, "for more than one reason. We're going to need officers like you in the new United States Air Force and a few people like me are singling out good candidates. This war's going to be over soon . . ."

"Has it been worth it, General?" Robinson asked suddenly.

"Has what been worth it?" Sutter replied, scowling at the interruption.

"The losses. This huge operation. Two hundred thousand men. Thousands of airplanes. The Eighth Air Force. Ruined cities, dead civilians. Has what we've accomplished been worth the cost?"

Sutter glared at the younger man for a moment and then his face softened. "Believe it or not, I've given a good deal of thought to that question. The short answer is, yes, it's been worth it. It would have been worth it if all we'd done is destroy the German Air Force. Right now, except for this Messerschmitt 262 pop-up, we've done that. If we hadn't, there wouldn't have been an Allied invasion and Germany would still rule the continent. It took control of the skies to make those landings possible and to drive through France and Germany and we've given it to our armies. We forced the Germans to switch from bomber to fighter production to defend Germany and then we overpowered the fighters, nothing fancy, mainly by outnumbering them when we forced them to come up and meet us. We took the pressure off England—except for those rocket bombs, of course.

"And, of course, there couldn't have been an invasion if we hadn't torn up the Germans' railroad marshalling yards and their whole damned transportation system. We stopped their resupply operations. And we've finally knocked out their oil, their energy supply, which we should have done a year ago instead of screwing the pooch trying to knock out their aircraft production. If we hadn't been so goddamned dumb we would have realized that it didn't matter how many planes they built if we could deprive them of fuel. The same thing applies to their tanks and trucks, of course. G2 estimates that, even if we and the Russians don't advance another foot, the German army will literally run out of gas and have to stop operations within the next four months."

Sutter smiled sardonically. "Oh, some fool—more likely a committee of fools—will come along after the war and say, 'but look, you lowered German production overall only by ten percent or whatever. It actually went up during the middle of the war.' But, if they're fair, they'll also point out that, until 1943, Germany never made a serious effort to *go* to full production. They had always planned on a short war and, until they gave Speer the job, they never really mobilized their resources. The Germans are an inventive people, but I'll tell you something that'll sound strange. They're *inefficient*. They've screwed up their production system, starting with their priorities, all the way down the line. In the beginning, because Hitler and Göring appointed war heroes instead of professional managers to run their war industry. Now, from what we gather, Hitler's calling all the shots on what gets produced, and he's made the wrong choices. People think of the British as bumblers and the Germans as efficient; it sounds crazy, but it's just the other way around. Look at what the British have done with radar; they're ahead of the Germans and us, too, in nearly any application of electronics you can think of. And their research gets fed quickly into production. Not so, apparently, in Germany. And neither country has America's production resources. In the end, that's what's made the difference. The Germans are beaten. And, after the war when the histories are written, they'll say that the Eighth Air Force played an important part in their defeat."

"After the war," Robinson mused. "What will they say then when they see the destruction we've caused? I can't think of a German city we haven't leveled. How many civilians have been killed in the process? What will they say about *that*?"

Sutter waved his cigar in exasperation. "Colonel, when you've got to knock out factories, railroad marshalling yards, all the logistical aids to fighting a long war of attrition—that's the kind of war we've got here—you're bound to hit civilians. Because those things are located in and around cities. The government buildings in Berlin, of course, are right in the center of the city. You've also got to define 'civilians,' for

God's sake. Are the workers in the factories making the airplanes *civilians,* as such, or are they as important to the war effort as soldiers in the field? At any rate, we aren't *trying* to kill civilians, as the Germans are doing with their rockets in London. Or, if the truth be told, as Bomber Harris is doing with the RAF's night raids. That was a bad idea to begin with, but Churchill bought it from an Oxford professor who convinced him that the RAF could 'de-house' a third of the German population and break the people's morale. A very bad idea. And we aren't raping women and shooting old men and boys the way the Russians are doing in the German towns they're taking. You should see the reports we've been getting. They'd curl your hair."

Sutter looked grimly at the younger man. "Keep in mind, too, that the Germans set the standard for behavior in this war. They had no earthly excuse to bomb Warsaw and Rotterdam and Coventry. We aim at the things that help Germany fight. We grind away at it, bit by bit, day by day. And when they're shooting at us and the weather's bad, we don't always land inside that thousand-foot circle." Sutter chuckled mirthlessly. "The Germans are making us do a sloppy job. If they'd just let us bomb their factories and yards without shaking us up so much, we'd be a lot more accurate."

"Actually, it's a pity we haven't had something bigger, more authoritative, to bring this war to a quick end. But we don't." Sutter smiled thinly. "I almost forgot. This will interest you. What's your middle name, Robbie?"

"Moltke," Robinson said, puzzled.

"I know. Well, we've intercepted a list of the German jet pilots. It includes just about all the old guys we've learned to fear and respect. But there's a young one there, too—one Karl von Moltke."

"Oh my." The portrait of the elder Moltke flashed across Robinson's mind. He heard Aunt Adda retelling the Moltke story. 'You should go to Germany some day and look up your family.'

Sutter was peering at him quizzically. "It sounds as if he could be a cousin of yours."

"He probably is." He heard Aunt Adda's voice : *I'll bet he looks just like you.*

———

The Fieseler Storch touched down at Templehof just as the first rays of light appeared in the east. Moltke breathed a sigh of relief as he taxiied toward the boarded-up terminal with Sergeant Willi Steiner beside him.

Moltke was accustomed to being the hunter, not the hunted. Skulking along at low altitude in an unarmed reconnaissance plane to avoid enemy aircraft seemed ignoble. It also made him uneasy. But the Storch was all that could be made available to carry out Galland's orders.

"We need to make the request in person," Galland told him. "Memos are just locked in the safe, if they get that far. Speer will be there to make a demonstration of that new rocket of his, so we might as well give the Führer (did Galland put a sarcastic emphasis on the word 'Führer'?) a rounded presentation on air defense. Describe how we propose to make the coordinated jet-prop attack on the bombers and why it's important for us to use all of our resources to do it. We need his permission to commandeer the entire fighter arm for the big blow, *der grosse schlag*. Remind him that the Americans have a history of retreating, even halting operations, when we inflict big losses on the bombers. Do you have any questions?"

Moltke opened his hands, palms up, in an involuntary gesture of perplexity. "Just one, Herr General. I don't mean to be impertinent. But—why me? I'm a junior officer in this squadron of experts."

Galland smiled. "Look, Karl. Ever since our so-called mutiny, my name and the name of every other pilot in the old group has been *dreck* to Adolf Hitler. Anything I said would be automatically discounted right now. We need a new face and new name, and you're perfect for the job. *Moltke*. That's enough to freeze even the Supreme Commander in his tracks. You're also a Prussian, and the Prussian officer has always stood up to the King. You're the man to do it, believe me."

"I'll do my best, Herr General," Moltke said. Later, when he told Elise he would be going to the *Reichskanzlei* in Berlin the next morning, she clapped her hands.

"Oh good," she said. "I hope you'll have time to do a small errand for me, Karl. I'll write it down for you. I need some pills for that cramping I've been having and I can't get them here. Go to Dr. Margot Hoffmann. You remember her; she was my gynecologist in Leipzig. She's in Berlin now and this is her address; it's near the Zoo at the southwestern edge of the Tiergarten. I hope she's still there; if she is, I'm sure she'll remember me and give you the pills."

The resourceful Willi had a Volkswagen jeep waiting for them at the airport when they arrived. Willi jumped behind the wheel and consulted a street map as Moltke got in beside him.

"The *Reichskanzlei* is just a short distance north of here," Willi said. He was wrong, and the reason horrified Moltke beyond words. The wide streets and avenues were gone. There were only twisting paths through mountains of rubble. The proud city of Berlin was a blackened, soot-covered ruin. Whole neighborhoods had disappeared. Thousands of bomb craters pock-marked the landscape. Windowless, roofless buildings stared blankly at them as they passed. The trees that remained were bare and seared from intense heat. Civilians in patched, threadbare clothes, heads down, made their way through the wreckage. Moltke shook his head in wonder and horror. *God in heaven, this is what they have done to us,* he thought. *This is what we have done to ourselves.*

At the western end of the *Unter den Linden,* the eight-story Brandenburg Gate, though chipped and pock-marked, still stood, its twelve Doric columns intact. Nearby, behind piles of rubble, stood the three-story *Reichskanzlei.* The walls and golden eagles that hung over the entrance were pitted and scored. In front of the building lay a huge bomb crater full of stagnant water.

But the sentries at the entrance were immaculately dressed. They snapped to attention as Moltke told Willi to wait and got out of the jeep. Inside, an SS officer greeted him, checked an appointment book and said Moltke would receive an audience with the Führer immediately following a meeting the Führer was having with Colonel-General Heinz Guderian.

"Guderian," Moltke breathed in awe. No general, including Rommel, commanded more respect than the tough *panzer* leader who had revolutionized modern warfare with his use of tanks. A guide was detailed to take Moltke to the Führerbunker. He was led to the basement and out into the garden. He remembered visiting it years ago after winning his Luftwaffe commission.

Then, the *Reichskanzlei* garden had been a magnificent design of well-tended shrubbery, trees and flowers with walkways, beautiful fountains, a teahouse and greenhouses. Now it was a wasteland pocked with craters and strewn with chunks of masonry, smashed statuary and uprooted trees. The windows were gone from the rear of the soot-covered building that faced it. At the end of the garden stood a block-house manned by two guards. They examined Moltke's papers and opened a heavy steel door for him to enter. At the bottom of a flight of stairs two SS officers greeted Moltke courteously, took his coat and apologetically took his pistol from his holster and patted him down for concealed weapons. He was ushered into a lounge whose ceiling lights cast an eerie yellow glow on the stucco walls. Furniture that seemed to have been assembled from different rooms had been placed along the walls.

To the right of the entrance was a door leading to a conference room and what clearly was a meeting of explosive proportions. Two voices were rising and falling. One was shouting, the other screaming. The door opened and a handsome but harried-looking officer stuck his head out and introduced himself as Colonel Otto Gunsche, the Führer's personal aide.

"We're having a bit of a problem, I'm afraid," the officer said. "You can wait out here, Colonel, or—it doesn't make any difference at the moment—come in and stand in the back of the room."

Moltke sidled into the conference room and pressed his back against the wall. Standing in the center on an Oriental rug was Guderian, hard-faced, broad-shouldered, dignified, every inch a soldier. Though the room seemed filled with people in uniforms, Moltke felt somehow that Guderian was the only soldier among them. Striding up and down in front of the *panzer* general on the edge of the rug was the Führer. He seemed close to apoplexy.

"Why did the attack fail?" Hitler yelled. "Because of incompetence, that's why! If Busse didn't have enough ammunition to do the job, why didn't you get it for him?" Hitler's face was enpurpled; his eyes bulged from his head. Foam flecked the corners of his mouth.

"This is nonsense!" Guderian shouted. "Absolute nonsense! I've already explained it to you . . ."

Hitler moved nose to nose with Guderian and screamed in his face. "Explanations! Alibis! That's all I get from you! It's all of a piece! I'm constantly lied to and tricked and misinformed!"

Guderian roared back and the two men shouted at each other at the tops of their voices. Finally, aides pulled at their sleeves, Hitler collapsed, seemingly exhausted, into a chair and Guderian left the room. Minutes later, he returned and everyone was ordered from the room except for the two men and Hitler's personal chief of staff. Five minutes later, the group was herded back into the conference room and the meeting resumed. Moltke noted that Guderian, his face a stone mask, sat at the rear of the room, staring straight ahead. For a numbing two hours, Hitler and his staff talked in agonizing detail about battle tactics and deployments on the Russian front. The Warlord ordered dozens of minute changes in positions, discussed the use of individual bridges, hills and villages as strong points, and countermanded the tactical orders of divisional and even company commanders. To support his decisions, he frequently cited streams of figures on available personnel, tanks and ammunition.

To Moltke, the scene became grotesque. Hitler had always been famous for his superhuman memory, but was he now remembering what really existed, or only what had been? No one raised such a question. Whenever the Führer expressed an opinion or issued an order, staff members would nod vigorously—almost, Moltke thought, like the toy birds he remembered as a child.

Finally, General Wilhelm Burgdorf, Hitler's adjutant, summoned Moltke. As he rose to walk to the front of the room, he noticed that Reichsminister Albert Speer had entered.

Hitler, now sitting erect in his chair, looked at Moltke with interest. "Well," he said, "I see why they've sent you. A Moltke." Hitler pronounced the name slowly as if savoring it. His voice became strident. "You come from a long and distinguished line, young man. Always be worthy of your name. I've studied Moltke and Clausewitz and read the Schlieffen papers as well. Which is more than most of my generals have done."

He looked at Moltke appraisingly. "Within your own sphere of operation, you've done very well, I'm told. The *Wilde Saus,* the *Sturmgruppe,* now the 262s that Galland and his bunch have caused so much trouble over. So tell me. What have you come to petition me for?"

Moltke carefully explained the rationale behind the request to restore communication between the jet squadron and Luftwaffe fighter command to plan a coordinated mass attack on the American bombers. Hitler heard him out without speaking or displaying any reaction. When Moltke was finished, Hitler nodded and said:

"A sensible plan; one we might undertake at the right moment. Right now, however, I have another mission for the Luftwaffe fighters. As a matter of fact, I think you should play a part in it. Can you still fly a Focke-Wulfe?"

Surprised, Moltke said: "Why—yes, my Führer." He hated having to use the salutation that now seemed groveling and hypocritical, but it was the way the man expected to be addressed.

"Good," Hitler said shortly. "Your presence and name may very well make a contribution. You'll be notified." Hitler scowled abruptly, seeing Speer. "Reichsminister," he called, "has this rocket demonstration of yours anything to do with Moltke here?"

"Not directly, my Führer," Speer replied.

"Well, then," Hitler said, waving a hand toward Moltke in dismissal, "you may go." Before Moltke could leave the room, Hitler turned toward Speer. "I'll agree to see this demonstration of yours of the—what do you call your new rocket? . . ."

"*Wasserfall,* my Führer."

"All right. I'll attend if it doesn't take too long. Where will it be and when?"

"Tomorrow, my Führer," Speer answered. "We've built a launching platform in a wooded area just west of here. The plan is to test the *Wasserfall* against one of the reconnaissance planes that come over in early morning."

Hitler nodded, seemingly bored. "Very well." His eyes brightened suddenly with anger. "Before you leave, Speer, I must tell you I've read this latest memo of yours asking me to rescind my order to destroy our resources wherever the enemy advances."

Hitler's voice hardened and rose in volume. "Let me be clear on this once and for all!" He pounded the arm of the chair, punctuating his sentences as he spoke. "If the war is lost, then the nation will be lost. There's no need to consider saving what people would need to live a primitive sort of life. It's better to destroy all these things, because this nation will have proved itself weak. The future will belong to the people of the East because they've proved themselves stronger. Those Germans who are still alive when the battle's over will be only inferior persons. The best will already have fallen. The others don't matter."

Moltke was leaving the room as Hitler spoke. As the final words were uttered, a feeling of desolation settled over him. *This man was, and against all logic and common sense, still is, our Supreme Commander. And we are lost. Lost.*

Outside the bunker, he found Guderian waiting for his car. As Moltke wondered whether he dare introduce himself, Speer emerged from the shelter and did it for him.

"Not too happy an occasion for any of us," Speer ventured.

Guderian sighed. "I've been sacked, as a matter of fact. While you were out of the room. I've been told to take six weeks' convalescent leave." The hard face cracked into a small smile. "They told me I'm not well. Keitel recommended my wife and I go to Bad Liebenstein. I told him this wasn't advisable because the Americans are already there. No, I think, in view of everything, I'll keep my movements to myself. The people down there . . ." he gestured toward the *Führerbunker* ". . . they're living in *wolkenkuckucksheim,* cloud-cuckoo-land. He and Jodl and Keitel; they move little paper divisions that aren't there any more, or that have shrunk to a company, around on a map."

Guderian's tone became contemptuous. "He thinks he can manage battles and campaigns from an underground shelter six hundred miles from the battlefield without seeing the terrain or experiencing the weather or responding to tactical changes. He denies us the right to maneuver—the one thing we're really good at; better than the Russians. So we have to stand and take their massed frontal attacks."

He laughed wryly. "Do you know, he actually called me to a demonstration of an 800-millimeter railway gun and told me it could be used to fire at tanks? Can you imagine? He was chagrined when I got the fellow from Krupp to admit that it took forty-five minutes to reload the thing. The reserves for the defense of Berlin have been outfitted with *Panzerfausts* instead of rifles. Each man has been given *one* round! What will they do when they've fired it? Use the bazookas as clubs?" The general sighed. "It's a terrible, criminal waste. Our men are dying by the thousands, by the millions—for nothing."

Speer nodded somberly. "You have my memo on his order to destroy everything?"

"Yes," Guderian said. "That was courageous of you; I'll do everything I can to help. Talk to my fellow generals; secure their agreement to ignore his order. The poor people who're left when this war is over will have to have some means of survival. We owe them that much. He can take his order and—" the panzer general halted and offered his hand. "I'll say goodbye."

Watching the general leave, Speer spoke pensively. "A good man. We have to think of the future now. I've a plan to smuggle the Berlin Philharmonic musicians out of the city. After the next concert." His face tightened in anger. "I'm trying to prevent them from tearing down my bronze lampposts between the Brandenburg Gate and the Victory Column. For an airstrip. Can you imagine such desecration? After all, I'll be responsible for rebuilding Berlin when this is all over." Speer's face relaxed. "I developed a plan to kill the Führer, you know. I was going to introduce poison gas into the bunker's ventilating system." He laughed briefly. "But I couldn't figure out how to get the gas into the intake stack. It's twelve feet high. A little mechanical problem like that." He shook his head. "Ah well. Adolf Hitler is Germany's destiny; it's fitting that they should die together."

Depressed and shaken, Moltke climbed back in the car and gave Willi directions to Dr. Hoffman's office. They picked their way along the southern edge of the Tiergarten. Moltke took one look at the once-magnificent 600-acre park and averted his eyes. What had been a lush forest was now a field of twisted and burned tree stumps.

The apartment building in which the gynecologist had her office was still standing, though boards had been fitted into window frames where the glass had shattered. Dr. Margot Hoffman was a slim, middle-aged woman with sad, searching eyes. She was wearing a frayed white coat. Sitting behind a small oak desk, she seemed to Moltke to have absorbed into herself the suffering of all the women of Germany.

When he gave her the note with the name of the medication on it, she lifted her eyebrows in surprise. "Medication for cramps?" she said. "Is that all?" Within a few minutes she had located the pills. But she handed him a second vial as well. "These are the ones for the last," she said.

"For the last?" he asked, puzzled. The gynecologist looked at him steadily for a minute and then said quietly: "I thought that's what you had come to ask for. It's what they're all asking for."

"I don't understand," Moltke said.

"Cyanide," she said. "It's called the KCB pill. It's the most popular prescription in Berlin at the moment."

He was aghast. "But why?"

"Rape," she said sharply. "That's why. Refugee women from the East are pouring into Berlin by the thousands. As a gynecologist I've examined hundreds. The ones who've survived. Many of them have been subjected to gang rapes by the Russian soldiers. The lucky ones have been raped by only one or two. Some women have slashed their wrists—before or after. A few have killed their children."

"Barbarism," Moltke breathed.

"Barbarism and revenge," she said. "The women say the Russians told them they were paying them back for the atrocities committed by German troops in the East."

"Not our soldiers, surely."

"If not, by the SS. Beatings, hangings, even burnings. Of Jews, partisans, any civilians who broke their rules. So now, with the Russians advancing on us, every female in Berlin between the ages of seven and seventy can expect to be raped. And many would rather take a pill beforehand."

Moltke looked at her levelly. "Are you advising your patients to commit suicide, Doctor?"

"I'm advising them to leave Berlin by any means they can. This is the way of last resort."

"And yourself, Doctor. Are you leaving?"

"My job is here, unfortunately."

"When the time comes, will you take cyanide?"

She hesitated. "I don't know."

Moltke rose, suddenly eager to leave. "I have to go."

She handed him the two vials. "Take the pills, both containers. In case the Russians get to you ahead of the Amis. No charge. Tell your wife. You owe it to her."

Moltke had reached the building entrance when sirens began to wail. A loudspeaker somewhere nearby began blaring the word "Gustav," apparently the code-warning for an air-raid alert. Antiaircraft guns on the edge of the city began to fire. A heavy, dull vibration began to make the ground, the buildings, even the air seem to tremble.

Moltke looked up. His eye caught silver glints from the bombers far above. He swore. The bastards were so confident now they didn't even bother to paint their planes in camouflage colors so they wouldn't catch the sun. A huge stick of bombs exploded at the edge of the city and black smoke gushed upward. Another stick moved closer. They were carpet-bombing. The explosions from the third stick were deafening. The ground rocked; he cried out involuntarily in a fear he had never felt before.

People were running to a nearby shelter. A hand grabbed his arm. It was Willi. "*Oberst, Oberst!* Come!" Moltke allowed himself to be pulled along the street toward the shelter. There was a horrible series of explosions close by and the ground swayed beneath them. His breath came in short gasps; his ears were ringing; his knees had turned to jelly. He was terrified.

They entered the shelter and pressed among the townspeople huddled together on benches. A terrible blast erupted overhead and the shelter shook violently. Dust and debris fell from the ceiling. People cried out; a frightened baby wailed. Moltke shut his eyes and clasped his hands tightly together. Violent explosions rocked the shelter for what seemed like minutes on end. Finally, the blasts began moving away.

As the dust cleared, Moltke saw a middle-aged man in a shabby civilian suit staring at him coldly. When their eyes met, the man turned to another beside him. "We've been wondering where the Luftwaffe is. Now we know." Someone snickered. Moltke felt his cheeks grow hot. A woman spoke up from nearby. "Why aren't you fellows up in the air shooting those bombers down?" she demanded. Abashed, Moltke cleared his throat. "We do what we can with what we have left." The woman made a derisive sound. "It isn't much good, is it?"

A man with a bass voice spoke next. "Fat Hermann said if the bombers ever got to Berlin we should call him Maier. As of today, I've calling him Cohen." Inexplicably, everyone laughed.

The sirens wailed the all-clear signal and the shelter door was opened. Moltke gratefully stumbled up the steps and outside with Willi. The bodies of three civilians, little more than bloody rags, lay a few feet from the shelter. Water gushed in a fountain six feet high from a broken main. The hiss of escaping gas filled the air. Nearby, an apartment building had collapsed in a mountain of loose masonry. Cries and moans came from inside. Ambulances clanged by.

Moltke, with Willi at his elbow, walked blindly to his left and found himself in the zoo. A zoo keeper ran up, wailing that the aquarium had been destroyed. Willi tugged at his sleeve. "Shouldn't we start back, *Oberst*?" Moltke shook his head. "I want to walk for a minute, Willi. To clear my head a bit." Several of the zoo buildings had been leveled. Zoo keepers ran back and forth. One, obviously a senior official, stood stock-still, tears in his eyes.

"Has there been much damage here?" Moltke asked. The man nodded. "Two buildings; many of our rare birds—beautiful, invaluable creatures. Nothing left but blood and feathers. Other raids have been worse. Only one elephant is alive out of nine. My animals are starving—starving! We can't get the meat and fish we need and the pumps can't bring us water with the electricity knocked out."

The zoo keeper raised his arms and let them fall despairingly. "What happens when a bomb breaks open the lion cage?" he asked imploringly. "What of the gorilla, the hyenas, the bears? Should we shoot them? I don't know that I can. I just don't know." He put his hands over his face and wept.

Numbed and speechless, Moltke turned and walked away. They reached the jeep and found it intact except for a pile of loose bricks that had fallen on it. The vehicle was scarred and dented but still operable. "I'll try to get us to Templehof," Willi said. "Maybe they didn't hit the airport this time."

But they couldn't. They kept running into mountains of rubble. At one intersection they saw the body of a young soldier hanging from a lamppost. A sign had been tied to its feet. It said: *TRAITOR*. HE DESERTED HIS UNIT. One block further, they found the men who had done the hanging. They were a group of perhaps a dozen young SS men. The leader, a tall, blond sergeant, pointed his machine pistol at the jeep and ordered them to stop.

"Out of the jeep," he ordered roughly.

"Sit still," Willi said.

"Out, I say!" the SS man repeated. "We hang deserters here. And you look like two of them to me."

"You will get the hell out of our way!" Willi said loudly. "This is *Herr Oberst* Moltke, a Luftwaffe ace with thirty victories to his credit. How many of the enemy have *you* shot down, sergeant?" he demanded sarcastically. "Or do you kill only Germans? The *Oberst* has had business here with the Führer himself." Willi yanked his pistol from his holster and pointed it squarely at the SS man's face. "Now stand aside or I'll shoot your face off. *Now!*"

The SS man swore, became irresolute and then turned his back and walked away. The others followed him. Willi looked at Moltke, smiled contemptuously and drove away.

As they rerouted themselves from one detour to another, they drove past a building that was burning out of control. "Stop!" Moltke said. The decision was instantaneous. He fished the container of cyanide pills out of his pocket and threw it into the fire. Nothing like that could or ever would happen to Elise. He would see to it. He had a far better solution.

# Mutual Losses

ERGEANT Willi Steiner stood in the hallway next to the great room of the lodge and waited for Moltke's call. He could hear Elise von Moltke sobbing and the sound saddened him because he liked his colonel's lady. He felt sadder still at the prospect of leaving the dashing young officer he had served for the past three years. But, as always, he would do what Colonel Moltke ordered him to do.

Willi Steiner had the short, broad-shouldered physique and heavy face of a Saxon peasant. He acknowledged his heritage with a certain pride. The land near Leipzig which the Steiners had farmed had been granted to them generations earlier by the Moltke family. The Steiners had been treated well over the years by the nobility and, even after the Republic and Hitler, he had remembered the Moltkes with respect.

As a private first class, he was delighted to be assigned as batman to the young Karl von Moltke. They liked each other from the start; the relationship between them had always been an easy one. Moltke always joked that Steiner was "my factotum, my Figaro—the man who can fix everything and arrange everything, and has." And Moltke had seen to it that Willi was promoted to corporal and later, over some Luft-waffe objections, to sergeant, with corresponding increases in pay.

Willi Steiner had come to believe, with some reason, that he had become the young officer's guardian as well as his orderly, mess officer and cook. How often had he foraged for fresh food when official stocks offered only malt coffee and tinned meat? How many times had he improvised a *Bauernfruhstuck,* a peasant's breakfast of diced ham, scrambled eggs and fried potatoes, when the colonel rose early or returned late? Willi saw to it personally that Moltke never lacked for what he needed or wanted, that the mechanics took extra care with his aircraft, that on trips like that terrible one to Berlin, he returned safely. He had saved Moltke's life when they were threatened by the ma-rauding SS men. Moltke was an ace in the air but, in some ways, he was a bit helpless on the ground.

Now, Willi reflected, that close association was about to end. He opened the door a crack so that he could find out how far the conver-sation had gone. Obviously, the *Oberst* had told her the plan.

Elise von Moltke was sobbing. "Why, Karl?" she wailed, raising her voice. "I don't *want* to leave you. I want to *stay* with you." She turned to her husband and her eyes widened in alarm. "Something has hap-pened to make you suggest this. What is it? Tell me!"

Moltke shook his head. "Nothing, my dear. At least, nothing new." As she opened her mouth to reply, he took her by the arms and led her gently to the couch before the stone hearth. Willi had set a log fire to burning to take the chill out of the room, and it was crackling and burning fiercely.

Moltke drew his distraught wife down beside him. "Listen to me, Elise. The Amis have already taken Frankfurt from the West; who knows when they'll begin pushing south? And the Russians are moving toward Berlin from the east. You can't imagine conditions there. The Berliners are being bombed to pieces every day by the Amis and yet they're praying that the Amis will somehow get to Berlin ahead of the Russians. They won't, though.

"Sooner or later, one or the other is going to move into this region. And, to top it off, now we have the Americans and British buzzing overhead all the time. You know how badly they've hit Munich. Who knows when bombs might fall on this lodge?"

Elise shook her head angrily and balled her small hands into fists. "Karl, there's nothing new in any of this. There has to be something else—some further reason why you want me to go now. Tell me what it is!"

Moltke sighed. "Look, Elise, the situation I've described is deteriorating every day. That's what's new about it. Right now, we have freedom of movement in this area. A month from now, even a few weeks from now, it may be gone. And, I have to tell you this, I find myself worrying about your safety while I'm flying. That's a dangerous thing to do. You know how outnumbered we are. My very best chance of doing my duty properly, and surviving, is to devote my full attention and energy to it. I just can't do that if I have to worry about your safety."

"Oh, Karl," she sobbed. "I try not to be a burden to you."

He smiled gently and took her in his arms. "The burden isn't of your making, *liebling,* but of my own. If I cared less about you, it wouldn't be so great. This is why I want you to let Willi take you to Switzerland now. The family deposited money in a bank in Zurich long ago. It's been sitting there gathering interest for a long time. The Swiss are famous for protecting the privacy of their depositors. Your name is listed along with mine as owner of the account. The bank has a specimen of your signature. They won't be concerned with your citizenship. As a matter of fact, you'll be carrying a Swiss passport. Willi will destroy your German passport, and his, when you've crossed the border. You'll retain the Moltke name, but remember to drop the *von.*

"They speak a godawful dialect in Zurich called *Zurideutsch;* you'll get onto it. But the books and papers and radio are all in standard German. If you're ever pressed, you can speak French. You speak it well and it's commonly spoken in western Switzerland. You won't have any trouble. Really, the country is a melting pot, particularly now. But even before the war, the language differences in Switzerland were so great that people living in one mountain valley couldn't understand the people living in the next valley."

She stared at him incredulously. "You arranged all this without telling me. Why?"

"Insurance," he said shortly. "We lost the war when our colossal idiot of a Führer declared war on America. The Amis have one thing that nobody else in the world has: inexhaustible resources. Ours, obviously, are extremely limited. They always were. When the Americans began filling the skies with airplanes and outfitting their fighters for long-range bomber escort, we stopped being able to defend our cities. We'd already lost the ability to defend our ground troops. That's when I decided it was all over."

"But Karl," Elise said slowly, "even assuming I was willing to do all this—go to Switzerland as you say—how would Willi and I get there? What about the borders? And, I know Willi has always been very loyal to you, but do you really trust him that much?"

Moltke nodded vigorously. "Willi Steiner is as devoted to me as, in point of fact, I am to him. He's tough and straightforward and when someone like that gives you his loyalty, you can count on it. And Sergeant Willi Steiner is also an accomplished dog-robber."

"What on earth is that?"

He laughed. "I see I've neglected your military education. Every army has them. It means improvising, making do, being resourceful. Seeing to the needs of your superior or your unit. If you can't get food or supplies through normal channels, you get it some other way. I can't imagine a better person to get you across the border. He'll go with you and take care of you; from now on he's your Uncle Willi. As to the border, I've spoken to a friend or two and spread a bit of money around. A lot of that's going on these days." Moltke frowned. "There's always some element of risk, of course, but I think we've managed to make it a small one. A great deal smaller than staying here. It's all arranged. Willi will drive you to Friedrichshafen . . ."

"That's close to Lake Constance. Is that . . ."

"Exactly. Willi's made arrangements to take you across the lake by motor launch. From the Swiss side it's a short jog to Zurich." He lifted a finger. "There's a fallback plan as well. If for any reason Willi doesn't like the setup when you get to Friedrichshafen, he'll drive you on to Lorrach."

"The *Schwarzwald*."

"The Black Forest, yes. From there you can cross the border to Basel. Believe me, there shouldn't be a problem."

"And what about you, Karl?"

"I'll move back into the barracks with the other pilots, where I belong. When this is over—I don't think it'll be long now—I'll join you. If we get our chance to use the jets properly—the Führer has held up the plan again—we have a good chance to stop the daylight bombing. That will give Germany time, and maybe, just maybe, we'll be able to depose the madman and negotiate a liveable surrender. If not, I'll make sure I'm taken prisoner by the Americans. All of us are planning on that." *We don't mention the more likely probability that we won't live long enough to surrender.*

"Oh God." She began sobbing again and melted against him. He held her tightly and rocked gently back and forth. In a few minutes she composed herself. "I'll do as you say, Karl. When we arrive in Zurich, I'll have Willi send you back a message. And you'll communicate with me just as soon as you can."

"Of course. Just as soon as I can."

Moltke made their goodbye as casual as possible, as if she were leaving for a weekend with a friend. But even as he joked lightly, giving her an affectionate squeeze and a light kiss, his heart cried out in pain. He *loved* this woman. He wanted to fall at her feet, embrace her knees and groan in despair, as he had heard the Eastern peoples did when the SS invaded their villages and separated families for forced labor. But he could not, for her sake or his own. Centuries of stern breeding forbade it.

He had come close to telling her of his deepest feelings just before she left, but, even though he had rehearsed the words, his throat closed on them as he prepared to speak. Now he said them silently to himself.

*There is one more thing I want to say to you. I love you very much—your beauty, your intelligence, your good heart, even your name, Elise. When I hear it, you know, I think of Cyrano. When he lay dying in Roxanne's arms —he wouldn't have said "dying"—he told her how sweet it was to have loved her. 'Across my life,' he said, 'one whispering silken gown.' When I think of that, I think of you. Across my life, one whispering silken name. Elise.*

He would liked to have said it, but it was impossible. It would have been too emotional, too mawkish, too *final.*

After he had put her in the car, he and Willi shook hands with all four hands. They didn't speak. There was nothing more to say. Moltke shook his head slightly and smiled when Willi's eyes filled with tears. He patted the squat sergeant on the back and opened the driver's door for him. From somewhere, Willi had got his hands on a black Mercedes to take them to the border; it would identify the occupants as important personages with whom it would be unwise to meddle.

When the car wound up the road and down the hill, Moltke turned back toward the lodge. A feeling of calm resolve settled over him. Everything was in order, or nearly so. All he had to think about now was attacking the destestable Flying Fortresses. He had become convinced that it would probably be his last act. By now, all the aces assumed they would soon be killed. But they had endured too much to consider dying very important. All that mattered was to make their final attack a crushing one.

———

It was a beautiful day in England and all across the continent for someone who didn't want to fly. The cloud cover was ten-ten, solid all the way from the ground to 40,000 feet. Visibility was zero–zero throughout the island and over any conceivable target. Everyone and everything was grounded. Even the birds were walking.

Robinson knew he shouldn't feel as relieved as he did, but he was. The forecast was for forty-eight hours of unbelievably foul, lovely weather. It allowed him to leave the base and make a long-postponed trip with Sandra to visit her father in Harpenden. They sat in their compartment, holding hands, as the train slid cautiously through the fog at half-speed.

"I'm so glad you had this stand-down so you could come with me today," Sandra said.

He nodded, "So am I. Nobody's flying anywhere today."

"That last mission. Was it—difficult?"

"Amazingly, no," he said. "We didn't have any casualties at all. A real milk run."

"Why so amazing? You've taken a great many on other raids."

"Not lately," he said. He paused momentarily. "It was amazing because of the target. I suppose there's no harm telling you; it was Berlin. When everybody comes back from a raid on Berlin, you know the war's just about over." *Except for the damned 262s,* he said to himself.

She grinned. "I'm so excited about today, taking you to meet Dad after all this time," she said. "The two of you will get along smashingly, I know you will."

He smiled. "To tell you the truth, I'm feeling a little intimidated by the prospect of meeting the old gent."

She squeezed his hand. "He's the one who should be intimidated, meeting a great, glittering brute like you for the first time. But you're right, in a way. The Brigadier's rather a small man, small and slight, but he has a certain, I suppose you would say, dignity about him that can make him seem a good bit larger than life."

"What will we talk about, do you think?"

She laughed. "That's an easy question. After we've done with the niceties—how are you, tell me about yourself, young man—we'll be talking about the Brigadier's specialty and passion: military history. I daresay, by the time we leave, you'll know a good deal more about this war you're fighting than you can imagine."

"That will be welcome, I'm sure," Robinson said. "There are times when I'm not exactly sure I know exactly *what's* going on." He pulled a scrap of paper from his pocket. "For instance, what is this all about?" There was nothing on the paper but the neatly handwritten words:

*He who thinks that the living entity is the slayer, or that the entity is slain, does not understand.*

"Do you have any idea who left it for you?"

"Not a glimmer. Somebody slid it under the door of my office. It's Eastern, I think. A fragment of a poem. Somebody apparently is trying to send me a message, if that's what it is." He smiled ruefully. "Funny in a way. Here I am a major in English lit and this is the closest thing to poetry I've touched or thought of in a long time. Well, except maybe that one little line from Housman that seems to creep into my mind once in a while."

She looked at him sidelong. "I'm sure I know the one. 'Give crowns and pounds and guineas, but not your heart away.' "

He chuckled. "That was a low blow. No, this one:

*By brooks too broad for leaping*
*The lightfoot boys are laid . . .*

Sandra's eyes became soft. "Oh, I know the rest:

*The rose-lipt girls are sleeping*
*In fields where poppies fade.*

She straightened. "But don't you see, that little message is saying absolutely the opposite of Housman. It's as if the person who sent it to you is reading your mind."

Robinson looked at the words again, compressing them. " 'He who thinks that the entity is slain does not understand.' Death isn't the end, is it? That would be nice to believe."

Retired Brigadier General Harold Brooks greeted them at the door of his modest house, a ten-minutes walk from the train station. He was, as Sandra had said, small and slight. But the Brigadier had the erect bearing of a career military officer—Robinson found himself standing straighter, though the ceilings were low—and the old man wore his tweed shooting jacket as if it were a military uniform. Brooks' hair was iron gray and neatly brushed at the sides and he wore a neatly clipped gray moustache. His eyes were remarkably like Sandra's.

Within minutes, it seemed, Brigadier Brooks had deftly cross-examined Robinson about his home, family, schooling and military service, and, over a glass of sherry, was probing Robinson's views about America's contribution to the war.

"I know we're not very popular here in England," Robinson said, "and I think it's easy to understand. And there's the business of our men and the English women." He looked uncomfortably at Sandra.

"But I think the contribution is undeniable. We sent supplies when you needed them most urgently, even though our president had to make several end-runs around Congress to do it. And we're here in force now, in the air and on the ground. It seems to me that your toughness and our help are the two reasons why England is still free today. You may not agree with that."

"Quite right, I don't," Brooks said. "But not for the reason you may think. England remains England today entirely by courtesy of Herr Hitler."

"I don't understand."

"Reconstruct the events at Dunkirk, Colonel. It was 1940. Hitler's tank divisions smashed across Holland, Belgium and France within two weeks. An incredible feat, all the more so because they were outnumbered in men and equipment." The small man's eyes shown with obvious respect. "They squeezed the BEF, our entire expeditionary force—I'm speaking of all our troops and all our armament—into a tiny pocket of beachfront at Dunkirk. The Germans had one army group facing our troops and another group at our rear. Our people put up a strong defense, of course—we always do that—but there was really no hope. It was death or capture for the British army. The French army already had been defeated."

"But your flotilla of small boats rescued your troops from the beach," Robinson said.

"Ah, but you miss the point, my boy," Brooks said, extending a professorial finger at the American. "That happened only because we were granted three days in which to do it. When our defeat was imminent, Hitler ordered his tanks to halt and pull back out of cannon range."

"I'm afraid I've heard nothing about that," Robinson said. "My attention has been on my own part of the war."

"Of course. But that halt order—historians will be gabbling about it for decades to come, you'll see—was the pivotal point of this war. We know from intelligence sources that General von Rundstedt feared a mythical flank attack by the remnants of the French army. We've also concluded that Hitler, while an exceedingly bold man in his military concepts, becomes surprisingly timid in the execution of his plans. I expect it's because he lacks staff experience of any kind. He felt justified in indulging that timidity because Göring boasted that his Luftwaffe would wipe out our troops without use of the army. The RAF made that impossible and our army escaped, almost unscathed, to Britain."

"And that one blunder made all the difference."

Brooks sipped at his sherry for a moment. "Actually, there were two. Even though we had our troops back, they were a demoralized lot—why wouldn't they be?—and all the more because, except for one division, they returned empty handed, with no arms at all. I was a member of the anti-invasion force at that time. There were no rifles or ammunition, no field pieces, not even hand grenades in the whole of England. In my sector, our equipment consisted of a van and two shotguns." For the first time, the dignified little man raised his voice. "If Hitler had ordered his paratroops and glider troops to leapfrog the channel and seize an airfield or two, bringing in two or three airborne divisions behind them—we know that the Inspector General of the Luftwaffe urged him to do this—our navy couldn't have stopped them. The RAF would have had to commit all of its reserves to an unfavorable series of air battles. On the ground, there would have been literally no one to oppose them. The German divisions could have fanned out like a brush fire, living off the land as many of your troops did in the South in your Civil War, and taken London. Churchill has said himself that he had no doubt they would have found English friends who would quickly set up a government favorable to Germany."

Robinson, fascinated, leaned forward. "If that had happened, England would have gone down and the entire continent would be in German hands. We couldn't have set up our bomber bases or staging depots here. We couldn't have invaded. The war would have gone on for—my God, forever."

"Quite right. And it might, eventually, have become an immensely more bloody war for you than you could possibly imagine. If, in fact, you had got into it at all."

"And all of this, you believe, hung on Hitler's timidity."

Brooks reflected, stroking his moustache with his slim fingers. "There was an additional factor, and one day we may find that it was the most decisive of all. Hitler had always expressed admiration for the British. He said many times that we knew how to govern. Germany and Britain together should rule the world, that sort of thing. We understand that, when his officers protested his halt order and then recommended the cross-channel attack, he said that the British were a reasonable people and that that sort of action was unnecessary. Britain would quickly come to terms with Germany and accept Germany's dominion over the continent. He actually proposed as much to Churchill. I'm afraid he misread our character rather badly."

Robinson laughed. "An understatement, if I've ever heard one."

Brooks nodded. "But I should add that we still would have been in dire peril if you hadn't come to our aid. Your President Roosevelt is a bit of a magician. Despite your neutrality laws and your Congress, he had one million rifles with ammunition and a thousand artillery pieces on the way to us one week after Dunkirk. Of course Hitler neatly solved your president's problem by declaring war on America after Pearl Harbor, didn't he? And then you chaps followed and set up shop here."

Brooks stared moodily at Robinson for a moment. "I don't think you could possibly realize how desperate our situation was. Consider your own specialty, bomber command. All the world knows of our gallant Spitfire pilots, and how they won the bloody Battle of Britain, now spelled in capital letters. Not many, I'm afraid, know what our boys have endured in RAF Bomber Command. Our Lancasters, as you know, are far, far larger than your B-17s and 24s."

"I know," Robinson said. "The RAF officers I've met look down their noses at us. They carry bomb loads two and three times bigger than ours."

"Yes, but you see, our bombers have achieved that capacity at the expense of speed and firepower. In contrast, your B-17s are literally what you call them—Fortresses." The Brigadier paused a moment as if to decide whether to say more. "I know that your boys, and you personally, have had it hard, Colonel, at least till recently. But I wonder if you know how much worse it's been for the young men in RAF Bomber Command. Command has always told new crewmen that their tour of duty was thirty missions. What they failed to tell them was that, till rather recently, no one survived long enough to fly thirty missions."

"I didn't know it was that bad," Robinson said.

"Well, you see, we always knew that our Lancs couldn't defend themselves by day. That's why they've always flown at night. But we found to our dismay that surviving at night was nearly as impossible as surviving by day. Searchlights, night fighters and antiaircraft fire have taken a dreadful toll of our bombers. And I'm terribly afraid that a great deal of this, this *attrition*—a lovely euphemism for blood and death, don't you agree?—has been wasted."

"Wasted, sir?"

Brooks took a deep breath. "Your high command knows what I'm about to tell you, but I'll ask you, as a matter of decency, to treat this as confidential. Now that Allied troops have moved so far inland, we've had an opportunity to verify bombing results. We have been shocked and, I must say, saddened to find that only one out of three of our nighttime bombers actually dropped its bombs within five miles of its target. Seems hardly worth the price, does it?"

Robinson, thinking of the names burned into the roof of the officer's club, felt a sharp pang of despair. "I'm terribly sorry, sir."

Brooks nodded and smiled faintly. "Your boys have done better than that, but even if they hadn't, you chaps have soaked up enough of the opposition to make it easier on the RAF crews. They're hitting the target a sight better and living longer these days because of you. We're all living longer because of what America is doing for us, Colonel, and we'll be eternally grateful for it."

In spite of himself, Robinson felt a lump in his throat. "Thank you, Brigadier. And now, thank God, the war is nearly at an end."

Brooks nodded but looked with intense seriousness at Robinson.

"Yes, it's winding down, but I hope you chaps don't become as complacent as some of ours are. Anyone who's studied the Germans as I have will never underrate their capacity in war, regardless of the circumstances."

Robinson smiled grimly. "I can testify to their capability in the air, Brigadier. I suppose I've always considered the Luftwaffe their elite corps, just as we've tended to think of the Air Corps as a special group within our military services. But I would think that Montgomery's Tommies and Patton's Third Army ought to be more than the equal of any troops the Germans can put on the field."

"Oh dear," Sandra said, standing in the doorway, "you've just put your foot in it, Colonel Robinson, and I was about to say that dinner's ready. I'm afraid you've just touched on the Brigadier's special interest."

Brooks smiled and waved at her. "Oh, do give us a minute more, won't you, girl? The hare will wait a bit; the vegetables, such as they are, can wait forever, so far as I'm concerned." He turned back to Robinson, his expression serious. "Let me tell you something that isn't generally known. Mark you, it won't be published for a time. The War Ministry has analyzed every significant battle that's taken place since the beginning of the war. Our analysts now estimate that the German foot soldier inflicts a fifty percent higher casualty rate on the American and British foot soldier than they inflict on him. On the Eastern front, intelligence tell us, German soldiers are inflicting casualties on the Russians at a ratio of eight to one, even as they retreat."

"Good God," Robinson said incredulously. "Why? Are they just naturally better suited to fighting than we are?"

"No," Brooks said. "Not when you look at their performance prior to this century. The Germans fought very poorly in your Civil War, for example. One German unit actually had to be broken up; its members were dispersed through other companies. No, it's the tradition, the training, and that's the product of the German General Staff. It goes back to the Prussian General Staff. Clausewitz, Schlieffen, Moltke."

"General Hellmuth Karl Bernhard von Moltke," Robinson said.

Brooks raised his eyebrows in surprise. "Why yes, Colonel. I don't mean to, um, condescend, but how would you know about Moltke?"

Robinson laughed shortly. "This is funny. He's an ancestor. Direct blood line. We have a portrait of him in the living room back home."

Brooks smiled faintly and stroked his moustache. "Fascinating. Doubly so when you consider your present position. And the fact that the Moltke family still exists in Germany. One in combat, I understand, another under a bit of a cloud. Well, now."

Brooks clasped his hands over one knee and rocked back and forth in his chair. He was clearly enchanted by the revelation. He seemed almost to view Robinson with heightened respect. "Your ancestor was a genius. He introduced the concept of mobility into modern warfare. He was the first to see the advantage of using railroads to move troops. He thought up the idea of having self-propelled artillery and integrating it with infantry. He was a pioneer in mobile mission tactics . . ."

"*Auftragstaktik,*" Robinson interjected.

"Why, yes," Brooks said, unconsciously assuming the role of a professor who is pleased with the response of a bright student.

"*Auftragstaktik.* They still have the power to utilize it, whatever their apparent resources. Do be careful, Colonel. Particularly of that new jet airplane they've got."

It was Robinson's turn to be surprised. "You know about *that,* too?"

"Of course. I have full access to the Ministry; I couldn't do my work otherwise. I consider that Messerschmitt a very dangerous contraption. They don't have many in operation, but they shouldn't need many, should they? Well," he said, rising. "I think we'd better go on to dinner while it's still being offered. Sorry for the delay, girl."

The conversation haunted Robinson as he sat at the dinner table. *So many have died. And another Moltke and I are waiting to kill each other.* He mechanically complimented Sandra and Brooks' housekeeper, Dora, on the country dinner of wild rabbit, homegrown potatoes and canned peas. In return, Brooks thanked Robinson for the contraband pound of butter and bottle of gin he had brought from the base.

Brooks spoke about Sandra at the end of the visit. She was reapplying her makeup in the bathroom while Robinson and her father waited by the front door.

"It's been a pleasure to meet you, Mitchell," the older man said. "Sandra's connected herself to a good man. I think." He paused a moment. "At another time, I imagine I'd be asking you about your intentions concerning my daughter. But I'm afraid that's all irrelevant somehow in wartime. Nor do I think you would know how to answer such a question even if I asked it. So, perhaps, all I can ask, as a loving father, is that you respect Sandra . . ."

"I do, believe me, sir," Robinson said.

"And for her sake, as well as your own, *stay alive.* That may seem an odd thing to say, coming from a military man like myself. But whether you live or die in the months remaining won't affect the outcome of this war. It will clearly affect my daughter. I don't want her to lose another man in battle. Stay alive, Mitchell."

Robinson's voice suddenly went hoarse. "I'll try, sir."

———

The Mosquito slid through the upper air at nearly three times the speed of a B-17. Lon Amundson chortled to himself. What a ball! The high-blown Merlins purred smoothly, smugly confident of their ability to meet any challenge. The sleek, twin-engined craft moved laterally at the slightest pressure of his feet on the rudders. The stick was feather-light in his hands. He had the feeling that he could pull it back and soar straight up to the moon that still hung like a silver coin in the morning sky.

Amundson looked at the altimeter. 39,000 feet. An absolute ball. It was Amundson's third weather reconnaisance flight in the British "wooden wonder" and he loved every minute of it. The light, elegant Mosquito and the heavily weighted B-17 were as different as day and night. *This,* he said aloud to himself, is the way flying is supposed to be.

He was almost as fascinated by the men of the weather group. They were skilled British Spitfire veterans of the Battle of Britain, a half dozen Free French adventurers, two Poles who had escaped from the East and three Americans, one with a terribly burned face. They lived together in a wonderful old stone mansion that had been comman-deered by the RAF for the duration.

His crewmate, a rosy-cheeked RAF captain named Paul Prentice, had briefed him on the recon missions. "Nothing to it, really," Prentice said over a gin-and-lime at the bar. "Our little Mossie carries no ugly guns, no nasty bombs, no excess weight of any kind—excepting, of course, the stone and a half I've put on since leaving the old squadron. All we have to do is climb high above the bloody battle and zip on over to look at the lovely cloud formations. Cruise about over the rubble your chaps expect to pulverize later in the day. Sample the temperature, wind drift, icing conditions, that sort of thing. Then we make our report, dash on home and bang our shilling on the bar. Piece of cake."

Their only worry was the ME 262, but the squadron commander had outlined the technique that had been developed for escaping it. The important thing was not to be surprised from above or behind. If one appeared, you simply pointed the Mossie's nose straight down and headed full-speed for the deck. Take it all the way down, the commander said. You might tear your wings off, he said casually, but what's the alternative? The point is that they'd learned the jet had no dive brakes and could become uncontrollable in a long, high-speed dive. Everything depended on vigilance.

Amundson was vigilant, though sometimes it was hard to keep his concentration focused on flying. His mind wanted to wander to Betsy. Her letters came in batches through the irregular military postal service. He would sort them out and read them according to the dates on which they were written.

Her letters were long and loving. *It's simply a miracle that you could come into my life and change it as you have,* she said in one letter. *It's so wonderful that I'm afraid of it. Please be very careful, Lon darling. I don't think I could bear it if this turned out to be a false spring.*

The sun was coming up, massive and red, and he was almost sorry to see it because, as it flooded the morning sky, it would make the moon disappear. The silver coin hung above him, pale, fragile and beautiful.

The explosion was shocking. It came without warning, seemingly from nowhere. It erupted beside him and threw the Mosquito sideways. The port engine disintegrated and the plane tried to roll over. Panicked, he fought for control. The second explosion seemed to come from within the airplane itself. It swelled massively and he felt himself catapulted from his seat. His last memory was looking up into the sky. He seemed to be soaring straight up into the beautiful moon.

———

The Führer grunted and turned away; the delegation followed him like a flock of sheep. Confused and agitated, Speer waited at the missile-launching site with his aides. The demonstration, clearly, had been a great success. Two *Wasserfall* missiles—it should have been one, of course—had destroyed the fast, high-flying Mosquito. What more could a reasonable man expect? Asking himself the question gave him a tingle of optimism.

Finally, one man appeared. To Speer's dismay, it was Reichsleiter Bormann. Bormann's face was impassive. He walked to within six feet of Speer, stopped and said formally: "The Führer has instructed me to say these words to you. 'As I have said many times, true strength lies not in defense, but in attack.'"

———

Two days later, the hammer fell for the second time. The news of Amundson's death had stunned Robinson, but he hadn't seemed able to absorb it. Then the letter arrived from Leila Crosby in Mahoning.

*I'm terribly sorry to have to tell you this, Mitch, but your Aunt Adda passed away this morning. She had a fall a week ago (there really wasn't time to notify you) then pneumonia set in. She hadn't been very strong, you know, and she died, peacefully, thank heaven, early this morning. I'll miss her terribly, as you can imagine, and I know you will too.*

Robinson smoothed out the letter and read it again, trying to find an emotion appropriate to the moment. He was sure he would feel it later, for her and for Lon. For now, he could summon up only a dull feeling of regret, a strange calm and a pervasive numbness.

———

"I thought we had this settled!"

The speaker was Lieutenant Kathleen McGinnis, nurse and principal assistant to flight surgeon Captain Harvey Benson. Hands on ample hips, she glared at the pear-shaped doctor who stood sheepishly before her.

At thirty-eight, Kathy McGinnis was not a conventionally pretty woman. But her strong features, ample bosom and muscular legs combined to create an earthy sexuality. She knew that the skinny flight officers she and Benson ministered to called her "earth mother." She rather liked the nickname. What she did not like, as she was reminding the flight surgeon, was to be patted and fondled in the office.

Benson raised his hands in surrender. "You're right, you're right, and I apologize. It's hands off in the office, the mess hall, out walking, et cetera. No fondling, no touching, not even a friendly pat. I agree. Just as long as you agree to remain mine in private."

"I agree to no conditions," she said, her voice falling to a purr. "But I think I've given you some reassurance in that department over the last six months I've been here. Although I'm not sure it's a good idea, the way you wheezed and puffed the other night. I don't want you having a heart attack in my bed."

"That would be embarrassing, wouldn't it?" Benson mused. "But imagine the prestige it would give you. You'd be able to write your own ticket in any medical department in the Air Corps."

She laughed, shaking her head. "I admit it's nice to feel so desirable. It was never this way in Des Moines."

"Nothing was ever like this anywhere. Or will be again. But," he sighed, shrugging into a white coat, "we might as well get ready for today's sick call. What've we got today, as if I can't guess?"

"Frostbite, colds, sinus."

"Sinus," he said. "I don't know how anybody lives in this climate without a cast-iron nasal transplant. I wonder how many crewmen have died from it."

"Died?" McGinnis said. "You're not serious."

"Oh yes," he said. "Imagine the sudden pain of a sinus block at 30,000 feet. There's no pressurization in those cabins. If a sinus block hits the pilot, he's going to be incapacitated. Like it or not, he's going to have to drop to a lower altitude to relieve the negative pressure. That's when the fighters pick them off."

"I had no idea. So if they have even a trace, we ought to keep them off the flight roster."

"Well, yes, in theory," Benson said. "But the fact is that casualties are pretty low right now. We've lost only three planes in the last three raids. Nothing like the old days. The other thing is, I've got personal orders from Robinson to fly every man from now on who isn't flat on his back. We're on a kind of perpetual alert. Scuttlebut is we're waiting for an all-out field order that could come at any time. And the way General Sutter keeps popping in and out to talk to Robinson I have to guess we're supposed to lead the parade."

McGinnis looked perplexed. "I can't imagine what all this fuss is about this late in the war. It seems to me we could just pack up and go home. Is Colonel Robinson really up to flying, do you think?"

Benson shrugged. "I'm better at treating people's butts than their heads, Kathy. I thought Robinson was going to fall apart when the word came about Amundson. But he didn't, somehow. He did keep to himself for a day or so, but since then he's been acting very matter-of-fact about operations. Too matter-of-fact. I've seen him a whole lot more jumpy before other missions. A lot more."

"Is it really official that Lon is dead?" McGinnis asked. "He was such a nice boy."

"Afraid so. There was another weather scout in the vicinity. He saw it. Said Amundson's plane just blew up, though he thought there were two explosions. That doesn't make sense, though. It had to be a mechanical problem, the gas tank or something. Flak doesn't go that high and it isn't that accurate."

Benson frowned. "I want to track Robinson after the war. And maybe two dozen others. Find out how their lives are affected by what they've been through here. That'll be my second book. The first one will come out of here." He pulled a desk drawer open and brandished a large gray notebook.

"I thought that was your diary. Not that I've read it."

"Actually, it's a collection of case histories—observations on what this new and peculiar kind of warfare does to young men. I'm going to call it *Dr. Benson's Notebook*. Or maybe something more dignified, like *A Flight Surgeon's Journal*. It won't be a quantitative study, though I can probably get some figures out of the army. But the fascinating stuff is qualitative—what we've observed and recorded in individual cases— what sort of projections we might reasonably make about the future of these young men."

McGinnis nodded. "If you want my opinion . . ."

"Along with everything else."

"One thing at a time. Physically, I think some of it's fairly clear.

These men are almost uniformly slim and skinny. Maybe they're that way genetically, maybe the hard work of flying those big things has kept them that way. It would be interesting to know which. As a group, they have abnormally strong back and upper arm muscles. Rather exciting, as a matter of fact."

"Now you're making me jealous. But go on."

"Except for exhaustion, they're a pretty healthy lot. I'm talking about their bodies, of course. But I think a lot of them are going to have chronic problems later in life. Sinus, certainly. Ear problems, too. Early deafness—I'm sure of that. And a higher incidence of tracheo-bronchitis than we'll see in the general population. And I think a lot of them are going to develop lower back problems from wrestling these big planes around. Maybe a tendency to circulatory problems, too. You can't get your hands and feet frozen as often as they do without suffering some long-term damage."

"Excellent, Kathy!" Benson said. "You ought to be my coauthor. But what about psychological problems?"

"Your turn. What's your diagnosis?"

"Well, I've given it a good deal of thought. I think we're going to find out that the Air Corps, especially the bomber groups, have produced more psycho-neurotics than any other military unit. The poor grunts in the infantry wallow around in the mud and live like Bowery bums, but at least they aren't jerked from one environment to another every day. Here, somebody wakes you out of a sound sleep in the middle of the night, when your energy and courage are at their lowest, and tells you you have to get up and go fight. You fly one of those monsters for eight hours up at 60 below zero and you get shot at by fighters and flak and then struggle back through horrendous weather. You're exhausted and dirty and in a state of shock and maybe you've peed in your pants and suddenly it's peaceful again and now you're supposed to shave and shower and put on your nice uniform and have a drink at the bar and take some aspirin for your headache and call the girlfriend and maybe go dancing and wonder if the orderly's going to wake you up again tonight. Being jerked back and forth that way is just too big a strain on the psyche."

"It must have been a lot worse before I got here."

"Robinson was a squadron leader at the time. A whole bomb group could turn over in a week or ten days. One kid sat in his barracks waiting for his friends to come back from a raid. When *nobody* came back, he took the train to London. A bobby caught him trying to jump off a bridge. We had to get him out of the brig and ship him home in a straitjacket. We've sent a lot of people home on hospital ships that were just full of cages to hold deranged young men.

"And then there are the dreams. I have one case history where we had to separate the pilot and copilot of one crew, put them in separate barracks. They were sharing the same nightmares. The pilot would yell out to feather No. 4 engine and it would jerk the copilot into the same dream. *He'd* yell out that No. 4 was feathered."

"Yuk. That's creepy."

"Well, all my stories aren't that grim. Take the one about Mickey Walsh, everybody's perfect Irishman. A handsome, fun-loving young man. He got his primal organ stuck in an oil can up at altitude. It was about 60 below up there and the foreskin froze to the metal."

"My word. Why did he have it in an oil can, if it isn't too much to ask?"

"The relief tubes are big, cumbersome things and they often freeze up there. So the pilots ask the crew chiefs to punch holes in empty oil cans and they tuck them under their seats for when they need to go."

McGinnis laughed. "What happened?"

"He had to pull it loose or lose it. The whole thing would have frozen like a rock. So he lost a good deal of foreskin. His girl friend was an innocent young English girl. He had been trying hard to persuade her that he needed her virginity more than she did. And suddenly he was unable to—what shall we say?—press his case. Even an impure thought was painful, as a stray erection reminded him. He didn't tell her about his disability, of course. But his behavior changed. He had become sweet and considerate. She was very pleased. She thought he'd had a change of heart and become a gentleman. He was back to his normal predatory self in about a month.

"But Mickey's little story has a serious point. When these kids haven't been flying, they've done everything possible to live it up. Eat, drink, make Mary and Jill and every female possible, for tomorrow you die. It becomes a hard habit to break. I think that a lot of them are going to be a pretty restless lot in later life. Fidelity, I think, may be difficult for many of them in marriage."

"What do you think will happen to Colonel Robinson?"

"Well, he's had it harder than most. I think he could turn into a zombie if something isn't done to help him out. He comes from a small town and it isn't as if he has a business or profession or even family to fall back on."

"I guess that part's not unique, is it?"

"God, no. When this war is over, there'll be hundreds of thousands —what am I saying?—*millions* of people trying to make sense out of their lives, find something worth living for."

McGinnis sighed. "Well, I hope *he* finds it anyway."

———

General Adolf Galland, flushing red with anger, struck his fist heavily on the desk of his makeshift office. "I can't believe the Luftwaffe could be given an order this stupid! Especially now, when we need to throw everything we've got against the bombers." He jammed a long Brazil in his mouth. "This way—we're just pissing away the last of our strength."

Karl von Moltke stood before him, head down. "I'm sincerely sorry, Herr General. I tried to convince the Führer but . . ."

"Oh the Führer be blowed!" Galland grated. He motioned Moltke to a chair. "It isn't your fault, Karl. You did what you could. At least he heard you out. The fact is that he doesn't understand air power. The only use he sees for it is ground support, the sacred Stuka concept, the flying artillery. The fact that we're being bombed to pieces is *our* fault."

"He said your plan to make the coordinated attack with the jets and prop fighters was a good one . . ."

Galland waved him off. "But not at this time. I know. So we're to peck away at the bombers here and there while every available prop fighter and bomber in the Luftwaffe is thrown into ground support to cover the army's retreat from the Rhine." Galland glared at Moltke. "Do you have any idea what the odds against your aircraft are going to be? A hundred to one? Five hundred to one? And he wants *you* detached for this mission to lead a Focke-Wulf *gruppe*. I can't believe it!"

Galland's voice fell and he stared sightlessly over Moltke's head. "The last time the Luftwaffe fighters were given an order like this was in the Ardennes campaign. It was suicidal. We lost over three hundred airplanes. Three hundred! And all the materiel we had been storing up for air defense. Never mind the criminal diversion of our armored divisions from the eastern front, where they would have made a difference."

Galland's voice rose abruptly. "Now it's all happening again, only worse! We're short of pilots and fuel. We need every drop of gasoline we can lay our hands on for the attack on the Boeings." He picked up the orders and waved the sheets of paper around angrily. "Attack bridges, forward airfields, even troop concentrations! Ignore enemy fighters! Did you read that? Ignore enemy fighters!" He laughed; the sound was like the bark of a large dog. "And our fighter pilots have been trained for air combat only!"

The general looked at Moltke somberly. "There's nothing wrong with getting killed for a good reason, we all expect that. But getting killed for nothing . . ." He shook his head. "I'm not going to notice whether you obey that order."

Moltke smiled. "It comes directly from fighter command. I'll go." He rose. Galland rose with him and extended his hand. "Break a leg then. And come *back*. We'll still strike *der grosse schlage*. The real one."

---

Galland was right. The mission was a disaster. After flying the jet, Moltke found himself horribly frustrated with the old propeller-driven Focke-Wulf. He loved the way it jumped off the ground and the ease with which it handled. But when he needed speed, real speed, it simply didn't have it. And he needed great speed to press home the attacks on the ground targets and evade the incredible numbers of American fighters that swarmed over the battlefield.

The Luftwaffe had assembled 2,000 aircraft for the mission. They included all available twin-engined bombers, groups of fighters that had been equipped with bomb racks and bombsights and converted into fighter-bombers against the will of their pilots, groups of ME 109s and FW 190s ordered to support the bombers and attack all possible enemy targets, even several squadrons of night fighters.

Since a thin overcast lay a thousand feet above the ground, Moltke took his group in low, using it for cover against the Mustangs and Thunderbolts that otherwise would have fallen on them from above. The low-level attack on the portable bridges and forward airfields was like flying into the mouth of hell. Moltke, dry-mouthed but wet with sweat in his flying suit, fought with all his will against the temptation to panic as unbelievable barrages of rapid-firing flak came up to meet them. The tracers became eerie globes of colored lights that formed long arcs from the ground. If this was what the bomber pilots put up with, Moltke thought, they must be crazy.

Within minutes of arriving in the target area, the scene became a confusing jumble of smoke and fire and airplanes flying in all directions. Several groups of American fighters had descended to the deck to meet them head-on, even though the flak was bursting all about them.

As the smoke thickened, finding a suitable target to attack became nearly impossible. Avoiding collisions and preventing Ami fighters from getting on your tail took almost total concentration. Moltke's wingman, a young pilot named Fassbinder, was hit early. A flak burst struck the gas tank and the Focke-Wulf blew up in an explosion of bright red and black. Moltke cursed, hunched his shoulders involuntarily and dropped his nose to fix his gunsight on a column of tanks moving eastward along the autobahn. His cannons thumped and he saw flashes against the metal of the tanks as he swept past. As he swung around, a Mustang crossed in front of him and, in instant reflex, he led it just enough to score a clean hit. He clearly saw the pilot slump over in his cockpit. The Mustang plunged vertically into the ground and blew up.

For a few moments, it seemed as if the Luftwaffe would hold its own and perhaps even inflict some substantial damage against the enemy positions and airplanes. But, as though a vengeful god had lifted his hand, a large sheet of overcast dissolved and sunlight poured down on the attacking Luftwaffe airplanes.

Disaster followed. Hordes of enemy fighters that had been circling above now fell on them like hungry hawks. Moltke seemed to be surrounded by Mustangs. Everywhere he looked, no matter which way he banked, an enemy fighter was turning toward him. Twisting, clawing, firing, he shot down another Mustang. But, from nowhere, something ripped one of his wings. A moment later, a stitch of machine gun bullets smashed his instrument panel. And then something struck him hard on the side of the head and blood began trickling down his face.

Moltke bent the throttle to the stop, pushed the nose down till the propeller was kicking up dust from the ground and headed for a murky patch of low cloud that still hung on the eastern horizon. Looking back, he saw two Mustangs converging on him. His heart hammering against his chest, he quickly flipped through his options. Trying to reverse course would only prolong the danger and, if one of the Mustangs failed to get him, others would quickly join the chase. Jinking back and forth would only delay the inevitable for a few moments. And he was too low to bail out.

Suddenly he remembered a ruse that Galland had pulled successfully on two pursuers in an earlier engagement. Without further thought, Moltke fired all his weapons—his four cannons and two machine guns —straight ahead. The explosions shook the Focke-Wulf and sent blue smoke streaming behind him. Abruptly, the two Mustangs sheared off and left him.

Moltke cried out in relief and wonder. It was exactly as Galland had said. The Amis either thought that the Germans had developed a fighter that fired backwards or that another German fighter had pulled up behind them. He had escaped. Using the cloud cover to shield him, Moltke managed to stagger back behind the German lines before his engine conked out. He said a quick prayer, settled the crippled airplane into a flat glide and headed for a thin patch of woods he saw up ahead. There! He saw two stout trees just about the right distance apart. Dropping the flaps and raising the nose to slow the airplane, he steered the fuselage of the Focke-Wulf neatly between the trees. The trunks snapped the wings from the airplane with a loud crunch and the fuselage, braked to a near-halt, dropped heavily into a pile of resilient brush. The fall knocked the wind out of him, and Moltke sat in the wreckage for a moment before he smelled gasoline and recognized the danger of fire. He climbed out, feeling wobbly and slightly ill, to find a German farmer staring at him, open mouthed.

"Are you a German?" the man said wonderingly, as if speaking to an alien from another planet.

"Of course I'm a German," Moltke said testily. "Can't you see by my uniform?"

The peasant's mouth still hung half open. "Shot you down, did they?"

"Yes, my God, what do you think? I landed from Mars? Where is the nearest telephone?"

"Telephone?" the farmer asked, as if hearing the word for the first time.

Galland laughed heartily when Moltke told the story that night as his head was being stitched at the airfield's one-room surgery. There was no laughter the next morning when the casualty reports came in. The Luftwaffe had lost another four hundred planes; much worse, they had lost more than three hundred pilots.

"It doesn't matter how many planes we lose," Galland said gloomily. "Speer will make more. But he can't make pilots and, under present circumstances, neither can we." His voice rose in frustration. "Do you know how our kids are being trained now? They're taking off and landing on fields that are under attack! Can you believe that? Do you know how many hours of flying time they're getting before they're thrown into combat? *Fifty.* There isn't enough octane gasoline to give them any more."

Galland shook his head. "Fifty hours. Barely enough to learn how to fly straight and level, never mind deal with bad weather or, God forbid, an enemy airplane."

Next morning, the general assembled his aces and told them what he intended to do. "If our leaders"—he gave *leaders* sarcastic emphasis— "fail to approve the plan for a coordinated attack on the bombers within the next forty-eight hours, I propose to contact the commanders of the Luftwaffe fighter groups directly and win their agreement to stage the attack anyhow, regardless of orders. I think many of them will follow me. Does anyone here disagree with this?"

No one spoke. A few of the older aces smiled. Galland nodded. "That's it, then. We'll do it on our own."

# CHAPTER NINE

# Broken Bonds

ADOLF Hitler was deeply depressed. He had finally admitted to himself that Germany was beaten, which meant that *he* was beaten.

It was late April 1945. The Russians were massing for an enormous attack from the east; his generals estimated that their forces included thirteen separate armies and 1,500,000 men. But, of course, his spineless generals always exaggerated enemy strength. They also insisted that the Russians would soon invade Berlin. He knew better. The advance on Berlin was only a feint; their real target would be Prague. One of his staff officers had recalled Bismarck's statement that whoever controlled Prague controlled Europe. He immediately elevated the man to field marshal and ordered four panzer units that had been held in Berlin to be sent south for the battle he expected there.

To the west, the Americans had already crossed the Elbe, little more than an hour's drive away. They seemed to be sitting on their hands. No matter. All that remained now was the need to set the record straight. He would write his will and, equally important, a political testament to leave for the Germans of the future.

Earlier, he had made a series of audio recordings, with Bormann operating the machine, to confess the mistakes he had made. Yes, even *he* had made mistakes; he freely admitted it. Ticking them off on his fingers, he reviewed them.

Putting his faith in Mussolini was an important one. The man had turned out to be a blundering incompetent whose military misadventures in Greece had necessitated a German rescue and delayed the attack on Russia—later, events proved, fatally.

Misreading the character of Great Britain was another mistake. The Jew-ridden, half-American drunkard—Churchill—had been given the chance to make Britain a true world leader; together, Germany and England could have ruled the world, put all of Europe to work in their service, built an autobahn to India, exploited the natural riches of Africa, found limitless *lebensraum* in Russia and made South America a cornucopia of profit.

But Churchill had been too small-minded to grasp the opportunity. Now England would become a minor player in the contest among nations. The Soviet Union, against all reason, would become a major one. And what of America, that mongrel race? Those who criticized his decision to declare war on the United States failed to understand that the Jew, Roosevelt, had already decided to make war on Germany. Why else would Roosevelt have pulled one trick after another on the American Congress to give arms to Britain and Russia in violation of American law and the will of the legislature?

And, he admitted, he had sent Germany to war too soon. There simply hadn't been enough time to mold Germans into the revolutionary ideal. Too many of the senior people—especially the generals— came from an earlier generation. Their thinking and behavior were petty bourgeois. Consequently, he was confronted, over and over, with incompetence, cowardice and betrayal.

The common thread that ran through it all, however, was the pernicious influence of the Jews. One thing was certain. No one could any longer accuse *him* of being unfair to them. On the contrary; he had been scrupulously open and honest with the Jews. He had warned them he would exterminate them if they fomented another world war. He had even been decent enough to give them a nation-wide demonstration of every good German's enmity toward them on *Kristallnacht.*

Yet they stayed in Germany. Those who tried to leave were denied visas by the countries they sought to enter. He laughed bitterly. It seemed that Germany's position was shared by others, after all, though they were too hypocritical to admit it. No, the Jews deserved everything they got, and any German who said otherwise, even today, would immediately be packed off to a concentration camp.

His political testament would be generous to the German soldiers who had made so many sacrifices. He would beg them, whatever the odds, to fight to the end. From their blood would spring the seed of a radiant renaissance—he said the words aloud, liking their sound—a radiant renaissance of National Socialism to create a true community of nations in the future.

He would make the appeal to the men on the front lines, the gunners in the remaining tanks, the Luftwaffe pilots. The pilots! What had happened to those Luftwaffe jet aces? What were they waiting for? He would tell Bormann to send them an order immediately to implement that plan the young Moltke had presented. The Luftwaffe had failed Germany so far. This time, he would tell them, they must get the job done. If they perished in doing it, that was entirely fitting. He couldn't recall exactly what their job was to be; however, that was secondary to the goal of sacrificing themselves.

For himself, he would set a moral example by remaining in Berlin. His staff had pleaded with him to escape southward through the narrow corridor that still existed between the Anglo-American and Russian armies and set up an *Alpenfestung,* a National Redoubt, in the mountains. But he refused. Berlin was the heart of Germany and so its fate and his were inseparable. For now, all he wanted to do was to lie on his sofa with his new puppy, Wolf, on his chest. He would stroke the puppy and call its name over and over. In the evening he would bring his secretaries in, feed them sweet cakes and talk to them, often all night. It was a way to ease the loneliness. And he liked to have company during the unspeakable air raids.

Dwight Eisenhower was deeply depressed. He knew he shouldn't be, since the Allies were clearly on the verge of victory, but the joy he should have felt was being drained away by political bickering and a growing horror at the inhumanity his troops were encountering as they advanced.

He had heard vague reports about concentration camps and, like any commander who receives dozens of unsubstantiated and sometimes conflicting reports every day, he tended to discount them. The reality, he had just discovered, was far more terrible than anything he could have imagined. He and Third Army commander General George Patton had just returned from Ohrdruf, near Gotha, the first such camp to be liberated by the Allies.

The visit assailed all of the senses so strongly it was hard to tell which was worse: the sight of the emaciated inmates, the sound of their weeping or the stench of the living and dead. He interviewed several inmates through an interpreter and was sickened by their stories of starvation, cruelty and bestiality. He steeled himself to walk through every foot of the camp so that he could say that he had seen the horrors first-hand; no one would be able to say later that the stories were propaganda. In one room he had found the bodies of thirty skeleton-like men who had starved to death. The normally jaunty Patton had refused to enter, saying he would vomit if he did.

When he left the camp, Eisenhower immediately cabled Washington and London, urging that journalists and members of Congress and Parliament be brought in to view the horrors for themselves. Then he ordered the townspeople to come and tour the camp. The next day, the mayor and his wife hanged themselves.

Similar and larger camps were found as the armies moved eastward; this fact alone made him feel that his broad frontal strategy was the right one. It would liberate these dreadful places. In solitary moments, he pondered the meaning of the cruelties he had seen. They seemed incomprehensible, the work of a deranged people. But if a cultivated people like the Germans of the twentieth century could be educated (the word seemed grotesque) to act in such a manner, couldn't the people of any nation? The thought was chilling.

Churchill, as usual, put it best. In their last telephone conversation, the Prime Minister said that "crimes have been committed here that find no equal in scale and wickedness with any that have darkened the human record. Every bond between man and man has perished in this war. This wholesale massacre exceeds in horror the rough-and-ready butcheries of Genghis Kahn." Churchill said he had jotted the words down and intended to use them, or something close to them, in the history of the war he intended to write.

Other parts of the phone conversation were equally uncomfortable. Eisenhower was forced to say, clearly and unequivocally, that, as Supreme Commander, he no longer considered Berlin to be a major military objective. Churchill argued passionately, as he had done before, that it was of paramount importance to the peace following the war that the Allies capture Berlin before the Russians did. But Eisenhower was implacable.

He had outlined his strategy a few days earlier in a cable he had sent to the Allied Military Mission in Moscow to deliver to Stalin. The fact that he had sent the cable, as well as its contents, had enraged the British military commanders and upset Churchill. But all he had done was to outline his strategy and ask the Soviet leader to do the same so their armies could efficiently join hands at an agreeable meeting place.

Instead of plunging on to Berlin, he said, he would encircle and destroy the German forces defending the industrial Ruhr. The next task would be to divide the remaining enemy forces by joining hands; he proposed that Allied and Soviet soldiers meet along the Erfurt-Leipzig-Dresden axis. A secondary advance would be made in the Regensburg-Linz area to prevent the consolidation of German resistance in the Redoubt in southern Germany.

The nagging concern about what was happening in the south triggered a question: What was the status of the Eighth Air Force's planned attack on the German jet fields that had been discovered there? Even at this late date, those jets could still play havoc with the Allied advance. What was the Eighth waiting for? He would tell Tedder to tell Anderson to get the job done, ASAP. Meantime, he would order the Ninth Army to advance no further than the Elbe to avoid colliding with the Russians at Berlin.

What he hungered for most at the moment was a good bridge game.

The night he had made a redoubled slam against those two hot-shot colonels his aide had dug up for him in Paris was the last time he had really enjoyed himself.

———

Short, swarthy, pockmarked, almost Asiatic in appearance, the Premier of the Soviet Union sat in his second-floor inner office in his sand-colored building near the white brick bell tower of Ivan The Terrible. It had grown dark outside. He stared at the paper that the American and British envoys had just delivered to him from Eisenhower. He had listened to them and then told them that the Allied plans seemed very sound. As to his own plans, he said, he would have to withhold comment until he could consult with his staff.

The wording of Eisenhower's message was clear enough. The American was saying he would drive north and south, hold still in the center, and leave Berlin to the Soviet forces. Stalin picked up the phone and ordered Marshals Georgi Zhukov and Ivan Koniev, the two toughest generals in the Red Army, to report to him the following day.

The true meaning of Eisenhower's message, he had decided, was the opposite of its words. The *soyuznichki,* the little allies, were lying. They intended to race the Red Army to Berlin. But they would not succeed. He would ensure that that particular dish was eaten by Soviet soldiers and not by any others.

When that had been done, he would see what he could do about acquiring some of the wonder weapons his intelligence staff kept gabbling about. The Americans, rumor had it, were working on some sort of super-bomb. He would have to wait and acquire that weapon later; he would find a way. Meantime, he wanted to get his hands on some of the new jet-propulsion aircraft that had been attacking the American bombers of late. He was sure the Americans would race him for them, too. Their capacity for intrigue and deception was endless.

———

Major Ed Carlino held a contrary view. To him, the Western mind was straightforward and relatively uncomplicated, with one aggravating exception. The exception was standing before his desk now in a taut, backward-bowed posture of attention.

"Google!" Carlino shouted, "I could hang you up by your thumbs for this!"

"Yes sir," Google said.

"I could have you court-martialed and sent to the brig for the next twenty years!"

"Yes sir."

"Falsification of official records, conspiracy to defraud the government, misappropriation of government funds—hell, that could get you thirty years!"

"Yes *sir*."

Carlino stared at the slight junior officer. "There's only one reason I'm not sending you up on these charges right now. Do you know what that is?"

"Yes sir. I mean no sir."

"It's because you've been flying copilot for Colonel Robinson and because we're on alert for an important mission. I don't have the time to do the paperwork on you and I don't want to disrupt the colonel's crew at this moment. Otherwise I'd do it like a shot."

"Yes sir."

Carlino scowled and leaned forward as if trying to see inside Google's skull. "Tell me, Lieutenant, because I would really like to know. Why, exactly, did you pull this latest stunt with that dog of yours? Opening a 201 on him—I mean *it*—and putting it on the squadron payroll?"

Google paused; the truth was much too complicated. "Well, sir, Wushu had flown with me on a couple of raids and all, and, well, it just seemed like a good idea at the time."

Carlino sighed and nodded. "It seemed like a good idea at the time," he said slowly. "The universal reason." He sat up straight and jabbed a stubby finger at Google. "All right," he barked. "I don't have any more time for this. It's against my better judgment, but I'm going to let you off this one last time."

"Yes sir."

"*One last time,*" Carlino said deliberately. "Next time it's—" He drew a finger across his throat in an unmistakably Sicilian gesture. "There had better be no more tricks. Do you understand? *No more tricks.*"

Google nodded vigorously, his small face knotting into an expression of intense seriousness. "Yes sir! No more tricks."

"Dismissed."

Google saluted, executed a smart about-face, and marched from Carlino's office, expelling his breath sharply. He had had a close call this time. He had better stick to the military business at hand. He frowned and shook his head. Problem was that, when you've been cultivating a reputation for eccentricity for a long time, you tend to become what you've been pretending to be.

No more tricks, the major had said. On the other hand . . . Walking toward the barracks, he began smiling to himself. When events have already been set in motion—he imagined the whole cosmos turning on the wheel of life—it's difficult to stop them. It would probably be unwise to try.

Rita had told him her father would be at some kind of farmers' meeting out of town in the days ahead. And the thought had occurred to Barney that, maybe just this one time, the non-coms might really like some fresh milk. The men were always bitching about the godawful powdered milk that came over from the States. He had persuaded Rita to let him borrow Daisy, her father's milk cow, for just one day. The plan was to tether it in the middle of the non-coms' mess hall, spread some hay around to make it feel at home and milk it for breakfast and maybe lunch and—well, Daisy's tenure would depend on how fast news traveled. The men would line up with their cups. That wasn't a *trick,* was it? It was more like a public service. You couldn't really call it a trick . . .

# CHAPTER TEN

# The Hunters

A Dodge truck and two jeeps full of armed MPs brought the big scale-model to the 205th war planning room in the morning. Robinson and General Sutter watched as they set it up on the conference table. Expert craftsmen had fashioned the model out of wood, clay and wire. The tiny airplanes, the buildings and all natural features had been painted. By the splashes of green and a patch of yellow and purple on a hillside—presumably denoting wildflowers—you could see that spring was coming.

"This is it," Sutter said. "We've named the target the Hornet's Nest. And, given the excellent weather report we've been handed, not to mention a sharp kick in the ass General Anderson gave me yesterday, you and I will lead the Eighth for a visit tomorrow morning. Before the general briefing, you'll want your lead navigator and bombardier to come in and study it." He paused. "In fact, you might want to bring in all your navigators and bombardiers." The meaning was clear, though unspoken. *In case the lead bomber, meaning us, doesn't make it to the target.*

Robinson took the news calmly. For some weeks now he had felt as if his nervous system had gone dead, as if he were on a sedative. Since it suited the task at hand, his numbness of spirit didn't concern him. "I've never seen one of these models before," he said.

"We make them up only for important targets," Sutter said. "They're accurate to every detail. We have some top-drawer photo interpreters at High Wycombe. They set up paired recon photos taken by the Mosquitos and Mustangs and look at them through a stereoscope. You've seen the old lantern-slide shows as a kid, I'm sure."

"Sure."

"Well, it's simply a refinement of that. They move the photos around until they appear to merge and create a three-dimensional image. Then, knowing the altitude from which the photos were taken and the sizes of common objects, they can determine precise dimensions of everything and give the figures to our craftsmen. Those guys were graphic artists in New York and Hollywood. They use the data to make big scale-models like this."

Sutter pointed to the features as he talked. "You can see the layout. This is apparently the primary field; most of the support facilities are here. The secondary field, with the flag markers in place, is over here. The schoolhouse, which we now identify as their ground control setup, the barracks, the old inn, here. Notice the builtup earth berms and the camouflage nets; they've been added to in recent photos, meaning they've acquired more planes and, presumably, more pilots—though the new pilots must be fairly inexperienced. We've pretty well killed off the rest. And see this little building at the top of the hill over here? It looks like a hunting lodge; it's probably an observation post."

"With all respect, General, how do we know that it's for real?"

Sutter looked up and smiled. "A good question, Robbie. The bastards have conned us into bombing the wrong targets more times than I want to admit. But we've learned through trial and error. First of all, objects on the ground, of any size, cast shadows. And the shadows move around as the sun moves. Simple observation, right? Well, it may seem hard to believe now, but we used to be fooled by shadows that were painted on the ground. Somebody finally pointed out to us, after examining pictures taken at different times, that something had to be wrong. Also, at different times and on different days, there are different numbers of people and objects—airplanes, trucks, cars—on the site."

The general picked up an envelope and shook a packet of eight-by-ten photos onto the table. He shuffled through them and then held one up for Robinson to see. "Here's the clincher." Robinson peered closely at the picture. A tiny, sleek, twin-engined aircraft was taking off. The shadow was clearly visible behind it.

Robinson nodded. "It's convincing, all right, General. And it certainly gives us a detailed picture of what we're aiming at. So what's the drill?"

"The drill is that we make a feint at Munich—we've been there lots of times before—but this time we use it simply as our IP, then we swing right onto the bomb run. And we carpet-bomb the whole area you see here. Nothing—I repeat, *nothing*—must remain standing. We want everybody and everything on that site destroyed, smashed flat. We want the airplanes and we want the pilots. And we want those fields to look like World War One shell craters in no man's land."

Robinson shook his head in wonder. "The whole Eighth Air Force, a thousand bombers, ten thousand men, maybe four thousand tons of bombs—all of it to hit one little target. It seems like—well, overkill. With all respect."

Sutter smiled faintly. "Overkill, huh? Let me tell you something, Colonel. If we'd known last year just how important that fellow Speer was going to be to the German war effort—the man's a damned production genius—we'd have sent the whole Eighth Air Force hunting for him. Just for *him*. Believe me. Knocking out these ME 262s—*and* their pilots—is just as important. Right now, more so."

———

Moltke watched as the mechanics and armorers fitted the new 55-millimeter rockets beneath the wings of the ME 262s. As some trucks unloaded the rockets, others off-loaded thousands of 30-millimeter cannon shells for the 262s' cannons.

The rockets had arrived just in time. Ground control had received an excellent weather forecast for the next morning, and an urgent order had been sent down from Fighter Command—they said it came directly from the *Führerbunker*—to fly the coordinated attack mission against the bombers.

At another time, this whimsical change of mind by high command would have surprised him. Nothing surprised Moltke now. He was still in a mild state of shock at the disaster that had befallen his elders. Steinhoff, that superb pilot, had proved that an accident could happen to anyone. He had struck an earthen bank on takeoff, caught fire and crashed. He had been terribly burned and was in the hospital. Galland had been caught off guard by a Thunderbolt that fell on him from above after the general had shot down two Ami medium bombers. A machine gun burst had crippled his aircraft and wounded him in the knee. Now he, too, was in the hospital, and Fighter Command, apparently acting on orders from above, had appointed Moltke to lead the crucial mission against the enemy. The leadership of what was to come would be his.

———

The British signal sergeant, who had been sitting in his van near the Rhine monitoring the radio frequency, copied the Enigma message and teletyped it, in his own code, to Bletchley Park. Because its call sign marked it as one of the messages that had been traveling back and forth between Hitler's bunker and German Fighter Command during the past two days, it was flagged for priority action. Six hours later, the cryptographers handed their letter pairings to the clerks, who ran them through the electromechanical *bombes*. Predictably, one of the machines stopped an hour and a half later and displayed the three-digit number that the Germans were using that day to mark the position of the code wheels in their Enigma typewriter.

An Oxford professor of mathematics set the three wheels of his copy of the Enigma into the positions prescribed by the numbers and typed out the encoded German message. He copied the clear text that appeared in the illuminated lampboard at the top of the machine and handed it to the watch officer.

Two hours later, the message was transmitted from High Wycombe to General Sutter at the 205th in a scrambled telephone call. Sutter took the call at the desk he was using in a corner of the war planning room. Afterward, he stared at his notes for a long minute and then lit a match and burned them in an ashtray. It was interesting, to say the least, that the JV 44 jet squadron, the very one they were after, would lead the Luftwaffe in a coordinated jet-prop attack on the Eighth Air Force in the morning. The hunter and the hunted would be one. It was also interesting to note that JV 44's leader was now one Colonel Karl von Moltke. Sutter would tell the 205th's air crews in their predawn briefing that the Luftwaffe would be making an all-out effort to stop them. But, he decided, he would not tell Mitchell Moltke Robinson that the leader of the ME 262 squadron he was dedicated to destroying, and who was dedicated to destroying him, was Karl von Moltke, almost certainly his cousin.

————

The orders that clacked over the base teletype that night were starkly explicit. Destroy the two airfields. Destroy all aircraft on the ground. Destroy the building that apparently housed parts and supplies for the ME 262. Destroy the barracks by the newer of the two fields. Destroy the inn. Destroy the schoolhouse that housed ground control. Destroy the hunting lodge at the top of the hill. Destroy anything in the vicinity that could house or help the pilots or support the German jet fighters in any way. Destroy the airfields themselves. Give them no place to take off, to land, to restore themselves, to rest. Spare nothing.

Robinson and Sutter scanned the orders together. Then Robinson gave wakeup and logistic instructions to operations and the two men separated to get a few hours' sleep.

As Robinson lay on his cot waiting for sleep to come, he realized that this raid would be a very different one for him. Instead of the familiar sense of dread, he felt a cool detachment about what was to come. He realized for the first time that he had lost his fear of death. That had drained out of him when he heard about Lon and, two days later, Aunt Adda. One had been his closest friend, the other his parent. They had been important parts of Mitchell Robinson and now they were gone. Others, also gone, had been smaller parts. Too much had been chipped away from him by now for him to have any great concern about the rest.

General Sutter had told him that this was to be his last mission and, for that reason or another, he had become certain that it was true. He would lead the mission to the best of his ability and there would be no more.

Robinson even half-believed that he understood the latest note from his anonymous correspondent. It was, apparently, a quotation from another Eastern sage. *Join the dust of the world,* it said. Today, it sounded like a good invitation.

———

Cigarette smoke hung in its familiar nimbus cloud over the men crowded into the briefing hut. The operations officer showed the men huge blowups of the reconnaissance photos. The ordnance officer said they would carry full bombloads of new 500-pound, RDX high-explosive bombs. The intelligence officer warned them that they would meet unusually heavy opposition in which the jets would attempt to disrupt their formation. Virtually every Luftwaffe field in central Germany seemed to be preparing for action. But the bombers would be accompanied by fourteen USAF fighter groups—Mustangs, Thunderbolts and Lightnings. Some of them would fly high cover, others would weave around the bomber formations, giving particular protection to the lead wing. Still others would protect them from below. Dissatisfied with even this reassurance, the men grumbled and sighed.

The weather officer said that, due to the sharp contrast between local air and ground temperatures at the moment, there would be heavy ground fog and clouds at the time of takeoff. The men groaned. But once they got aloft, the weather man said defensively, it would be clear all the way in and out. Visibility would be excellent for bombing and they shouldn't have any trouble getting back.

The group navigator and group bombardier, who had spent hours studying the scale model, gave them course, altitude and calculations for programming the bombsights. The briefing was nearly complete. Robinson invited General Sutter to speak to the men. Sutter strode to the podium and talked for several minutes about the importance of holding close formation—no matter how severe the attacks on them became—to maximize their interlocking fields of fire. He told them to

maintain external radio silence and to keep internal radio communication open. He admonished the pilots to watch their cylinder head
temperatures, the navigators to monitor their checkpoints, the gunners
to stay alert.

Sitting on the platform behind Sutter, Robinson noted that the men
hardly reacted. They had heard it all so many times. Their eyes were
glazed. Their minds filtered out any data that were necessary and ig-
nored the rest. A tickle of amusement, combined with a desire to
shock, rippled through him. Perhaps, this one last time, he should tell
them something that would wake them up, something they hadn't
heard before. He had only a half-formed idea of what he would say.

Robinson walked to the podium easily; he didn't posture and play
resolute leader as he had done in earlier briefings. He began speaking in
a low voice that increased in energy and volume as he continued. The
words seemed to flow naturally and he came to believe in what he was
saying as he heard himself speak.

"It's been easy for some time now. We've taken very few casualties.
Even the long missions have been milk runs. Today it will be different.
Some of us won't come back."

Heads snapped up. Some showed fear, some outrage that their group
commander would say anything so insensitive.

"Today's raid will be the most important we've ever flown. We've
been given the job of leading the Eighth on a mission to destroy the
last and very best of the German Air Force—their new jet fighters and
the best of their remaining pilots. As you know, they're first rate. And
they're going to commit everything they have to stopping us.

"We'll take the brunt of that effort because we're the lead group.
We'll get there first and they'll go after us no matter how big an escort
we have. Many of you replacements have found combat a lot easier
than you expected. Today it won't be easy. So this is what I want to
say to you.

"This is the day when we stamp out the last chance the Germans
have to prolong this war. If you live through this day and come home
safe, no matter how long you live or what happens to you in later life,
when this date rolls around, when this mission is mentioned, when
someone says the name of this group, you'll stand up straight. You'll

feel proud and you'll be justified in feeling proud. Because, from this day to the end of time, we will be remembered for what we do today. Only we in this room—we few—will have this privilege, this honor, this *cause* for enduring pride. But first we have to go to Germany and earn it. Will you?"

The last two words were sharp, a challenge. The men sat stunned. They always stood when the national anthem was played, but they did it casually. They felt no particular thrill at seeing the flag. They were professionals, not patriots. Now the "old man," the weariest professional of them all, had confronted them with something new, something confusing and troubling.

"I said we have to go and earn it! Will you?" They stirred. The voice came again like a whiplash. *"Will you?"* And then one man yelled: "Yeah!" And then a second, and a third. And someone began clapping and soon everyone in the room was standing and shouting and waving his arms. Only one man stood still, a beatific smile on his face. Robinson didn't have to look to know it was Barney Google.

———

The last of the Luftwaffe aces listened intently as Moltke spoke from the front of the main room of the inn.

"We'll go in first to tear up the formations and open the way for the prop fighters, and we'll go in *kettens* rather than *schwarms*—the three-ship formation is better suited to the jets than the four. Three *kettens* to a *staffel*—nine ships in three flights in loose, echelon formation. Each *staffel* will attack a bomber group. We'll blow holes in the Boeing formations. First with rockets, then with cannons. When the formations break up, the 109s and FWs will jump on the bombers. We won't try to reassemble our *staffels*. After the initial attack, it'll be every man for himself. It's all been cleared with headquarters, to the extent that's important."

Moltke looked with momentary fear at the faces of the pilots sitting before him. The old aces, hard-faced, leathery, impassive, could have been the fathers of the young men whose fresh, open faces looked at him so expectantly. For days before the briefing, he had wondered what he should say to them. If General Galland were here, and if he were speaking only to his old comrades, he would tell them they could get off their arses and follow him or stay at home, for all he cared. They would smile tolerantly, clap each other on the back, adjust their well-worn gear, and get up and fly.

That wouldn't work with the young ones. What could he offer them? Reassurance? He had none. Comfort? None. Inspiration? They had to be given *something*. He had looked up the Schiller he had read as a student. It made him laugh hard, though the act of laughing was strangely painful. *Against stupidity*, Schiller said, *the very gods themselves contend in vain*. Goethe was equally relevant and inappropriate: *If I work incessantly to the last, nature owes me another form of existence when the present one collapses.* And there was always Nietzsche: *I give you Superman*. That would have been appropriate in the demented atmosphere of 1939. Hardly now. After a bit, it came to him in a surge of ironic humor. How often we Germans still turn to the British for inspiration! he marveled. It was his favorite passage from Shakespeare; he could quote it by heart, and would.

"From a military standpoint, the war is probably lost," he said in preamble. A few of the younger pilots scowled, clearly offended. The older ones sat impassively, revealing nothing of their thoughts. "The Americans and Russians will soon meet at the Elbe. Berlin is under siege. So why bother? There are several answers, I think. One is that neither victory nor defeat can be guaranteed till the last shot is fired. We may not have a big chance, but it's still a chance, to stop the bombing and give our armies and factories time to recover, probably here in the south. And then who knows? Perhaps we can negotiate a better armistice, at least." *And rid ourselves of the demon,* he thought.

"Another reason, perhaps a more realistic one, is that this may be the last chance we'll have to fly the ME 262. We're fighter pilots, some of us are aces, and we may not have the pleasure and privilege again to experience *dei grosse Fliegerei.*

"And there is still another reason, if you need one. Some may call it pride, but it's more than that. It was best stated in a play in which an English king told his soldiers why they should be happy to fight an enormously superior French army. I will quote his words to you:

He that outlives this day, and comes safe home,
Will stand a tip-toe when this day is named,
And rouse him at the name of Crispian . . .
From this day to the end of the world,
But we in it shall be remembered:
We few, we happy few, we band of brothers . . .

Some of the pilots looked at him uncomprehendingly. One seemed
puzzled. Another laughed. But the eyes of several shone with pleasure.
Moltke smiled. "Break a leg," he said.

# CHAPTER ELEVEN

# Remember This Day

THE fog hung over the field like a damp shroud. As the crewmen gathered on the hardstand by the nose of the airplane, Robinson looked carefully at each man's face as if to commit it to memory. Sutter, command pilot, flying right seat. Google, spare copilot and gunner. Doroshkin, navigator. Fisk, bombardier. Claiborne, engineer and top turret gunner. O'Kane, right waist gunner. Weaver, left waist. Hebert, radio operator. Furman, belly gunner. Bauer, tail gunner. They stood, frozen for a moment, a pantheon of ragtag warriors.

Robinson looked up at the silhouette of the four-engined bomber. It was as if he were seeing it for the first time. Or was it because it was the last? The shape of the aircraft seemed bulky and menacing and it looked impossibly large. He suffered a moment's doubt; when he climbed into it, would he really know how to fly it?

"Shall we preflight the airplane?" Sutter growled. Robinson nodded. He and the general walked to the crew chief, who was standing in front of the little hut he had built near the hardstand. A coal fire glowed inside.

Robinson made the introduction. "I don't believe you've met. General Sutter, this is Master Sergeant Callahan, our crew chief." The two men nodded gravely at each other, fellow mourners at a cemetery. "Colonel Robinson has spoken highly of you, Chief," Sutter said.

It was not unusual for even a general officer to go out of his way to pay a crew chief a compliment. Every flying officer knew that his aircraft's performance and, possibly, his own life depended on the crew chief's expertise and dedication. A dedicated crew chief might work sixteen or more hours a day. He and his assistants rebuilt shattered wing spars, patched flak holes, installed new instruments, overhauled engines, replaced propellers, strung new control cables and did the thousand things—including cleaning up blood, feces and vomit, when necessary —that made the bomber ready to fly the next day.

They walked slowly around the silent airplane, visually checking the fuselage, stabilizers, rudders, flaps, wings and landing gear. They sprayed kill-frost on the wings and control surfaces.

"Anything special, chief?" Robinson asked.

"She's ready, Colonel," Callahan said. "We had to do a good deal of work on those wings after all that jigging around you did last time." His voice took on a reproving tone. "You cracked some ribs and there was a hairline in one of the spars. They're okay now. Also, No. 4 engine's been running a little hot. We took it apart and put it back together. Runs up okay now."

"Thanks, chief."

"Would you officers like to come into my hut and get warm by the fire?" Callahan was extending a courtesy. It was understood that his hut was his personal property and that entry was by invitation only.

"We would indeed, chief," said Sutter. "Thank you."

The stove glowed a rosy welcome and they extended their hands to the heat. Callahan excused himself to attend to last-minute details. Sutter looked at Robinson, a small smile on his weatherbeaten face. "That was an interesting little pep talk you gave the men, Robbie," he said. "Kind of a shocker. But you forgot one thing."

Robinson looked up, puzzled. "What was that?"

"You didn't say, 'England and St. George.'"

Robinson's eyes widened. "You knew?"

Sutter grinned. "Yes, even old regular army types like me read occasionally. That was just about a perfect paraphrase of Henry's speech at Agincourt. Shakespeare might not have liked the translation but it was pretty good for a bomb group briefing. These boys haven't heard the words 'honor' or 'pride' for quite a while. Maybe they should have. Maybe we've forgotten something."

The crew chief entered the hut. "Sirs, it's time to start engines."

"Thank you for your hospitality, chief," Sutter said. They walked to the B-17. The gunners and radio operator entered by the door near the tail. Doroshkin and Fisk pulled themselves up into the nose hatch and crawled into the nose, lithe as cats. Claiborne swung up inside and crawled into the cockpit. He would stand behind the pilots until the engines were started.

It was time for the pilots. "After you, General," Robinson said. He locked his hands to make a stirrup. "Can I give you a hand up?"

Sutter looked at him reprovingly. "No thanks. Old and feeble as I am, I can still do it. Just." He reached up, grasped the edge of the opening, palms up, and quickly chinned himself, swinging his legs and body up into the hole. Turning over with a grunt, he landed inside the passageway between nose and cockpit. From there he crawled to the flight deck.

Robinson wiped his hands on his coveralls and grasped the metal rim. He was momentarily curious. The last half-dozen times he had tried to pull himself up, his arms seemed to go dead and his body weighed a ton. Sometimes he had to try two or three times. The last time, Callahan had unceremoniously pushed him up from behind. Today, his body was light. He swung up easily and rotated in midair to land on his hands and knees in the passageway.

In the cockpit, his hands seemed to move without thought. He buckled himself into his seat and plugged in his radio and intercom lead. He and Sutter silently spread their flak vests beneath their seats and arranged their chocolate bars on the dashboard. When they started the engines, he was struck by the sound they made as their crankshaft counterweights slapped back and forth. Just like the threshing machines on a Pennsylvania farm. No. 2 coughed and grumbled a bit, but, within minutes, all four engines were running. As the temperatures of the engines rose, the clattering became a roar.

Visibility was still zero-zero when it was time to taxi. A jeep with a luminescent FOLLOW ME sign on its rear rolled up. Serving as pilot fish to a blind whale, it led the bomber to the takeoff runway and took it far enough down the centerline so that Sutter could lock the tail wheel straight.

Robinson leaned forward and set the gyro compass, making sure that the indicator split the zero squarely in its center. He kept his eyes fastened on the indicator. Until they were airborne, he would look at nothing else. Sutter set the flaps at one-third for a short-field takeoff.

A green flare pierced the fog. "Go," Sutter said. Robinson stood on the brakes, held the wheel column hard back in his lap and slowly slid all four throttles forward. Sutter blocked them open with his left hand and Robinson kept both hands on the wheel. The Cyclones bellowed and the bomber shook and strained. When the sound reached a note of anguish, he released the brakes.

The big bomber rolled through the fog, pulling at the wheel yoke. Robinson held it back, keeping his eyes fixed on the zero. It swung a tiny fraction to one side. Robinson touched a rudder delicately with his booted foot to return the indicator to the center of the zero. Sutter called off the airspeed. "Sixty . . . 70 . . . 80 . . . 90 . . . 100 . . ." The bomber left the ground. Robinson eased the wheel forward and called for wheels-up. Sutter flipped the switch and the wheels rumbled up into their wells. They continued to spin and Robinson touched the brakes to stop them. "Flaps up," he said. Sutter milked up the flap switch a bit at a time. "Flaps are up," he said.

Fingerlike black branches of tall trees reached for the underside of the airplane as they struggled upward. At the head of the runway, the deputy leader released his brakes and began his takeoff roll.

When they broke through the clouds at 10,000 feet, Robinson felt the familiar shock. *It can move me, even now,* he thought. The sky above was an immense dome of deep blue. The sunlight was more brilliant than he had ever seen it. The cumulus clouds were towering mountains of virgin white. *I'll never see this again,* he thought. *Or maybe I will. Maybe this is where you go.*

Robinson turned toward Sutter. The older man's eyes crinkled between the top of his oxygen mask and the bottom of his helmet. What was he feeling? A hand touched Robinson's shoulder. He looked up. Google's face was hidden by the oxygen mask and the walkaround oxygen bottle that he had plugged into it, but there was no mistaking the large yellow eyes. He raised a gloved hand, extended a thumb and forefinger, pulled an imaginary trigger and then turned and walked across the bomb bay catwalk to midships. Two hours later, they led the bomber stream across the channel.

———

Standing outside the inn and looking over the field, Moltke took a deep breath. The air had turned warmer and become fragrant. Spring was coming and it promised to be a beautiful one. The hillside beyond was lush with yellow and purple wildflowers. He peered up toward the hunting lodge that he and Elise had occupied. It was empty now, a haunted house. To his surprise, he had received a letter written by her in Zurich and smuggled across the border. Apparently there was no limit to Willi Steiner's resourcefulness. He had read the letter ten times.

*I am ensconced in a very nice apartment, which I share with Uncle Willi,* she wrote. *He has been a wonderful friend and protector; you were quite right about him. We are completely comfortable here, though we share the same dissatisfaction. We both want very much to be with you, Karl. I hope your duties will be completed soon and you'll arrange to join us here. Meantime, I won't tell you to be careful. You've explained to me that being too careful is dangerous, as well as inviting bad luck. So I'll simply ask you to be lucky, my love. I miss you and love you.*

As he folded the letter and placed it in his breast pocket, a signal clerk emerged from the inn and stopped at attention in front of him. "Herr Oberst. Ground control reports that the Americans are approximately one hour from the German border. Is there a reply?"

Moltke nodded and spoke formally as the man made notes on a pad. "Tell them I request we wait until their destination is certain or can be predicted with high confidence. Tell them I consider it urgently important that we conserve every possible liter of fuel. We have one hour's fuel supply; I want to devote it to combat, not to waiting aloft for them to show up. We want sufficient time to get up to altitude and meet them, no more than that."

———

As the bomber stream thundered toward Germany, the crew of Sweet Sandra—Robinson had had the name painted on the nose after the base party—busied themselves with housekeeping chores.

Doroshkin, kneeling at his navigator's table in the nose, updated his log and rechecked his calculations. Upon him would depend the group's—perhaps the entire division's—accuracy, and the responsibility gnawed at him. He knew he was a superior navigator. He was glib and self-assured to the point of arrogance with his fellow officers, but he had always felt inadequate, and sometimes he cried in the arms of his chubby English girl friend while she made cooing noises to soothe him. He knew why he felt such low self-esteem and he didn't understand why he couldn't shake it off. He had been the intensely serious only child of nagging parents in Queens. He was the prototypical student who regularly made A's and was always afraid of failing.

Still, others had peculiarities, too. He felt a flicker of amusement at Fisk, his roommate in the bomber's nose. Fisk had already recalibrated the Norden bombsight three times and checked the nose guns. Now, yielding to the compulsive neatness that marked his behavior under stress, he began fussily to pick up scraps of paper dropped by the navigator. Afterwards, he scrubbed the plexiglass with a towel. He had been an offensive lineman in high school and had had a tyrannical coach who belabored his players to get short haircuts, tuck their shirts in and keep a neat locker. Maybe, Doroshkin reflected, he and Fisk weren't as different as he had thought when they first met.

Claiborne surveyed the engine instruments, hydraulics and fuel flow one more time and then climbed back into the electrically controlled top turret above and behind the pilots. He swung it around to search the sky, his big 50-caliber Browning machine guns pointing aggressively into space. The job of aircraft engineer suited Claiborne perfectly. He was good at mechanical tasks, working with his hands and getting into the guts of things. He had learned a lot in the Eighth. Now he had a postwar goal: starting up his own auto repair business.

At the right waist position, O'Kane made sure the ammunition belts were securely locked into his guns. Then he repositioned the ammunition box so he could quickly reload when the time came. He wanted to shoot down at least one of the bastards today. He had had a bad scare when that white-hot flak fragment slashed his arm on the Merseburg raid. Today he felt a deep desire for revenge. His old man had seen his buddies killed at Verdun and what he said was right: The only good German was a dead German.

The left waist gunner, Weaver, checked the ship's first-aid kit to make sure it had a full supply of morphine syringes and sulfa packets. A Mennonite from the midwest, Weaver had joined the Air Corps against the wishes of his pacifist parents. They had wanted him to register as a conscientious objector and do relief work, as many Mennonite farm boys were doing. Aerial combat terrified him, but he felt he owed his service to his country and to the oppressed peoples whom the church's relief programs were intended to serve. The Allies had practiced nonviolence in the Rhineland, Austria and Czechoslovakia, and all it had done was to increase Hitler's appetite and produce a vastly larger war.

Furman, the belly gunner, wiped oily residue from his guns with a cloth and wished for the thousandth time he had been born tall rather than short so he wouldn't have been bullied as a boy and, now, so he couldn't be stuffed into the tiny gunner's globule that hung beneath the airplane. He hoped that the undercooked oatmeal he had eaten for breakfast wouldn't swell up in his stomach and intestines in the low atmospheric pressure aloft. If it happened, there was nowhere to go but in his flying clothes. His larger fear, a constant one, was that, someday, the turret would get stuck in the down position; he would neither be able to crank it up nor climb out, and the ship would have to make a wheels-up landing. It had happened a month ago in another group. The pilot had talked to the belly gunner comfortingly for half an hour as they circled their base; but, in the end, he had to land the airplane. There was nothing else to do. Every belly gunner in the Eighth Air Force felt cold fear when he heard the story.

A few feet away, in the radio compartment, Hebert spread the notes on the day's radio frequencies across his table, tapped the sending key in the off position a few times to limber his fingers and made sure the safety catch was turned off on the single gun that projected rearward from the top of the compartment. He would dearly love to carry that big 50-caliber home to the boys in Louisiana when the war was done. Wouldn't they gawk with their pea shooters and shotguns? Of course, a lot of them had been using Garands for a long time now—the boys that were left.

In the bottom of the huge, soaring tail, lying prone, Bauer looked back at the vast aerial armada of the First Division as it glittered across the sky. The silvery metal of the replacement airplanes in the groups shone garishly against the muddy camouflage colors of the older ships. With the air war winding down, Pinetree had decided there was no need to repaint the new airplanes as they came in. Let the enemy see them more clearly; they could do little about them now.

Bauer wished he had a sketching pad and soft pencil so he could sketch the scene. He had gone to Pratt Institute for a year and he was a good illustrator. He wanted to do a drawing he could hang in the studio he intended to open later on. But that wasn't among his present duties. Instead, he adjusted his earphones and tapped the bottom of his oxygen mask to break loose any ice that might have formed there. Ice and burning cold. They hadn't told him that flying over Germany would be Arctic duty. A 150-mile-an-hour gale whistled through every pinprick and crevice of the unheated tail section. He hoped against hope that he wouldn't have to clear a gun jam bare-handed and lose fingers from frostbite. That would wreck the career of any artist.

Google, with nothing to do except fill in as spare pilot or spare gunner, sat on his parachute and visualized his Tai-chi until he had gone through all of the postures in his mind. Refreshed, he considered the two very different pilots in the cockpit. General Sutter tickled Barney. The old man, sitting placidly in the copilot's seat at Robinson's right, was an admirable warrior. He knew exactly what and who he was, a peaceable fighting man who had lived a good life and knew it. To him, every day he lived was a good day. If he died today, it would still be a good day.

But Colonel Robinson, who had always worried Barney, now puzzled him. Clearly, the man had lost the fear that had enveloped him for so long. Was it the notes that Google had been sending him? Was it the attentions of the nice blond lady, Sandra? Or was it—he didn't want to think it was—the death of Major Lon Amundson? If that was the reason, it meant that Robinson had given up, that he had lost his desire for life and declared himself dead. A warrior should, of course, resign himself to death. It was easy once he recognized that life and death were the same and that neither should be hoarded or avoided. But that was the point. To declare yourself dead so that you could live more fully was not the same thing as resigning from life.

If that was what Robinson had done, he might function competently as a warrior for the moment, but there would be little future for him.

Google frowned. He had been thinking about his own future for the past few weeks. He had loved military service—the discipline, the training and learning, the flying—above all, the experience of aerial combat. Soon it would be over. What would he do and where would he go? *This* was what he was born to do. He would consult the words of the masters and he would find an answer. Over the centuries, many unemployed warriors must have asked themselves the same question.

Google looked through the left waist gunner's plexiglass. The sky was clear and quiet. The flak batteries had moved back to the periphery of the fast-shrinking Reich. They, and the German fighters that would fall on the bombers, still lay ahead. Google smiled. It wouldn't be long now.

———

The voice was flat and metallic in the field telephone. "The pantechnicons have overflown Stuttgart and are now crossing the Danube north of Neu-Ulm. Their general course is east-by-southeast. They are now headed for your region, probably Augsburg or Munich."

Moltke took a deep breath. "That's close enough. Let's scramble. Reminder that JV 44 strikes first. Fighter Command groups to follow us. This is Rhineland One, out."

"Victor, Rhineland One. Understand you are scrambling."

Moltke zipped up his gray leather flying suit, tied his yellow silk scarf around his throat and strode toward the ready room. Minutes later, the pilots poured onto the field, the younger ones trotting and smiling broadly, the older ones walking, heads down in thought, like middle-aged businessmen going to work.

When he reached his aircraft, Moltke looked at it affectionately and surreptitiously patted the fuselage as if it were the neck of a prize stallion. He quickly inspected the control surfaces, snapped the slotted flaps in and out, checked to see that the rockets were in place on their rails beneath the wings and climbed into the cockpit. He cinched his belt and shoulder straps, buckled his helmet and attached his oxygen mask, plugged in his leads and turned the radio on.

Then he looked over the side, raised a hand and twirled his fingers. The mechanic started the tiny motors at the head of the engine nacelles and the turbines fired. Minutes later, he advanced the throttles, taxiied into the wind by the line of flags and looked back for his wingmen. They pulled up just behind him and to the side in echelon formation. Moltke nodded, closed his canopy and pushed the throttles forward. The turbines screamed and the three airplanes rolled forward on the grass field. Five minutes later, all of JV-44s jets were aloft and assembled in fighting formation.

———

As the bombers neared the Danube, the ground began winking like sunlight playing across a field of dew. Seconds later, barrages of flak bursts began to blotch the sky. At first, they were low, but they crept steadily closer till a descending blizzard of chaff turned the antiaircraft gunners' radar screens to snow. It would take them several minutes to switch over to geometric box patterns to bracket the incoming bombers. It wouldn't be hard. The flak battery commanders knew the bombers were approaching at 25,000 feet. The altitude had been radioed to them by reconnaissance planes. And, when it became apparent what the final compass heading of the bombers would be, all the gunners needed to do was to fix their sights on that oblong channel at flight altitude and fill it with exploding shells.

Robinson told his crew to stay alert and observe interphone procedure. Heavy concentrations of enemy fighters—ME 109s and Focke-Wulfs—were reported gathering up ahead and in the distance at three o'clock. What, he wondered, were they waiting for?

———

From 30,000 feet, with the morning sun behind him, Moltke watched the bombers creep toward him like a vast swarm of beetles. They seemed to stretch to the horizon. For a time, their changes of course had suggested they were heading toward Stuttgart, then Regensburg, then Augsburg, and now, apparently, Munich. But, if Munich were the target, they would have picked a spot some distance short of it as their initial point—their IP, as he had learned to call it—the place from which they would turn, open their bomb bay doors and begin their bomb run.

*That* was when he wanted to launch the first attack—when the bombers were forced to fly a straight line, when their tensions were the highest, when their fighter escort had to peel away and wait for them to finish their run through the target's flak. But where *was* the IP? They had nearly reached Munich and they were heading straight for it. It made no sense . . . His heart leaped. Unless . . . He said the words aloud to himself. Unless *we* are the target. Was that possible? Look! They were turning now! *Munich* wasn't the target; it was the IP! As the lead group turned and opened its bomb bay doors, the answer became certain. Munich-Reim, the air field and supporting buildings, the 262s and their pilots—*these* were the target! The cat and the mouse were stalking each other. A trickle of fear ran through him, to be followed by a surge of pride. *This* is how important we have become! To be the target of the entire Eighth Air Force!

Splendid! Then it would be, as it should be, a fight to the death, in honorable combat. He looked around. His *geschwader* of 262s bobbed gently on invisible currents of air. The Luftwaffe groups of prop fighters appeared as a tiny cluster of dayflies in the distance, the sun glinting from their cockpit hatches.

A feeling of the purest joy swelled in Moltke's throat and tears filled his eyes. He had been waiting all his life for this moment. It was what he had studied and trained and fought for: a climactic battle against a powerful foe. Today, only minutes from now, he would make his contribution to the long, aristocratic Moltke tradition: to fight, expertly and honorably, in defense of country. But not simply to fight. To fight with a degree of intelligence and individuality that bordered on art. To use one's experience to the fullest. *Auftragstaktik.*

Moltke felt only one regret. The descendents of all the other Moltkes could and did visit the scenes of their battles. They could walk the battlefields of Prussia and France and Russia and see what had happened there. But no one would ever walk the battlefield of Karl Walther von Moltke and retrace the tactics that had been used there. Nothing would mark the site. The fire and smoke and wreckage would disappear. The wind would blow, the clouds would move. Only the empty, silent sky would remain.

The sky was glorious this morning; the deep blue was etched delicately with traces of frozen cirrus. It was as close to heaven as a living man could aspire. It was a wonderful day to be alive; a wonderful day, if need be, to die.

Moltke turned on his gunsight. It glowed softly in the windscreen. The bombers were very near now. They seemed to stretch to infinity. Never in man's history had there been an armada like this. Never would there be one like it again. Weaving around the bombers, like swarms of bees, were group after group of American Mustangs and Thunderbolts and Lightnings. They flew high cover, they guarded the flanks, they screened the B-17s from below. No matter. They were the past, vainly trying to defend against the future.

An unexpected sound burst through the earphones. It was tinny but unmistakable. *The Ride of the Valkyrie.* Probably the Berlin Philharmonic. Moltke laughed gaily. Control was too clever to broadcast Nazi party songs today. Just good, solid, inspiring Wagner. It would do nicely.

Moltke moved his stick back and forth a few inches, rocking his wings. He depressed his mike button. "Tally-ho!" he called. Winging over, he wondered momentarily why the Germans used the British signal for a fighter attack. But they did. The Germans and Britons were so alike in so many ways. Only the Americans were aliens. And yet it was to America that the Moltkes who had left Germany had emigrated.

Where are they now? he wondered momentarily. He dismissed the thought from his mind to concentrate on the attack at hand.

Moltke dived at a shallow angle toward the leading bomb group and fixed his gunsight on the leader. At 1,000 yards he fired the rockets and swept through the formation. Climbing steeply away, he cursed. His wingmen's rockets had punched huge black holes in the lead formation, but the leader plowed past, unscathed. *He had forgotten to release the second safety switch on the rockets. They hadn't fired at all.* That's what comes of thinking of irrelevancies like American Moltkes rather than killing the bombers, he told himself. He swung around for another attack, scattering a flight of Mustangs like a flock of frightened geese.

The sky had become a vast tapestry of swirling airplanes. On this one day the fighters hadn't retreated beyond flak range; German and American alike, they flew right into it. As Moltke leveled out, two fighters collided nearby in a huge orange puff that slowly dissolved. The lead group's high squadron lay in his sights. He waited two seconds and released the twenty-four rockets beneath the wings. They streaked toward the B-17s, trailing long corkscrews of white smoke. An instant later, there was a massive explosion in the middle of the squadron. Two bombers disappeared. The wing of a third bomber— the propellers of its engines still turning—fell away from the ship. The carcass of the B-17 rolled onto its back and plunged into the smoke below. The remaining bombers spread apart, wallowing in fear and confusion; they would be ripe pickings for the oncoming 109s and FWs. Moltke swiveled in his cockpit; he didn't want a Thunderbolt to fall on him while he was gawking about. Now it was time to go to work with the cannons. He felt a personal animosity toward the commander of the lead group. He would save enough cannon ammunition to destroy it. It had the name of a woman painted on the nose and a triangular unit designation on the tail. But meantime, there were targets in front of him: he shot through the lead squadron of the trailing group, cleanly taking out the lead pilot and his crew with four 30mm cannon shells through the nose and cockpit.

Then he turned back toward the leader of the first bomber group. That pilot had led a charmed life too long. And he was *still* leading the battered bomber group toward the airfields. Most of the bombers had been shot away, but the others were still plowing slowly toward the home of JV 44.

————

To the crewmen of Robinson's group, it was as if Hell had suddenly opened its sulphurous mouth and spewed out a flock of demons. The flak was a heavy, boiling cloud. Chunks of metal tore through the airplanes and rattled against fuselages. *And right through the black cloud came those swift, ghostlike apparitions without propellers.*

The interphone instantly became a babble of frenzied voices reporting 262s and flak and falling bombers. Robinson sharply ordered the crewmen to lower their voices, to stop reporting casualties except within their own ship, to warn only of attacking fighters. But it proved of little help; attacking fighters were coming from all directions.

The ship shook with the thunder of the guns and the crack of exploding flak. A cannon shell ripped through the waist and exploded in O'Kane's chest, showering the interior with blood and bits of flesh and clothing. Weaver, blood-streaked and shocked, stood motionless at his gun position. Google stalked to him and shoved him toward his waist gun. Moving to O'Kane's gun, Google found it shattered. O'Kane was dead beside it and there was nothing Google could do to help.

"Bombardier to pilot; I've got it," Fisk said evenly. From his position in the nose, he took control of the autopilot and steered it, with minute corrections, onto the final bomb run. The open bomb bay doors created a heavy drag through the windstream and blasts of frigid air filled the cabin.

"How many of the lead group do we have left?" Sutter asked.

Robinson looked about. "At a guess, about a third of us. At least the bastards seem to be out of rockets. We're only two minutes from bombs away."

He shifted to the group radio frequency. "Close up! Close up! Do it now!" he ordered. The remnants of the lead, high and low squadrons moved toward the leader to form a single battered squadron for the bombing run. Every man knew that, without a tight and accurate bomb strike, all of the blood and horror would be wasted.

As Robinson spoke, an ME 109 deliberately rammed a nearby B-17 head-on. He watched the fighter plow into the nose, peeling the bomber's fuselage away like a banana. The fighter's wings folded and stuck amidships with the dead pilot. But the hot engine and its spinning propeller tore through the length of the bomber, slowly grinding the airplane and its crew to bits.

"Oh my God," someone said quietly.

A gray-green 262 whistled past the nose and a heavy explosion shook the airplane. The B-17 lurched and yawed. Robinson quickly adjusted the autopilot and returned to course.

"Pilot to nose. What happened?"

"Cannon shell," Doroshkin gasped. "Came through sideways. A piece hit Fisk, knocked him down. He's crawling back to the bombsight."

"Are we still on course?"

"On course." The answer, a whisper, was Fisk's. "Hold steady, please." A moment passed. "Bombs . . ."

"Are we bombs away?" Robinson demanded. "I say . . ."

"Bombs away!" The voice was Doroshkin's. "I'm closing the bomb bay doors. Fisk is down. I think he's had it."

"I've got the control now. We're turning off the target."

"Tail to pilot. A 262 at six. Coming fast." A gray-green object shot past. A cannon shell slammed through the back of the cabin and exploded. The blast threw Robinson into the controls like a rag doll. His chest struck the wheel yoke heavily. The B-17 nosed over momentarily; leaning back, he pulled it level. He felt a sharp pain in his chest and had to gasp for breath. *Broken ribs.* The B-17 began to turn to the left. He looked sideways. No. 1 engine was dead. Oil spurted from the nacelle; the propeller was windmilling.

"Feather One!" he grunted. Nothing happened. He turned to his right. Where General Sutter had been sat a headless torso. Robinson punched the button to feather the propeller on the disabled engine, stopping the turning blades and turning them sideways to minimize drag.

"Pilot to top turret!" he called. "Give me a hand . . ." He looked behind. Claiborne had slid out of the turret and was sprawled on the cabin floor. His face and chest were covered with blood.

"Pilot to . . ." A hand touched his shoulder. Google, his face encased in a mask and oxygen bottle, pulled Sutter's body from the right seat and moved into it. He plugged in the oxygen and intercom leads, found them working, nodded at Robinson and took the controls.

"Left waist to pilot. A 262 at three, level. Turning in. I'm going to try to get the bastard this time." The thunder of guns filled the ship momentarily. They ended abruptly as a cannon shell landed amidships. The jet whistled past again.

Robinson told the crew to check in. Fisk was dead in the nose, Sutter and Claiborne in the cockpit. O'Kane was dead and Weaver was badly injured in the waist. Doroshkin could still man the nose guns, Hebert the single radio gun, Steiner the tail guns. Furman didn't answer in the belly turret. Because of the repeated attacks, no one could leave his station to investigate or help. They were unprotected now from below and, if the belly turret wasn't working, from either side.

Robinson craned his head to look outside. Google saw what he was doing and depressed his mike button. "Looks like six or seven left in our group. If we take any more damage, we're gonna have to hit the deck. Get down in the treetops."

———

Enraged, Moltke swung the jet around in a circle and banked over at 90 degrees. Despite all the damage they had soaked up—the lead bomber group had been nearly decimated and could do little harm by itself—the remnants of the formation had led the bomber stream to the target. Their smoke bombs, dropped along with the high-explosive bomb load, trailed eerily to the ground from the spot at which they had been released. The Germans called the ugly markers "the fingers of death."

And here came the parade of beetles to bomb on them. Despite shattering attacks by the jets, destruction of the formations and ruinous follow-up attacks by the FWs and 109s—even deliberate rammings—the tidal wave of bombers rolled forward. There were simply too many to be killed off by the Luftwaffe force available. And the prop jets, with largely inexperienced pilots flying them, were being picked off, one by one, by the enormous swarms of Mustangs and Thunderbolts. Even some of the jets had gone down through collisions, lucky hits and mechanical malfunctions. A year earlier, it would have been different, but the Führer's crazy order had denied them the opportunity to strike the bombers with 1,000 jets and change the course of the war.

Red tracers reached out to Moltke's 262 from a marauding Mustang and he banked away, ignoring the fighter as he would a flea. As he watched, the oncoming masses of B-17s rolled over the JV-44 base and carpet-bombed it from one end to the other. The whole site erupted as if it had been mined from beneath with thousands of tons of dynamite. Succeeding waves of bombers came on and dropped their loads in the still-boiling cauldron below.

It was all disappearing before his eyes. Now there would be no safe place to land. Even if they could touch the ground without tripping over bomb craters and crashing, there would be no fuel, no parts, no qualified mechanics, not even a bed and food. Nothing. No future. The jets still aloft were—he grasped for an analogy—butterflies, or as Steinhoff had once said, dayflies, destined to flutter beautifully for a day and then, without the capacity to feed, expire.

He had never doubted this could happen. He might even have accepted it if he had had the satisfaction of destroying the lead group. But that had been denied him too. Now there was nothing left to do but kill as many of the enemy as he could in the minutes left to him. Perhaps the last bomber downed would raise the toll high enough to shock the Americans into suspending the bombing. Absent that, there was only revenge. He looked around. Great clouds of smoke and dust hung in the sky, but the battle was largely over. The bombers had dropped their bombs and turned toward home. Some of the American fighters were still on the scene, diving and firing on the hopelessly outnumbered 109s and FWs.

The German boys had done the best they could. And now, Moltke realized, a new sound was coming through the headphones. It was still Wagner, but something entirely different: the *Götterdämmerung,* the

twilight of the Gods. Moltke laughed angrily. It was entirely appropriate.

His fuel supply was low now but he still had a few cannon shells in
the ammunition compartment. He swung the jet westward to overtake
the fleeing bombers. He still had one score to settle: the lead bomber of
the lead group. By now the desire to destroy it amounted to an obses-
sion. He would ignore any accompanying fighters. If one hit him, so be
it. He had enough ammunition and fuel left to fight a single airplane,
and he wanted the leader of this murderous air army before the day,
and the dayfly, expired.

Moltke found the survivors of the lead group within five minutes.
First, it was important to be sure he had the right airplane. He pointed
the nose down and dived through the formation. *Yes.* There was a large
triangle on the tail with the English letter H inside it. Painted on the
side of the nose were two words. Moltke knew enough English to
recognize the word *Sweet.* The second word was a woman's name.
*Susan* or *Sally* or the British name *Sandra.* This was his enemy.

He pulled up, sailed well ahead of the formation and turned back. A
head-on attack was an elegant aerial maneuver, one in which the skillful Luftwaffe pilots had always taken pleasure in their FWs and 109s.
The ME 262 was considered much too fast to make such an attack and
then split-S in a half loop in front of the bomber. Well, he would see.
He wanted his last attack to be a testament to his skill.

Moltke leveled out to make a straight run at the nose of the B-17.
As he raced toward the bomber, he rolled the jet onto its back, pushing
the stick forward to hold his altitude. Upside down, the 262 screamed
toward the nose of the big brown bomber. Rapidly, the target grew
large. Winks of light began flashing from the chin of the B-17. Moltke
pressed his firing button and pulled the stick sharply back, falling out, a
few scant feet from the B-17, into a half-loop. As he did, centrifugal
force squashed him in his seat and something struck the jet a heavy
blow.

———

Two cannon shells tore the nose off the B-17, blowing it into an open,
gutted tunnel and killing Doroshkin. The bomber rose almost verti-

cally, stalled and fell off on one wing. It was spiraling downward when Robinson came to. The pain was intense. His left leg was wet with blood and his knee seemed to be smashed. With Google's help, he gradually slowed the dive. When he tried to level out, Google shook his head and shouted at him.

"Oxygen gone! Got to go down! Down!" He jabbed his gloved downward and pressed the wheel forward. The two pilots stood the big airplane on its nose. The airspeed indicator began winding up. *200, 220, 250, 275, 300.* The airspeed indicator went past the redline. The wings could shear off any minute. They also could be blown off by the malevolent 262. But where was he?

They leveled off just above the topmost branches of a stand of tall trees, both pilots tugging at the wheel. Google turned the trimming wheel to trim the airplane into a crablike attitude to compensate for the dead engine on the port side and to minimize the blast of air from the shattered nose. The three engines, pushed to full throttle and cranking at emergency war power, bellowed discordantly.

Robinson moved painfully in his seat. His breath came short against his damaged ribs; his shattered knee burned and throbbed. He pushed the mike button. "Pilot to crew. Where's the bandit?"

Hebert responded. "Radio to pilot. He's at four o'clock high and a mile or so out. He's sort of wobbling around out there as if he's got some kind of trouble. Nobody else in sight."

Google told the crew to check in. It was a brief communication. Besides the two pilots, Hebert was alive in the radio compartment and Steiner had survived in the tail. When Furman failed again to answer, Hebert left his position long enough to check on him. The answer was a short one. "Belly turret's gone. Shot away."

"Tail to pilot. The bandit's sliding around our tail, out of my range. Looks like he's coming round your side, pilot."

"Roger," Robinson said. A feeling of calm settled over him. *Let him come.*

———

Moltke looked at the flying wreck of the bomber in anger and admiration. He couldn't imagine having to sit there and take the punishment the crew had endured. The airplane itself was incredibly durable. He could think of nothing else in any air force that could take such a pounding and still fly. The nose was an open hole. The No. 1 engine was a blackened hulk and No. 2 was leaking oil over the wing. There was a gaping hole at the rear of the pilots' cabin and another, so large the fuselage should have split in two, amidships. Holes and rents appeared through the length of the fuselage. A third of the vertical stabilizer was gone. Yet the airplane flew, and now the bomber was lumbering along just above the trees, which made an attack by a faster aircraft hazardous for the attacker.

Still, this would have presented no real problem, Moltke knew, if it hadn't been for his own damage. The bomber's 50-caliber machine gun bullets, which had a greater range than the 262's cannon shells, had smashed the jet's port engine. The 262 still flew, but its lovely, unmatchable speed was gone. So was its graceful maneuverability. It would be difficult just to stay aloft.

Moltke turned the jet slowly to the right to make a beam-on attack on the pilot. The bomber's chin, top and belly turrets were gone, and so were the waist guns. Neither the single gun pointing rearward from the radio compartment nor the tail gun could protect the B-17.

Robinson watched through his side window as the jet swung around to attack him. Moving instinctively, he turned his wheel to the left to spoil the German's aim. It wasn't fast enough. The jet roared over the cockpit. Robinson shut his eyes, waiting for the explosion. Nothing happened. He opened them.

"He didn't fire!" Google shouted. He had never heard Google shout before. "He's got a jam. Or he's out of ammunition!"

Moltke shook his head in frustration as the jet sailed away from the B-17. The fire-control system was dead. Now even the cannons were useless. He looked at his fuel gauge. It showed empty. He made a wide turn to the right to circle the bomber again. There was only one thing left to do. But first he would close in and take a look at the pilot. He wanted to see the face of his nemesis. Careful to avoid the bomber's tail guns, he slid around to the left of the B-17 again and skidded carefully to the right until he was flying formation on the bomber. He dropped his wheels to slow himself to the bomber's speed. The jet mushed, nose up, through the heavy air, as it closed in on the B-17's cockpit. The 262 was very hard to fly in this manner. But he was a skillful pilot; he would manage. Slowly, Moltke stripped his helmet and goggles from his head.

Robinson felt as if he were flying in a surrealist dream. The German outside seemed to be trying to speak to him, to say something urgently important, he couldn't imagine what. And then he realized that the man wanted to look at him. Robinson pulled off his helmet, the useless oxygen mask still attached to it. Then he took off his sunglasses.

The jet staggered in so close he could see the German clearly. He would never forget the pale face that looked back at him. It was topped with dark hair, like his. It was slim and heavy-browed, like his. The eyes were wide-set; the nose was prominent, the mouth was full. All like his. He shut his eyes and opened them again. Was it his imagination? Was he in shock from his wounds? A chill shot through him. The portrait in Aunt Adda's living room had come alive and, in some unfathomable way, he and the man in it were peering at each other through a distorted mirror. The German's jaw dropped and he stared at Robinson, nearly losing control of the jet. The man nodded slowly, gravely, his face twisting in anguish. He looked as if he were about to cry. Then his eyes widened and his mouth opened.

"Look out!" Google shouted. "He's going to ram . . ."

Google wrenched the wheel to the left and stamped the left rudder with all his strength. The jet missed the B-17's flight deck and side-swiped the inside starboard engine. There was a terrible rending of metal. The bomber slewed violently and tried to roll over. Robinson and Google fought the controls. The B-17 clipped the branches of a tall tree, yawed helplessly for a moment and then leveled out. Google instinctively tried to feather the No. 3 engine, but it was pointless. The engine was hanging dead on its mount. A huge rent had been gouged in the wing. Beyond, Robinson and Google saw the German cart-wheeling over the trees.

Locked into his crushed cockpit with the world spinning crazily before his eyes, Moltke tried to pluck a last thought out of the chaos. His mind raced, flipping through the things worth remembering. The early days, the great times, his dead comrades, the tragic war, the *doppelganger* in the bomber, his ruined nation. *Elise.* The 262 plunged into a grove and exploded. The world became orange and then faded to black. Robinson, looking back at the smoke, felt relief and an incomprehensible sense of loss.

# CHAPTER TWELVE

# Last Landing

**T**HE torn and blackened B-17 staggered westward across Germany a few feet above the ground. The two working engines bellowed discordantly; the wind whistled through the open nose.

Robinson sat quietly, his hands in his lap, as Google flew. His chest ached and his knee burned as if someone was holding a red-hot poker to it. But it subsided into a dull ache after Hebert came forward at Google's order and jabbed a morphine syringe through Robinson's coveralls into his left thigh. The physical sensation matched Robinson's mental state. His mind groped sluggishly, like a blind marine creature seeking to understand what lay around it.

It had been a climactic battle that had become strangely and intensely personal. Robinson's thoughts rose to the surface and he considered the phenomenon. Throughout all of the fighting, neither he nor any other crewman he had known had ever confronted an enemy face to face. To them, the war, though bloody, was impersonal. A line from Henry VI flickered through his mind: *Oft have I struck those that I never saw /and struck them dead.*

Today, this last day, he had seen a face and, through some disordered working of his stunned and weary mind, it had become his own. Who was the strange man in the German jet with the familiar face who cared so much, and what was it he cared about? Robinson's mind settled into repose. The questions were beyond understanding. The battle. The man. The war. The fear. Himself.

"Spring is coming, Skipper."

The words roused him and Robinson looked to his right. Google, bareheaded, his face shining with sweat as he struggled to control the disabled airplane, was smiling at him. The big yellow eyes were larger than he had ever seen them.

"See those trees?" Google motioned with his head. "The tops are turning green. The grass down there; it's turning green, too." They thundered across a pasture and over a field of brown earth, making a farmer's plowhorse shy and spoiling the furrow. The farmer looked up at them, shading his eyes with his hand.

"Look at the cows over there," Google said. "And those nice little towns. Nice to see something that hasn't been wrecked."

"We wrecked Munich," Robinson said dully.

"We sure did."

"Joyce and Noonan got it there. Fighter attack '43."

Google nodded.

"Ulm," Robinson said.

"We passed it during the fight."

"Pellegrini got it at Ulm. Gas tank blew."

They sat silently in the howling of the wind and the engines.

"Nurnberg's up north," Robinson said.

"Northeast, yeah."

"Polderman," Robinson said, taking a deep breath. "Parachute bomb blew up in the formation. Nurnberg was a tank factory, I think. It's hard to remember what was there—in those places."

"You remember all the men, though."

"Yes. The men."

"We passed Stuttgart a while ago," Google offered.

"Bobby went down at Stuttgart. So did Montgomery. Collision."

"That's probably Ludwigshafen over there, what's left of it."

"We hit the marshalling yards there, twice, I think, in three days. A ground rocket got Campbell and Kaufman. And their crews. I should have mentioned the crews."

Google looked at the man beside him. "Up north there, Frankfurt."

Robinson started. "Frankfurt. We aimed at the clock tower. Best way to miss it, given normal error. It was the only thing left standing. Larson was hit over the target."

"I think that's the Mosel up ahead," Google said, peering through the oil-smeared windscreen. "We should be crossing the Ardennes in a bit. We flew that raid last Christmas, remember? When the Germans made that counterattack."

Robinson nodded. "Weather was bad. Got everybody screwed up. Planes landing all over England. Merrick got it . . ."

"A barrage balloon. On the way back."

"Yeah."

Google nodded toward the right, his face glistening. "We ought to hit the channel just south of Antwerp. That'll give me a fix."

"We blundered over Antwerp that day. Came out of the undercast and it was right below us. They got McElroy and Pekkinen."

Google grunted. "I'd sure like to put the lady down on this side of the channel, but we're going to need a long, long runway. We've got no hydraulics, probably no brakes, probably no landing gear. Too low to bail out and we can't climb." *And you sitting here like a dead man,* Google thought. *I'd never be able to get you out.*

Google grimaced. "Gonna get Darky to vector us to Landhaven, Skipper. Twenty-five thousand feet long. You can roll forever. Always wanted to land there. That fog dispersal system they've got. They burn gasoline in those open troughs, right beside the runway." He grinned painfully. "Damned clever, those Limeys."

Robinson stirred. "There were other places."

"Sure," Google grunted. "Berlin, Kassel, Schweinfurt, Regensberg, Hamburg, you name it."

Robinson frowned, distressed. "So many. Hard to remember all the people."

"Lost a lot of people in those places, Colonel. Tell you what. When we get back, we'll get a list and check it off, if you want. Then you'll remember them all."

Robinson nodded, his face relaxing.

They left the continent. The cold, choppy waters of the channel lay beneath them now. Google looked at the engine gauges. No. 2 was running hot and the B-17 was losing altitude inch by inch. Spray spattered the windscreen. They were flying only a few feet above the water. Barney pushed the throttles hard against the stops. Hebert was throwing everything possible from the airplane—guns, ammunition, supplies. It was as light as it was going to get. They were barely skimming the waves as they approached the chalk cliffs of England. Abruptly, the underside of the airplane struck the water. Miraculously, it bounced high in the air. Leveling out, Barney laughed aloud. They had gained nearly 100 feet. If they could just hold it.

Barney told Steiner to join Hebert in the radio compartment. He would be safer there than in the tail. Then he switched to England's distress frequency and asked for a bearing to Landhaven.

"Roger, B-17 calling," answered a clear-voiced WAF. "Steer 270 degrees for two minutes and look for a flare."

"Roger, Darky," Google said, carefully turning the B-17 to the new compass heading. A flare burst in the sky ahead. Landhaven's incredible runway came into view.

Barney felt a new pressure on the wheel. He turned to Robinson. The colonel looked like a man trying to wake from a deep sleep. "I'll take it in," Robinson said. "Last time."

Google looked at him and then nodded. "We'll take it in together, Colonel. Last time for both of us. I'll follow you through on the controls."

"Straight in," Robinson said. "Gear down."

Barney flicked the landing gear switch. "Negative. No landing gear. Have to make a belly landing beside the runway."

They approached the runway. "Flaps down," Robinson said.

"Flaps going down, maybe. Flaps half down."

"Full flaps."

"Negative. Don't have full flaps. We'll have to go in fast."

Google called the Landhaven controller, telling him tersely that they were coming in fast.

"Ball turret up?" Robinson asked.

"Ball turret's gone. Take it straight in now. As soon as we touch, I'll cut the switches. Begin flaring out now."

Carefully, gently, Google helped Robinson ease the wheel back. With his other hand, he pulled the throttles closed. The controllers in the Landhaven tower watched tensely as the battered wreck approached. It mushed, nose-up, to kill its speed, then settled into the foot-high grass beside the concrete strip. At 110 miles an hour, the belly touched the ground, rose a foot, touched again, scraped and began plowing through the grass and dirt.

The two working engines screamed in final agony as the long propellers gouged great chunks of earth from the ground and then bent backwards against the cowlings. Google and Robinson held the wheel back in their laps, like riders trying to rein in a monstrous horse. They stared straight ahead; there was nothing else to do. The airplane slid another fifty yards, groaning and shuddering. Then, abruptly, it plowed to a halt.

"Hold on!" Google shouted. As he knew it would, the B-17 nosed over, the torn nose catching in the soft earth. The hulk teetered, tail high in the air for a moment, and then fell backwards, breaking in two at the waist gun positions. Google slapped the switches shut and looked down through his feet. Tall blades of grass were sticking up through rents in the bottom of the airplane. The smell of gasoline spread through the cabin and, for the first time, he could smell the blood of the dead general that was caked on his coveralls.

"C'mon, Colonel. Get out now," Google said. "Through the nose. If you can't, I'll get out first and pull you out."

Google heard the sirens approaching. Looking around, he saw people coming from what seemed like every point of the compass. In firetrucks, ambulances, lorries, jeeps, even bicycles. People in asbestos suits and helmets were outside now, reaching through the window and nose, lifting Robinson to safety.

Barney Google clambered out, ignoring the shouting people around him, nodding at Hebert and Steiner, who wanted to shake his hand and thank him. He walked away a dozen yards and then turned and sat down in the grass and looked at the wrecked airplane. He smiled broadly and slowly shook his head. He felt like crying. It had all been so—so *majestic*. There had never been anything like it before; there would never be anything like it ever again. He was sorry about his crewmates losing their present lives, though they would return again in other forms. But the razor's edge of difference between what they called life and death was what gave combat its incredible beauty. He had loved every minute of it.

# CHAPTER THIRTEEN

# The Price

THE Supreme Commander grimaced briefly when the call came from the Prime Minister. The Berlin decision, which had strained their relationship so sorely, was now behind them and he hoped it wouldn't come up again. To his relief, Churchill opened with a different subject.

"My dear Ike," the PM said over the scrambled line, "I've just been talking to Bomber Harris here. As you know, with the Luftwaffe gone, our RAF boys have been bombing cities by daylight. But I really see no point in piling ruin on ruin. In my view, further destruction of German cities will only magnify the problems of our occupation forces. May I take it that you agree?"

"Agree completely, Prime Minister," Eisenhower said. "We'll be overrunning these same cities on the ground very shortly now. As a matter of fact, Spaatz has been shifting our heavy bombers to ground support missions for our army groups. If you concur, we'll issue a joint statement declaring that strategic bombing is at an end."

"I concur and I'll leave it to you to issue such a statement," Churchill said. There was a short pause as he apparently struggled with and yielded to the temptation to bring up the sensitive topic once again. "I understand that the Soviets are hitting Berlin hard from the air just now, as well as with their ground batteries. The city will fall, I should think, within a matter of days, perhaps hours."

"Yes, it seems that way," Eisenhower said carefully. Nothing more was said about Berlin and the conversation soon ended. Eisenhower pondered for a moment and then, swiveling toward the door, shouted: Lee!" When his aide bounced into the room, Eisenhower said: "Get Tooey Spaatz on the phone for me. I want him to issue a statement. The heavy bombing is over."

Smoke was rising in the east and the rumble of artillery was growing steadily louder. Reichsmarshall Hermann Göring listened to it for a moment, muttered a curse and pulled the master switch. He watched with pleasure as the wheels of the locomotive turned, picked up speed and began pulling the line of cars over the tracks and through the bridge toward the town. He closed the switch as the train pulled even with the station and the locomotive stopped precisely by the semaphore.

The Reichsmarshall loved the model railroad that stretched across the spacious attic of Karinhall, his palatial hunting lodge an hour from Berlin. He looked at it for a long moment and then beckoned to the two Luftwaffe soldiers who had been standing patiently in the doorway. Behind them in the hallway lay a stack of boxes and crates.

"All right," Göring said. "Pack it up. But mind you don't damage it. Make it fast, though."

He had wanted to play with the train a bit longer, but time was becoming a factor. The massive Russian forces would soon cut through von Mantueffel's Third Panzer Army like butter and overrun the area; shells could start falling on the estate at any time. If the Russians knew it was here, they would already be shelling it. He struggled to his feet and waddled slowly downstairs. Luftwaffe soldiers under the command of a shouting sergeant had already packed his paintings and furniture and antique silver and hunting trophies and were loading the crates onto twenty-four Luftwaffe trucks that were lined up by the front entrance.

The Reichsmarshall was well aware of what his fellow officers would say if they knew he had commandeered trucks and precious gasoline for personal use while tanks were being abandoned and Luftwaffe planes were grounded due to lack of fuel. But that was all beside the point now; one had to look out for oneself. He watched as his trunks of uniforms were being carried down the walkway. He had hidden his jewel box beneath the clothes in one of them.

Göring turned toward the trophy room and saw a corporal carefully packing his hunting rifles in a long box that had been made for them. "Wait a minute," he said. He picked up his favorite rifle, ran his fingers lovingly over the gold inlay, hefted it and then handed it back to the corporal.

Thirty minutes later, the truck convoy, flanked by armed motorcyclists, headed south. Göring stayed behind with an engineering officer and two aides. When the convoy disappeared in the distance, he took one last look at Karinhall and blew it a kiss. Then he walked across the road, bent over a detonator and pressed the plunger. There was an enormous blast and his magnificent masonry castle slowly collapsed into ruins.

He looked at the engineering officer and smiled. "When you're a crown prince, sometimes you have to do things like this." He climbed into his Mercedes and ordered the driver to take off. As he relaxed against the leather upholstery, his fleshy face contorted in a frown. He would drive south and find a safe place to wait for the Americans. But what uniform should he wear when he met Eisenhower?

———

The news announced over the radio by the War Ministry sent Londoners into the street to celebrate. Some, disregarding stern warnings from the air raid wardens, began ignoring the blackout rules. It wasn't the end of the war, certainly, but it was an important auger of victory: there had been no civilian deaths due to bombing or rocket attacks in all of England during the past month. The bottle clubs were packed that night with British and American revelers singing and dancing to

"The Lambeth Walk." Late in the evening, they embraced each other and danced slowly to "Lilli Marlene," the song that was popular in both England and Germany. There was a feeling of freedom and safety in London that hadn't been felt in years.

——

During the same evening, Beethoven Hall was filled with somber music lovers to hear the last performance of the Berlin Philharmonic. The orchestra played *Götterdämmerung* with a passion that had seldom been heard before. At the climactic moment, the majestic chords of the brasses and the crashing of the kettledrums signaled the collapse of Valhalla and the death of the gods themselves. The enormous volume of sound drowned out, at least for a few moments, the whining and booming of Russian shells that had begun landing just a few blocks away.

——

Next morning, the 100-foot-high, heavily fortified flak tower that dominated Berlin's zoological gardens took a terrible battering from Russian artillery and the howling *Katushka* rockets. How the poor people inside it were able to stand the shock and noise was beyond her understanding. And there was a constant danger of an errant shell or rocket striking her nearby apartment building.

Nevertheless, sitting at the dining table in her flat, Dr. Margot Hoffman determinedly served her friend, Ilse Buchwald, a lunch of sausage and lentils that had been made possible by the allotment of an extra food ration, apparently in celebration of the Führer's birthday. Afterwards, crouching and starting whenever a shell landed close by, they sipped the coffee they had been hoarding separately, ounce by ounce, over the preceding weeks. They were careful to leave a little in the bottom of their cups. Then, kissing and wishing each other Godspeed, each of them swallowed a cyanide pill.

——

In the pock-marked tower fortress, thousands of hysterical civilians were packed together on the floors and stairways. The place reeked of sweat, human waste, urine, disinfectant and rotting bodies. More than a thousand were dead, some of them casualties of the shelling and some of them suicides. The shelling was so intense that it had become impossible to take the bodies outside.

Stacks of amputated limbs spilled out of containers in the operating room of the tower's hospital. The crashing of high-explosives against the walls and steel shutters was almost intolerable. But escape had become impossible. The only options left were to surrender and run the risk of a massacre or hope that a German or American army would arrive and end the siege.

————

Below the tower and a few hundred meters distant, zoo keeper Otto Naumann looked despairingly at the carnage. Shells had been landing at random in the zoo all morning. Birds were flying in all directions; some, crippled, were dragging themselves along the ground. Nearby, in the shattered monkey house, a baboon screamed in anguish. There was no food, no electricity, no water for the aquatic animals. Soon they would die. Seeing that the lion cages were damaged, he had shot five of the animals. The experience had so sickened him that he had resolved never to do such a thing again.

A sixth lion, a magnificently maned male named Wotan, was pacing his cage, roaring incessantly in fear and anger. Wotan was Naumann's favorite and he knew the animal must be terribly hungry. Yet he had nothing to feed him and, when the Russians arrived, they would almost certainly give Wotan a bullet rather than meat.

"What can I give you, my dear?" Naumann asked. "There is nothing left." But there was, and in a dreadful instant he knew what it had to be. It was simple justice. Naumann closed his eyes and quietly said a prayer. Then, speaking reassuringly to the angry lion, he slowly undressed. When he was naked, he walked to the door of the cage, unlocked it and stepped inside. He just had time to pull the door shut behind him.

————

It was time. Life in the Führerbunker would serve no further purpose. The barbarians had won. Russian tanks and troops were only a block away. They had occupied the Tiergarten and reached Potsdamer Platz. A few things remained to be done. The Supreme Commander ordered that his beloved Alsatian, Blondi, be destroyed. Then he lined up the members of his staff in the passageway and shook hands with each man and woman, bidding each goodbye. At two o'clock in the afternoon, he took lunch with two of his secretaries and his vegetarian cook. It was one of his favorite meals—spaghetti with a light tomato sauce. His bride, Eva Hitler, née Braun, remained in her room.

After lunch, he returned to the Führer's suite and closed the door. He and Eva embraced and carried out the plan they had agreed on. They sat down and said a last goodbye. She placed a cyanide pill in her mouth and quickly drank a half glass of water. As she did, he raised his .380 Walther semiautomatic pistol to his head and pulled the trigger.

———

In the fog of war, particularly on a shrinking battlefield and when the conflict is in its final agony, communications break down and it becomes hard to tell friend from foe. So it was that a flight of surviving German prop fighters fell upon a convoy of German trucks driving south and strafed them mercilessly, destroying seven and forcing the others off the road.

A few miles distant, a squadron of British Typhoon fighter-bombers came upon a column of British prisoners-of-war who had just been released from a prison camp and, thinking they were German troops, bombed and strafed them, killing scores.

And fifty miles to the west, American Mustangs mistook low-flying American twin-engined bombers for German JU-88s and shot down three of them before they realized their mistake.

———

It was quiet, eerily quiet, in the English Midlands. At the dawn of nearly every morning for the past three years, thousands of airplane engines had coughed, bellowed and roared throughout the region like a fantastic assemblage of predatory beasts. Now, sitting in his jeep at the end of the 205th's long runway, Major Ed Carlino heard only the sighing of the wind through the trees in the rolling hills beyond the empty base. He had never heard the sound before. It was strange but not unpleasant; the day would be sunny and the spring air was warm and fragrant with the promise of rebirth. Yet he felt confused and restive.

For the twentieth time he pulled the piece of teletype paper out of the pocket of his leather jacket and smoothed it on his knee. It was two weeks old but he was still carrying it around to remind himself that it was true. The message was signed by General Carl Spaatz.

*The advances of our ground forces have brought to a close the strategic air war waged by the United States Strategic Air Forces and the Royal Air Force Bomber Command.*

Most of the bomber groups, he knew, had been flying mid- and low-level ground support missions, much to the alarm and disgust of the air crews. Neither the B-17 nor the B-24 Liberator had been designed for such a role. But that experience was a brief one; those operations had shut down, too. At this moment, heavy bombers were clearly unnecessary in the European Theater of Operations. The mission boards that covered the walls of the war planning room were empty; Carlino had never seen them empty before.

At some airfields, there had been isolated tours of bombed-out battlefields and cities for members of ground crews. They took off exhilarated and came back appalled.

The 205th had been exempt from all duty since the Munich-Reim raid for the simple reason that the group had been decimated—airplanes and crews alike. Only five B-17s had returned to the base that day; four more, including Robinson's and Google's ship, had landed or crash-landed elsewhere and survived. Most of the surviving personnel were already in Liverpool, waiting for a ship to take them home. Google had been given a B-17 to ferry home to Langley Field in Virginia via Gander Field in Newfoundland. Before he left, Carlino invited him to have a last drink at the officers' club. "Barney," he said, dropping the detachment of rank, "this group owes you a great deal, even if you have been a royal pain in the ass at times." He laughed. "Of course, that was probably all to the good, too. It lightened things up a bit around here. I was ready to kill you, and I mean literally, after we had settled the business with your dog and then you brought that goddamned cow into the noncoms' mess hall and milked it and it shat all over the floor. But, God knows, you saved Mitch Robinson and those two other guys that day. I owe you personally for that."

"How is the Colonel?" Google asked.

Carlino's smile faded and he looked into his gin-and-lime.

"Well, physically, he's going to be okay fairly soon, I think. Of course they did reconstructive surgery on that knee and it's going to take a lot of therapy before it's anywhere near what it was. Mentally, that's another question. The psychiatrist up at Diddington said that Amundson's death pretty well took the life out of him and then that last raid, and that weird encounter with that 262 pilot seems to have affected him. Frankly, I don't think that psychiatrist knows anymore about it than we do."

Carlino looked at Google appraisingly. "In some ways, you know more about all this than anybody. What do *you* think?"

Google's large eyes blinked and became reflective. He knew what he had seen but he wasn't about to discuss it with a conventional-minded Westerner, not even the major. A certain kind of German would understand—after all, a deep vein of mysticism ran through the German character. Adolf Hitler had intuitively tapped into it; without it, he never could have mesmerized the German people as he did. And it was the Germans who had created the legend of the *doppelganger,* the phantom double. But the concept of multiple incarnations was distinctly Eastern. In some way, perhaps, the Wheel had altered its cycle. But there was more harm than good in trying to understand it. As the opening words of the *Lao tzu* said: *The way that can be spoken of is not the constant way. The name that can be named is not the constant name.* So he chose other words from the *Lao tzu* to answer Carlino.

"There's an old saying that if you temper a sword to its very sharpest, the edge will break." He paused and said slowly: "I think that Colonel Robinson has to start over, to find the way . . ."

"The way?" Carlino asked.

"To come back. Or become—whatever he'll become. It's nothing that anyone else can do."

It seemed an unsatisfactory explanation to Carlino at the time, but, the more he thought about it, it made a strange kind of sense. And it became the gist of what he told Sandra when they met for lunch in the old dining room of The Swan in Bedford. She was distraught, which didn't surprise him.

"When I saw him in the hospital," she said, her voice trembling, "it was as if there was some sort of barrier between us, as if I was trying to communicate with someone through a pane of glass. He smiled and was polite—the way we're polite to a stranger or acquaintance—not to a . . ."

"A lover," Carlino said gently.

"Yes, a *lover*," she said fiercely. "Perhaps I've been a fool to think it could last. But I told myself, he's been hurt very badly." She looked at him accusingly. "And now you'll be sending him home, and I shan't have a chance to be with him, to care for him." She groped for words. "To find out if we still—if something still remains of what I thought we had."

Carlino smiled and raised a hand as if to ward off a blow. "It's standard operating procedure, to send a wounded man home in cases like these. Not my decision or anybody else's." He leaned forward and looked at her earnestly. "I'll be going home soon myself, Sandra— Steubenville, Ohio, isn't all that far from Mahoning, Pennsylvania, you know—and I'll keep track of what's happening. But, right now, there's nothing either one of us can do for Mitch Robinson. As you say, he's been hurt, and only he can get over it. I'm afraid it's entirely up to him."

He took her slender hand in his stubby fingers and squeezed it gently. "But if what you and Mitch had was—is—real, it seems logical to think that it'll still be there when he recovers." *If he does.* "Meantime, my dear, we have to try to pick up the pieces of our own separate lives. It's all we can do."

He hadn't been of much comfort to her, he knew. Nor, for that matter, had he done much to calm his own confusion. He put the piece of paper back in his pocket, looked at the lovely rolling hills of the

English midlands and tried to analyze his feelings. It was as if he had been the deputy mayor of a thriving small city and suddenly, without warning, the city's principal employer had gone out of business and all the inhabitants, including the mayor, had been transported somewhere else. With them had gone his job, his very reason for being.

Was that a good analogy? No. There was no possible analogy to what had happened here, he decided, and there could never be one. The great masses of bombers had never been seen before and would never be seen again. Meantime, alone in a place abandoned by history, he had lost his vocation, and he felt profoundly adrift. He tried to tell himself that his feeling of disquiet was absurd; the base was closing down because the war was won. Wasn't that good news, the very best there could be? Yes, of course, he told himself, but it didn't allay his anxiety. He had been doing something important for more than three years; suddenly it and everyone associated with it was gone.

He would pack up and leave the following day and what would remain? Only weather-worn, empty buildings and oil-smeared runways. He would also leave behind—because he had to—the names of the men and missions that had been burned into the ceiling of the old officers' club. He didn't know what would happen to them; probably some clod would tear down the ceiling and throw it away with the rest of the debris when the base was put to another use.

Even so, Carlino felt—no, he *knew*—that it wasn't right for the base to be abandoned when the ceiling was missing the names of all the men who hadn't returned from Munich-Reim. If he left without seeing to it that the story told by the ceiling was complete, the names of those men would—well, they wouldn't actually *haunt* him, surely—*that* thought was ridiculous, but they would always *weigh* on him. They would always remind him, somehow, in odd, inconvenient moments, that he had had the opportunity—they would call it the responsibility —to add their names to the list and he hadn't done it.

Carlino shivered and swore at himself. He had always thought that it was Google who was the mystic. He started the jeep and drove to his office and picked up the casualty list. Then he walked to the officer's club. The place was empty when he arrived. He took off his jacket and tie and started looking for the tools he would need.

# CHAPTER FOURTEEN

# Mahoning

ROBINSON hobbled out to the side porch of the old house, stopping once to lean on his cane. He was dressed in chinos, loafers and the old blue mohair sweater that Aunt Adda had washed and put away for him.

Robinson had felt unprepared to see the Amundsons, though he knew he would have to do it eventually. Olaf Amundson, Lon's father, took the initiative. One week after Robinson returned to Mahoning, the elder Amundson came to the house with his younger son, Steve. Seeing Steve was a shock to Robinson. He remembered him as a mischievous, dirty-faced kid. Now Steve Amundson was a man, broad-shouldered and chunky, more like his father than his dead brother. But Mitch would have recognized the eyes anywhere. They were Lon's.

"We know what you tried to do for Lon, Mitch," Olaf Amundson said, sitting on Aunt Adda's tasseled sofa. "The Amundsons won't ever forget it." The old man's voice, slow and deliberate in its Scandinavian accent, faltered for a moment. "You tried to help my boy. Now we want to help you, any way we can."

Robinson tried to smile and reply. But his emotions, like his physical movements, were slow and sluggish.

The elder Amundson studied him for a moment. "You don't have to think about it now, Mitch," he said. "There's plenty of time. You look tired out. Thin, too. We want you to come out home for dinner Sunday noon. Will you do that?"

Robinson went because he knew he had to. It had been years since he had been to a Sunday dinner in Mahoning. He rummaged through his closet, looking for something to wear. His old sport coats hung on him. Finally he put on his cream-colored Army dress slacks and his dark brown jacket with the 8th Air Force shoulder patch, the silver pilot's wings, and the row of campaign and medal ribbons. It would be the last time he would wear it. It would be a sort of tribute to Lon, and he thought the Amundsons would recognize it as such.

When he arrived, Frances Amundson clung to him and cried. He patted her and murmured incoherent words in her hair. Olaf laughed and then wept briefly. Steve hugged him hard and grinned broadly, almost, Robinson realized, as if he were greeting his brother.

Before dinner, the men drank straight shots of rye whiskey at the kitchen sink. They were learning to sit at the country club bar and drink in mixed company, but the habit hadn't taken hold yet at home. Frances Amundson drank nothing till after dinner, when she joined them in a glass of her homemade elderberry wine.

The family nagged gently at Robinson to eat their mountainous menu of Scandinavian and rural Pennsylvania cooking. Atop the white tablecloth on the heavy red oak table Frances Amundson placed platters of herring and stuffed eggs and tiny spiced meatballs, a glazed ham, potatoes scalloped in cream with a crinkly brown crust on top, smoking ears of corn, tomatoes still warm from the sun, hot homemade rolls, a pound of unsalted butter and a flaky-crusted rhubarb pie.

At first dutifully, and then with appetite, Robinson ate until his shrunken stomach ached. After the meal, they sat on the front porch and watched the hill behind the country club change colors as big summer clouds sailed above it. He half-expected to see some kind of warplane fly out of them, but the sky remained wonderfully empty.

He realized that Olaf was talking to him. "Other side of that hill, we're going to put up some real nice houses," the older man said. "When you get so you can walk better, I want you to come out and take a look. This war, it's been like an earthquake here. So many people went away. The ones that stayed behind, they had to take over, no matter what kind of people they came from, what kinda work they'd been doin'.

"Then the young men began comin' back. Some of them. They had seen other places, *mixed*. They have new ideas about—oh, everything, the way we are to each other."

"What Pop is sayin' is that the old fences have come down," Steve volunteered. "Example, we belong to the country club now. Think about *that*. Swedes and Hunkies belonging to the *country club*!"

Except for occasional contacts with the Amundsons, Robinson stayed at home. He treasured the silence that hung over the house.

He slept heavily at night and sometimes during the day. In late afternoon, he would sit in the chair across from the one Aunt Adda had occupied. When the shaft of sunlight touched the Moltke portrait, his eyes would turn to it. He was sorry, though he wasn't sure what for.

After dark, he exercised the leg by walking uptown, keeping mainly to the back streets. He didn't want to talk to the townspeople. He knew it was irrational but he resented their innocent eyes and soft bodies. He had never known a fat pilot; now, obesity, even physical softness, repelled him.

Robinson tried to think about Sandra occasionally. It was as if she had been stored away somewhere, like a piece of beautiful sculpture that gathers dust in a museum because the curator hasn't found a place for it. There was no woman in Robinson's life until Donna arrived. Indirectly, her arrival was Frances Amundson's doing. Frances Amundson had engaged a cleaning woman to come to Robinson's house once a week to clean and wash and dust.

"You're not going to live in a pigsty, Mitch Robinson," she said. "I'm not going to let you." He almost said "Yes, Aunt Adda."

So a pudgy-faced, middle-aged woman named Aggie came to the house every Tuesday morning and flailed through upstairs and downstairs with bucket, mop, rags and carpet sweeper. Aggie was, Robinson realized, a remnant of Mahoning's one-time servant class. Now that she was emancipated from live-in labor, she free-lanced from house to house.

One Tuesday morning the doorbell rang and Robinson went to the front door to let her in. His heart leapt when he looked through the heavy glass pane. "Katie!" he said incredulously, pulling the door open. He realized his mistake as soon as he saw the girl clearly. To begin with, Katie would have been much older by now. And, though this girl had the same blooming skin, dark blond hair and blue eyes, she was taller and had an athletic physique.

She smiled as he stared at her. "I'm Donna," she said. "Aggie's niece. She's sick today so she sent me to do the cleaning. Can I come in?"

Robinson stepped back wordlessly and she walked past him and entered. He shook his head at his stupidity, thinking this young girl could have been Katie. Donna was wearing a striped sports shirt, denim skirt and sneakers.

Turning, she smiled. "You thought I was somebody else. Sorry to disappoint you." Her smile seemed to say she knew she could hardly disappoint any man.

"No, no," he said, feeling awkward. "I mean, it's fine. Please come in."

He hobbled into the study and sat down heavily in an armchair.

The rehabilitation program at Pittsburgh had helped a good deal, but there were days when the knee ached badly.

She watched him from the doorway. "Can I get you some coffee or anything, Colonel Robinson?"

He reacted instinctively. "Don't call me that, please."

"Mister Robinson, then? Mitch? Shall I call you Mitch?"

"Fine."

"Okay then, Mitch, can I get you something?"

He shook his head, embarrassed. "I've had breakfast. Besides, you don't have to wait on me. You came to . . ."

"I came because Aunt Aggie was sick, remember?" she said, hands on slim hips. "I don't mind waiting on you, Mitch. I wait on tables during the school year to pay my tuition and board at State and I do whatever work's available when I'm home in the summer." She paused and smiled. "Besides, I was glad, taking over for Aunt Aggie today."

"Why?"

"Because you're kind of a mystery man, y'know. The handsome war hero who comes home and lives alone in his big house. Kind of sad and romantic."

"Romantic."

"Uh-huh. Well, you're unusual, y'know, and there aren't many unusual people around. When there are, they stick out like . . ."

"A sore thumb."

"Like a handsome, mysterious war hero. Call me if you need anything." Smiling, she walked away and began cleaning the downstairs. Robinson picked up the Banner and tried to read it. Soon, he put his head back against the top of the chair and closed his eyes.

The girl was poking him gently in the shoulder, and he realized he had fallen asleep and the light in the room had changed. "I thought I oughta wake you. It's one o'clock, past time for din—lunch. I almost said 'dinner.' Like the local folks. Think you could make it back to the kitchen? It's nice and sunny there. I'll have a bite with you if you don't mind."

"Sure," he said, rubbing his eyes. When he arrived in the kitchen, she was setting the table. "Looks like Costanza's sent you down some fried chicken. That okay?"

"Fine," he said, sinking into one of the hard-backed kitchen chairs.

She laid out the chicken, cut up two potatoes and set them to frying in butter, and sliced one of the big beefsteak tomatoes that had come in the last bag of groceries.

"This is really great," she said. "What do you want to drink? There's some milk in there. And beer. What's that in the bottom of the frig?"

"A bottle of white wine, I think," he said. Steve Amundson had brought him a supply of beer and wine. "Open it if you want to."

She rolled her eyes and laughed. "This isn't exactly the cleaning lady's everyday lunch. But sure, why not?" She fished in the kitchen drawer for an opener and found two glasses in the cupboard. Pouring two glasses, she held one out to him, smiling, and raised the other. "I'll offer a toast. To a new friend."

They clinked glasses and he dutifully repeated the toast, feeling ridiculous, like an adolescent aping Bogart. *Here's looking at you, kid.*

Come to think of it, he thought, as the cold wine tingled in his mouth, she does look a little like a young Ingrid Bergman. He told her so.

"Oboy!" she laughed. "This is some day. I come to the mystery man's house to clean and I wind up drinking wine and being told I look like Ingrid Bergman. I oughta come here every day."

He toyed with his food and sipped at the wine while the girl ate heartily. A short time later, he was surprised to find that the bottle was empty. He didn't feel tight, just heavy and langorous. And uncoordinated. When he pushed the chair back to get up, the bad leg crumpled under him and he fell heavily to the linoleum floor.

"Oh Mitch!" Donna said, slipping to her knees beside him. "Are you all right?"

He straightened the leg gingerly and sat up. "I think so. The leg's a little unreliable sometimes. And I guess the wine got to me a little bit."

"Well," she said, rising, "let me pull you up. I'll help you upstairs so you can lie down. I think you can use a nap."

"I'm too heavy," he grunted, trying to get up.

She pulled him up strongly, threw his arm over her shoulder and slid an arm around his waist. "Listen, Hunkies may not be smart, but they're still strong."

"You're a—it's still called that? I don't even know your name."

"Bortz. It was shortened; no foundry foreman could have pronounced the old country name. Sure I'm a Hunkie. These days we're kinda proud of it." She swung around. "You gotta lotta bedrooms up here. Which one is yours? There? Okay, here we go."

They moved to the big bed together. He turned, hopped and sank into a sitting position. Donna stood over him, looking at him for a moment. She reached out and smoothed the hair from his eyes. Then, as if she had come to a decision, she gently pushed him backwards and slid down beside him. Her mouth, soft and warm, covered his. Slowly, still kissing him, she unbuttoned his shirt. When it lay open, her hand moved down his torso. He convulsed at her touch and then relaxed. Sensing no further response, she looked at him searchingly. Then she rose, slipped off her shirt and skirt, discarded her bra and peeled off a pair of lacy white pants.

Making a ceremony of the act, she pushed her long blond hair from her eyes, inhaling to make her athletic rib cage expand and her full breasts rise. The triangle of hair at her pelvis was dark blond. Her body was a rich tan except for white strips across her breasts and lower belly.

For a millisecond, he was transported to the day in London when he first looked at Sandra's body. She had protested at first; then, at his pleading, Sandra dropped her robe, threw her shoulders back, opened her arms and displayed herself for him. Donna was showing him her body proudly, on her own initiative.

"You have a beautiful body," he said.

She smiled. "I know. I think you're beautiful, too. I want to see more of you."

Moving to the bed, her long hair falling in her eyes, she stripped his trousers, shorts and sox from him. Then, deliberately, she eased herself atop him and began kissing him again. His hands closed lightly around her back and he softly returned her kisses. But the act was more friendly than amorous and she knew it. The warmth of her mouth was pleasant, but he remained passionless. After a few minutes, she stretched out beside him and held him quietly in her arms.

"I'm sorry," Robinson said at length. "It isn't you. It's just the way I —I've become."

"It's all right, honey," she said, cradling his head against her breasts. "I didn't come here for that, anyway. The subject just came up some-how. Are you comfortable?"

"Yes, very."

"Do you want to talk some?"

"Not really."

"Then why don't you close your eyes and try to sleep some more? You look pretty heavy-eyed. I'll just lie here with you."

He closed his eyes, relaxed completely and drifted off to sleep. The sun was low when he woke. Donna was sitting up on one elbow, watching him.

"Hi. You slept real well."

"Yes, I did," he said, feeling refreshed, tasting the fragrance of her skin, conscious of the softness of her breasts. "You're very comfortable to be with. I hope that's not too weak."

She laughed a low, throaty laugh. "Well, maybe that comfort will be available again." She rose and began to dress. Fastening her skirt, head down, hair hanging in her eyes, she laughed aloud. "God. When I think of the guys that have busted a gut trying to get into my—skirt. And wouldn't you know that the untouchable—" she pronounced the words delicately—"would want the unattainable."

He sat up and reached for his shorts. "You mean the un-do-able."

She shook her head. "I don't think so. Not that I've had much experience, but I know you've been through a lot. And I *am* a woman. I'm supposed to be intuitive or something. And, even if I'm not, it doesn't matter right now anyway."

She turned at the door. "Would you like to take another nap like that sometime soon?"

He paused, seriously considering the question. "I think I would."

"Good," she said, flashing her bright smile. "See you."

It became a habit. Day after day, she would come to the house— usually in mid-afternoon—and they would talk a little and then lie on his bed, quietly.

Then one day she didn't come. The afternoon stretched out for an inordinately long time and the even rhythm of the house seemed to have been disturbed. At sunset, he put on a sweater, picked up his cane and walked toward the west end. It was the longest walk he had taken since he had been home. When he returned after dark, he was sweating heavily and his knee was throbbing. He ate a pickup supper from the refrigerator and took a hot bath. He slept badly that night.

The next afternoon at two o'clock the phone rang. Without preamble, she said: "Can I come down?"

"Yes." She hung up.

When she came in the door, she put her arms around him and kissed him soundly. Then she leaned back in his arms and looked at him. "I didn't come yesterday so you could see if you missed me. Did you?"

"Apparently."

The small ritual of undressing was concluded quickly and they lay beside each other. "Let's us talk a little bit," she said, her face on the pillow facing his.

"All right," he said. "Tell me about the men in your life."

She grimaced. "That isn't what I had in mind. But okay. My steady last year was Skinny Garner."

"Garner. I used to box with his older brother. Hell, it was probably his father. Was he your first?"

"You mean sex. Yes and no. It used to be called petting—heavy petting. Everything but. It almost drove him nuts. I helped him when I had to, when he couldn't stand it any longer. But he never got—where he wanted. I didn't mean to be a tease. I just wasn't ready. And I didn't want him later on to be able to say, oh yeah, Donna, I used to bang her. He might have said it anyway, but, if he did, he knew it wasn't true."

"That made a difference to you."

A spark showed briefly in her eyes. "Yeah, it did. Some things haven't changed *that* much. I don't want to be used. And I haven't been."

"Nobody?"

She smiled sensually. "I have a super surprise for you, Mister Robinson. I'm a virgin, believe it or not. At least technically I am."

"Good God."

She flashed her wide smile, leaning over him, her hair falling in his face. "You thought I was a real sex machine, didn't you? You *know* you did. Well, I am, honey. I'm a brand new model. A couple of workmen have—um—oiled it up a bit and maybe touched the bearings. But it hasn't been used."

"And here I am—useless." He looked at her quizzically. "Is that why you . . ."

"No, nooo," she protested. "I came here without knowing, remember? Then when we had that lunch and I helped you upstairs, you were so, so sweet and vulnerable, you didn't try to wolf me or anything, I just really wanted you right then and there. But that's enough about dull ol' me. Tell me about the Hunkie girl you thought I was that first day."

"Katie."

"Yeah, Katie. My ethnic sister. Tell me about her."

He took a deep breath and told her about his adolescent passion for the Polish girl. About the overwhelming thrill of crawling into bed with her that first night. About the awful night in the car when he got sick and Lon took his place in the back seat. Donna exploded in a fit of giggles over that. She grew somber when he told her how Aunt Adda caught them in bed together and kicked Katie out of the house.

"You were nuts about her."

"Yes."

"Yeah, but do you know something? I don't think you really *loved* Katie. You had no basis for love, not real love. You were a kid, hot and horny, and she was an older woman. I think you were overwhelmed, as you put it, with your first sex. And the idea of being in love." She paused. "Were you in love with Betsy Bowers?"

"Jesus," Robinson said. He told her about Betsy, about the nights at the country club, about how he introduced her to Lon. Suddenly, in a rush, he was telling Donna about Lon.

Robinson's voice became harsh as he told her the end of the story. "The dumb sonofabitch," he grated. "He could have quit flying, he was entitled to. But he just *had* to go into that recon force. I *knew* better. I could have stopped him and I should have. And I don't even know for sure what killed him." His throat closed. "I can't talk any more right now."

"It's okay. Just relax now. Close your eyes. I'll hold you. Let it go."

He lay against her for a while, feeling her arms around him, breathing the fragrance of her breasts. As he sank into sleep, it began to rain. He could hear it spattering against the windows. He had been asleep for a short time when he realized that the light was bright against his eyelids.

He opened his eyes to see where the light was coming from and he was staring through the windscreen into the sun, heading east across the channel. The group was rocking and weaving around him on tides of air. They were only ten minutes inside the continent when the first attack came, like a crack of thunder, out of the sun. Two B-17s blew up nearby; the high squadron above was shattered by a wolfpack of fighters.

Heavy antiaircraft fire penetrated the formation from below. Orange and black bursts filled the air. The wing of a B-17 windmilled
slowly past like a wind-blown pod. A body, falling from above,
bounced off the nose of his airplane in a shower of blood. He pounded
on the wheel. *This isn't real!* he screamed. *It's a goddamn dream! I'm not
supposed to have this dream anymore! I'm not supposed to!*

The copilot touched his shoulder as he was yelling and he turned
and looked at him and quailed. The copilot was Lon, but his face was
covered with blood. Then the dream changed because he couldn't bear
it. The copilot became Google, and he was pointing across Robinson
to the left. Robinson looked and his blood froze. It was himself, no, it
was the German, no, it was himself in a German uniform, flying a 262
out there on his wing. The man who was himself kept shouting to him
but the wind was howling so loudly he couldn't hear what he was
saying. A huge explosion tore both airplanes apart and he felt himself
falling.

Sandra was shaking him. No, it was Donna. "It's all right, honey!
It's all right, baby! We're having a thunderstorm, that's all. You were
having a nightmare." She pulled his head against her again, rocking
him like a baby. After a moment, she said: "Tell me about the dream."

A savage thunderstorm crackled and boomed as Robinson told her
about the dream. Speaking in a flat, dry voice, he told her everything: about the fear that had grown within him like a malevolent
cancer, about the loss of his men, about his continuing grief over Lon's
death, about the last raid and its mind-shattering conclusion, about
Sandra and his inability to penetrate the murk of his spirit to know
whether he loved her or not. Donna said nothing as he talked. When
he was through, they lay together quietly. Robinson was exhausted; his
mind seemed to have gone blank. Nothing at all to think about. Nothing. The sound of the word was comforting and he repeated it silently
to himself.

When he woke again, it was dark. His right arm was curled around
her bare shoulders and her head lay between his shoulder and neck. For
an instant he thought she was Sandra.

"Donna," he said.

"Hmmm."

"You overslept. You should have gone home."

"Nope," she said. "I called the folks a while ago and said I was visiting a girl friend in Dubois. I'm going to stay here with you tonight. If it's all right."

She gently turned her face toward his and kissed him softly, her lips parting. He was surprised to discover that he wanted her. Abruptly, he pulled her to him; her pliant body moved into his. The bed became uncomfortably warm. He grasped the sheet with his free hand and threw it aside.

For the first time in their relationship, he became the aggressor. He kissed her hungrily, his hands ranging over her body. She writhed slowly at his touch. His lips closed around a taut nipple and he gently stroked her body.

His mind and body seemed to have come alive. He felt extraordinarily alert; it was as if a film had been cleared from his field of vision. He was conscious of the pumping of his heart, the powerful flow of blood in arteries and veins, the strength of flexing muscles, the erotic texture of skin against skin. He realized he had become hard, even swollen. Her hand strayed to him and closed around him in surprise.

"Oh my God," she said. "You're ready. You're really going to, aren't you?"

"Yes."

"Oh jeez, I'm scared."

"Want me to stop?"

"Oh no, no. I want you to. I'm just scared."

He started to move atop her but she pushed him back. "Not that way, not yet. Let me do it, the first time."

Her body gleamed in the half light as she straddled him. "Oh jeez, Mitch, it hurts. I don't know if I can . . ." She pushed down harder, determinedly. "Oh." She began moving strongly, plunging atop him.

"How is it now?"

Her words came in short gasps. "At first . . . it hurt . . . now . . . oh God . . ." Abruptly, she threw her upper body down against his, moaning.

He held her close. "Hold on tight. I'm going to turn us over." He rolled over so that he was atop her. "Put your legs around me. Hook them in back of my ankles. Then move them up. Find out where it feels best."

In a moment, her legs were wound tight around his waist. "Oh this is even better," she gasped. "Even better." She held him tighter and tighter. Suddenly, with a cry, she convulsed, becoming a creature of teeth and claws. He climaxed at the same time and they moved together mindlessly.

Then he was lying on his back and Donna was huddled beside him. Their bodies were slick with perspiration.

"How do you feel?" he asked.

"As if I've been turned inside out. Fluttery, achy, wonderful. How do you feel?"

"Wonderful," he said truthfully. The scratches in his back stung from the salt in his sweat and his abdomen ached as if he'd blown a cylinder head. But he felt like laughing, wondering if Lazarus had laughed. "It was the first time for me in a very long time."

"It was the first time for me, ever. Coming from inside that way. Unbelievable."

When she kissed him goodbye in the morning, she murmured: "I love you." She paused, her eyes warm. "Oh jeez, don't look so worried. It's my first time, remember? I have to be in love with you for a while. You're my—Katie."

The days and nights passed as if in a dream. Robinson felt as if he had become a teenager again. Donna turned up with a diaphragm she had acquired from a doctor in Dubois and they made love nearly every day. She also cooked huge meals for him. Robinson found himself talking and joking like a boy; the first time he heard himself laugh he was startled. It was as if the sound had come from someone else. And, curiously, when he wasn't with her, and sometimes when he was, he would think about Sandra, remembering *their* nights, *their* talks.

And then, one day in August, there was an enormous shock. It was late afternoon and he had just walked out to the side porch when a church bell began ringing. Then other church bells began ringing. A moment later, the town's fire siren began wailing. "What in hell?" he said aloud. He heard running feet and the paper boy, wide-eyed, sprinted up the walk, threw his copy of the Banner at him, and yelled: "It's over! It's all over!"

Quickly, Robinson unfolded the paper. The headline stretched all the way across the page. It was the biggest and blackest the Banner had ever displayed. It said:

THE WAR IS OVER

Beneath it was a two-column sub-head:

*Japan Surrenders After*
*We Drop New Kind of Bomb*

He sat down and eagerly read the story. A B-29 had dropped an entirely new kind of bomb on a city called Hiroshima. Three days later, a second bomb of the same kind was dropped on a place called Nagasaki. Two bombs, two cities. Afterwards, the Emperor had gone on the radio and announced Japan's surrender.

He frowned as he read what it said about the new bombs. They were called "atom" bombs. The one that was dropped on Hiroshima was said to be 20 kilotons and that was supposed to be the equivalent of 20,000 tons of high explosive. Could that possibly be true? If it was, it meant that one airplane had carried the explosive power of two all-out raids by the entire Eighth and RAF. From what he could gather, the first bomb had flattened Hiroshima and the second had destroyed part of Nagasaki. Cities had been flattened before, but the unexpectedness of the explosion and the very fact that one bomb dropped by one airplane had caused it apparently had created an enormous psychological shock that had quickly brought the war to an end.

Then a terrible thought stuck him. *If we had had that bomb a year ago in Germany, we could have dropped it on Berlin and stopped the war. We'd have killed 100,000, maybe 200,000 people, but we'd have saved millions and millions of lives. All those men on the battlefields who died during the last year of the war would still be alive. All those civilians. All those people in the concentration camps. All those men in my group. They would all still be alive. Lon would still* . . . He choked off the thought; it was too painful to bear.

The thought haunted him for the next two days. When Donna called, he told her he'd like to be alone for a while. She said she understood. On the third day the doorbell rang and he felt an instant's irritation. She had come anyway. But the figure he saw through the vestibule glass was short and chunky and dressed in summer Army khakis.

Robinson gasped. "Ed!"

"Colonel Robinson, I presume?" Carlino said. In the curious way male friends behave when they haven't seen each other for a long time, they pounded each other on the shoulders and back.

"I can't believe it!" Robinson said. "Where in hell have you come from?"

"I took the train from Washington, actually. I've been detailed there for a bit; I'll tell you about it. But, when the news came over the ticker about the Japs' surrender, I just had to knock off for a day and come visit."

Robinson drew him into the living room and they sat facing each other. "I'm glad you did, Ed. What're you up to?"

"I've been detailed as part of a survey team that's leaving for Japan right after the surrender ceremony to survey the bomb damage." Carlino laughed aloud. "Which is a hell of a lot better than the assignment I had up until three days ago."

"Which was what?"

"Which was a B-29 group on one of the forward islands. I was being rotated to the Pacific theater along with a couple of million other unlucky souls. Operation Olympic, our planned invasion of Japan, no less. G2 says the Japs have moved as many as six million fresh troops back from China to defend the mainland. And they've had thousands of kamikaze planes that've been sitting, waiting for us, in underground hangers. It would have been an incredibly bloody mess, even worse than Europe. And now, thank the Lord, it's all over. The new bomb did it."

Robinson went to the refrigerator, opened two bottles of beer and handed one to Carlino. "Is it really as powerful as they say?"

"You get a hell of a lot more explosive power with this weapon but it's indiscriminate. For the same tonnage, you could do more damage with the bombs *we* dropped. Example: According to our estimates, two of our conventional bombing raids on Tokyo killed about 225,000 people—two and a half times more people than G2 says were killed in the Hiroshima and Nagasaki raids. But it took maybe 250 of those big B-29s to do it."

Robinson shook his head in wonder. "What do you think, Ed? Does this mean an end to war, big wars?"

"I think it means the end of major wars of attrition," Carlino said. "Over these last three years, we've had to knock out factories and roads and railroads and canals and ports and airfields and oil refineries and every damn thing on the landscape because they all contributed to the enemy's ability to wage war. Now, with this so-called atomic weapon, all you'd need to do is to knock out the other side's ability to deliver *his* atomic weapons. There won't be any percentage in hitting cities. So, in that way, it could be good. But the higher good would be if adversaries decide that messing around with this kind of power is too risky. That would be the best use of this kind of weapon—to keep a major war from developing."

They sat silently for a moment. "What're you going to do now, Mitch?" Carlino said. Robinson shrugged. "I don't know, Ed. But I'm finally feeling alive again. How about visiting here for a while? God knows I've got a lot of room. I'll show you the sights. All two or three of them."

"Well, I'd like to, buddy, but duty calls. I'll stay in touch, though. And, speaking of being in touch, have you given any thought to writing the lady in England? I had a letter from her some time back, asking about you."

Robinson's heart leaped. *Sandra.* "I guess I wasn't ready, but it's funny I've started thinking about her again. What did she say? Is she well?"

"She sounded fine. She's still single and she sounds as if she's still interested in that dashing flying officer she spent so much time with."

"Well, there's not much dash in me these days, but, yeah, maybe I'll get in touch—when I figure out what to say."

Carlino looked at his watch and rose. "I hate to drink and run, but I only wangled one day's leave, and in half an hour there's a train going to Pittsburgh, where I can catch the Washington flyer. I'll call you when I get back from Japan. Great seeing you, Mitch, even if it was short and sweet."

Carlino's brief visit helped lift the gloom that had enveloped Robinson. That Sunday, Mahoning was the site of a county-wide celebration. The high school band played at the bandstand in the park and the town fathers shot off the biggest fireworks display ever seen in western Pennsylvania.

That night, he and Donna lay on their backs on the golf course green atop Country Club Hill and looked up at the giant pinwheel of stars rotating around the North Star directly overhead. He showed Donna how to locate the North Star—its proper name in the Air Corps navigational course, he explained, was Polaris—by sighting along the pointer stars at the end of the cup of the Big Dipper. Then, one by one, he called off the names of the summer constellations that Aunt Adda had taught him: Saggitarius, Scorpius, Aquila, Libra, Lupus.

———

The cosmic pinwheel had turned only a little that night when Elise von Moltke walked onto her balcony at the edge of Zurich, sat in her lounge chair and looked up. Since the weather had grown warm, she had acquired the habit of waking late at night and sitting on the balcony for a while. It was a time when she knew she could be alone, and alone she felt close to Karl. She had taken to imagining that he was up there somewhere; perhaps he was one of those glittering lights that winked down on her. She didn't examine the premise closely; it comforted her and it made it possible for her to talk to him.

She had already told him how Willi, at great risk to himself, had got across the border and back and established the fact of Karl's death. She had apologized to Karl for not wailing and tearing her hair like a Greek heroine when Willi gave her the news. For she had known for months that Karl was bound to die; the way they parted made that very clear to her. In a real sense, he had died when Willi drove the car from the hunting lodge that day. She had wept a Danube full of tears then; there was really nothing more to cry about now.

In fact, she felt a quiet joy. For the baby, *their* baby, had begun kicking inside her. Her body was swelling noticeably now and her skin had acquired a beautiful glow.

It would be a boy, she knew. *So you're not dead at all, my love. You will be here in a very short time, you'll see, and your name will be Karl.*

———

Donna went back to college in September. Sitting on the side porch during their last meeting, she wept briefly and then, characteristically, smiled. "You know what they say about all good things."

"It's OK. It's time you were with people your own age."

"I know," she said. "Same goes for you. Like that lady love in England, maybe."

"We may be very different people now."

"Uh-huh. Well, maybe she was just a fling, during your time over there."

"She was more than that."

"Maybe she looked good over there but she doesn't stack up too good against the home-town talent."

"Sandra's a very good-looking woman."

"Okay, she's good-looking, but maybe she's not so bright."

"No," he said stoutly. "She's highly intelligent; well-educated, too."

"Good-looking and smart, okay. But kind of boring, huh? Not much fun to be with."

He laughed. "No, actually she has a good sense of humor; she was a lot of fun to be with."

Donna turned and hit him in the chest. "Well, knucklehead, you'd better hope she hasn't found somebody else to replace you."

Robinson smiled. "Maybe I should get in touch."

She hugged him briefly. "I'll never forget you, Mitch."

"I'll never forget you either, Donna," he said. "You're a super-woman."

She laughed. "Superwoman. That's nice. Well, if I am, as the song goes, you've made me what I am today." She kissed him again. "And I'm not sorry. Bye, lover."

She broke away and, without a backward glance, walked down the porch steps and up the street.

After Donna's departure, Steve Amundson arrived in his battered 1940 Ford pickup truck. Minutes later, he and Mitch were at the rim of green valley.

"Remember, Pop told you at dinner how this whole valley belongs to us," Steve said. "We've been buying it, a parcel at a time, over the last three years. Now the war is over we're going to build a whole village here—the biggest thing that's ever been seen in these parts. We need help and we want you on board from the start."

Mitch slowly shook his head as Steve described the project. Steve would handle design, financing, permits, cost estimates and the like; Olaf Amundson would run the building supply operation. And they had recruited Ed Carlino, who promised to supervise the building process and manage the office once he returned from Japan and received his discharge.

"You don't need me," Robinson said.

"I need somebody who'll take overall charge of things here and deal with the community and outside businesses. This is no get-rich-quick land speculation deal, Mitch. We've got to grow right."

"Steve, there must be fifty guys in town with better qualifications than me—*and* more enthusiasm for the job."

"I don't think so, but it doesn't matter. You're family, Mitch." Steve grabbed Mitch by the shoulders and shook him gently. "Think about it and call me tomorrow. OK?"

———

Robinson made the phone call just before noon the next day. Then, hearing the mailman, he walked to the front door and found a letter. It bore a San Francisco return address. Opening it, he read:

*Dear Chief,*
*Got your address from Army records and thought I'd write. Hope you're feeling good by now, your leg and everything. We sure had a doozy that last*

*time out. I've taken a job flying D-3s for old Chiang out in China. No retirement pay but $10,000 a year (lot of money, right?) plus a house and a couple of servants. Imagine that. It ought to be fun and I'll be where I can visit the temples and talk to the old warriors and all that. Maybe you figured out by now that I'm the one that sent you those notes. I hoped they helped you some. I'll toss one more at you. The last thing that Buddha said before he left the earth was Strive Mightily. Of course you've gotta decide what to strive for. But I think it's a good thing to live by.*

> *Good luck always, Chief,*
> *GOOGLE*

Robinson smiled, re-read the letter, folded it carefully and put it in his shirt pocket. Then he walked uptown, leaving the cane hanging in the closet, and had himself measured for three suits. He also picked out three pairs of slacks and a pair of new shoes. He figured he'd eventually fill out enough to wear his old sports jackets. Next stop was the Farmers' bank up the street where he deposited the back-pay Treasury checks that had been in his wallet for the past three months.

Finally, he walked over to Murray's Ford dealership and put in for one of the back-ordered new models they were starting to advertise. Once he had signed the contract, Dick Murray shook hands with him and smiled and said: "It's real nice to see you lookin' so good, Mitch. I'm real glad you've got your health back and you're goin' to work for the Amundsons."

"Where did you hear *that*?"

Murray shrugged. "Oh, you know how things get around town. Tell you what else I heard this morning. Your ex-girl friend, Betsy Bowers? She's got that Red Cross job she was after. Maybe you already know about it. Hear she'll be leavin' for England in a couple of days. You came back, she's goin' over. Funny, isn't it?"

"Yeah," Robinson said. "Funny."

Instead of going home, as he had planned, he walked over to the Bowers' house on Pine Street. The old porch looked warm and friendly; the hanging swing was still there, still empty. He rang the bell. Betsy answered and quickly opened the door. They looked at each other for a moment and then hugged lightly.

"I gather you've heard," she said as they sat on the couch. She looked thin, older; her skin seemed dry. He realized they were sitting in the same positions as when he first kissed her.

"Just now. That you're leaving for England. London, I imagine."

"To begin with," she said. "Then they tell me I'll be going on to the continent to help with the relief work."

He grunted, thinking of the bombed-out cities, the misery of the concentration camps, the millions of homeless refugees. "There's plenty to do. It could be a lifetime job."

"Well," she said, smiling faintly, "I'm looking for a new life and it sank into my skull some months ago that maybe the best way to find it is to go somewhere where I'll be busy thinking about somebody else and not about me. I've done all the thinking about me I want to do. For a long time."

They sat silently for a long minute. "Bets," he said finally, "I just want to say that I—that I'm very sorry, terribly sorry, for . . ."

She held up her hand. "It's okay, Mitch. It's all behind us now." She paused for a moment as if deciding whether to say what was in her mind. Then she smiled. "We did have a good time back then, didn't we?"

He nodded. "We sure did. It was great."

"Yes, great." Another pause. "I don't want you to try to answer what I'm going to say. Just don't say anything at all, please. I was very much in love with you, you know that. You also know, and I always knew, that you really weren't in love with me. You *liked* me and we had good times and enjoyed a nice physical relationship. When you left for the Air Corps, I knew that would be the end of it; even so, it made me bitter when I didn't hear from you. I had lost you and it made me bitter.

"And then Lon appeared and something extraordinary happened. We fell in love." Her voice broke briefly; she struggled for a moment before going on. "Those few weeks he was home were the most wonderful of my life. I feel as if I lived a whole lifetime during those few weeks. I'm grateful for that; so grateful."

She smiled. "Maybe you can take some credit for it, Mitch. You awakened me to love, after all, and when the real thing came along I was ready for it."

"And then I lost *him*, too. I've loved two men and I've lost them both. Now I'm going to try to give something to the people who need it most. I can't lose them all."

Her words hung in his mind as he walked home. *I can't lose them all.* He began to walk faster. There was so much to think about, so much to do. On the way home, he began thinking about what to say. When he arrived, he saw the late rays of the sun beginning to slant through the windows. He went to the kitchen and made himself a rye highball. It had a clean, malty taste that bit the tongue slightly and created a pleasant warmth in his stomach.

He carried his drink into the living room and sat. The light streamed through the windows, reddened the cherrywood pillars in the hallway, touched the clock with a patina of gold.

In a moment, the light touched Moltke's portrait. The face gleamed and seemed to come alive. Robinson looked at it and felt an unexpected feeling of kinship. He raised his glass to it. When the war was long over and time had dissolved the hatred, he would go to Germany as Aunt Adda had wished and find the remaining members of the Moltke family. He wanted to know their names, see their faces and, particularly, ask about Karl von Moltke.

It was growing dark. He rose and walked into the library that Uncle Ralph had used as his office. He sat down at the oak desk, snapped on the goose-necked lamp and pulled a piece of writing paper from the drawer. He had to discard two fountain pens before he could find one that would write.

*Dear Sandra,*
*You told me to get in touch with you after I'd spent enough time by myself to sort out my feelings. I think you meant if and when I returned to the land of the living. Well, I finally have. The Amundsons have offered me a job, helping them build and sell houses and, on a larger scale, helping our town to grow. I don't know whether I'll be any good at it, but I've told them I'll give it a try.*

*It's possible I'll be able to help them, but I think they'll do more for me than I can ever do for them. I have no idea what the future will bring, but at least I've come to recognize that there can be a future. And I'd like to ask you if you'd like to share it with me. You and I came together under the special circumstances of war, living in a fearful country under attack. You fell in love with a stranger who seemed romantic to you because of his differences and maybe because of a certain standing he occupied as an alien in your country. Here, I have no special standing. But here, you would be very different. You're a product of an old and highly sophisticated urban culture. You can walk, literally, in the footsteps of Shakespeare and Johnson and Byron and Housman, too. Every day you look at buildings and remnants of man's past that have lasted hundreds, even thousands of years. Here in America, in Mahoning, anything that's lasted for more than a hundred years is probably an arrowhead. And soon now, with this war over, everything in America will become brand-new again. Let me assume for a moment that you haven't come to your senses and decided to spend the years ahead with Roger or Nigel or Rex. If that's the case, if the foreigner you once loved still interests you, consider this offer: come to America, to Mahoning. Come live with me and be my love, as Will said so perfectly.*

*If you're willing to entertain this proposal—it* is *a proposal—I owe it to you to tell you what you'll be in for. First, the climate. On the whole, it's better than England's, though roses don't grow as well here. It's not as damp as England and it gets cold earlier. But the summer is absolutely beautiful, sunny and warm. The fall is beautiful, too. More than half of Pennsylvania is forestland and we have all the trees you have there—oaks and elms and flaming maples and pines and hemlocks.*

*The winter can be pretty nice. The snow can be thick, but we have tobogganing and skiing on country club hill. Sometimes there are horses and buggies on the roads. People here know how to drive their cars in winter and the state snowplows come through like clockwork. The worst time is slush time from March up to about April. I have to admit that's pretty dreary.*

*Now the people. Mainly, they're good, simple people from all kinds of ethnic backgrounds. They're Costanzas and Amundsons and Robinsons and Bortzes and Schwartzes. We used to occupy distinct levels of class that dictated who we associated with and what we did for a living. The war seems to have eliminated all that. We're all equal now, the way the French claim they want to be. But I do have to tell you this: we're still pretty provincial. A few drive to Pittsburgh to see plays during the season at the Nixon Theater. A few have even been to New York. But America in September, 1945 is still primitive in many ways.*

*Now you may be reading this and asking yourself: whatever is the fool talking about? Does he think I spend my days in museums and my nights in theaters? No, but I want to be sure you understand. In London, you can go to a performance at the Old Vic, and see Olivier, Richardson, Gielgud and Sybil Thorndike, in repertory, no less, and then you can go to the Ritz or Claridge's or Brown's or the Savoy for tea. You can look up and see Big Ben or go down by the river and look at the White Tower or have an ale in the pub where Dickens did his writing.*

*Here you can turn your head from nearly any point in town and see the Banner building, all seven stories of it. It's the highest thing in town. You can go to a movie at the Winslow and to Gleckler's for a drink (if you're a man).*

*The country club is nice, though. It's an old rickety building with a big porch around it. The surrounding hills are as beautiful as any you've seen, and there's a natural spring nearby where you can drink the finest water on earth. The food is an assortment of German and Scandinavian and Italian and Lithuanian and Polack—I've got to remember to say Polish. Taken all together, it's what we call American cooking. No offense, but it's a lot better than you get in England.*

*I know you'll like the old house. I've described it to you before so I won't do that again. But it's rich and warm. It's waiting for new lives to be lived here. It rejected my earlier effort to blend into the furniture. It wants new stories to be told, new personalities, new memories to add to the old ones.*

*The people here will be fascinated by you. Your physical beauty would be enough to accomplish that, of course, but your speech will boggle their minds. Nobody has ever sounded like that here, made every word crisp and understandable.*

*At this point, you may be asking yourself: what could possibly be my reason for travelling to such an odd-sounding place? One reason is that I think we would enjoy being together, continuing what we began back in London. And there is another reason why you might want to come. I've come to realize— and I apologize for being such a slow learner—that I love you. If honest effort on my part will give us a good life together, rest assured that I will—as a wise friend has advised—strive mightily. I'll be waiting to hear from you.*

*Yours,*
*Mitch*

*P.S. I hope the Brigadier is well. I'd be pleased to have you bring him with you, if he'd like to come. We have plenty of room here, and he and I can have long talks about military history if you're willing to put up with it.*

Sandra Brooks had just reached the street when the postman arrived and handed her the letter. When she saw who it was from, she turned, climbed the stairs to her flat, sat down and opened it. She read it through three times, wept briefly and then laughed.

There was so much to do. She would have to break the dinner date with Roger. How could Mitchell possibly know that she had been seeing a man named Roger? She would have to call the Ministry and tell them she was quitting. They had been lovely to her, particularly since the Brigadier's fatal heart attack, but they really didn't need her anymore.

She would have to call a few friends and tell them why they wouldn't be seeing her for a long while, at least. She would have to settle with her landlady and temporarily store her few worthwhile pieces of furniture. She would have to renew her passport and phone the American Embassy to ask if they required a visa. She would have to go round to her bank and draw out her money. She would have to make her travel plans.

But first she would telephone America. The British phone system was dicey enough as it was. Just imagine the difficulties of getting all the way through to a tiny place called Mahoning in a state named Pennsylvania.

I *beg* your pardon, miss, the operator would say. It's in America in a state named Pennsylvania, Sandra would reply. Rather near a city called Pittsburgh. It's spelled M-A-H-O-N-I-N-G.